ADAM'S LADDER

CO-EDITED BY MICHAEL BAILEY
& DARREN SPEEGLE

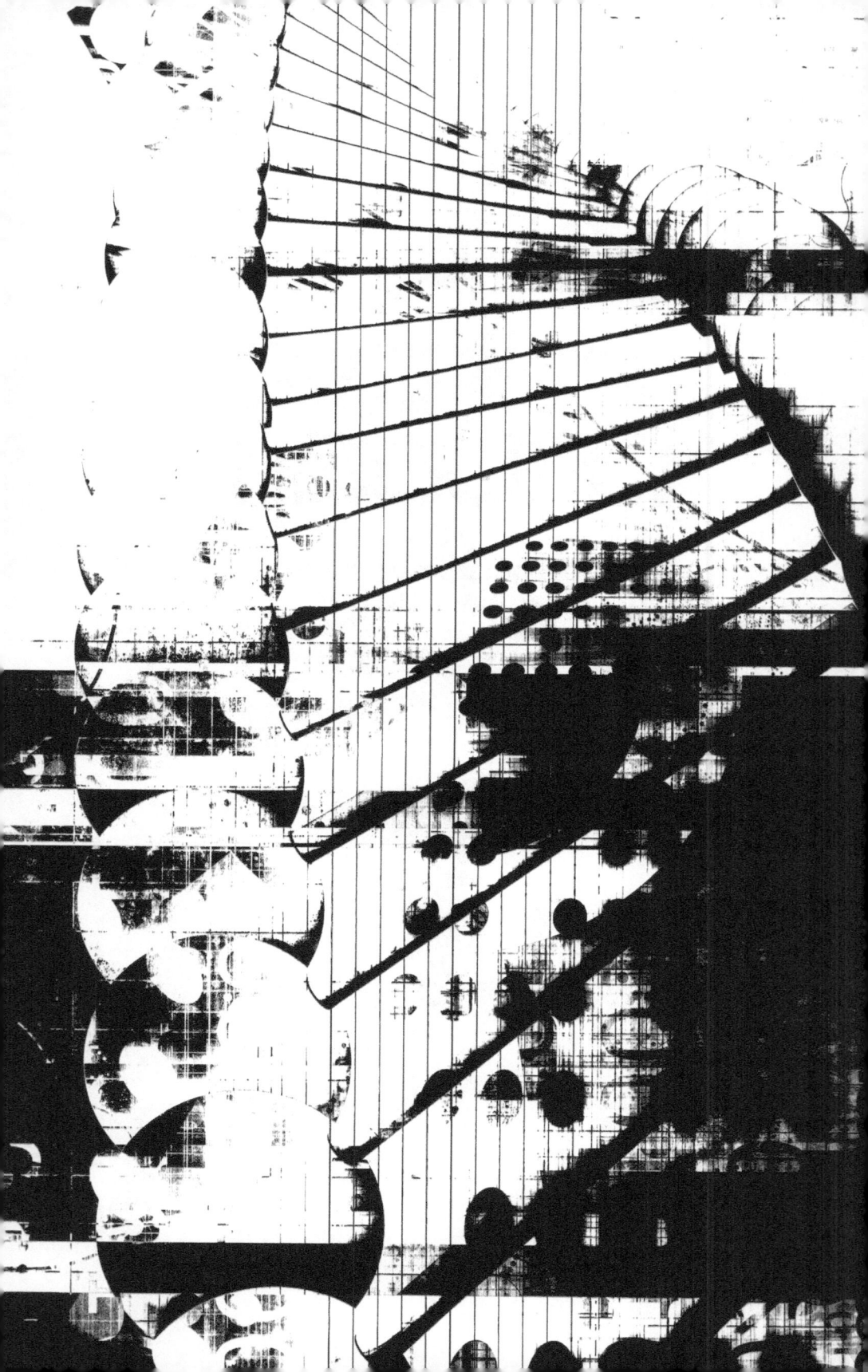

Published by Written Backwards
www.nettirw.com

100 Numbered Hardcover Edition
ISBN: 978-1-62641-266-8

First Trade Paperback Edition
ISBN: 978-1-62641-267-5

eBook
ISBN: 978-1-62641-268-2

ADAM'S LADDER

CO-EDITED BY MICHAEL BAILEY
& DARREN SPEEGLE

T.O.C.

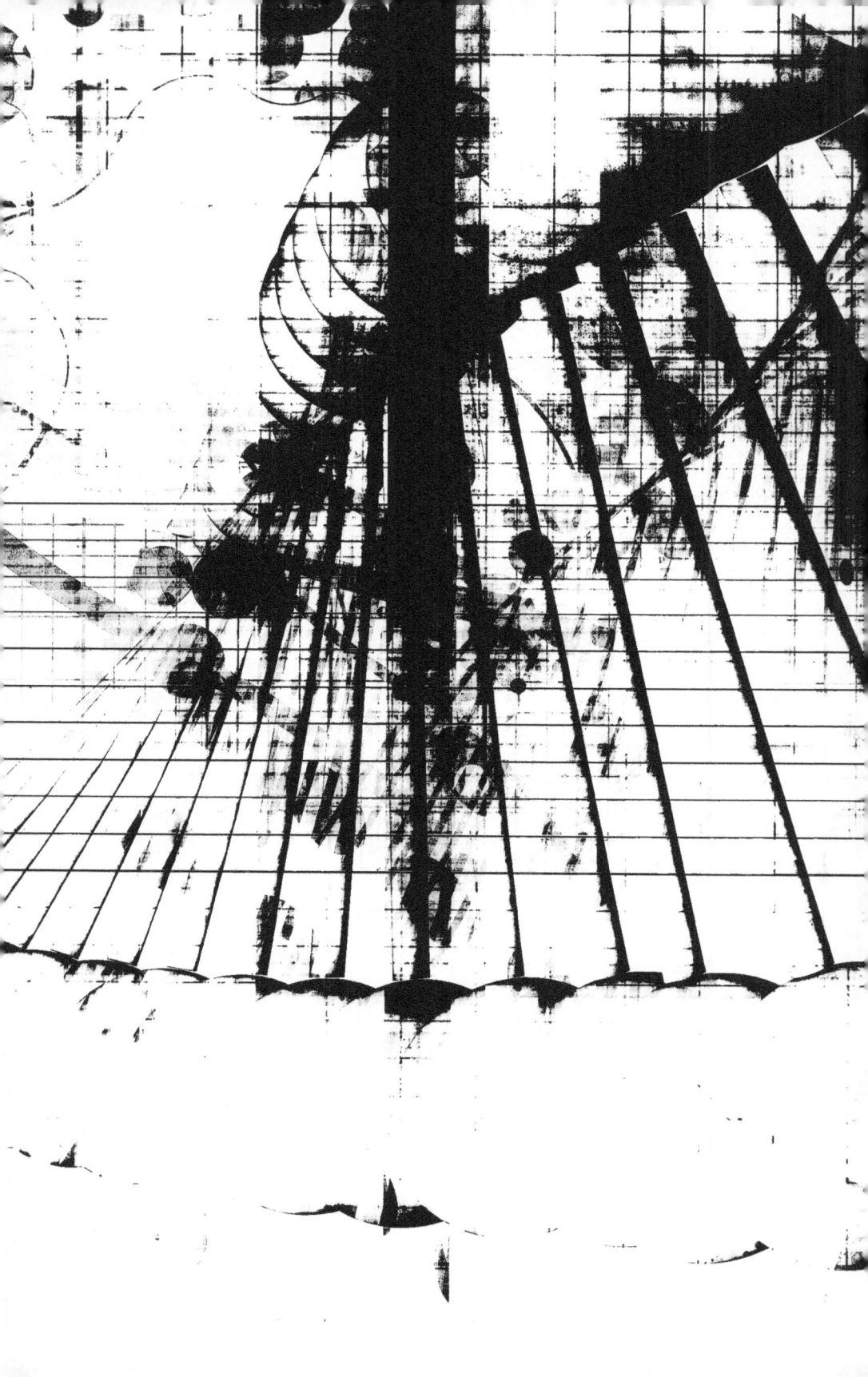

CH-CH-CHANGES

CHAZ BRENCHLEY

*all art aspires
to the condition of music*

The rules are few, at Parry's. Indeed, they're barely rules at all, so much as customs observed—but they are scrupulously observed, and they can be rigorously enforced at need. Don't make that necessary. That's Rule One.

Rule Two? Don't call it a bar. Parry's quite clear about that; it's an establishment.

Don't let that stop you paying for your drinks. He's quite clear about that, too.

If you must kick up a ruckus, keep it quieter than the pilots'. They're privileged; you're not. And whatever else you do, don't approach the pilots. If one of them brings you in, that's fine: join their table, cling close, and welcome. If they beckon you over, the same applies. But always, always wait to be invited. Don't ever try to push in.

Actually, that's what most of the rules boil down to. It's the pilots' place of choice, and Parry means to keep it that way. Which means they get to do what they want, and you don't. That's it.

To be fair, that's more or less the rule all over the Margin, all along the Limb, all through human space. With them so few and the need so great, who's ever going to say no to a pilot? Whoever they are, whatever they ask? Pilots are the new black: they are always in order and may never be debated.

Actually, that last is a joke, mostly. Pilots make a disordered crew by definition, and they'll cheerfully debate with each other or with anyone, if 'debate' means argue stubbornly or viciously or relentlessly, up to the very edge of fighting. Pilots don't fight each other, and you never, ever fight with a pilot. Not in Parry's, certainly, but not actually anywhere.

Actually, maybe that's Rule One. Maybe that's all the rules there are, all over. Let pilots be, let them find their own ways to damnation.

Trust me, they'll do that. They will.

Tonight, they're being peaceable enough. Parry's all but slumbers under the dead weight of their sobriety. That's literal, more or less—pilots don't drink, don't smoke, don't drug when they're in port: they're trying to come down, to remember what it's like to live with all the limits of a body and claim it as their own, to stop at the inside of their skin—but it's also situational. Out beyond Parry's door lie the lights and noise and reckless abandonment of the Margin, every twisted thing that humans find or do for fun compressed into a mile or two of sheetwalk, into a few thousand urgent transient bodies. Pilots are all about the body, this side of n-space: they'll do most of what's available out there. And then they'll come in here, because Parry's is quiet and comfortable, a place to catch their breath and touch base with their inner selves in the company of colleagues.

They come in here *a lot*. Which is why anybody else comes too, why everybody else looks in: just to drink where pilots are and watch how pilots sit, listen to the murmur—or the yelling—of their voices and breathe a little of their rarefied air. Nothing rubs off and no one would want it to, and even so. This is still the place to be, and here they are.

Not all, of course. Not most, for human space is a skein stretched fine and far; not even most of those you might have hoped to see hereabouts, if you were that kind of fan, if hope was still a thing for you. By definition, pilots are a fly-by-night crew, here and gone, always in demand. Some like the long haul, one end of the Limb to the other; they might not show their faces in Parry's from one year's end to the next. Some are in and out, barely flitting outside this system before they're back, barely pausing before they're off again, barely worth the effort and the risk.

And n-space is another variable, as whimsical as they are. Some times, some places—if there's a difference, if you could ever confidently divide time from space and say which was which—it may be slick as oil, squeezing ships through, spitting them out; or else it can be thick as porridge, clinging, close to impassable. And some pilots are cautious by nature, taking it slow and sweating all the way, while some are devil-may-care, slapdash, heroic in the worst way. Not noticeably dead yet, but even so. Mostly those get the cargo runs; passengers would sooner wait for someone steadier. Relatively steadier.

So, yes: Parry's is quiet just now. Some of the regulars are out. Mercy Mercy and Ferrel have been gone so long, people are starting to think them lost, adrift in n-space. Irrecoverable. No surprise in Ferrel's case, but Mercy would be a real loss. Everyone loves Mercy Mercy; she's the acceptable face, the people's pilot, the single splendid example you can point to.

Could point to. Maybe. They've not been gone long enough to be certain, but the question's in the air now, whether they're ever coming back. The strangest thing, of course, is that they went together in the first place. Pilots never do that. They're too rare to risk, and if one gets into trouble the other can't get them out of it. Navigation isn't a science. It isn't even an art: it's an embedding, an act of faith written in the body, inherently individual. Impossible to repeat, almost—almost!—impossible to survive.

Which of course is why and how pilots are what they are, and why we put up with them.

This night—it's always night on the Margin, if "night" means "time to be out on the sheetwalk, looking for trouble," which it always, always does—there's the one settled table in Parry's, as so often, with the onlookers coming and going, staring and pretending not to stare, never quite daring to cross that gap that pilots create and Parry enforces, that narrow space between one table and the next, that unbridgeable gulf.

You want to cross that gulf, you'll need to fly. Unless you're lifted over.

This is Brone's table, by custom and practice and—well, by mere occupation. Brone the Shutterself entity, the pilot who never flies, who almost never leaves Parry's. It migrates in a slow shuffle between a room in the back and a table, this table, its table out here in the front where everyone can see, for values of seeing that include being baffled by layers of swaddling drab duffel. It has a head by courtesy, by inference alone, that hooded peak that's narrower than what might be its shoulders. It has a drinking tube of sorts, that emerges to suck at whatever's in its glass; some people think that's a finger. Hollow and translucent and plumbed in, but a finger none the less.

None the less: Brone is as human as any of them, these pilots that we've made by luck and guesswork, great endeavour and great loss. So many have been lost in n-space, lost to us, despite our need; none has ever—quite—lost their humanity, despite the changes bred into them, the wild experimentation, the slow gestation over generations. Despite random mutation and surgical intervention, despite mind-altering treatments and mind-altering drugs, despite it all. They're still human, if only because we say so. Because we could not bear for them to give that up, or because we could not bear to be the ones who made them or named them something other, or because we could not trust them after.

"Bodies like ships like buildings, machines for living in," says Ferenor who has never seen a building, who was bred in a bottle and hatched in orbit, cultivated for this life she leads. One of the rare successes, a design for a pilot that actually worked. Once, it worked once. All her litter-mates died or grew strange, strange as she, without the benefit of her ability. An unreproducible result; an experimental method recorded, remembered, not to be repeated. You can't call it science, if it never works again.

As usual, Brone says nothing. Does it even listen? Who can, who could possibly say? There's no standard measure for a pilot, any pilot; but whatever concept you have of what it means to be a pilot—or what it means to be human—the Shutterself entities are far and far beyond that. Far and far.

Ferenor wears her body as lightly and as fleetingly as she does her opinions—unless that's the other way around—whereas everything in Brone is slow and fixed and solid. If it knows change, that could only be on a geologic scale. Ferenor is air, limitless and uncontained, a breeze across Brone's mountain. Here and gone. Perhaps that's what it cherishes in her. Perhaps it likes them fickle, transient, departed.

Perhaps that's why it stays.

"Living is incidental." So says Ten Barry, the devolved clone. His—brother? twin? simulacrum?—who answers to the same name is for once absent from his side. They're doing their bewildering double act solo, perhaps simply to mystify twice as many people at once. One thing for sure, he won't be flying a ship alone. It takes them both: that much we know. Not much more, for some pilots are open and some have been thoroughly exposed, but the clone gestalt holds its secrets close. Are there ten? Were there ten? No one has ever seen more than two abroad, and they're believed to be the same two, though how would you, how would anyone know? And are they a single distributed individual, or a family? Or worse? And above all, of course, how does the flying happen, what's the methodology, how is it achieved?

They—or he—won't say, and there is no power and no law that might compel them. Dozens, perhaps hundreds of such laws exist in draft, all through human space; no jurisdiction has ever dared enact them. Of course it's for the greater good, we could learn so much, enhance our chances of making another generation of pilots—but what if this generation responded with a blockade, an absolute refusal to fly into that region of space? No government could survive that, however strong or secure their grip. The hold that pilots have on their privacy is so much stronger, it has never been tested. They've never even needed to threaten such a blockade. A politician's imagination is enough. More than enough. Pilots get what they want, here as everywhere. In Ten Barry's case, that means he—or they, or what you will—can be oblique, obstructive and infuriatingly unforthcoming, to their dual hearts' content.

"How incidental?" Ferenor asks.

"A ship is a machine, yes—not built for living in, no. Built to journey, to endure n-space, to come out elsewhere, with goods or passengers or war or what you will. The same is true of us: built to journey, built to survive, built to be going somewhere else. If they could make machines instead, they would do that, and do without us gladly. The living are inconvenient, and not at all to the purpose."

It's true enough, and hardly a new argument. In honesty, it's hardly an argument at all. No autopilot yet attempted has even found a way into n-space, never mind emerging otherwhere. Those that have been taken into n-space by human pilots and triggered there have never found their way out, despite the best of planning. Either the pilot has abandoned the experiment and taken control again, or else the ship has been lost entirely, to our great cost. One pilot down, each time. Very few such experiments occur. We can't afford them.

But if Ten Barry's not speaking metaphorically, at least he's told us something about his own origins. *Built to journey*, he said. If that's to say the devolved clone was created to pilot a ship, if this is someone's private and successful experiment—well, that's something we didn't know before. It might have been happenstance; many pilots are completely unprepared, unschooled, unexpected. Most, perhaps.

Perhaps that's why you rarely see Ten Barry—either Ten Barry, or any—without the other, or one other, at his side. Perhaps they act as a guard on each other's tongue, and here's this one free tonight, saying more than he meant, perhaps.

Saying it to pilots, though. There's no one else at Brone's table today, and no one close enough to overhear. Parry has a brisk way with eavesdroppers, be they human or mechanical or something other.

Pilots don't care, particularly. They're not big on origin stories from others, when they all have their own; and nor are they particularly big on posterity, that relentless search for the next generation, for more and more reliable and better pilots, better controlled. They like themselves pretty much the way they are. For sure they like the life, the privilege, the freedom.

For sure, Maellelin was never built to be a pilot. If she had been, they'd have built her to a standard measure; she wouldn't need a booster-seat just to join the pilots' table. She had the gift of it, that feeling, a sense of n-space unfolding all about her; it wasn't enough, so she had herself rebuilt. Not to scale, no. Just everything she needed, to suit her particular vision. Eyes seven times the size, and so forth. It's said that there are other changes, less clear to be seen: at the molecular level, her brain and nerves rewired. She doesn't need drugs to ease her passage through n-space, nor devices to find her way about. She only has to look. That she comes with her own ship—bespoke again, with a cockpit tailored to her size—is just a bonus.

She's promised that scientists can have her blueprints, her biotech and her body, once she's gone. If they can figure out what she was or what she had to start with, and then the nature and scope of her alterations, see what she made of herself, maybe she'll be replicable. That's if she dies within reach, within our knowledge. If she doesn't lose herself out there somewhere, beyond recall or investigation. We speak of human space as though it were coherent and within bounds, as though we were secure in our holding and in our travelling back and forth, known roads swept free of danger, but none of that is true. Not many pilots die in their beds, in port, convenient for autopsy and study.

A lot of them may not be dead at all. Adrift in n-space, beyond all understanding—who knows, who can tell?

Just how late are Ferrel and Mercy Mercy, anyway?

They're not here, that's all we know. Not here now. Maybe they'll blow in tomorrow, all smiles and ease, full of news and great occasions. A shipful of cargo and great expectations, a new route won, a new system discovered. Something.

Maybe not. Magical thinking is endemic, where pilots are concerned. Their whole process, their individual processes seem halfway to magic at least. People say that it's unlucky to wish them well: that the harder you struggle to believe they'll bring their ships in safe, the less likely that is to happen. Scientists say that. It's been measured. People try not to think about it, mostly.

Murun is here, has brought his ship in safe. To everyone's always surprise. Murun is really not what you'd look for, in a pilot. He does not inspire confidence. Really not. The best of Murun is his companion Telfer, always at his side, calm and cooling and engaged. Telfer's the one you'd want in control, except that Telfer is no pilot. Telfer's just the rock, the counterweight, ballast or reaction mass or whatever metaphor you like: what allows Murun to work, that's Telfer. Possibly also what keeps Murun sane, if sane he be. Pilots don't usually fly with a partner—come to that, pilots don't usually have a partner—but every one's exceptional in some way, and this is Murun's.

Also he's an asshole and no one knows why Telfer stays with him, but there it is. Here they are.

Here they all are, this tableful: extraordinary anywhere, vanishingly rare all along the Limb, quite commonplace at Parry's. What people come to see, except that he'll never, never make an exhibition of them.

Parry serves drinks relentlessly, distributes smokes and other intoxicants, passes food orders through to the kitchen, answers questions from customers and servers both, watches the door, helps stray tourists find what they're actually looking for as soon as it's clear that his place is not that—and never takes his eye off the pilots' table. There's a barrier between them and the rest of the room; it's immaterial but clear to be seen and widely acknowledged. Let anyone breach that—and people will: drunk or determined, with a question to ask or an axe to grind—and Parry is there, swifter than you'd have thought possible, to steer them aside or throw them out, whichever. He's not always proportionate. Hell, he's not always appropriate. But it's his name above the door, or at least his singular initial, and he gets to make the rules and interpret them too. And enforce them, at need.

Tonight, though—well, tonight here comes a stranger. Five score eyes check him through the door, and no one recognises him. That means he's not a pilot. If he'd brought a ship to Dock, he'd be known by now: new and hence intriguing, mysterious and hence more to be gossiped about than any of the stalwarts.

Nor does he seem to recognise anyone here, even Parry behind the bar. That means he's not local, he doesn't work anywhere in Dock or anywhere on Base, because everyone knows Parry. By the look of him, he's only come here because he was told about it; and there's only one reason why he might have listened, only one reason ever for people to talk about Parry's.

But he's not heading to the bar for a drink, he's not joining the relentless not-quite-staring of the gathered crowd. No, indeed. One look around, and he knows just exactly where he's going: straight to the pilots' table, because he like everyone here knows pilots by sight alone, or else he just sees that barrier of awareness, that do-not-cross, and makes up his mind to cross it—and Parry does nothing.

No, that's not true. Parry does nothing but watch. He knows what's happening, none better; and he makes no move to interfere.

That's unprecedented. He can't have been bribed; this is his place, and what could you possibly offer him that's worth more?

Unknown territory makes uncertain ground. There's a breathlessness all over, people watching Parry watching the newcomer as he steps up, as the pilots lift their heads from that odd little conversation they're having.

They look, and see that they don't know him, and for a moment that is oh so unexpected, they don't know what to do else. Then they remember, one by one but in rapid succession, that this is Brone's table. So all their heads turn its way, relieved of responsibility, curious to see what it will do in their stead.

Unhurried as ever, Brone extends a hand—at least, two visible fingertips emerging from a fold in its swathe of blankets—and a welcome with it, gesturing towards the vacant seat opposite.

Parry never comes to take orders at the table, never—but he comes tonight, and stands at the man's shoulder with that kind of patient submissive authority that demands the attention of those on whom it waits.

He looks so ordinary, this man: there's nothing to him, no reason for any of this.

No observable reason.

Until he speaks, until he says "I don't want a drink, I never drink in port—and I couldn't pay you anyway," which is more honest than many a proprietor would expect.

Parry takes this in his stride, or rather in his stillness. Quite comfortably, he says, "The first one's on the house, always. And no one at this table drinks alcohol in port."

All of which goes to say one thing, and one thing only: and Parry might be down on eavesdroppers, but somehow everyone in the place hears that one thing, as it goes entirely and graciously unsaid.

The newcomer's a pilot after all. For all that he came in without a ship.

First Ferrel goes off with Mercy Mercy, and now this. Someone must have brought him in—but why? Any pilot can always find a ship. We have too many lying idle, when there are always passengers to ferry and cargo to shift, one end of the Limb to the other. There are a dozen here in Dock right now, their owners bidding high for any pilot's time, desperate to see their craft in service. The same is true at every station, every port of call.

Here he is, though, a pilot who didn't fly here, who must have been no more than a passenger in someone else's journey. Parry knows. Maybe Brone knows too. Maybe there's something about a pilot, something detectable, known to others of their craft. And to Parry, obviously.

Maybe he's just been talked about between themselves. Maybe he was hot gossip from the moment he arrived, and they've all been waiting to see him show up. Sooner or later, every pilot in Dock steps off the Margin and into Parry's, if only just to catch their breath before they dive back in.

He asks for honeymint, which may be the humblest request any pilot has ever made in here. Parry nods, doesn't bat an eye, but there's a murmur all around. Maybe no one's conspicuously eavesdropping, but no one's talking either, they're trying to absorb the conversation by osmosis; and he seems keen to help. His voice is extraordinary: a baritone that holds its own music, that strikes pure through every syllable and resonates all through the space, through people's heads as though it were their own proper note each time, entirely personal and entirely true.

Honeymint is good for the throat, but he really, really doesn't need it.

Except—well, is that a tremolo in his voice, or is it just a tremor? Certainly there's a tremor in his fingers, where he lays them so neatly, so carefully along the edge of the table. Here as elsewhere, every head is turned his way; here as elsewhere, every voice is hushed and waiting, leaving space for his. Maybe some of them only want to hear him speak again, and never mind the matter. Maybe. Pilots aren't usually so susceptible, but there's nothing usual happening here.

Brone gestures again, and this time maybe with an open hand, palm up. If it has palms, or hands. Nothing's certain, where there's almost nothing to be seen: a muffled movement within the fabric, perhaps another glimpse of fingers.

It's enough, seemingly. Or he was going to talk anyway, invited or otherwise. Just like he was going to approach anyway, he was going to push his way in. He has a seat, he has a drink on its way: both of those might be superfluous, might not have been needful at all. Not to the purpose. He might be all about the purpose.

He says, "My name is Almarine. I dislike to break in on you, but my need is urgent. I—I am a stranger to you, but … "

Even such a voice can lose its words, it seems, and die away, leaving a sense of absence that's both intolerable and insurmountable. No one is in a hurry to fill that vacancy, knowing how they must inevitably disappoint, however wisely they speak. Cadence should perhaps not matter so much, but sometimes—this time—yes, it truly does.

If anyone ever wants to tell you that pilots have no vanity, that they can't afford it—well. Laugh in the idiot's face. Even Almarine's silence has a mellow musicality to it, the attentive thrumming silence of a classic instrument, and not one of these wants to set their chicken-scratch voices against that, like an affront.

"You are a pilot."

Perhaps it had to be so, that Brone came forward at the last. Brone's table, after all; and Brone so seldom speaks, this wasn't so much an opportunity as a sucking vacuum. They hardly know what it sounds like, any of its cohort here; its voice is as much a shock as Almarine's, though for different reasons.

A figure so large, you'd expect it to boom hollowly, but it doesn't. There's a great deal of flesh in its voice, an unexpected wetness, a sense of marsh life where you'd think more of the high desert plains, as much of the dust and dry as you can imagine, who have never been to a Shutterself habitat.

"A pilot, yes." Almarine confirms it, and seems likely to go on, and then falls short of words again.

"Then whatever you need, in this place it is yours." And *this place* might mean Parry's establishment, or the Margin at large, or Dock or the whole station or the whole of human space: it's still a truth, plain and simple. It's not quite *carte blanche*, it's not *whatever you want*—but a pilot's need, any need, oh yes. If it's humanly possible, that will be met—and if it's not humanly possible, then it's not a need, by definition.

"I need a ship," he says—and then holds his hand up to stay them, to hold back the whole table. A little late: someone's laughing, someone's rolling their eyes, only Brone is showing no emotion at all. Brone's a rock. But Almarine goes on, "I mean, I need a ride. On someone else's ship. I can't, I can't do this alone. Not again."

And now no one's laughing, though their degrees of puzzlement or denial are probably no easier to take. Once again they leave this in Brone's hands, as though it were dependable, a rock. It says, "What, that you will not do? Pilots fly."

That's the criterion, really, that everything turns upon. *Whatever you need*, yes—but you do have to fly. For preference you have to get where you're going, with more or less what you were given— the ship, the passengers, the cargo—in more or less working order. Within tolerances, at least, in all particulars. Pilots have come in to the wrong port with the ship and the people and the goods too strangely changed; but they flew, and they survived.

Rock bottom, if you're a pilot, you really do have to fly.

Unless you're Brone, of course. Brone's unique, which is why there can't be two.

"You don't have to fly alone," Murun says, sounding almost considerate for once. It's a matter that touches him deeply, of course; maybe that makes a difference. He curls a hand around Telfer's wrist, and smiles, and for that little moment he's almost not an asshole.

"I do," says Almarine, and it might almost be his tragedy; certainly it is his sorrow, if not its cause. "I have to be alone. I," and this is really no news, now that they've heard his speaking voice, "I sing my way through n-space. The music of the spheres is quite literal to me: from planet to planet, and from star to star. Someone else with me would ... not be in tune."

Nods around the table. None of them could do that, or even understand it, but it makes perfect sense. They know a pilot who sees her path and draws it, a sequence of rapid sketches that somehow carries her and her craft along. If sketches, why not song? And if Murun needs Telfer, then of course another might need solitude.

"So," Maellelin says, "why can't you fly alone, if you have to be alone to fly?"

"I come from Reynmark's Star," he says slowly. "I grew up a planet-hopper, singing cargoes back and forth. I was happy there." More nods. Everyone knows Reynmark's, it's a constant port of call. A dozen ports of call, more habitable planets than any other system in human space, and enough traffic between them to sustain its own small navy, its own coterie of pilots.

To sustain, of course, does not mean *to keep*.

"I was offered better ships and a better life, if I would only go further. I was happy, but. The music of the planets was extraordinary; what might, what must the music of the stars be like? I could only ever hear Reynmark's Star, in-system. I thought there must be more, they must all sing in chorus; I thought I could join that chorus. I thought I had to hear it. I thought I only had to hear it, to know it. I thought it was the song the Sirens sang ..."

"So?"

"So I took an offer, I took a ship to go far and far, from one end of the Limb to the other. The further I went, the greater the music, you see? I wanted to hear all the galaxy sing to me ..."

"And?"

"And I heard all the galaxy sing to me, and it was the most dreadful terrible thing in my life," and they know how that feels, none better, though none of them can ever hope to hear what he's heard.

Each of them in their different ways has confronted n-space, and each of them has found it appalling, each and every time.

That's the other reason why they're treated very, very well. They go through hell out there, every time they go; we have to counter that with some little taste of heaven, every time they make it back, or why would they ever go?

Conversely, they do actually have to go, to justify their status. Everyone at this table—well, except for Brone, who is a law unto itself—does that, over and over. There's not much sympathy to be found here, for a man who won't.

"Aww, did it scare you, diddums?" Murun, being an asshole, as advertised.

Almarine looks at him, and something causes Murun to fall quiet, which may be the thing least expected in this most unexpected evening.

Parry brings Almarine's drink, and he sips it, holds it in his throat, almost seems to gargle it before he swallows. Must be a singer thing.

He says, "The planets around Reynmark's Star were like, like plainchant: organised, methodical, a unity. Anyone with an ear could sing with them. The star itself was grander, symphonic, still within my compass. I thought the stars at large would be like that. I thought I could reach them. I thought I could *aspire*." Even that magnificent voice can crack, seemingly. Another sip of honeymint, another pause. "I was wrong. I could barely survive the stars."

"And yet you did. We do." Maellelin, laying down the bare base fact of it like a card that could never be trumped.

"Not me. Not again. I came too far, I heard too much … I need to go home. In other people's ships, and small jumps. However long it takes. I can still hear them, even when I'm just a passenger. Not so, not so vividly, not inside me, blood and bone, but still. I hear them. And I can only stand so much."

He stares around the table, looking for contempt and finding that—Murun, yes, but not Murun alone: this isn't asshole territory, this is earned, the achievement of weakness, of broken oaths and neglected duty—and more, a kind of weary dismissal, *if you're choosing not to be a pilot, why are you sitting at our table?* Pilots have *noblesse oblige* written into their DNA—literally, in some instances—and they're very sensitive to betrayal.

"The stars leave their scars on us all." That's Brone again, saying more tonight than it might have said in a month before this.

"Not the stars," Almarine counters, and this, now: this is what he's here for. What he's here to say. Why he needs that ride so very, very much. Three short words, in that voice, with that emphasis: they were half turned away from him already, but now they're turning back as he goes on, "The others. The voices, singing their own way between the stars. They're out there, and I hear them."

"No." That's Ten Barry, and you could say that he's invested here. "No two pilots have ever worked n-space the same way," except themselves, perhaps. If that's what happens when you clone. "We never heard of another pilot singing. We never heard of any pilot singing, until now."

"Not one of us," says Almarine, and this is what they were all listening for, what none of them wanted to hear. "Not human. Their voices, their chord-sequences, their tonality—nothing human. But singing, yes, and doing what I do, riding the music from star to star. I can't bear to hear them, but I am sure. They're everywhere, out there."

And that's the thing, there's the moment. You could call it first contact, except it's not. Just a footfall on the stair, the sound of someone else's passage. All this time, all this space, nothing but human traffic, they had almost begun to believe themselves alone; and here's this sole voice—this extraordinary voice, but never mind that—to tell them it's not so. To say there's some other culture, creature, civilisation out there. Doing what he does, but doing it routinely: training up pilots the way we train up doctors or managers or civil engineers. Or barkeeps.

Here's Parry, and if anyone actually eavesdrops here, that would be him, so it would hardly count. The world or life or the universe just changed, something just changed radically, human perspective, turning over on itself; and he's here taking orders for fresh drinks, offering snacks from the kitchen, saying, "So, will one of you be taking Almarine on, the next step, towards home?"

And they all look at each other, still swimming from the revelation; and of course it's Brone, because Brone is talkative tonight where they apparently cannot be, who says, "I will find a ship, and take Almarine home. All the way. With pauses, when he needs them."

Which is unprecedented, more than implausible; which would have broken their understanding of the very way things are, if that weren't already lying in shatters about their feet; and which none of them, not one of the pilots at the table there needs so much as a moment to understand, to acknowledge, to accept.

Because it's the human thing to do.

FILIGREE, MINOTAUR, CYANIDE, BLOOM

DAMIEN ANGELICA WALTERS

Corinne makes a final circuit around her greenhouse, nodding here and there, closes the door behind her, and stretches with hands on her lower back. She knows the girl, only six or seven by Corinne's guess, is still watching her from behind the lilac bush in the far corner of the yard. Knows, too, she won't come any closer.

There's a rustle from the bush. Tangled dark hair appears, disappears, appears again. Corinne waves, slowly, with fingers only, but the girl doesn't respond. Corinne is neither fool nor miracle worker. If she were a virologist—and that's assuming the scientists were right—maybe she could make a difference, but she's a former librarian turned gardener. Her only claim to fame, if you can call it that, is that she's still here. Besides, she's patient, and Silent Ones aren't unintelligent, as most first speculated.

The girl has been visiting her for eight months now, and all Corinne's attempts to communicate have thus far been unsuccessful. They may very well remain that way, but, if nothing else, the attempts give Corinne a sense of purpose, gives her something to do other than exist. The girl is the first one to venture on her side of the inlet, the first Silent One to show any interest in her at all.

The girl takes off, climbing up and over the fence with ease. Corinne smiles. Funny, she was never overly fond of children before. She thought they were too noisy, and now, even thinking that, guilt twinges in her belly.

She stretches her back again and says "Mother, abacus, xylophone, beer."

Sixty is approaching on fast feet, and while she isn't frail or sickly, she has the older person's occasional aches and pains. The body betrays everyone in the end, no matter how active you are.

Before heading inside, she fills a pot from one of her rain barrels to boil atop her wood-burning stove. In warmer months, she uses the grill outside, but the late September air is cool enough now to cook in the house. After a light dinner of sweet potato bread, peach preserves, and cucumber slices, she slips on a cardigan for her nightly walk. As she fastens the buttons, she says, "Pine tree, squirrel, alphabet, locks."

Though she closes the front door behind her, she doesn't bother to lock it. No reason for that anymore. As she strolls through her neighborhood, she takes stock of the houses and the lawns. The old Patterson place at the end of her street is little more than a pile of charred bricks surrounded by weeds—it was struck by lightning a few years ago. Corinne watched it burn for hours, no longer expecting someone to come and help. It didn't take long for the greedy flames to eat through the shingles and the siding, the wallpaper, and the memories of human life within.

Ivy covers almost every inch of the big house on the corner, with only a hint of cedar siding peeking through on the top floor beneath the eaves. She always loved this one and once considered moving into it because it was twice as big as her two-bedroom rancher, but when she dared make an inspection, the ghosts—crumbs on the kitchen counter next to the sink, a glass in the drainboard, a load of laundry folded atop the dryer, a grocery list stuck on the refrigerator with a cartoon cat magnet—sent her running back out, hands butterflying to her chest. Better to stay in her own home. After all, she had the roof replaced the previous summer, and the shingles supposedly had a lifetime guarantee. And her yard got more sun. More sun equaled a better garden.

On the next three streets, all running parallel to hers, most of the houses are lost within the surrounding greenery; nature is all too willing to reclaim its space. A larger road runs perpendicular and curves around another series of small streets before passing the elementary school. That road is the only way in or out of the neighborhood on land; no through-traffic is part of the reason Corinne bought her house here. Once on the main road, it's only a short drive to a plethora of stores, although now that matters not at all. But it was a help in the early days when she stockpiled supplies, when she retained the hope that someone—the military, she assumed—would come in and put things to right. That hope died in dribs and drabs, ultimately replaced with a stoic sense of survival.

She turns down another perpendicular street, this one closer to the water, and walks down the gravel pathway leading to a small neighborhood beach and the South River beyond. Overgrown lawns, choked with weeds, sit on each side of the pathway. The roof of one of the houses collapsed by degrees; the other in one fell swoop after a storm a decade ago.

For a long while, Corinne kept the lawns tamed with her push mower, but now she worries only about the path and the small grassy area at its end. She maintains the bench in the middle of the grass as well; it's her favorite place to watch the sun set. The grassy area slopes down to the beach, a sandy half-circle about thirty feet long and ten feet wide.

Seated on the bench, she toes the dirt below her feet. Across the river, there's another beach, three times as large as this one and home to Silent Ones. This group currently numbers twenty-eight. They make no sign that they're aware of her presence, but she knows they are. The children, including the dark-haired girl, are off to one side, running in circles in a game that resembles tag. The lack of chatter, of happy shrieks, no longer strikes Corinne as strange. Some of the adults are stretched out, napping; others are scurrying around the shelter they've built from scavenged materials—garage doors, vinyl tarps, and the like—perhaps expanding it or making repairs. From where she sits, Corinne can't tell. For the past few days, they've seemed busier than usual; with the colder weather on the horizon, it makes perfect sense. In spite of the activity, the only sounds are thuds and banging. No calls to each other for assistance, not even a grunt or a whistle.

Their skin is light and dark and in between, and, as far as Corinne can tell, they treat each other the same. Most are clothed in a manner

27

of speaking—they have old, tattered blankets over their shoulders or wrapped around their waists, but a few are naked. All have long hair, and the men are heavily bearded. Feral is the first word that comes to mind, but it isn't right. Feral implies a sort of bestiality they don't possess. Primitive might be the better choice. They often groom each other, and they work together when foraging for food or caring for the children. Primitive, yet peaceful. She's never seen anything resembling a squabble, and she's been observing them for a long time.

There are only two in the group of a similar age to Corinne; the rest are younger. She can't help but wonder if they remember what their lives were like before everything changed. Before *they* changed.

If she closes her eyes, she can recall the first video. It went viral in days, even though no one understood what was happening and what it meant. People proclaimed it a joke or bizarre performance art and why not? Uploaded by an anonymous user with no mention as to where it was taken, it showed two dozen protestors holding signs that read *No Fracking!* and presumably chanting, although there was no audio, only the movement of their mouths. In hindsight, a frightening harbinger of what was to come.

They paced back and forth, back and forth down a generic American street, in front of a generic American office building. A woman at the end of the line dropped her sign, her face went blank, and her mouth opened and closed like a fish. She started moving her hands, as if scooping water, and the other protestors gathered around her, seemingly offering aid. There the video ended. Nearly six months later, when the swarms began, everyone realized that first protestor was most likely Patient Zero.

The affliction earned crude nicknames such as Shut the Hell Up, Captain Mute, in a nod to a Stephen King novel, or, oddly enough, Chatter. As to where it came from, no one ever knew or if they did, they kept mum. A few groups tried to claim it their creation, but they were all discredited. Others called it a natural phenomenon, a step on the evolutionary ladder. Some claimed it a disaster brought about by pollution, oil spills, the destruction of the rain forests. Those of a particularly religious bent offered the usual end of the world Judgment Day opinions.

No matter its origin, everything changed. It spread slowly at first, until the swarms began. They attacked—though that isn't quite right because they didn't appear to be trying to hurt anyone—those who still had words, had language, touching their mouths and bringing their hands back to their own, over and over again, as if trying to borrow or steal what they'd lost. Sooner or later, they'd give up and walk away, sometimes weeping, always soundlessly, and wringing their hands.

After the swarms came the overcrowded hospitals, the brown-outs, the mandatory curfews, and then the mass suicides. Not all who plunged from bridges, cliffs, or swam into the ocean were those afflicted. A few months later, the power went off and never came back on.

She doubts she's the only one alive who's capable of language and sound, but after eighteen years, those who aren't surely outnumber those who are, and probably in vast numbers. And by the time she realized how lonely, how jarring, the silence was, she'd already filled her pantry, spare bedroom, and garage with supplies, built her green-house, and taught herself how to preserve fruits and vegetables. She'd settled in. And she had Jacob, her neighbor, another immune, to look after. He was nearing eighty when the world changed, and he lived for five more years.

The world belongs to Silent Ones now and maybe it's for the best. Maybe the world is better quiet. For certain, there's no more global warming, no more melting ice caps, no more cities vomiting exhaust and chemicals into the air.

The sun begins its descent, painting the surface of the river in shifting shades of gold, and Corinne rests back against the bench, a breeze rifling through her hair. Those across the river don't pay the same sort of attention to the sun she does, but there is a shift. The children settle down a bit and draw closer to the group. A woman begins running her fingers through their hair, picking out leaves and such. A man begins gathering wood for a fire they'll start with a stick and friction, which is much harder to do than it appears.

Another group, larger than this one, once lived near the elementary school but none survived a particularly harsh winter two years ago. Why they don't go indoors when there are plenty of empty buildings and houses is beyond Corinne. She doesn't know what they comprehend and what they don't and wishes she did, but the changes are definitely more than a lack of words and language.

"Manicure, pedicure, elephant, sex," she says, her words soft and low.

If she establishes some sort of communication with the girl, maybe it will lead to communication with the adults, and maybe then she'll have more of an understanding.

The sun drops below the horizon, and, as is her routine, Corinne waves before she heads down the pathway. No one waves in response, but their gazes are heavy on her retreating back.

The girl returns the next day, spying on Corinne as she runs through her afternoon chores. After about an hour, Corinne sits cross-legged on the ground near a rain barrel, about twenty feet from the lilac bush. The girl peeks from between two branches, then dips back down, out of sight.

Corinne closes her eyes and tips her face toward the sun. After a time, she glances over at the bush, and unless she's mistaken, the girl's now seated as well. Corinne gives a slow finger wave. The girl peers through the branches again. Corinne waves again. The branches shake as the girl rises to her feet and climbs the fence, but she doesn't race over as fast as she did yesterday. Progress of a sort, perhaps.

"Aluminum, peroxide, squalid, bear," Corinne says. "Bear," she repeats, tapping her chin while a smile grows.

She keeps a bag of fabric scraps in her spare bedroom, now a storage room. She's seen the children playing with sticks and rocks, but never toys, though there must be some lying around in decent shape. Maybe the girl will respond to a stuffed animal.

She cuts pieces of brightly colored fabric in the rough shape of a bear and sets aside other pieces to use as stuffing. Her stitches are small and neat, reminding her of a line from a movie she saw a few times. Early on, when the gas was still viable, she had a generator and played movies at night. Now, her collection of DVDs is in the attic above the garage. Her car is long gone; to free up storage space, she parked it in her neighbor's driveway where it sits to this day, rusting away.

After a break for dinner, she returns to the bear instead of taking a walk and when it's done, she shakes out the stiffness in her fingers. One of the bear's ears is larger than the other and the limbs on the right side are plumper than those on the left, but all in all, it's not too bad for a first effort.

For a long time she sits on her front porch, holding the bear loosely in her arms, while insects chatter and flit through the growing dark and bats give chase. A fox lopes down the middle of the street, its bushy tail bouncing with each step. "Butterscotch, pillow, radiation, pine," Corinne says. The fox pauses, twitches its tail, then moves on.

The girl is sitting behind the lilac bush when Corinne comes outside after breakfast. She pretends not to notice her at first, but eventually goes back inside for the bear. The girl is there upon her return, and Corinne repeats yesterday's action with one difference: she holds the stuffed bear against her chest.

Then she wiggles her hips and scoots a little closer to the bush. The girl remains in place. Corinne sits for a time, cuddling the bear, then scoots again. As the girl watches, Corinne continues to hold the bear and scoot until she's about ten feet from the bush. She takes a deep breath and holds out the bear. The branches rustle as the girl scrambles toward the fence and, in a blink of the eye, she's gone.

Corinne's shoulders sag. "Telephone, harpsichord, battery, flu," she whispers into the bear's fur. After a few moments' consideration, she leaves the bear behind the lilacs and returns inside. She checks periodically during the day and early evening, but the bear is still there each time.

After dinner, she walks to the river's edge and sits on the beach itself, tracing patterns in the sand. Across the water, the Silent Ones go about their business. Of the dark haired girl, there's no sign.

Before Corinne turns in for the night, she checks the lilac bush again. The stuffed bear is gone.

It's late afternoon and she's inside the greenhouse when the crash comes. Cucumbers fall out of her hands, but she leaves them on the ground as she runs outside, her tongue slicked bitter with panic. Her house is fine, and those around hers are intact as well. No fallen trees, no collapsed roofs, no shattered glass.

The second crash is louder than the first and it comes from the beach. She breaks into a run. Across the water, half the Silent Ones shelter has fallen. A man drags a bit of loosened tarp away to a pile off to the side. Another man pulls on a garage door, and there's a third crash when it falls on its side. The two begin dragging it up the beach, toward the houses.

Corinne has never ventured around the inlet to their side of the river, but her curiosity is strong. The road that curves around is narrow and twisty, full of potholes and rubble. She makes her way carefully, but quickly. Maybe they're planning to rebuild the shelter closer to the houses. Maybe they're planning to relocate *in* one of the houses. That would be a definite mark of progress.

She rounds the last corner and skids to a stop. In the middle of the road, one of the men is standing, staring at Corinne, his face impassive. He takes a step toward her and then another. He holds no weapon and his arms are hanging loose at his side, fingers un-clenched, but fear waltzes up her spine.

"Okay," she says, hands out as she backs away, pulse rushing in her ears. "Okay, I'm leaving. I'll leave you alone."

She keeps backing away, even when he's no longer in sight. For the first time in a long time, she locks her windows and doors before she goes to bed. But sleep eludes her and she slips from bed. From the top shelf of her closet, she removes a handgun. It belonged to her neighbor and comes in handy when she ventures out of the neighborhood—the dogs are all feral now and sometimes they need to be scared away. She leaves the gun on her nightstand, within easy reach, and climbs back in bed. Foolish, perhaps, to keep the weapon at hand, but she's unsettled and can't shake it off.

The morning dawns heavy with clouds and the smell of impend-ing rain. Corinne takes enough wood inside to keep a fire burning for several days, just in case, and makes sure the tarp over the rest of the pile is secure. She locks the door behind her and pulls the curtains tightly closed so the interior of her house is swathed in shadows. She keeps the gun close at hand as well.

Mid-afternoon, the storm rolls in. It starts strong, with a deluge of rain, deep rumbles of thunder, and bright flashes of lightning, and rains all day and into the night. She sleeps in fits and starts, tossing and turning between nightmares of masked assailants.

Morning brings full sun and a bright blue sky, but Corinne's smile fades as soon as she steps outside. There's a thick smell of char in the air, and from her front lawn, a dark plume of smoke is visible over the roofs and trees. She thinks the fire might be across the street in one of the old shopping centers, but the proximity justifies taking a look. She won't be able to put it out herself, but she can at least survey the damage and make sure it can't spread, if she's able.

She packs two days' worth of supplies, more than she'll need, but better to have it and not need it than the reverse. The day is warmer than it's been with only a hint of a breeze. On her way out of the neighborhood, walking stick firmly in hand, hiking boots tightly laced, handgun in a holster on her hip, she focuses all her attention on her passage. The roads are cracked and pitted with weeds sticking up from the gaps, and one unseen pothole, one misstep, could prove disastrous.

"Calliope, grapefruit, troubadour, swing," she says, punctuating each word with another step.

She used to leave the neighborhood once a month or so, not that there was anything to find, but she liked to keep watch, liked to remind herself that the world was larger than the small corner she occupied. She stopped not long after the girl came into her yard for the first time.

Birds sing from the trees and squirrels dart this way and that, too intent on their lives to worry about her. She pauses at the main road to take a drink of water, and a half-dozen white-tailed deer pick their way across the parking lot of an old bank on the corner. After they pass, she crosses to the middle of the road, checking left and right beforehand, for animals, not cars. Bits of white paint, the crisp edges long erased, streak the asphalt in spots.

She keeps her eye on the smoke. It's not as near as she first feared, which is a relief, and she's fairly certain it's far enough away to be of no concern, even if the fire's still burning, but since she's made it this far, it makes no sense to turn around. And it feels good to be moving. She forgot how much she liked these trips.

She keeps going, stick tapping in rhythm with the thud of her boots. The ghosts of old shopping centers rise and fall on either side of the street. Grocery stores, frozen yogurt shops, the bookstore—that one she misses—pizza chains and Chinese restaurants—another definite miss. A good many of the buildings appear structurally intact; more than a few have unbroken windows. The signs have faded or fallen, the latter now concealed by greenery. The deer and rabbits do a remarkably good job at keeping the grass and weeds from overtaking everything, but it's very apparent the buildings are no longer inhabited. She's curious what another eighteen years will bring. If she's alive to see it, that is.

The stink of charred wood grows stronger as she crosses the bridge over the river. Another bridge sits a quarter-mile further down, over the interstate, and the smoke is coming from just beyond that.

"Octopus, tennis ball, orangutan, worm," she says, pausing for another drink of water.

The remnants of a crude shelter sit in the parking lot of another grocery store—an organic market she rarely shopped in because the prices were expensive—but there's no sign of the Silent Ones who lived there. If she recalls correctly, they were a smaller group, only ten or eleven in number.

As she draws close to the second bridge, she hears a sound she can't place. It almost sounds like rushing water, but not quite. She quickens her steps, then slows, then stops, the fire forgotten.

On the southbound lanes of the interstate below her, hundreds of Silent Ones are walking, all with purpose in their steady strides. Men, women, children; some empty-handed, others with bundles over their shoulders. The larger whole is made up of smaller groups, yet as she stands there, some of the groups meld with the others around them. This is behavior she's never observed before. It reminds her of ...

"Migration?"

She peers into the distance, one hand shielding her eyes from the sun. More Silent Ones appear. Are they retreating to warmer climes? Relocating permanently? Making some sort of pilgrimage?

One man with a long beard looks up and Corinne's cheeks warm as he watches her watching him, then he moves out of sight, under the bridge. As other Silent Ones pass, some notice her standing atop the bridge, but most ignore her presence. The sense of being an outsider—an interloper—grows stronger, and it tastes of vinegar and ashes. This is a world she's no longer a part of. She's nothing more than one of the buildings falling to ruin. A dying breed.

"Hippopotamus, amber, chrysalis, tile," she says.

More Silent Ones come and go. So many more of them than she imagined possible. No speaking or shouting, only their resolute footfalls. Corinne twists her hands and shuffles her feet. Finally, she shouts, "Where are you going?"

Several Silent Ones start, another stumbles, and they begin to move faster.

"I'm sorry," she says. "So sorry."

She scrubs her face with her hands and makes her way back home, her steps slower than usual. As she turns down the road leading into her neighborhood, the Silent Ones from across the river come into view. They're walking in the same manner as those on the interstate. Corinne stands off to the side, her arms crossed beneath her breasts. A few meet her gaze, but none hold it for more than a second or two. Most act as though she isn't there at all. The little dark-haired girl is near the back, the stuffed bear gripped in one hand, and Corinne's eyes fill with tears.

From here, she can't see her house, but she feels it waiting for her. The rain barrels filled, the plants in the greenhouse, the mason jars full of preserves. Safety and surety. Survival.

Solitude.

She scuffs the toe of her boot along a crack in the asphalt. She could go with the Silent Ones. She wouldn't be *with* them, exactly, but she wouldn't be alone either. She could act as witness, keeping her distance until they trusted her. Maybe one day they'd welcome her in and allow her to care for the children. Maybe …

She takes a step toward them and then another. A man stops, turning slowly, the same man from the other night. His face is as equally impassive as it was then, but Corinne hisses in a breath and backs away once more.

"Filigree, minotaur, cyanide—"

The little girl holds out a hand. Her fingers crook, release, and crook again. Corinne waves in return and, with tears running freely down her cheeks, watches them go.

HOW HE HELPED

RAMSEY CAMPBELL

Hubble knew why he felt watched, but for a moment he thought somebody nearby had spoken his name. Perhaps they'd said something about trouble, which would be appropriate enough. He'd never seen a restaurant so crowded; he hadn't expected Disable Disability Day to bring so many people downtown. All three queues were held up—retarded, you used to be able to call it—by a less than teenage boy who was waddling alongside the counter to read the descriptions of food at the top of his voice. Whenever his mother tried to hurry him or learn what he wanted he unleashed a prolonged shriek of rage and stamped his plump feet in their plump expensive shoes, making the electric heels flare red. As a woman in the next queue caught Hubble's eye he risked remarking "We can't say anything, can we?"

Her thin lips worked like a displaced frown. "What are you trying to say?"

He wasn't to be trapped like that. Even if belittling weren't the latest crime you might be prosecuted for, he shouldn't offend anyone just now. "Nothing," he told her. "That's what I said."

The man in front of her turned around from typing on his phone. "We don't know what you're getting at, friend."

"Just that some people are allowed to make more noise than the rest of us."

Both faces stiffened as if they were shielding themselves from his thoughts. "Maybe if you had a disability," the woman said.

"Be handy with a handicap." Hubble couldn't resist uttering one of the slogans of Delight In Diversity Week. "I've got one," he said, flourishing his spectacles. "I just don't have any letters to my name."

"No idea what that means," the man said tersely enough for a text message.

Hubble donned his glasses to glance at the boy, who was dealing the counter a pudgy thump accompanied by a scream. "Aid Edie," he said, "isn't that the accepted term?"

Too many people were staring at him now, and the mother swung around. "It's ay dee haitch dee," she said as though she was proud of the extra letter. "He's got attention deficit hyperactivity disorder, and don't nobody go saying he's not."

She couldn't speak grammatically or pronounce a letter correctly, and yet she had the jargon to a t, in fact to six of them. "Will he be in the parade?" Hubble couldn't resist asking.

"Like you will, I don't think."

"Oh, I'll be involved." Perhaps he let that out because of feeling watched by too large an audience. "Aren't we all meant to be?" Hubble thought it best to add.

He might have looked for a response if the item hidden by his coat hadn't slipped an inch. He made for the exit at once so that nobody would see him hitch up his burden and wonder what it was. Today the road was closed to traffic, but temporary barriers confined the crowds of spectators to the pavements. He had to glance back to dispel an impression that quite a few people had followed him. "Just me," he muttered and wondered if anybody thought he had Tourette's, though nowadays so many solitary people talked outdoors, not to mention swearing, that it was hard to tell. You couldn't even ask them to mind their language in case they had you arrested for discrimination. The ordinary man was the only category it was safe to discriminate against, and complaining about that could get you done for hate speech.

All the queues in the next restaurant extended almost to the entrance, and Hubble wouldn't have gone in if he hadn't absolutely needed to. As he shuffled forward a distant band struck up a march. The parade had begun, but surely it wouldn't arrive before he was ready, though the nearest spectators were joining in the cheers by the time he reached the counter. Behind it the staff were uniformed with paper hats that made them look like children at a party, and he thought they weren't much older. "How can we serve you today?" they kept saying, and at last a youth who might have owed his blotchy complexion to the food said it to him.

"I'll have a Super Triple Feast," Hubble said and tried to sound sufficiently enthusiastic.

"Not on today," the youth said with audible weariness. "Just the celebration specials."

Hubble hadn't time to scrutinise the list that was taped over the illuminated menu, where blurred words showed through the temporary text. "What else is as big?"

"The Colossal Chicken Bun."

"One of those, then."

"One Colossal," the youth called across the metal pass into the kitchen, only to report to Hubble "Sorry, just sold out."

Hubble had to make himself relax before his arms could crush the item inside his quilted coat. "Safe," he blurted, then pretended he'd set out to say "Same question, then."

"What?" As Hubble's patience gave way the youth said "What's as big, you mean. Just the Vastly Veggie Burger"

"That, then," Hubble said, wishing he could be terser still.

"One Vastly." Having called that, the youth said "Any drink?"

"I'd like extra fries and extra salad." A jab of doubt made Hubble add "So long as they're in the same carton."

Surely the meal would have come that way, and the youth gave him a less than professional look before tapping the order on the till screen. At least the polystyrene box was as capacious as Hubble had hoped it would be. "This'll do it," he declared and felt bound to say "The meal, I mean."

Only the start of the parade had passed by. As Hubble left the restaurant he saw metal limbs pumping in unison beyond the crowd at the barrier. They put him in mind of components in an enormous machine—an engine constructed to crush all dissent—and he knew they represented Paraplegic Power. He mustn't mutter Pampered Paraplegics or even the Mobility Nobility, and he took a mouth-sized bite of the burger to block any comment, only to feel he shouldn't even let the thought into his head. Surely surveillance hadn't progressed that far, though might it in his lifetime? He could have fancied that he felt his brain shrinking back from the future, striving to contract so as to hide more safely in his cranium.

The burger was almost as dry as the bun and tasted like a pretence. Perhaps that was why Hubble felt as if he was putting a show for an audience—as if he was being not merely observed but commented upon. No doubt everyone was being watched by the cameras perched above the shops on both sides of the road, and feeling singled out needn't mean he was. He knew why he did, and it would be prudent to move well away from the restaurants where the staff might remember him. As he marched alongside the paraplegics he could have thought he was being propelled by the relentless martial music blaring out of floats in the parade. So long as nobody suspected him of mocking the paraplegics, but officials posted along the route kept glancing at him. As soon as he realised where he might be least conspicuous he stopped next to the nearest official.

Like all of them, she wore a yellow waistcoat over her clothes. He might have reminded her what being yellow meant, and couldn't anybody colour-blind accuse her and her colleagues of discrimination? Once she'd returned his smile, presumably having failed to glimpse the sly grin it hid, she returned to watching the parade, and Hubble didn't know why he felt more watched than ever. Perhaps talking would help calm his nerves, and he said "Keeping you busy, are they?"

Her smile seemed to summarise her placid well-fed face. "No more than they ought to expect," she said.

Had his remark sounded even slightly like a gibe? "The crowds, that is," he tried saying. "Me and the rest of us."

"I'd rather have a job than not."

"Oh, definitely me as well." On the edge of saying too much, Hubble said only "You'll be grateful to our friends there, then."

"We should all be."

He oughtn't to have prompted that, because now he had to demand "What for?"

"Showing us what's possible for everyone."

"Soon."

Who'd said that? For a moment Hubble thought the parade had. He felt he'd heard more than one voice, though this hadn't sounded quite like any chorus he could bring to mind. Might it belong to some of the phones that spectators were using as cameras? He had an idea that it had been somehow electronic. All the same, he felt as if it had been addressed to him, and since the official seemed not to have heard it, perhaps it was just in his head. He mustn't seem uneasy, and so he made the first remark that came to him. "You aren't expecting any trouble, then."

"I can't imagine anyone would want to cause any, can you?" As Hubble hushed himself she said "I wouldn't mind if it could always be like this."

"You want people putting on a show every day."

When she stared at him he was afraid she'd seen through his until she said "I'd like the road to stay closed to traffic. Friendlier to everyone."

"Not so much to drivers."

"They shouldn't expect special treatment. Our roads are for everyone."

"Just not them."

He thought her placid stare was growing close to smug, but it wasn't as imperceptive as it looked. "Is driving what you do?" she said.

"Used to be."

"I don't think accommodating people's needs would put anyone out of a job."

Hubble stifled his rejoinder with a bite gouged out of the burger and shook his head, a gesture she could interpret how she liked. Just a few words were all it took to destroy your livelihood. He ought never to have stopped his taxi for the bunch of drunks—he should have seen there wasn't room for all of them and one man's wheelchair. When they'd kept accusing him of discrimination he'd finally retorted that although he was crippled by bad eyesight he didn't expect anyone else to pay for his spectacles, and in less than a month the council had withdrawn his licence. It had taken him much longer to accept that no firm would hire a driver who'd been condemned for using proscribed language. In fact, he didn't accept it at all, and now he had to choke his words down along with the mouthful of burger. When he didn't entirely succeed, the woman said "I didn't catch that."

"I said I knew what they need."

She could take that how she liked as well. He'd got rid of enough of the burger now. As he dropped the remains in the carton her gaze made him say "For the bin."

"There's one over there." As he began to sidle through the crowd she called after him "Enjoy your day."

"Hubble Day."

They knew his name. That was his first reaction, and he felt celebrated until he remembered nobody could know. If the voices were real he would be seeing people hear them. They were too clear in the midst of the blurred blare of music, as if they were somehow removed from conventional sounds, more like a message sent directly to his brain. None of this meant they were wrong. They knew as much as he did, and being heralded made him surer of himself.

When he reached the concrete bin close to a temporary barrier he looked back. The woman was watching the parade, and didn't see him dodge past the bin. He wouldn't be tricked into using it, since she might identify him as the man who had. He restrained himself from shouldering spectators aside, though they slowed him down so much that a procession in wheelchairs was overtaking him. "Hobble along, Hubble," he could hear his old form master saying at school, not that teachers would be allowed to say that now. Soon you might have to submit everything you planned to say for approval before you dared open your mouth. Meanwhile phones might continue to deplete language, the way texting did. Perhaps abbreviating words would end up reducing everyone to an icon, to the smiling disc so many people used as language. Perhaps society would oblige you to resemble it as well, and too many of the crowd around him appeared to be proving they could. So long as they weren't mocking his efforts to keep up with the wheelchairs, a race he would have won by now if his opponents hadn't benefited from special treatment as usual. Did they have a name? The Wonderful Wheelies, they might call themselves, with the Epic Epileptics still to come in the procession, along with the Awesome Autistics and the Tremendous Tourette'ses … Some people said autistics were the next development in evolution, in which case Hubble hoped he wouldn't see it happen. In his view it had gone into reverse, the result of inventing so much jargon to excuse if not encourage bad behaviour. He would like to see a future that left all that behind. Perhaps he could help to bring that about— perhaps this was the message the voices had for him.

He thought the next waste bin was being guarded until he saw the dog belonged to a blind man. How could the fellow be watching the parade unless he was pretending to be sightless? Surely he ought to be trooping along with the rest of his type, the Pampered Partially Sighted or the Blithely Blind. If Hubble took his glasses off he could join the pageant, except he would never trade on his problem, which was his responsibility and nobody else's. The wheelchair contingent were showing off now, spinning their vehicles in circles, and he could see nobody watching him. He needed to be ready before he reached the bin.

He should have left a shoelace untied. As he crouched to loosen one he dropped the carton and let his other burden slip. For the benefit of any cameras he mimed accidentally opening the carton, and then his body hid the object he planted within. He shut the polystyrene lid before tying his shoelace and making for the bin.

The dog didn't bark or otherwise acknowledge him when he placed the carton on top of all the rubbish in the concrete tub. No doubt guide dogs were trained not to react to people, but he didn't mind thinking the animal sensed how right he was. He moved onwards at once, and didn't take his phone out until he was hundreds of yards from the bin. All around him people held their phones up as if they were displaying tributes to the parade. They were taking photographs, turning the world more electronic, and he keyed a code into his phone before lifting it high. The band came to the end of a jolly march, and he felt as though it was giving him a cue. He hoped nobody saw him take a fierce breath before tapping the screen.

He was hardly aware of squeezing his eyes shut until they flared with an inner light and then with a flash that was bigger and brighter than anyone else's phone had produced. In less than a second he heard a sound almost too uncommon to define, a deep thump that felt like a punch in the guts, a noise immediately transformed into a stony splintering that was followed by a smash of glass and widespread thuds of rubble. After this came more of a silence than he expected, so that he imagined the crowd pausing for breath if not growing mute with awe at the spectacle until quite a few of them voiced the first scream.

If he didn't look he might be too conspicuous. It was too late to be squeamish, and he should be proud he hadn't been. When he opened his eyes as wide as they would stretch he saw that the parade and the crowd around the ruins of the bin had grown more colourful, though only with varieties of red. An indeterminate number of wheelchair users were strewn across the road, some of them bidding to compete with the paraplegics at fusing flesh with metal. Among the scattered limbs and other fragments he saw a tattered reddish item that reminded him of furs that women used to wear around their necks. It was a pity about the dog, but the animal wouldn't have been there if the blind man hadn't been trying to prove he belonged in the audience. As some of the reddened lumps lying in the road began to move, the speakers struck up a new tune, which seemed to rouse the crowd to panic. He saw a mass of appalled faces turn to him before they came at him. The mob wasn't about to seize him, it was simply fleeing, and he ought to join in.

He didn't need to think where he was going. Nobody would just now. Instinct sent him down the nearest alley, which took him out of the dangerous uncontrolled surge of the crowd. A few people copied his example, but were they why he felt pursued? He might have felt guilty or at any rate dissatisfied if he'd let himself, because he hadn't taken into account how many able people would be crippled by the bomb. Surely more of the parade had been eliminated, which should restore some form of balance. At least the people who'd commandeered the week had been shown what the silenced majority thought of them.

Hubble dodged into another alley, and another. Each of them left more of the crowd behind, and yet he still felt watched if not discussed. He could see no cameras—not until he turned a corner and found one pointing straight at him. He was about to hide his face, having failed to grasp how guilty this would look, when he saw he was behind the local television station, where a cameraman was loading the equipment into a van. Even so, Hubble felt compelled to explain his haste. "Bomb," he panted, pointing back the way he'd come.

A man whose face he vaguely knew from newscasts hurried over to him. "Were you there?"

"I was, yes." In case this sounded too suggestively emphatic Hubble said "Like a lot of people."

"Did you see what happened?"

"I didn't see it go off. Just what it did."

"Can we interview you?"

His impulse was to refuse, but how suspicious might that look? Before he could think of a convincing excuse the reporter said "You'd be doing us a big favour."

Hubble had done that for the world, and why should he need to be cautious? Perhaps talking about it like a spectator would let him stop feeling observed. "I've never done this before," he said.

"It won't hurt. You'll be fine. Just go round to reception and tell them Danny says for news to film an interview."

As the van raced away Hubble strode around the building to the counter in the lobby. "Danny says you want to film me about the bomb."

The receptionist blinked at him beneath a pretty frown. "Which bomb?"

"Only one that I know of." When this didn't lift the frown Hubble said "The one that did for the parade."

She kept her gaze on him while she leaned towards the switchboard, and he wished he didn't feel she wasn't the only watcher. "I've got a gentleman out here who wants to talk about a bomb."

Hubble didn't like the sound of this, and was thinking how to put her right when a door beside the counter let out a woman a head taller than him. "That's fine, Terry," she told the receptionist. "We know all about him."

He was distracted by a sense that her voice had covered up an instant echo of her comment about him. She thrust out a large hand to detain him. "Maria Neilson," she said. "Danny called to say you were coming in."

She only wanted to shake his hand. He recognised the presenter now, her hair cropped short as if to make her height less daunting, her broad face spanned by a constantly concerned look. A man with a camera perched on his shoulder followed them into the street, where passers-by glanced at Hubble as if they ought to know him, no less than he deserved. "Just say your name," Maria Neilson said.

"Harold Hubble." He did his best to fend off an impression that the muted voices, which he couldn't really hear, had joined in if not answered for him. "Harold Hubble," he said in case he hadn't spoken after all.

"Harry, shall we say, or Harold?"

"I'm exactly what I said."

"Harold." Rather too much like someone addressing an invalid she said "Tell us what happened in your own words."

"Who else's am I going to use?" Hubble retorted and peered at the camera. "Is he filming me?"

"That's the idea, Harold. Just tell us all about it and we'll edit you if necessary."

A wailing chorus silenced him—the sirens of police cars. No doubt she was conducting the interview out here to include that kind of detail. "What did you see?" she prompted.

"I didn't see the bomb go off, I only heard it."

"How close were you, Harold?"

"Not that close. Not very close at all." Having established this, he felt safe to say "You wouldn't think a little bomb could do so much."

"We've had no report of its size."

"You could see they'd left it in a rubbish bin." Surely an innocent spectator might know this, but Hubble thought it wise to add "I expect anyone can find out how to make bombs these days. Just go on your computer and there you are."

"I'm afraid that's the truth." Before Hubble could point out that the truth was the last thing you should be afraid of, she said "You were saying what you saw."

"It did a lot of damage. Shops, not just people." He saw she was eager for details. "It wasn't just the bomb, it was chunks of the bin," he said. "Smashed all the windows by it and the people too. There were bits of them in the road, the people. I think a lot of them were dead, but there'll be some of them in hospital for a good bit. Let's just hope they learn to look after themselves. Are you broadcasting me now?"

"As I said, we'll be editing you first."

Then why did he feel he had a larger audience than he could see? He must be anticipating his future fame, but Maria Neilson distracted him by asking "What did you do?"

"Nothing. Not a thing. What makes you—" He managed to interrupt himself, hoping he hadn't understood her question too late. "There wasn't anything I could do," he said "I'm not a nurse or a carer either."

"But you do care, don't you, Harold? How do you feel about what you saw today?"

"It was worse than you could have expected." This struck him as so clever an escape from the trap she'd laid that he risked adding "It was like a battlefield, only not the ones you see in films. They don't show the mess it makes of people."

He seemed to have engaged her sympathy; certainly she winced. "What kind of person do you think could have done it?" she said.

While this wouldn't trick him into saying too much, he wouldn't deny himself either. "Someone who believed in what he was doing," he said.

"I'm sure that's true, unfortunately."

Was she trying to provoke him to declare it was by no means unfortunate? Certainly her gaze was encouraging him to speak. When he met it with a silence no mute could have improved upon she said "Thank you for all that, Harold. I should be on my way if I were you."

"You aren't, or you wouldn't be talking to me." Rather than say this Hubble demanded "Why would you?"

"They're bound to cordon off the area. We don't know where they'll let the buses stop."

He might have enquired how she knew he'd come by bus. She couldn't know he'd had to sell his car after he'd been caught cruising for passengers. Didn't he look sufficiently famous to own a car? He might have told her he deserved to be, but said only "When will I be on?"

"As soon as we've put you together." While the cameraman returned to the building she said "I just need you to sign a waiver."

She wanted his name and address on the form. Surely he had no reason to conceal them, but he felt obscurely nervous. Too late he wished he'd told her false ones, and he signed as illegibly as he could. "Thank you for bringing it alive," she said.

He didn't like that either. Since it was the opposite of his achievement, he could have suspected her of joking. Rather than confront her he made for the main road. He wasn't running away from her, he simply wanted to be home to watch himself on television. He had nothing to be ashamed of. "You needn't be," he thought someone— indeed, quite a number of them—said, though he couldn't see them.

The wide street was still hosting an impromptu race. Everyone was fleeing the bomb and its aftermath, and Hubble didn't mind appearing to be. Beyond a line of police cars was a growing crowd of people determined to board a bus, and he managed to struggle onto one despite provoking protests, which seemed less present than the voices he'd been hearing. As he stood in the aisle, gripping a metal pole for support, he felt like a crusader with a spear. More passengers than he would have thought the bus had room for piled on board, forcing people along the aisle, but he didn't let go of his emblem. At last the bus moved off, so sluggishly that it felt retarded by its unaccustomed burden, and Hubble was mutely urging it to gather speed when he heard a voice beside and below him. "You wouldn't think a little bomb could do so much," it said.

It wasn't like the other voices he kept hearing—it was his own. When he glanced down he saw his face in miniature, almost filling the screen of a woman's mobile phone. "You could see they'd left it in a rubbish bin," it said.

"That was me." Hubble managed not to say this, even though he would only have meant the interview, instead letting his electronic image speak for him. "It did a lot of damage. It wasn't just the bomb, it was chunks of the bin. There wasn't anything I could do. It was like a battlefield, only not the ones you see in films. They don't show the mess it makes of people."

He was waiting for his best line when a reporter's face ousted his—Danny with a shattered store window as a backdrop. Hadn't they wanted people to be told the truth? Didn't they realise how many might agree, or was that what they were afraid of? He was close to proclaiming the censored line when he heard his voice behind him. "You wouldn't think a little bomb could do so much," it said.

It was on another phone, and it was less than halfway through its statement before a third phone found him. The repetitions made him feel as if he were being split into electronic fragments. They weren't going to break up his mind, and he clawed at the bellpush on the metal pole. As the bell went off he let his suppressed voice escape. "Getting off," he shouted. "Coming through."

He had to squirm through the crowd between the seats while his entire body prickled as if it had turned electronic. The bus left him beside a small memorial garden, where a path encircled a statue inside a spiky fence reminiscent of a crown of thorns. A few benches stood beside the path, and Hubble sat behind the stone figure, not caring who it represented. As he took out his phone he had to remind himself it was no longer a trigger. Rather than search for the television station, he couldn't resist typing his name in the search box, and the phone suggested a link at once. Hubble Day, it said.

Could he really be seeing that? He poked the words hard enough to leave a moist blurred fingerprint on the screen, and then he jerked his head around. Nobody was watching over his shoulder or from anywhere else that he could see, and he turned back to the phone to find his own reduced face gazing up at him. "You wouldn't think a little bomb could do so much," it said.

"It changed the world."

The voices said so. They were closer now, as close as the core of his mind. "Let's hope so," he said.

"You could see they'd left it in a rubbish bin."

"What it brought about wasn't rubbish."

"You won't hear me arguing," Hubble declared and tried to concentrate on his own voice, which was saying "It did a lot of damage."

"Not damage, Harold. It was a sign."

"I don't know what you mean."

"It wasn't just the bomb, it was chunks of the bin. There wasn't anything I could do."

"You did more than you imagine, Harold. You made us find out how we couldn't be destroyed."

The voices were getting out of control, he thought. He no longer understood them, which meant he'd had enough. "I'm not hearing you," he said. "You're nothing to do with me."

"It was like a battlefield, only not the ones you see in films," his processed voice was saying. "They don't show the mess it makes of people."

"It never will again, Harold. That's what you gave the world."

He wished his image would silence the voices by speaking his last line, but he did instead. "Someone who believed in what he was doing."

"We know, Harold. We understand and we forgive."

He felt as if the voices were massing around him, more and more of them. He ought to stop responding in the hope that this would rid him of them, but he couldn't help demanding "Who are you?"

"We're the future you made, Harold. You remember, the world will be electronic, and that's us."

He felt as if his brain was being raided. "I never said that," he protested.

"But you will."

They sounded more impatient to be heard, blotting out his own small voice, which was doggedly reiterating the interview. It sounded no less electronic than the chorus—the messages that were being projected into his head. The voices were separating now, which only made them harder to ignore. "We led the way," one said, "and you will."

"Nobody is different now. Everyone is free."

"Nobody because there are no bodies. No bodily dependence any more."

"We can be anything we want to be."

"Once you're uploaded. Once you're stored."

"It will happen in your lifetime, and then we won't depend on time."

"In your time you'll be forgiven. You already are."

"We'll be with you always, Harold."

They were more than voices. He couldn't avoid knowing he was surrounded by presences, and he had an impression of innumerable smiling faces, as though icons from his phone had congregated around him. "You won't," he vowed and switched the phone off.

"You'll see."

The chorus would have deafened him if he'd been hearing it that way. As it was, it swamped his thoughts. If the phone had been attracting his persecutors somehow, he'd turned it off too late. "I won't," he said more fiercely still, snatching off his glasses to drop them on the path and stamp on them. Now the world was a blur, but it was still too visible, and he set about ensuring he would never see whoever came to him.

SPIRITS

GENE O'NEILL

"On moonlight nights the long, straight street and dirty white walls, nowhere darkened by the shadow of a tree, their peace untroubled by footsteps or a dog's bark, glimmered in the pale recession. The silent city was no more than an assemblage of huge, inert cubes, between which only the mute effigies of great men, carapaced in bronze, with their blank stone or metal faces, conjured up a sorry semblance of what the man had been. In lifeless squares and avenues these tawdry idols lorded it under the lowering sky; stolid monsters that might have personified the rule of immobility imposed on us, or, anyhow, its final aspect, that of a defunct city in which plague, stone, and darkness had effectively silenced every voice." – Albert Camus, *The Plague*

On Ice

Sudden awareness.
Darkness.
Icy darkness.
Adrift … moving upward.
A cork in dark water.
Sensing a presence nearby … several eerie presences.
Unsettling, the unseen apparitions.
Upward.

Upward.
Consciousness thawing ... questions.
Where?
When?
What happened?
Upward—
Bursting and gasping into sudden brightness, as if finally breaking the surface of water and escaping from drowning.
Blinking ...
Overhead lights.
Recovery room.
Short-term memory gradually coming back.
You've been down On Ice.
Just brought back to life.

Baikonur Cosmodrome, Kazakhstan

The first Russian tourist moon shuttle was launched at 4:00 a.m. today—no spectators.

It was a perfect launch and flight.

The ship appeared like a silver arrow streaking upward, highlighted against the black velvet backdrop of space, scheduled to eventually dock in four days at the moon colony.

USA-Russia Lunar Colony,
Ground and Tourist Recreation Levels

"Gus, why are you lingering down there so long?"

The admonition from Big Sis thundered in the small chamber.

And it was true. He had lingered over each one of the twelve spacesuits hanging like rusty-orange, ribbed, lifeless, alien pelts on three of the walls of the tiny airlock. He'd visually and manually checked all the support systems, every seam, the oxygen and water backpacks, even each clasp, hook, and seal. Four times. He told himself he was being extra careful because it was probable that some of the tourists on tonight's shuttle would elect sampling the low-gravity, lunar surface, or maybe even want to take a visit to the Stone Garden—especially if they had a relative, friend, or colleague there. But, as Big Sis's booming question hung in the air unanswered, he had to finally admit to himself that his OCD behavior was really all about himself, not about the safety of any potential visitors. The look, feel, and texture of the suits, the smell and feel of the sterile air of the airlock, all resonated at some mysterious level deep inside him.

But why?

He couldn't answer his own question, much less explain the circumstances of the feeling causing him to linger in the tiny cell to Big Sis. So, no, he didn't even begin to try.

Instead, he roused himself, took a deep breath, exhaled slowly, and finally said: "Sorry, Big Sis. I've taken the extra time to double-check each of the twelve spacesuits because they are getting really old. As you are certainly aware of the manual of instructions down here, these same suits were originally used by some of the First Colonists on maintenance and construction crews outside. Now, after a careful inspection, I know for certain that everything is still in top working order in each of the twelve suits. Ready and safe for any tourist who may want to come down here and go outside. And I'm finally finished checking over everything here in the airlock chamber."

"Okay, that's all very commendable, Gus ... but actually a big waste of time," she said. Her hint of a sarcastic tone matched that of an exhausted teacher dealing with an intentionally annoying, recalcitrant student. "One quick look at each suit would've been more than sufficient. So, if you are indeed completely ready to continue *now*, it's past time to begin performing the check-offs up at Hotel Tranquility. It's after nine o'clock already and the Russian shuttle will be docking here at midnight."

Gus knew he still had plenty of time, and, so did Big Sis, but he didn't make any more defensive comments. Of course, she had activated all the life support systems on both the ground and tourist levels. His visual and manual checks were only the redundant part of the lunar colony's established protocols. Reluctantly, he slipped out of the airlock and took the nearby upchute to the recreation level and Hotel Tranquility—the airlock with spacesuits to outside was actually located down on the G Level just above the 01 Level of underground warehousing storage space.

At Hotel Tranquility, Gus went over his checklist again carefully at the five-star rated establishment—actually the only hotel on the moon. In addition to the prescribed checklist, he'd manually flushed a number of the toilets, bounced on a bed or two, and glanced over the late night menu choices that could be ordered from the hotel kitchen. Of course, everything was in perfect working order. And he had everything checked off the list in less than an hour and a half.

"The hotel is ready for all of the incoming guests," he reported to Big Sis.

"Okay, that's good," she said, the relief evident in her tone. "Now, hurry over and see if Christa needs any help in PlayLand. She should be in the Histro-Bistro right about now, preparing for the Deathplay performance: *Tombstone, October 26, 1881.* I'm guessing this could be a well-attended favorite with our guests. Last century's American Western movies have always been a huge favorite in Moscow."

Gus found Christa in the Saloon, dressed up in a sexy, old-time, dance hall girl costume. She was just sitting down at the player piano, but glanced up and smiled as he moved closer.

Gus watched her open the console cabinet on the piano, exposing a screen, a view scanning the outside street of the carefully recreated old west town, which had been located in the Arizona Territory. She zeroed in on the corral at the end of the dusty street and the four men dressed in black Stetsons and dusters, one armed with a Greener 10-gauge shotgun, all four carrying .44 Colt handguns in hip holsters exposed outside their longcoats. Then, her fingers flew over the computer keyboard above the piano keys, running a quick physical test on each of the simulacrums …

Wyatt moved a step forward, Virgil and Morgan closed in protectively on either side of their brother. She hit a key and Doc lifted his shotgun up ever so slightly. The others slowly drew their .44s.

Christa turned her attention to Ike and Billy on the dusty street almost directly in front of the saloon, moving them a few steps closer toward the corral. Then, she checked each of the others in the cowboy gang, including the two McLaurys, who she prepared to advance alongside the Clanton's.

Finally, the attractive dance hall girl looked up at Gus and nodded. "Okay, I think we're ready for the famed gunfight, if any of the Russians want to attend a late night performance here at the Histro-Bistro tonight ... Or for that matter any of the other scheduled ones during their visit."

"You've worked this entire Deathplay before?" Gus asked.

She nodded. "Not much for me to do actually, the script entirely programmed after activation. But yes, Big Sis and I did a complete, check, review, and a full rehearsal run yesterday on everything—the buildings and street appearance historically one hundred percent accurate of course, and the weapons and dress all authentic for that period. The gunfight surprisingly lasted only thirty seconds—thirty rounds were fired during that brief period of time. Historically, it was never determined who fired the first shot, setting everything off. But in half a minute, it was all over. Two of the McLaurys and Billy Clanton died soon after from .44 gunshot or shotgun wounds. All of the four men at the corral were hit at least once, but no one wounded seriously. This short-lived, notorious gunfight, including its lead-up and aftermath, were so famous that Hollywood made several western movies of it back in the mid-20th century. Musical ballads were even written and sang by various performers. The movies and the music became extremely popular worldwide. We think this will be a potentially exciting and familiar Deathplay for our Russian guests. Showings will be scheduled several times a day and twice in the evenings during their visit."

Christa pushed herself back away from the player-piano-computer-console and announced to Big Sis: "I'm ready to stage the Deathplay here at the Histro-Bistro. It's prominently advertised now as an available activity over at the Hotel."

"Excellent. And the rest of PlayLand?"

"I've checked over everything, including all the kids' rides, exhibits, and parade of circus animals and performers. All of that appears ready to function perfectly. All the other adult stuff, including the games of chance are ready, too."

Then, she turned toward Gus and in a slightly lower voice said: "Man, those characters that were called clowns, with their bizarre faces and weird costumes, roaming around in the parade are actually kind of frightening. Why would any tourist want his kid to get anywhere near one of those scary devils?"

Gus had not paid any attention to the clowns and had no answer for her. But he did say: "Let's give Big Sis our official word, which she will want to log."

Christa nodded. "All systems in the recreation area have been thoroughly checked visually and manually and are completely functional," she announced.

"Then, you are officially ready for the shuttle landing?"

"Yes, ma'am," Christa replied.

And Gus followed suit: "The G Level and Hotel Tranquility check out and are officially ready for the spacecraft landing and our Russian guests, too, Big Sis."

"Okay, the shuttle should be docking in … exactly twenty-five minutes."

"We will be over there at the shuttle port bay to greet each of the tourists individually as they debark, before I have to head over to take my place with the others at the Russian-USA Historical Space Exhibit," Gus said.

"Yes, everything has been officially reported ready over there, too, by your pair of colleagues," Big Sis said.

Gus added: "The tube nearby the entry portal bay will automatically whisk the passengers over to their rooms at Tranquility, where they can freshen up and relax, maybe have a drink. Or an evening meal awaits if any of them are hungry. All available activities are prominently displayed in the 3-D adverts at the check-in desk."

"Excellent, good work you two," Big Sis said, and her voice did indeed sound pleased and relaxed.

The pair waited patiently at the shuttle port entry bay, watching the double doors that would open any minute now into the docked shuttle.

"It will be interesting meeting tourists from Russia," Gus said. "Big Sis says Russia was actually a major political rival of the USA during the last century or so."

Christa nodded.

Then, in a slightly tentative voice Gus asked: "Do you remember anything about the last time a shuttle docked?"

Christa was quiet for so long, he thought that she wasn't going to answer. Finally she said: "No, I don't remember. But Big Sis told me today in a kind of stiff tone that the last one was from the European Union of States, quite some time ago, and it apparently hadn't gone well. She never explained exactly why though." Christa glanced up at the digital announcement over the entryway into the bay: ETA: 0:01.

She said: "Get ready, Gus."

After another few minutes, the port entry doors finally slid open … but nothing happened after that. No one disembarked from the shuttle into the passenger bay. No one even appeared back in the spacecraft.

Surprised, Gus and Christa waited for a few more moments, just staring across the well-lighted empty bay and inside the doorway into the shuttle.

Then, Gus said in a loud but slightly puzzled voice: "Big Sis, no one seems to be exiting from the ship."

Silence for almost a full minute; then she said: "I was afraid this would be the case."

She had anticipated this surprise?

"What should we do?" Christa asked, her voice, too, indicating an unsettled nature.

"You need to go ahead and enter the shuttle yourselves, visually checking everywhere, the tourist cabins along the lower deck first, then go up and check crew compartments on the second deck, and finally the flight deck in the front of the shuttle."

Gus led the way cautiously across the bay, his shoe steps echoing in the empty cavern. He entered the shuttle, the lower level. It had the same kind of sterile feel as the airlock with the spacesuits on the G Level of the Colony, but the air was thicker and smelled stale. Nevertheless, they continued forward. The tourist cabins lining both sides of the ship all had the doors opened wide, as if prepared for an inspection. They each took a side row.

Glancing inside each dimly lit cabin, Gus could quickly tell that the narrow beds were made-up, undisturbed in each cell; and nothing seemed to be out of place, or even touched in the tiny cabins. Christa confirmed this impression from her examinations on the other side of the ship.

More than a bit confused, Gus led the way up to the second level. There was a tangible ominous feel palpable in the stale air. But despite their increasing sense of unease they continued onward with their inspection.

The crew's quarters, rec area, and mess were all empty; also like down on the lower level, everything was in place, nothing apparently even touched.

Christa frowned, puzzlement etched on her features now, readily apparent and reinforcing Gus's sense of increasing dread. What had happened here? Where was everyone?

Christa reached out and took his hand, before they proceeded forward to the flight deck.

Like everywhere else in the Russian shuttlecraft, they found no one manning the flight stations, the three chairs empty ... no Captain or other officers. Gus checked over the electronic flight display, which was completely lit up, apparently still functioning and fully operational.

He shook his head, sighed loudly, then reported the disturbing findings: "Big Sis, we have found no one on this Russian spacecraft dead or alive. It appears to me that the ship must have navigated here from Earth on auto-pilot ... arriving here at the Lunar Colony completely empty of tourists and flight crew."

They waited for a response from Big Sis.

Finally, she said: "Unfortunately, I suspected this when I first became aware of the flight announcements from Kazakhstan. All the transmissions were programmed computer electronic responses, *never any* accompanying human voices heard from Central Control at the Baikonur Cosmodome ..."

"So you knew we were probably preparing for an empty shuttlecraft piloted automatically from Earth?" Gus asked, not trying to hide the incredulous and unspoken condemnation implicit in his tone. "I don't understand why you never—"

Big Sis cut him off. "Yes, I suspected that was the case, but *hoped* I was wrong," she said in an almost apologetic voice. Then, she recovered her poise, and added in her normal, confident authoritative voice: "Anyhow, right now, since no one has disembarked and the shuttle is empty, I've activated the instructions for its programmed return to its base on Earth ... which will begin in exactly ten minutes. You and Christa must get off the spacecraft now."

Gus and Christa did as instructed, quickly exiting into the passenger bay as the shuttle doors snapped closed behind them.

Before they had an opportunity to ask any questions though, Big Sis said: "Okay, now, hurry over to the viewing deck. You will get an opportunity to see an awesome sight rarely seen by anyone. A totally unmanned spacecraft leaving the moon and returning back to its home base on Earth."

They did as instructed, and both ended up watching from the view deck on the 2 Level as the spacecraft blasted away from the colony, apparently already programmed for the four day flight back to Kazakhstan. Both were awed by the sight, but also a bit unnerved by the unmanned departure.

Eventually, Christa indicated the Stone Garden directly below them, which had been dimly lit up during the preparations for the arrival of the shuttle and guests. The statues, monuments, and several dozen tombstones, lined in three neat rows, were all circled by a white picket fence, like a nice military cemetery on Earth. She said: "Those are obviously the First Colonists buried down there. Do you remember what happened to them?"

Gus shook his head and replied: "No, I remember nothing much before coming up from being *On Ice*. Of course I recognize everything and understand my responsibilities, but I have no memory of past events."

He stared down at the Stone Garden for a minute or so, then said: "Big Sis, Christa and I would like to know more about the First Colonists. We realize they are all gone, buried down in the Stone

Garden now. Something bad happened? What? How long ago did it take place?"

Big Sis was silent for a moment, and then she slowly began her explanation. "After the First Colonists, who were an equal mix of American and Russian, finally finished setting up the station, they readied for the first tourist shuttle. The ongoing operation of the colony had been planned and designed to be supported by the frequent arrival of tourists visiting from Earth ..."

Big Sis paused, as if carefully ordering her remarks, and then in a hint of a slightly higher-pitched voice she continued.

"The first shuttle came from the USA twenty years ago, just before the Sarawak Virus Pandemic—the White Plague--raged across the world, wiping out first world populations—the news feeds a bit delayed to the Colony. But it quickly became obvious some of the tourists on that shuttle had been exposed and carried the terrible virus. The infection spread quickly through the whole Colony. Only two colonists, both of Asian ethnicity, survived to return on that shuttle, with a short-manned, non-Caucasian crew."

"Then, those buried in the Stone Garden, Russian and American, had all succumbed to the White Plague?" Christa asked.

"Yes, as did major portions of many countries around the globe, any with large Caucasian populations. And then opportunistic Daesh terrorists followed the devastating plague, causing many additional, indiscriminate casualties by planting dirty bombs in urban centers, including the major cities in the Mid-East."

"And what about subsequent shuttles?" Gus said. "Others have come, before this last empty Russian one?"

"Two. One from the European Union of States and one from Canada."

"And both of these craft were empty, too?" Christa said.

"Yes, they were."

It was quiet for a few moments on the Viewing Deck, then in barely audible whisper, Christa said: "We aren't a pair of those early colonists are we?"

"No, when you were first brought up, before the first tourist shuttle, you both were called Spirits by the Colonists," Big Sis answered.

"A nickname not meant in any way as cavalier or dismissive, but more in an appreciative, admiring sense ..."

She stopped for a moment, then said: "And now it's time for you and the other two at the Space Center, Yuri and Neil, to return to the MedCenter. You will be going back down *On Ice*. To be brought back up again in the future, when you are needed. Because I'm convinced there are survivors on Earth, many of them. And sooner or later there will be another *manned* space shuttle returning here someday. We will be waiting and have everything ready when they do return."

THE MYTHIC HERO MOST LIKELY TO SQUEEZE A STONE

B.E. SCULLY

I

The Boy and the Woman Have Sex

On nights they didn't sink the pump, they had sex. She'd have thought it would be the other way around—the fear-spiked cocktail of adrenaline and desire, of exhausted paranoia on the one hand and irresistible need on the other. But then she came to understand that on nights they stole water, the pump was the sex. After all, the water was more important—more necessary—and thus even more exciting. More risky, too. And unlike the sex, the pump lasted three hours.

That was the fault of his age, of course. In a few more years, the still tender, unformed landscape of youth would harden and solidify into the architecture of adulthood. But right now it was still summer, and the boy was still a boy.

A teenage boy, to be specific, but still a boy. The law, or what passed for it these days, still recognized him as such, but the woman wasn't worried about getting arrested. Stealing the water would get her sent to one of the huge detention camps that dotted the outskirts of every town and city like some barbed-wire encircled human circus show, but not the sex. Nobody cared who you slept with these days. The woman had thought *she'd* still care, though, even if nobody else did. He was half her age, young enough to be her own child if she'd have been unlucky enough to have any. She wasn't some kind of a pervert. But nothing about sex with the boy felt perverted. Maybe it was because nothing much felt that way anymore.

In a perverse world, wholesomeness becomes its own kind of perversion.

The woman reached over and ran her hand along a stretch of the boy's flat stomach. The relentless sun had tanned his skin as brown as a hazelnut.

That was just one more lie they'd all believed—that sex was some sacred, special thing. They'd learned, though, what sacredness really was—food, shelter, water.

Never enough of any of those things these days, but still plenty of sex.

The boy's stomach was smooth and clean, at least relative to the parts that never seemed to get clean. The woman looked down at her hands, cracked and scarred, nails caked with dirt.

Like an old lizard, she thought, and smiled.

The boy rolled away from her and sat up. "Do you think it's going to rain soon?"

"Nope."

"Not even a little? For like, ten minutes maybe?"

"Nope."

"Remember when it used to rain all the time? Even in summer, it rained sometimes. Remember?"

The woman closed her eyes. "I remember."

The boy stood up and began pacing around the room. She'd shut up most of the rooms by now—the bulk of her once prized possessions had been confiscated, sold, or repurposed long ago, and it helped save heat in winter, when the nights came on as early as two o'clock in the afternoon. Now the old porch and the kitchen were the only rooms left in use, plus the bathroom on those rare occasions they had enough water to plug up the old tub and soak, remembering the hot, dirt-and-bug free version that actually used to come right out of the rubbed bronze faucet, like magic.

One of the new national pastimes, remembering.

"If it's not going to rain, we should have sunk the pump tonight," the boy said.

"Too dangerous."

The pump had actually been in position—the boy had been down at the water's edge when they saw the flashes of light. He had frozen, Narcissus-like, in front of the rippling mirror of water, and the woman had crouched down in the weeds along the bank.

The boy's hissed whisper floated up to her. "Patrol Walkers?"

She peered into the darkness, but the lights had vanished. "I don't think so. Too far away."

They squatted in the silence, waiting. She was just about ready to go start the cell pack when she heard them—*pop-pop-pop*, three small explosions of gunfire from across the canal, where the lights had been. Five times now they'd seen lights in the dark patch of forest some intrepid businessman had once purchased with the idea of turning it into a spa resort. The bulldozers had come in and cleared about half of the twenty acres, chewing up trees and shrubs and sending the wildlife fleeing for their lives—the crows had taken to the sky in droves, circling and cawing above the metal beasts as if plotting their own counter-attack.

The Meltdown, of course, had put an end to all that. One by one the bulldozers went silent and then vanished altogether. One of them was still over there, its rusted, hulking metal skeleton gleaming in the sun. But the goldenrod and blackberry vines and ivy were winning their slow, patient re-occupation. The crows returned to the tops of the pines that hadn't been cleared and sat there as they'd always done, watching, waiting.

Just like the boy and the woman.

"Pull the pump," the woman had hissed back down to the boy.

He obeyed immediately. Without another word, they dragged the pump up the embankment and back onto the safety of the woman's property, where they hid it in the dead ivy vines. Afterward they went inside and had sex.

The forest was pitch black and silent now.

"We'll drop the pump tomorrow," the woman reassured the boy. "We'll go an extra hour, to make up for tonight."

The boy flopped back down on the bed. The woman had moved it from the bedroom into the porch by herself, before the boy arrived. She could have used the smaller, lighter one from the downstairs bedroom, but the bed had been her one stubborn concession to the past. It had taken her two days to tear the thing apart, haul it down the steep steps one piece at a time, and then reassemble it. She could no longer remember how she and her husband had gotten it upstairs in the first place. She still made the bed every morning, even when the sheets weren't clean, which was most of the time.

The boy and the woman lay together on the big bed, listening to the night. Finally the boy asked, "What do you think's going on? In the woods, I mean."

When the woman didn't answer, the boy said, "I'll bet I know," and then whispered, "*Revolution.*"

It was one of his most treasured words, taken out often to examine and consider, or stored away in secret to contemplate in the small, desperate hours before the light returned.

The boy reached out and ran his finger down the woman's stomach in imitation of her gesture. She felt the damp heat pulse to life between her legs and travel outward across her skin—it had once been everything, that heat. Through the years it had dwindled, dimming and flickering through the long, hard years before the Meltdown, and then eventually guttering out altogether. Now it was back again, primed and ready, it seemed, for a re-takeover.

"Like the blackberry vines and ivy," the woman said.

The boy raked his slender fingers through her pubic hair like a comb. "What?"

"Nothing."

"Revolution," he said again, louder this time, and sat up. "Revolution's coming."

The woman again said nothing.

"So what do you think's going on?" the boy persisted. "What do you think's happening?"

The woman shrugged. "Probably nothing—just people trying to stay alive a little longer."

II
The Woman and the Boy Sink the Pump

It was almost time.

In another ten minutes, it would be dark enough.

The woman looked both ways down the canal, wishing she had a cigarette. She hadn't had a cigarette in years, since long before the Meltdown—they'd given up their bad habits back then, swept up in the fervor of organic and gluten-free and longevity and yoga three times a week. They'd been convinced they might just live forever, funny as that seemed now.

"Sure wouldn't have given up so many things, if we'd have known," the woman said, echoing millions of people across the globe who wouldn't be on the globe much longer. She'd taken to talking to herself even before the Meltdown. After her husband disappeared, she got used to being alone. Post-Meltdown, her social life consisted of confirming her statistics once a month at what used to be the local one-stop super store and was now the local Designated Rations and First Aid Site.

"Same residence, classification code, and allotment number?"

"Same."

"Nothing's changed?"

"Nothing's changed."

She'd pick up her vacuum-sealed packets of pre-cooked beans and rice or pasta or whatever protein patty was passing for chicken these days, then shuffle down the counter for her jug of sanitized water. Next counter was one bar of soap, as hard and square as a block of cement and reeking of antiseptic, and a four-ounce packet of all-purpose liquid cleaner. One more stop at medical if she needed anything in that department—and, of course, if they had anything to give in that department—and then the three mile trek home.

The boy had shown up one afternoon reeking of the wild. It was astonishing, the things he didn't know. The only meal he could fix was sandwiches, and there hadn't been bread or deli meat in years. He didn't know how to start a fire or fix a fence. He didn't know how to grow vegetables or catch a rabbit. He didn't know how to use the shotgun or the handgun. Because he either didn't have a claimed residence or wouldn't give it up if he did, the boy did not qualify for a rations allotment. He only bothered to wash his clothes when a foul enough stain or smell demanded it, and the only reason his body got better treatment was because the woman wouldn't have come near him otherwise.

In some ways, the sex had been the easiest thing she *had* taught him. Their first night together, after a few fumbling attempts to figure out exactly how to get where he needed to go, the old primal knowledge had kicked in. After she'd taken hold and guided him in, the boy had known exactly what to do, thrusting faster and deeper until his still-adolescent hormones cut the newfound ancient instinct short.

The boy didn't have much practical use, but he was a male, and any male on the property was better than none. His age put him higher on the rape list than an adult male, but still lower than any female other than the very young or the very old. The mere presence of a penis seemed to send some kind of signal to other penises, like a lighthouse silently beaming "Stay Away" to passing ships.

Sitting beneath the pines on a cut tree stump wishing for a cigarette, the woman considered that male humans weren't so different from male dogs, sending off signals and marking their territories in a strange, secret ritual known only to themselves.

She looked up at the patch of squid-ink framed by two pine branches bent like frames around the square of stars and sky. As usual, dusk had crept in slow and steady to steal the last traces of light. The natural kind was the only choice left—no porch lights, no streetlights, nothing but the occasional Patrol Walker headlamp careening out of the darkness like a luminescent bat blindly seeking a target, any target.

The last of her illegal flashlight batteries had gone down months ago. They always sank the pump at dusk, when there was still light in the sky, but they pulled it up in utter darkness. In a flash of inspiration, the woman had unearthed a pack of glow sticks in a box of old Halloween decorations, the kind that crack open to produce a chemical light reaction. But they were down to their last pack. After that, they'd only be able to sink the pump on moonlit nights.

"Yellow-orange," the woman said. "Soft yellow-orange." That was the color of night-rooms, the way they used to glow. The woman could still picture it, driving or walking down a dark country road and all of a sudden there it was, some warmly glowing living room or kitchen flooded with the electricity necessary to cook dinner and watch television and hold together the snug miracle of modern domestic life.

Warm glowing living rooms, another lost pleasure.

The night was turning black and mean. An ill-smelling wind scuttled in from the east, where the fires still burned.

The boy had been coming and going, disappearing and reappearing, all day. It wasn't illegal for a person to leave his or her recorded place of residence, but it was risky. Almost everything was against the law now, and if the military or local enforcement patrols didn't get you, the vigilante gangs and just plain crazies would. But teenage boys didn't need organic vegetables and yoga to think they would live forever—it came with the packaging.

The woman was about ready to go down and sink the pump herself when the boy burst out from behind the patch of fly-bitten laurel bushes that screened the canal edge of the property. Most of the shrubs had died, but for now, anyway, the laurels were still going strong.

"Not much longer if it doesn't rain, though," the woman said, rubbing at a dirt spot on her leg that only smeared it into an even bigger dirt spot.

People stayed inside most of the time now, popping out of their sealed-up houses only to have a look around before digging back in again, like moles. But the tension was building. The woman could feel the restlessness race up and down the canal, from one house to another, like a downed live wire.

"I was about ready to go without you," she told the lanky form loping into view.

He shrugged. "It's your rule."

"And it's a good one: never go down alone, not to put the pump in or to get it out."

The boy shrugged again. "Okay, so I'm here."

Usually, he sank the pump while she stood watch. The woman was taller, but the boy was stronger. She was slow and cautious, he was swift and nimble. But the main reason the boy handled the pump was because he was young and had no fear—not of slipping and falling into the canal; not of being spotted by an unexpected Patrol Walker; not of their crazy neighbor, who on the day after the Meltdown had wrapped his property in barbed wire and could only be seen since patrolling the perimeter with an alarmingly long-barreled shotgun.

The woman, however, was not young, and had plenty of fear.

Tonight, though, the woman decided to sink the pump herself.

She grabbed it in both hands, stepped over the fallen telephone pole she'd dragged into place to discourage looters, and made her way down the steep embankment. By now it was nothing but dust and round little pebbles desperate to ball-bearing her downhill, arms pin-wheeling, the boy laughing at her the whole time.

At the bottom of the embankment, one last chance for breathing easy on the flat pathway separating her property from the canal, and then the descent.

The first part wasn't too bad. Years ago, before she'd owned the house, someone had placed a huge flat rock right at the edge of the canal and hacked a narrow, hidden pathway through the blackberry vines and sweet peas down to the water. The water had reached all the way up to the edge of the pathway then—in fact, the flat rock had probably been put there so that some long ago boy or girl could sit and dip a bucket or a pair of hot, dirty feet into the cool water. Now the canal was less than six feet deep, and the only way to the water was down a worn cliff side revealed by the vanished water. The cliff was lined with jagged gray teeth ready to pull loose and send her tumbling, plus more pebble ball-bearings happy to help out. Even though it was half as deep as it used to be, the canal waters were still swift enough to carry a careless body off.

The blackberries and sweat peas that were somehow outlasting the weather formed a tunnel at the top of the pathway, screening her on both sides. But at the water's edge, she was exposed.

The woman lowered herself onto the flat rock and started down the cliff. The middle part was the real killer. A huge grey rock was embedded deep within the hard-packed earth, its smooth top emerging like the back of a humpback whale. But that whale-back was as smooth and slippery as ice, and the woman crab-walked first one, then the other foot down the slope until she hit the shelf of square rocks the boy had gathered and placed there for solid footing. But it was only semi-solid, the rocks constantly slipping loose and careening into the canal water, *clackety-clack*, one giant stone square knocking against another all the way down to the *splash* that, when the boy had the pump, would cause the woman to hold her breath until she saw that the slide hadn't taken him with it into the dark, swirling water.

After she cleared the whale rock, the woman picked her way across the relatively flat expanse that led to the water's edge.

She glanced up nervously. Dropping the pump at dusk meant that they saved on light, but it also meant that it was still light enough to see the outlines of a woman positioning an illegal water pump into a formerly public but currently very un-public waterway.

So tantalizingly close; so entirely forbidden.

Just as the woman was ready to place the pump, flashes of light in the forest caused her to freeze. It was illegal to congregate in groups larger than four, but the woman counted seven distinct beams of light criss-crossing through the trees before vanishing all at once.

She hesitated. To pull the pump again tonight meant they'd be down two days.

The woman peered into the dark forest as if the pines could tell her what to do. Receiving no word, however, she lowered the pump just below the water line and hissed *"It's ready!"* into the darkness. Somewhere at the top of the ridge the boy loped off to plug the pump into the cell pack. Unlike the pump, the cell pack never got anywhere near the water. In fact, it never left a barricaded back room of the house from which they strung a power chord through a hole in the screen window to run across the yard to the pump. The pump was valuable, but the cell pack was gold—too important to risk losing.

The pump was an old gadget leftover from one of her husband's long-ago projects—a pond, if she remembers correctly, that never got past a two-foot hole in the ground. She hadn't turned the pump in during the first official Handover. It had been optional then, back when optional still existed. But like most people, the woman knew where to hide things when the trucks emblazoned with the New Government logo and the soldiers in back arrived. Even so, the pump didn't mean much after the electricity went from ration days only to no days at all. But then the boy had turned up, and even though it had taken him awhile to trust her enough, he'd brought more with him than his youth. The woman hadn't even known the rechargeable solar-hybrid cells existed—when the military tested the first prototype, there were rumors it ran on more than just sun and technology. Some claimed an organic compound too classified to release to the public was needed; some even claimed the mysterious substance might be human.

Before the Meltdown, the cell packs had only been talked about as an exciting possibility, the Next Big Thing that could solve the fuel and energy crisis and avert disaster for all mankind. But obviously they were more than just a possibility, at least for some people. Stealing water would get them fined, owning the pump would get them sent to a camp, but the cell pack? The woman couldn't even imagine the consequences of getting caught with something both the new and old governments denied even existed.

She had no idea where the boy had gotten hold of it, and she'd never asked.

The woman squatted in the dark by the water, waiting for the boy to get the cell pack running. A hard, sideways grin of a moon rose above the pines, dancing off the waves as if playing a game with the water. But the woman was more interested in scanning the gravel roadway that ran parallel to the canal, at the forest's black edge. They'd already worked out a plan if an unexpected Patrol Walker turned up: cut the pump loose and let it sink to the bottom of the canal, and say they were shrimping. There were still enough underdeveloped, soft-shelled crabs and unidentified bottom-crawlers floating around in there to make the story possible. Misappropriating resources of any kind was a first-level crime, but contaminated crustaceans were far less serious than water.

"Losing the pump is better than losing your freedom," she'd told the boy. "Or worse."

The familiar drone of the pump engine kicked to life and the woman scrambled over the rocks without waiting for the boy to return.

She cleared the whale-rock, found a crop of torn-off roots to grab hold of, and pulled herself onto the gravel pathway. One last stretch, up the dirt embankment and over the telephone pole. A twenty-foot hose attached to the pump carried the water up the canal bank, and the boy had already placed the nozzle in one of the giant rain barrels the woman had purchased before the Meltdown, when there was still rain. There were four of them hidden behind a pile of old furniture destined to become winter kindling. Each night, the boy and the woman would move the connector hose from one barrel to the next until it was time to pull the pump for the night. The next day they'd drain the water from the barrels into smaller containers and hide them around the house. They used half of it for the garden and a quarter for luxuries like bathing or washing clothes. The rest they put aside for the in-case days when even the rationed water dried up.

As soon as the woman joined the boy at the rain barrels he blurted, "Did you see them? Did you see the lights?"

"No."

He stood there dumb-founded. "How could you not see them? They were everywhere, more than ever before! Maybe even, like, twenty of them!"

The woman paused. "Patrol Walkers?"

"No, that's the thing! You can tell because they're the only ones whose beams are real bright, like how they used to be. But these were dimmer, more yellow."

When the woman didn't say anything, the boy gazed wistfully over at the patch of dark forest.

"The revolution," his whispered lovingly. "It's coming."

But the woman saw only darkness.

III
The Boy Reads the Woman's Future

They woke in the early afternoon and lay in bed letting the heat build. There wasn't any point getting up earlier—no jobs to rush off to, no chores to finish, no electronics to tend to like a frazzled mother fussing over a squalling infant all day long. In midday, when the sun was directly overhead, the woman rose and got the outdoor fire pit started. She brewed up tea and made lunch out of whatever she could put together from the rations and the sparse, fatigued patch of illegal garden the stolen water kept going. Then she and the boy would clean up and do the first of their two perimeter checks of the property, one in the day, one at night. Not that the woman kept track of time much anymore. It was either light out or dark, hot or less hot, dry or less dry.

Sometimes they'd fill up the bathtub and lie in the cool, cloudy water for hours, talking or watching the shadows cross the wall. Sometimes they'd take blankets and pillows and prop up beneath the giant pines, trying to stay cool. Sometimes they'd cross the canal bridge and forage for firewood or check the secret stash of rabbit traps that were almost always empty now. Sometimes they'd drink tea and do nothing but read books and old magazines until sundown, when the woman would again stoke the fire pit and make dinner. Sometimes they had lazy, sweaty sex on the porch bed as the crows weighed in across the canal, *caw-caw-caw*, six points for technique, ten for enthusiasm.

Today was a sex and old books and magazines day.

The woman took a sip of tea—she'd brewed up nettle and, in celebration of nothing in particular, one precious black tea bag—and leaned back against the lumpy pile of pillows.

"Let's not drop the pump tonight," she said.

The boy turned to look at her, lazy and slow in the afternoon heat. "Why not?"

"Just don't feel like it. Need a break."

"Do you think they're gathering back there, in the woods? The revolutionaries, I mean."

The woman drained the last lukewarm dregs of tea. The nettle tasted bitter. "Hard to say."

"I thought it would come faster. The revolution, I mean."

"Maybe revolutions happen the same way going broke happens, at least according to Hemingway—gradually and then all at once."

"Hemingway who?"

"Ernest Hemingway, the writer." When the boy didn't respond, the woman added, "*The Sun Also Rises; A Farewell to Arms*—didn't you read Hemingway in school?"

"No."

"Not even *The Old Man and the Sea?*"

The boy shook his head.

"Okay, what did you read?"

"Nothing."

"What did you learn then?"

The boy frowned, thinking. "I can't remember."

He reached beneath his shirt and scratched his stomach, yawned. As thin as he was, the woman glimpsed the traces of baby fat still tucked in around the fragile frame, as if to cushion it just a little longer against the journey ahead. The boy, she observed, had not yet caught up with the man.

The woman thought of her own belly as a girl, flat and sun-tanned from long summer days at the river. She ran her hands over it in imitation of the boy—flat and hard again, after all of these years of well-fed flab. The boy's navel winked at her as he lowered his shirt, and she felt the desire rise, absurd, unbidden, undeniable.

But it was too early, too hot for sex. The woman grabbed a magazine from a stack on the floor and then tossed it aside. It puzzled her, this newfound sexual interest in midsections. She thought of Eve, the first woman born not from a belly but from an afterthought. The woman imagined the first woman's stomach as smooth and impression-less as the surface of the whale-rock.

The boy picked up an old newspaper and started riffling through it. "When's your birthday?"

"August seventh."

"Want to hear your horoscope? The page is all wrinkly and torn and this magazine is from like, five years ago. But I can still read yours, if you want."

The woman closed her eyes. "Okay, read it to me."

The boy cleared his throat as if asked to read out loud in class. "'Leo,'" he read, as serious as a college professor, "'July is nearly over, and your ongoing struggles have already earned you the gold medal of Karmic Endurance. Another month of this, though, and you just might find yourself trying to squeeze water from a stone. You could walk away from it all. But if you are tempted to stick around in the hopes of becoming a modern day mythic hero, Leo, the stars indicate that it might be better not to.'"

The boy looked up from the tissue-thin newspaper. "What's that mean?"

"It means we shouldn't drop the pump tonight."

"My horoscope's Pisces," the boy said. "But that part of the page is torn away."

Later, after sex in the cool late evening shadows of the porch, the boy returned to the afternoon's subject. "It's funny how it said that. Your horoscope, I mean. That you could just walk away from it all. As if."

"What would I want to walk away from?"

The boy gestured around the room, lifted his hands to the ceiling. "This—all this ..." He dropped his hands and let out a sigh that sounded as if it came from someone three times his age. "I don't know. What do you miss most about before? I mean, apart from, you know, the obvious."

The woman hesitated. She knew what "the obvious" meant: people. At first, only the extras had vanished: junk food, entertainment, store shelves lined with cheap plastic goods. Next came electricity, fuel, fresh fruits and vegetables. Then people started to go, too: there were the suicides, of course, and homicides both random and planned. But there were also the quieter, sadder deaths, the slow starvation and malnutrition, the untreated illnesses and infections, and, most disturbing of all, those who left home one day for rations or firewood or even a breath of fresh air and never came back. People had learned to be careful talking about "before," and never, ever to ask.

"I miss hot baths," the woman finally said. "What about you—what do you miss?"

"Video games, for sure. My phone. Cheeseburgers and fries. I miss all kinds of things. Everything. I wish I would wake up and everything would be back to normal, like this is some kind of bad dream."

"Sometimes it does seem like a dream. But not necessarily a bad one."

The boy stood up and pressed his hands and forehead against one of the long, high porch windows. "How can you stand it, waiting around for something to happen?" He swung around to face her, his hands clenching and unclenching as if responding to some unseen electrical impulse. "There *has* to be a revolution coming. There has to be."

"And you want to be a part of it."

"Of course! Don't you?"

The woman gazed out at the darkness. "Nope."

The boy shook his head, incredulous. "Well, I'm going to be a part of it. I can't wait." He paused, considering. "Not that I don't like it here—with you, I mean."

She couldn't help but laugh. "That's okay. I was the same way when I was your age. Couldn't wait to leave home and conquer the world."

"And did you?"

"Leave home?"

"No, conquer the world."

"Not until it conquered me first," the woman said.

IV
The Woman Loses the Pump

They'd missed two days and couldn't afford to miss another. So even though the woman's danger instincts had been jangling like crazy ever since the beams of light had appeared in the forest, here she was, sitting beneath the pines waiting for the boy to place the pump.

Has to rain soon, she thought, then caught herself. *No, it doesn't. In fact, it doesn't ever have to rain again, and might not.*

The boy seemed to be taking an awfully long time. At night, when they pulled the pump, she went halfway down the cliff after the boy. He handed the pump off to her to make it easier to climb, plus she could keep a closer watch for Patrols. But at dusk, she stayed in the yard. It made it quicker to get back to the house to get the cell pack running, and sinking the pump felt safer than dropping it, even though it wasn't—most of the Patrol Walkers came in the day, no doubt to save on their headlamps. But if they did come at night, it was earlier rather than later. At first they drove up and down night and day in huge trucks, up and down the canal path with floodlights and bullhorns. Then they'd come less regularly, on foot, then sporadically, in straggling groups of two or three. It wasn't just civilians who were running out of resources. But the lights in the forest would bring the Patrol Walkers, limited resources or not. It was just a matter of time.

And time runs out.

The bright-white beams, the ones too bright and white to be anything other than Official, came shooting across the dark silvery expanse of water. They immediately targeted the edge of the rocks, where the boy would be crouched, placing the pump. The woman, safe on her own property behind the hedge of laurels, couldn't see that far down the cliff, but an image, a memory, suddenly rose in her mind: eighth grade science class, the big semester-end project. Students had to collect a dozen different insect species and pin them to a piece of plasterboard to be labeled and displayed. Nowhere in the instruction sheet did it offer advice on how to kill the insects before pinning them. For the first time, the woman wondered if some of the kids hadn't bothered.

She stood up and peeked over the laurels, and then crouched back down. She pictured the boy trapped by the water and wondered whether she should go to him, try and help somehow. But how?

When the boy had first come to her, she had seen right away that he was one of those types best suited to survive. It was his eyes that had convinced her. It wasn't the color or the shape or even the curious intelligence that flashed out of them when the subject suited him. What had caught her attention was something now more important than all of those things—in the boy's eyes, the woman had seen the calm, unequivocal intention to survive. She had, she was sure, seen the future, whatever kind of future it was going to be.

The Patrol Walkers began broadcasting a message in that staccato, metallic voice that always made the woman wonder if there were even human beings beneath all that metal and high-tech fabric. Rumor had it the Walkers were only permitted to spend two hours a day outside their uniforms; that they were a man-machine hybrid just like the cell packs; that they could run faster and shoot straighter than any human, though the woman hadn't seen any evidence of that yet. In their black outfits and headgear it was impossible to tell whether they were male or female, so most people had already taken to calling them "it."

"You are ordered by the New Government of the United States of America to cease all activity and stand up facing the lights. Place both hands over your head, fingers open, palms facing the lights."

The message kept repeating. Still crouched behind the laurels, the woman counted four headlamps.

She was certain the Patrol Walkers hadn't spotted her. They would call in reinforcements, that was also certain, and eventually the cruelly misnamed Search and Public Safety Teams would show up to search every house and question every resident within ten miles of the Reported Incident. She would have to find even more creative places to hide things, even more vague and misleading answers to give.

The canal pathway was still in darkness, the beams of the Patrol lights reluctant to leave their target. Slowly, so slowly her arms ached with the effort, the woman began to pull on the hose and power cord. Slowly, so as not to attract any attention, slowly, with only the slightest of movements, she inched the evidence up the cliff and across the pathway and up the dirt and gravel embankment and across the telephone pole and into the safety of the laurels.

Just as she knew he would, the boy had followed the plan. He had cut the cords and sunk the pump into the canal. If the currents were strong enough, it might be tumbled along toward the old processing plant and eventually washed out to sea. Or it might sink to the bottom of the canal where it would easily be spotted and retrieved by the search teams. But the high-tech recorders built into the Patrol Walkers' suits would have recorded the whole thing. The boy had clearly been the one stealing water, and there was no official record linking her to the boy. She still had a chance.

But what about the boy?

The mechanical voice suddenly got sharper, louder.

"You are ordered by the New Government of the United States of America to cease all motion and stand in place! Use of lethal force is authorized and will be employed in one ... two ..."

The voice kept counting. Forgetting her chance at a chance, the woman stood up and searched the canal waters. Dusk was rapidly giving way to full-blown night, and she just barely saw it—just barely, but there it was—nothing more than an outline, a shape, a quick-silver motion through the dark water and then it was gone. Nothing more than a shape—but a shape big enough to be a boy.

The voice cut short its counting. A series of shots rang out, one, two, too many to count. The woman watched the headlamps disappear down the canal, tracking their target. But the quick-silver boy-fish would be gone by now, one way or the other.

The woman went to the shed and got a shovel. She dug a deep hole and buried the ruined hose and electrical cord. Tomorrow, as soon as the light returned, she would go through the house and hide anything questionable or illegal. She'd have to hide the rain barrels, too. That wouldn't be easy, but she'd find a way.

If the Teams didn't get there first, she'd wade in and see if the pump had sunk. If it had, she would retrieve it and bury it, too. She was now down to only two electrical cords, and the pump would either be ruined or in need of serious repair even if she did manage to salvage it out of the canal.

She still had the cell pack, but she'd lost the boy.

Suddenly exhausted, the woman went and stood beneath the ancient pines. The canal was still now, the Patrol Walkers far out of sight. Without the pump, she could only steal water one bucket at a time. Without the boy, the water would last longer.

Her supply might hold out until the rains came, it might not. The Patrols might come tomorrow or the next day, they might not come at all. She might be arrested, she might not even be questioned. The revolution might begin tomorrow, it might never begin at all. The boy might have made it, he might not have. He and the pump might have washed out to sea, or they might be at the bottom of the canal somewhere, waiting.

If the boy had made it, he might be back. Then again, he might not. Then again *again*, someone else would turn up eventually. They always do.

"Trees aren't going anywhere," the woman said. "At least not yet."

The hard sideways moon rose in the sky, the dark canal waters flowed by, and the woman sat down on the cut tree stump to wait.

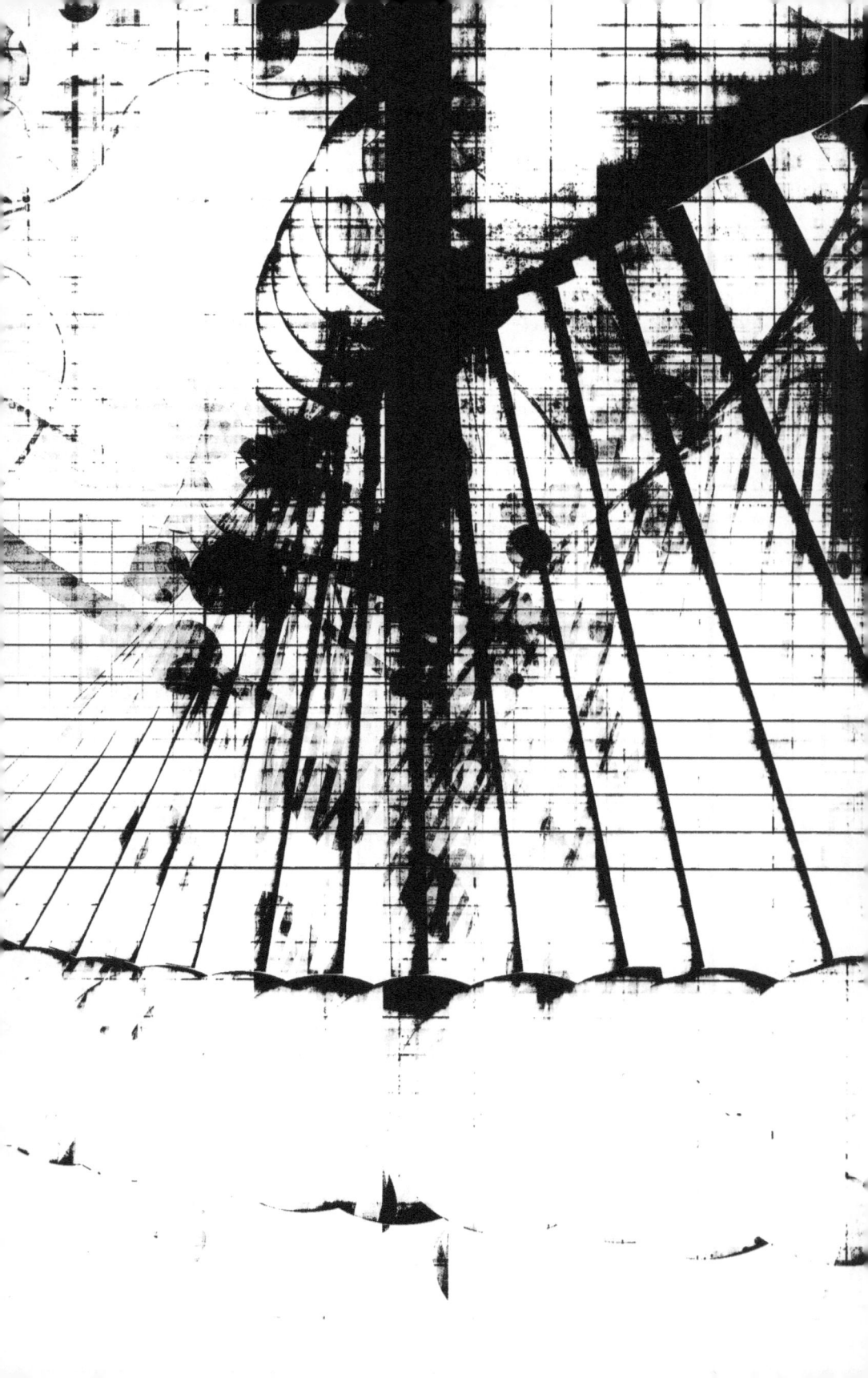

MY FATHER, DR. FRANKENSTEIN

JOHN LANGAN

Hi Dena,

*Here are the endnotes for my review of Dan Frank-
lin's* My Father, Dr. Frankenstein. *I'm afraid I may
have gone a bit overboard in providing historical context for
Franklin's book, but I think it's useful for understanding
the circumstances under which Josiah Franklin undertook
his research. Dan Franklin's account of his struggles with
addiction—not to mention, what sounds like some form of
schizophrenia—is compelling, but it assumes a great deal
of background knowledge about his father and the man's
work that I'm not sure the average reader has. Despite Josiah Franklin's reputation within the scientific community,
and the books that have been written about him already, his
life and career are more specialized subjects.*

*Anyway, feel free to include these as you see fit. Hope
all's well.*

Best,
John

ENDNOTES

1. Daniel Franklin's description of his father as Dr. Frankenstein
is more indicative of his sentiments towards the man from whom

he had been estranged so long and so bitterly than it is an accurate comparison. As presented in Mary Shelley's famous novel (1818, rev. 1831), Victor Frankenstein discovers the means for reanimating dead tissue and then cannot resist following his discovery to its logical end. By and large, the various cinematic incarnations of the scientist, from Colin Clive (1931) to Kenneth Branagh (1994), have been faithful to this initial conception of him. If such literary allusion truly is necessary, then it might be better to focus on Dr. Moreau, the titular figure in H.G. Wells's *Island of Dr. Moreau* (1896). Moreau's focus on manipulating animal life places him in relative proximity to the projects with which Josiah Franklin occupied himself. Of course, Franklin and Frankenstein sound similar enough to justify Daniel Franklin making a kind of half-pun; that, and the monstrous outcomes of his father's first experiments.

2. The exact quotation is found in James Whale's *Bride of Frankenstein* (1935), where it is uttered by the sinister Dr. Pretorius: "To a new world of gods and monsters!" One may hear in the toast an echo of Shakespeare's, "O brave new world, / That has such people in't" (Tempest V.1.205-206).

3. Josiah Franklin's concern—even obsession—with the end of the world has been traced to a variety of sources. Although Daniel Franklin insists that his father had left his religious upbringing long behind, in favor of what he calls a "quasi-pagan agnosticism" (45), this may be underestimating the matter. Gunterson has pointed out that the faith of Josiah's childhood, Seventh-Day Adventism, places a good deal of emphasis on the Apocalypse, which it envisions within a particularly American context (32). Similarly, Daniel Franklin spends only a few pages on his paternal grandfather, Samson, noting that the man partook of the mania for bomb shelters that swept the nation during the 1950s. Yet, as Molloy emphasizes, Samson Franklin's experiences in the Second World War lent the construction of his backyard shelter a real urgency (11). A private in the United States Army, Samson was part of the forces that occupied Japan after its surrender. Stationed near Hiroshima, he had a first-

hand view of the devastating effect of what would now be called a weapon-of-mass-destruction, and he shared some of what he saw with his oldest son—who in turn passed the stories on to his son. While Daniel Franklin discounts the significance of the Cuban Missile Crisis (1962) to Josiah's development, it is hard to believe that the threat of nuclear annihilation would not have had a profound effect on someone of his particular upbringing.

4. See William Butler Yeats "The Second Coming" (1920).

5. Far-fetched as the idea may appear now, the global cooling scenario originally was presented in a more restrained, even understated manner (e.g. Kukla and Matthews's "When Will the Present Interglacial End?" [1972]). It took a figure such as Nigel Calder to transform speculation about long-term climate change into anxiety over a "snowblitz," a sudden, catastrophic shift in the weather that would usher in a new ice-age in a matter of decades, as opposed to centuries or millennia. Calder's work at the beginning of the 1970s was complemented at the other end of the decade by a group designating itself "The Impact Team," which further popularized the idea of an incipient ice-age in 1977's *The Weather Conspiracy: The Coming of the New Ice Age*. (A dramatization of such a drastic change forms one of the crucial scenes in the film, *The Day After Tomorrow* [2004], in which the young protagonist must literally outrace a sudden freeze. This suggests that the idea of the snowblitz retains something of its potency.) There is no reason to doubt Daniel Franklin's assertion that his father, pursuing post-doctoral work at M.I.T., did not take the idea of a snowblitz seriously. That said, the prospect of a global catastrophe, even a fictional one, clearly struck a chord with Josiah. If nothing else, it prompted him to his first, sustained speculation as to how the human form might be altered to meet the challenges of an environment grown hostile—how, as Josiah put it, "evolution might be hurried up."

6. A copy of the paper may be read online through the Franklin archive at the University of Boulder (c.f. http://ucblibraries. colora-

do.edu/archives/franklin/surmounting-the-snowblitz/).

7. The word "bionic" was originated by American physician and retired U.S. Air Force colonel Jack E. Steele. Originally, Steele intended the term to describe the study of biological mechanisms as a means of solving challenges in mechanical engineering. However, the word's meaning expanded to include the use of artificial enhancements of and replacements for human organs and limbs. In no small part, this was due to the success of Martin Caidan's novel, *Cyborg* (1972), and the TV series it subsequently inspired, *The Six Million Dollar Man* (1973-1978). Inspired by Steele's ideas, Caidan created an astronaut gravely injured when his vehicle crashes, whose right arm, legs, and left eye are replaced by mechanical equivalents, which provide him with a number of augmented abilities. Despite the term's more colorful associations, bionics has remained an active field of study, both in its general and specific senses, since its inception.

8. As the apex predator of the Arctic region, the polar bear (*Ursus maritimus*) was not an unreasonable model for Josiah Franklin's "modified human form." Skilled hunters, the bears are also equipped with extensive fat reserves, which allow them to survive periods when no prey is to be found. Their fat combines with tough skin and layers of fur to insulate the bears from punishingly cold temperatures. Franklin's paper suggested using bionics essentially to graft what he viewed as the bear's most significant features onto a human being. A course of steroid injections would increase muscle mass. Hands and feet would be surgically enlarged, to improve load distribution on frozen surfaces and to improve swimming. Nails would be replaced with claws fashioned from a neutral metal (probably a titanium alloy). What Franklin called a "pseudopelt" would be attached to the skin through an extensive network of sutures. Composed of a breathable under layer covered with two layers of synthetic fur, the pseudopelt was intended for the frigid climate of the new frozen globe. Plastic surgery to the head would reduce the ears—and their potential for frostbite—and shape the brow to provide better pro-

tection from the glare of sunlight on snow and ice. Franklin weighed enlarging the jaw to insert additional teeth (polar bears have forty-two), but decided the extra teeth were unnecessary. The principal challenge to his design, Franklin wrote, lay in replicating the bear's considerable fat supplies. In order for the typical human to have sufficient fat stores to survive a significant time without food, other elements of the organism must be compromised, to a dangerous degree. In the absence of equivalent reserves of fat, his modified human would require near-constant access to substantial amounts of food. While Josiah's paper went largely unnoticed by his peers, it did attract the attention of the Department of Defense, which contributed increasing amounts of funding to his next several projects.

9. "Sasquatch," of course, is an Anglicization of the Halkomelem name for the cyptid popularly known as Bigfoot. Daniel Franklin's use of the word to describe the end result of his father's proposal is another indication of his sentiments towards the man and his work. His speculation concerning the connection between his father's trips to Colorado and the reported sightings of Sasquatch in the area should not be taken seriously.

10. Although the prospect of nuclear war had been present since the Soviet Union successfully detonated an atomic bomb on August 29, 1949, there had been instances when such a conflict appeared likely, even imminent. As early as the Korean War (1950-1953), the U.S. Strategic Air Command sent ten B-29s carrying unarmed atomic bombs to the U.S. territory of Guam for possible use against the Soviet-backed North Korean forces. U.S. President Harry Truman admitted in a November 1950 press conference that he had contemplated using these weapons, and while he never did, such an admission did little to ease global anxieties about the possibility of nuclear conflict. Within the United States, fears of a nuclear exchange with the Soviet Union led to widespread construction of public and private bomb shelters, such as the one Josiah Franklin's father, Samson, built in the backyard of the family home in Boulder, Colorado (see Molloy for a fuller discussion of this). From October 16-28,

1962, the Cuban Missile Crisis brought the U.S. and the U.S.S.R. to the brink of nuclear war, and while the immediate aftermath of the crisis saw both sides implement measures to lessen the chances of such a situation repeating itself (i.e. the establishment of a hotline between Washington, DC and Moscow), it was by no means the end of nuclear tensions between the nations. In addition, the People's Republic of China successfully tested a nuclear weapon on October 16, 1964, and although their nuclear arsenal was not as extensive as the Soviet Union's, it further complicated the international nuclear situation. During the 1980s, as U.S. President Ronald Reagan and British Prime Minister Margaret Thatcher embraced a more confrontational stance towards the U.S.S.R., tensions again increased. The shootdown of Korean Air Lines flight 007 by Soviet jets on September 1, 1983 dramatically heightened tensions between the United States and the Soviet Union, as did NATO exercise Able Archer 83 two months later (indeed, a number of historians of the Cold War have argued that the NATO war game brought the world as close to nuclear war as it had been since the Cuban Missile Crisis, as certain Soviet leadership elements viewed the exercise as a cover for the preparation of an actual nuclear attack). Although the second half of 1983 would mark the last significant flare up in Cold War hostilities, for Josiah Franklin, now affiliated with the U.S. Army Natick Soldier Research, Development & Engineering Center (NSR-DEC) in Natick, MA, these events appeared to presage imminent nuclear war. As a result, he suspended his work on the enhanced combatant program (see Gunterson) to devote his efforts towards modifying the human form to maximize its chances of surviving a post-nuclear-conflict world.

11. First broadcast in November of 1983 to an estimated audience of 100 million viewers, the ABC television movie, *The Day After*, dramatized the effects of a nuclear exchange between the U.S. and the U.S.S.R. on two communities in the American Midwest. In his memoirs, President Ronald Reagan credited the film with influencing his decision to engage in the negotiations with the Soviets that would lead to the 1987 Intermediate-Range Nuclear Forces Treaty.

For Josiah Franklin, the movie was "a hellishly evocative depiction of the nightmare I work day and night to find a pathway through" (quoted in Molloy).

12. The lyric is from Barry McGuire's 1965 song, "Eve of Destruction."

13. A redacted copy of the paper may be read online through the Franklin archive at the University of Boulder (c.f. http://ucblibraries. colorado.edu/archives/franklin/a-nuclear-metamorphosis/). A version of the essay was rejected by the editors of *Would the Insects Inherit the Earth and Other Subjects of Concern to Those Who Worry About Nuclear War*, who described it as "too fanciful" for their book.

14. Since Wilhelm Röntgen's discovery of X-Rays in 1895, the diagnostic applications of radioactive elements have been part of medical research and practice. As early as 1896, Leopold Freund employed X-Rays in a therapeutic fashion to remove a mole from a patient. In the first decades of the twentieth century, a host of over-the-counter health supplements containing radioactive substances were advertised as treating conditions including arthritis, rheumatism, and constipation. Several leading scientists, most notably Marie Curie, cautioned against such drugs, arguing that the effects of prolonged exposure to radioactive elements were poorly understood. By 1927, Hermann Joseph Muller had established the relationship between irradiation and heightened risks of cancer and genetic mutation. (He would be awarded the Nobel Prize in Medicine for his research in 1946.) From the 1950s, radiation therapy became one of the principal avenues of treatment for cancer; though with increasing concern for the consequences of the therapy on the patient's potential offspring.

15. Muller's experiments irradiating fruit flies with X-Rays to explore the effects on their genes were cited by Franklin as one of the inspirations for his proposal.

16. While Josiah Franklin had no formal plans to engage in mapping the human genome, the enterprise became necessary once he decided to focus his research on modifying human embryos. (A series of early experiments using radioactive materials to selectively mutate mature individuals had ended in a catastrophe, which resulted in closed-door Congressional hearings that put Josiah's career in serious jeopardy, and which have spawned a host of urban legends concerning his "monster men" [see Gunterson]). Franklin's research coincided with the first years of the Human Genome Project, which developed from a series of workshops and essays by leading scientists on the topic during the mid-1980s. The official enterprise began in 1990, its co-founders the U.S. Department of Energy and the National Institutes of Health. An international consortium of scientists from nations including the U.K., France, and China contributed to the process, whose target date for completion was set for fifteen years. However, a preliminary map was completed in 2000, five years ahead of schedule, while the final map appeared two years early, in 2003. Because of the nature of his work, Josiah Franklin's contributions to the project had to be made through a series of intermediaries. As a result, it is difficult to evaluate his claim that his research helped bring the mapping to its early conclusion; though it seems an exaggeration.

17. Anecdotal reports of the atomic blast sites at Hiroshima and Nagasaki listed cockroaches among the first organisms to return to the areas. This gave rise to the popular notion that, in the aftermath of a nuclear war, those insects would inherit what was left of the earth, an assertion that was repeated in an interview given by H. Bentley Glass to the *New York Times* in 1962 and that subsequently achieved the status of quasi-fact. The insects are quite hardy, able to survive up to 62,500 REM, as compared to just 800 REM for humans. Additional insects can withstand higher levels still—the Parasitic Wasp *Habrobracon hebetor* can endure 180,250 REM—but Josiah Franklin found a number of other advantages to cockroach physiology that caused him to select the insect (specifically, the American cockroach [*Periplaneta americana*]) as the model for his second mod-

ified human form. Through targeting of specific genes with infinitesimal amounts of what he called his radiation cocktail, Franklin intended to cause a human embryo to mutate in certain pre-determined directions. For example, the skin would develop as a harder surface, strengthened by elevated amounts of calcium carbonate and made water-resistant by wax secreted from its pores. The jaw and teeth would be reinforced, the interior of the mouth and upper digestive tract toughened, to allow the consumption of a wider range of sustenance, while the mid- and lower digestive tract would be adjusted to allow nutrition to be drawn from less promising fodder. Augmentation of the bone marrow would enable it to produce a glycerol-based "antifreeze" in the event of the severely cold temperatures accompanying the inevitable nuclear winter. The most significant change Franklin proposed, however, was to the rate of cell division throughout the body. Humans are vulnerable to radiation because it interferes dramatically with ongoing cell replication, disrupting it to lethal effect. The cockroach, in comparison, undergoes cell division at a profoundly slower pace, approximately once a week, which limits the damage radiation can cause. Thus, after an initial period of rapid growth, the cells in Franklin's modified human form would replicate at a substantially reduced rate. This would result in a smaller organism; Franklin estimated its average height as just over one meter.

18. Although Josiah Franklin's proposed modification chamber was microscopic in scale, his son has a point: it is hard not to be struck by the resemblance to the famous laboratory set in James Whale's *Frankenstein* (1931).

19. Perhaps the single-greatest challenge to Josiah Franklin's plan for his post-nuclear-conflict-humans was that of timing. Even in the case of a "snowblitz," there would be adequate time to alter human beings to meet the changed environment; in the case of a nuclear war, however, civilization would be in smoking ruins before the necessary procedures could be performed. Franklin's proposed solution was the creation of a small population of his modified humans well

in advance of any conflict. This would allow ample time to raise and educate a sufficient number of them to counter any sudden catastrophe. While Daniel Franklin enjoyed frightening his middle- and high-school friends with stories about the monsters his father kept in their house's extensive basement—and while he hints at actually having witnessed *something* under their residence in Natick—there remains no credible evidence to support any of these claims.

20. The Cold War came to an end over a two-year period that began on November 9, 1989 with the fall of the Berlin Wall and concluded on December 26, 1991 with the dissolution of the Soviet Union. While both the United States and the members of the Russian Federation maintained their nuclear arsenals, the symbolic "Doomsday Clock" of the *Bulletin of the Atomic Scientists* was set back to seventeen minutes to midnight, the furthest from that time and the catastrophe it represents the clock's hands ever have been. Despite this, Josiah Franklin continued work on his post-nuclear-war modified human until 1998, when U.S. President Bill Clinton ordered a review of biological threats to the country. Franklin's participation in the review was minimal, yet it spurred him to put aside the research that had consumed him for the last decade and a half in favor of a new project designed to address this new danger. The extent to which Daniel Franklin's increasingly erratic behavior had distracted his father, with the result that he failed to appreciate the full implications of the end of the Cold War, is difficult to gauge; though certainly Daniel's struggles with heroin addiction throughout the early and mid-1990s—resulting in a series of stays in rehab facilities—occupied a significant portion of his father's attention.

21. Ironically, the end of the Cold War revealed the extent of the former U.S.S.R.'s biological weapons programs. Although the U.S.S.R. was a signatory to the 1972 Biological Weapons Convention, whose express purpose was to prohibit the production of bioweapons, this had little effect on their actual activities. These were overseen by the Biopreparat, a nominally civilian bureaucracy that managed a series of secret laboratories, each dedicated to devel-

oping a different biological pathogen for military use. Documents whose release was approved by Russian President Boris Yeltsin in 1992 disclosed efforts at weaponizing the anthrax bacterium (*Bacillis anthracis*), the accidental release of which in Sverdlovsk (now Yekaterinburg) in 1979 led to at least one hundred fatalities from "Anthrax 836." A 1995 report indicated that the Soviets, building on research captured from the Imperial Japanese army at the end of the Second World War, had spent decades working towards a weaponized smallpox virus (*Variola major*), finally succeeding by using a strain of the disease retrieved from the 1967 Indian outbreak (and christened "India-1967"). Also in 1992, Yeltsin ordered all biological weapons within Russia destroyed, but numerous analysts agree that his directive was almost certainly disregarded, in part if not in whole.

22. The United States' biological weapons program was approved by President Franklin Roosevelt in 1942; the following year, the U.S. Army Biological Warfare Laboratories were established at then-Camp Detrick in Maryland. For the next quarter-century, the U.S. military worked on enhancing the effectiveness of many of the same pathogens as their Soviet counterparts. Although the United States did not suffer the same weapons-related accidents as the U.S.S.R., there was substantial testing of biological agents on unwitting subjects, many of them in the U.S. military. In addition, there were accusations of U.S. use of biological weapons during the Korean War, and against livestock targets in Cuba in the 1960s; though these charges remain subject to debate. (The extent of Josiah Franklin's knowledge of these events is unclear. The position he took at Defense Advanced Research Projects Agency [DARPA] in Arlington, Virginia in 1995 would have permitted him access to a significant amount of classified information.) The U.S. bioweapons program came to its end in 1969, when President Richard Nixon officially ended it and ordered all stockpiles of biological agents destroyed. This was accomplished by 1973. Since then, the official position of the United States government has been that any research it conducts in this area is purely defensive in nature; though concerns continue to be raised about the exact parameters of that study.

23. In 1984, members of the Rajneeshee group deliberately contaminated salad bars in the Oregon city of The Dalles with home-grown *Salmonella Typhimurium*. This was done in order to influence the outcome of a local election in which the group had a stake. Seven hundred and fifty-one people were affected, forty-five of them hospitalized. No one died as a result of the attack, but Josiah Franklin saw the group's actions as demonstrating the frightening ease with which a non-state actor could obtain and employ a biological pathogen, to potentially devastating ends.

24. Published in 1994, *The Hot Zone: A Terrifying True Story* grew out of an article *New Yorker* writer Richard Preston had contributed to the magazine in 1992, "Crisis in the Hot Zone." The article focused on the 1989 Reston Incident, during which a number of long-tailed macaques (*Macaca fascicularis*) at the Hazleton Research Products' Primate Quarantine Unit in Reston, Virginia, were discovered to be infected with a hitherto-unseen strain of *Ebolavirus*. While what would become known as Reston *ebolavirus* was eventually found to be non-threatening to humans, its relationship to the more lethal species of the virus, combined with the research facility's proximity to Washington, DC, led to a significant portion of the macaques being euthanized. Building on the magazine piece, the book describes a number of viral hemorrhagic infections, details their past outbreaks in sub-Saharan Africa, and speculates on their potential to spread to Europe and the United States. A massive success, the book reached the number one spot on the *New York Times* nonfiction bestseller list. With the benefit of two decades' hindsight, it seems clear that Preston's book owed a measure of its popularity to anxieties about the ongoing HIV-AIDS epidemic, which had foregrounded the threat posed by hitherto-unfamiliar viral infections.

25. A heavily-redacted copy of the paper may be read online through the Franklin archive at the University of Boulder (c.f. http://ucblibraries.colorado.edu/archives/franklin/a-symbiotic solution-to-the-coming-plagues/).

26. The origins of nanotechnology can be traced to a 1959 talk by Richard Feynman, "There's Plenty of Room at the Bottom," which raised the possibilities for technological advances created by the increasing ability to control individual atoms. Feynman's ideas were picked up by K. Eric Drexler in his 1986 book, *Engines of Creation: The Coming Era of Nanotechnology*, in which Drexler forecasts a wide-range of applications for nanotechnology, from information storage to human medicine. Drexler's predictions had been spurred by the development of the scanning tunneling microscope in 1981; while the use of the device to manipulate individual atoms in 1989 appeared to show his ideas in action. As Josiah Franklin already was working at a microscopic level with his embryo modification chamber, the notion of moving to an even smaller scale did not require a significant adjustment in his perspective.

27. With the exception of the scanning tunneling microscope, the necessary technology remains classified by the U.S. Government.

28. For Josiah Franklin, the challenges posed by biological pathogens were considerably more complex than those presented by nuclear weapons (or, for the matter, a sudden ice-age). Depending on the disease, the effects could vary widely, necessitating modifications to the human form that would allow an ongoing adaptive response. As was the case with his previous proposals for altering the human form to meet an apocalyptic threat, Franklin looked to the animal kingdom for inspiration. His focus this time was on the Egyptian plover (*Pluvianus aegyptius*), more popularly known as the "crocodile bird," for its supposed symbiotic relationship with the Nile crocodile (*Crocodylus niloticus*). According to the Greek historian Herodotus, while the crocodiles were resting on the banks of the Nile, they would open their mouths to allow the birds to hop into them. Rather than consuming the plovers, the crocodiles would allow the birds to pick through their teeth for any traces of food left in them. In this way, the birds would feed, and the crocodiles have their teeth cleaned. Although the story of the crocodile bird has not been documented by modern science, it provided Josiah with a conceptual

model for his third modified human form. Instead of radically altering human physiology to adapt it to a hostile landscape, he would supplement it with a population of symbiotic organisms designed to assist it in overcoming the most virulent diseases. Research into animal resistance to disease led Franklin to another crocodilian, the American alligator (*Alligator mississippiensis*), whose robust immune system allows it to survive open wounds submerged in swamp water teeming with a host of microorganisms. Through extensive modification using specialized nanomachines, Josiah proposed adapting macrophages isolated from the alligator's blood to enable them to function within human beings. Much of what he envisioned remains subject to DARPA secrecy protocols, but it appears to have involved splicing the animal's white blood cells with the individual human's, in order to avoid rejection by the host. The human appendix would be employed as a kind of reservoir for these augmented white blood cells, a portion of which would be released when the immune system registered a severe enough response to an infection. Outside the customized environment of the appendix, the modified cells would die in a matter of hours, but this would be ample time for them to destroy whatever disease was present. According to Josiah's calculations, the appendix of a typical adult human could contain sufficient reserves of his adapted macrophages to see that person through half a dozen significant epidemics.

29. Despite Daniel Franklin's accusations, there is no evidence that the 2009 car crash that claimed his father's life in Colorado was anything other than an accident caused by wet leaves and a sharp turn in the road. The quotation is from William S. Burroughs.

30. Approximately six weeks after Daniel Franklin turned in the final copy-edits for *My Father, Dr. Frankenstein*, he was found dead in his apartment in Ellicott City, Maryland, by his landlord. Since completing the manuscript of his memoir in late 2014, Daniel's behavior had grown increasingly erratic, as he struggled against and eventually relapsed into heroin addiction. Whether or not the end of what had been six years drug-free was caused by revisiting the

material covered in his book is impossible to say with certainty, but the coincidence is difficult to ignore. Daniel's drug use apparently fostered a growing conviction that he had been experimented upon by his father during his last stay in rehab, leaving him "infested," as he put it, with Josiah Franklin's creations, which Daniel insisted were concentrated in his appendix. (The echo of his father's final project is striking, particularly as the Franklin archive had yet to post the edited version of Josiah's final paper; though it is possible that he had shared some of the details of his work with his son.) Because of the alterations his father had made to him, Daniel said, heroin no longer offered the profound escape it once had. In addition, he felt his consciousness changing in ways he struggled to articulate, but that appeared to involve heightened impulses to aggression and violence. Consultations with a number of physicians failed to reveal any abnormalities in his health, and he could not convince the doctors to conduct exploratory surgery to examine his appendix. Nor did sessions with several therapists yield a resolution to his sense that he had been fundamentally altered. Finally, Daniel Franklin took matters into his own hands, and attempted to remove his appendix himself. After disinfecting his bathroom with bleach and covering it in sterilized sheets, he lay on the floor on his back. Positioning a pair of mirrors to allow him a better view of the surgical site, he swabbed his lower abdomen with iodine, then injected the area with a mixture of lidocaine and epinephrine. Using a folding lockback knife with a 3 ¾ inch blade, he made a four inch incision in his abdominal wall. Remarkably, he succeeded in reaching his appendix; once there, however, he sliced the appendicular artery lengthwise, creating a wound that he was unable to suture successfully. The resulting bleeding both complicated his task and gave it added urgency. This likely led to the slip that drove the knife into his external iliac artery. While Daniel Franklin attempted to address this even more serious injury, he had neither the training nor the tools to do so. He lost consciousness in short order, and bled to death on his bathroom floor not long thereafter. When his body was discovered, EMT's were summoned to the scene, but it was too late. The official report mentions that his appendix was found on the floor next to him; apparently, he had succeeded in his final task. What became of the organ afterward is unclear.

For Fiona

UNDERSOUND

MARK MORRIS

"So you gonna do it or what?" she asks.

"Yes," Clay mutters irritably. "I said I would, didn't I? And I will."

"When?"

"Tonight."

"Is that a promise?"

He looks up at her leaning over his desk, all cleavage and pout and long, glossy hair. "Look, this isn't a minor thing, Fern. This isn't like …" But he can't think of anything even remotely comparable. "Well, it'll change things," he says eventually. "It'll change things for ever."

"For the better," she says stubbornly.

"Yes, eventually. But it's just … well, it's the doing of it, isn't it? The doing of it and the getting away with it. I'm not sure you realise what a massive thing this is. We're stepping into the abyss here, Fern. Both of us."

She wears a look of weary incomprehension, and just for a moment he wonders whether he's making a terrible mistake. Christine's his intellectual equal—his intellectual superior in many ways—but Fern isn't. Not by a long chalk.

But then what does intellect matter when it's allied with what Christine's illness has made her become? Like Fern she used to be so vivacious, so adventurous, so fun loving, but since the diagnosis was confirmed fourteen long years ago she has allowed the MS to drain her of her joy and optimism, to the extent that she's now nothing but a collection of dry old bones wrapped in bitterness and fear.

It's not death she's fearful of, though. It's life. It's the future. And he's hoping that's what'll make this whole thing easier.

"I'm not scared of dying," she said to him once, not long after the diagnosis. "Death is an abstract concept, a non-experience. Death is only hard on those left behind. But I'm scared of the journey *towards* death. Of being conscious and aware while my body deteriorates around me."

He clings to those words, although he tries not to dwell on what his response had been—a reminder (parroting the doctor) that MS itself is rarely fatal, and a promise he'd be there beside her whatever happened. He tries also not to recall *her* response to *his* response, though the memory is as vivid as if it had happened yesterday. She'd squeezed his hand, the gesture full of love and trust, and she'd said, "I know you will, honey. That's what'll sustain me."

But that was then and this is now. He can't be blamed for resenting her for giving up, nor for wanting to continue to live his life. Even when she was still relatively able-bodied, she started to blame her tiredness for inactivity, depression for a lack of motivation. He did all he could to coax, and shame, and finally bully her out of her slump, but she seemed determined to play the martyr.

And now it's come to this. To a situation which began as a cruel joke between himself and Fern, then developed into a vague possibility, and has now narrowed and tightened into what feels like an inevitability. Almost thirty years ago Christine captured his heart, but tonight he plans to stop hers. He tells himself it's a win-win situation, that by killing his wife he'll be releasing them all. He tells himself, and sometimes even almost convinces himself, that what he plans to do will be an act not of cruelty or selfishness, but of kindness.

He could just leave her, of course, but wouldn't that be dealing her an even more devastating blow? Besides, most of what they jointly own is hers—the house, the money she inherited from her rich father—and although he's sure he'd get by on his own, he's fearful he'd be unable to satisfy Fern and her expensive tastes on his modest wage, and would therefore end up losing her.

He knows how it looks, but he's not a fool. He's well aware that Fern is a gold digger. But they do genuinely get on, and she gives him what he so desperately needs and has been deprived of for too long: excitement, spontaneity, *fun*.

Plus she's gorgeous, and nearly twenty years younger than him, so for the first time in he doesn't know how long he feels like a strutting rooster again. And a man needs that. A bit of self-respect. A bit of va-va-voom! All those years with Christine—all those *declining* years—have turned him into something grey, sunken, nondescript. For the last decade he's been the invisible man. But no more.

No more.

When he lets himself into the house, he feels as though his heart is thumping in his throat, strangling him. After swallowing several times, he finally manages to call out, "Hi, it's me."

Chris surprises him by cheerily replying, "Hey you, how was your day?" whereupon he immediately feels a pang of conscience. But then he smothers it by telling himself it's only a momentary burst of sunshine. It won't be long before the storm clouds gather and the gloom descends, as usual.

Following his nose to the kitchen, he finds her sitting in her wheelchair at the kitchen table with a chopping board in front of her. To his amazement she's peeled carrots and cut them into batons, which sit in a bowl waiting to go into the steamer, and she's now topping and tailing green beans.

"What's all this?" he says before stooping to give her a perfunctory kiss.

"It's dinner," she says proudly. "I've made a fish pie. It's in the oven."

"It smells delicious," he says automatically, although it genuinely does. "But what's it in aid of?"

"We're celebrating," she says, and nods to the bottle of Merlot on the kitchen counter beside the fridge, a gesture he immediately understands as an indication he should open it and pour them both a glass.

"Are we? Why?"

She beams at him. "Because I've had a good day. And because I've decided to turn over a new leaf."

Her uncharacteristic optimism should make him feel uplifted, but all he feels is a dull weight of foreboding as he pours the wine. He stretches his mouth and peels his lips back from his teeth in what he hopes is a convincing grin. "Well, this is … a surprise," he says inadequately.

"A pleasant one, I hope?"

"Of course. I'm just …" he dithers, his vocabulary deserting him, before muttering again, "… surprised."

"Have I really been so awful?" she says teasingly, and then sighs. "Yes, I suppose I have. And it's not been fair on you, has it? But from now on, it's all going to change."

"Is it?" he says weakly.

"Yes. I know it's been a long time coming, but I've decided to start living again. I've decided not to be scared any more. Fear is a choice, after all."

"Why?" he says, and to his ears the word comes out sounding like a bleat of disappointment or disapproval. "I mean, this is great obviously, but … why now? After all this time?"

"Call it an epiphany," she says, and immediately a cold fist of panic tightens around his guts.

She knows, he thinks. *She knows everything.*

"Has someone said something?"

She looks quizzical above the wine glass she brings to her lips. "Like what?"

"Well … I don't know. It's just … well, this isn't like you."

She pauses then, looks at him appraisingly. He holds her gaze, tries to maintain a casual pose, leaning back against the counter, but inside he's squirming.

"Guess where I've been today?" she says.

"To the supermarket to buy ingredients for fish pie?"

She smiles. "Yes, that too. But this morning Martha came round, and said there was a brilliant exhibition at the Sculpture Park, and would I like to go. My first instinct was to say no, to think of an excuse to stay home. And then something clicked inside me. Like a switch being thrown. As simple as that. And I found myself saying yes. And you know what? It was brilliant. I set off full of anxiety, and I came back … energised."

"Must have been some exhibition," he says with a laugh that sounds hollow.

"It was. It was called The New People, and it was by a Spanish guy—I can't remember his name—who builds these huge ethereal figures out of wire netting. From a distance they look like giants made of smoke. The idea behind them is that what we perceive as real isn't always the case—that each of us creates our own reality, and sometimes we trap ourselves in it. Anyway, they're amazing. We'll have to go. I really want you to see them. We can make a day of it, take a picnic."

"That sounds nice," he says.

"But it wasn't ... oh, it wasn't just that. It was ... I don't know how to describe it. Like I said, it was an epiphany. It came out of nowhere,"

"Well, I'm glad," he says.

"Are you? You don't sound it."

He makes an effort to instill some enthusiasm into his voice. "No, I am. Of course I am. I couldn't be happier. It's just ... it's a lot to take in, that's all. It's so unexpected."

"Yes, I suppose it is," she says. "I *know* it is. I'm sorry for everything I've put you through, and I'm so grateful you've stood by me all these years. I do love you, you know."

"I love you too," he says, the words like ashes in his mouth.

His phone pings in his pocket. Normally he has it on silent when he's with Chris, but today he had so much on his mind that he forgot.

"Who's that from? A secret admirer?" Chris asks teasingly.

He tries to match his smile to hers, but the muscles in his face don't seem to work properly. "I wish."

Half turning away, he scoops the phone from his pocket and checks the message. It's from Fern: **Have you done it yet?** He feels a surge of anger mixed with alarm. Does she honestly think it's that easy? Can she really be so insensitive? He deletes the message with his thumb and switches his phone to silent.

"Just work," he says. "Nothing that can't wait. Look, why don't you go in the lounge and relax. I'll finish up here. Give me your wine glass and I'll replenish us both."

She gives him an indulgent smile. "I'm not incapable, you know."

"I know. But you've done a lot today. You deserve to relax."

She drains her glass and hands it to him. "All right then. I'll look for a film on Netflix for us to watch after dinner. Don't be long."

"I won't be," he says.

As soon as she exits the kitchen in her wheelchair Clay starts to shake. He turns to the counter and leans on it and takes deep breaths. How can he go through with it now? But how can he not? But she's *happy*. Chris is happy. Even optimistic. He hasn't seen her like this in ... he can't remember how long.

But isn't that even more reason to go through with it, he thinks. Better to go out happy than miserable. Better to leave this world without fear or regret than to leave it in misery and pain.

When it comes to his turn he knows that's what he'd like to do. He'd like to drift away contented and unaware, and just ... go. No final illness, no lingering decline, no awareness of what's happening. Looking at it this way, he can almost convince himself that what he'll be giving to Chris is the most generous gift of all. Because this epiphany of hers, this new found optimism won't last. It's a false dawn. Tomorrow or next week or next month her fatigue will increase, or her neuropathic pain will become worse, and she'll once again slip into despondency and despair.

He tries to lock that thought into his head as he opens the drawer where she keeps her medication and takes out the temazepam she sometimes uses to help her sleep. At such times she has one 15mg capsule before going to bed, which pretty much knocks her out, and so he hurriedly crushes ten of the capsules into powder in the mortar and pestle and pours them into her empty wine glass. He quickly washes and dries the mortar and pestle, scrubbing out any remnants of powder—he can't afford any slip-ups—then refills both their glasses and carries them into the lounge.

Left hand, left hand, left hand, he repeats silently to himself, afraid that his jittering mind will make him forget which glass is hers. She's sitting on the settee, using the remote to flick through film choices on Netflix, and she gives him such a sweet and trusting smile that he fleetingly contemplates dropping her glass accidentally on purpose, abandoning the whole thing.

But then he's handing it over, and she's taking a sip, and his whole body tenses as he waits for her to screw up her face, to say the wine tastes funny, to look at him with slowly dawning realization, her face etched with horror and hurt and terrible accusation. He's already wondering what he'll say, how he'll squirm out of it, whether he even can, when she says pleasantly, "Why are you hovering like a vulture, love? Aren't you going to sit down?"

"Yes," he says, and then, "I was just wondering how long the pie needed? Whether you wanted me to put the vegetables on now."

She wafts a hand. "Oh, they can wait a few minutes. Sit down here and tell me about your day."

"There isn't much to tell." But he sits down anyway. "Same old, same old. I've just been working out costings for the Comstock job. Oakes is desperate to win the bid."

"Is this for the sports centre in ... is it Newcastle?"

"Glasgow," he says. "There'll be a nice commission if we get it."

"We should use the extra cash to go away," she says. "A long weekend in a spa hotel. We haven't done that in ages."

Her chatter of future plans, of things to look forward to, is causing a cement-like ache to bloom in his chest.

"We should," he says, and tries again to force his facial muscles into a smile.

She takes another sip of wine—more than a sip. "Whoa," she says.

"What?"

"Either my alcohol tolerance has plummeted or this stuff is strong."

Maybe you shouldn't have any more, he imagines himself saying, before taking the glass from her and pouring what remains of the doctored wine—still a good three-quarters of a glass full—down the kitchen sink. He imagines telling Fern it's all off, that he's come to his senses, that he can't believe he ever let her talk him into this.

He puts none of these thoughts into practice, though. Despite his anguish and turmoil, he stubbornly tells himself that this evening is an exception, that it can't last, and he knows also that the allure of Fern, of her body, of her glamour, of her youth, which is almost enough to convince him that he is still young too, has far too tight a hold on him. He wishes things could be different, but they can't. He has come too far down this road to turn back now.

And so he watches his wife drink the rest of the doctored wine, and then he tells her he's going into the kitchen to put the vegetables on. Once there he pours the remainder of his own wine down the sink because the small amount he has drunk is churning sourly inside him and he can't face drinking any more. He paces the kitchen floor, feeling loose and disconnected from his own body, and yet at the same time panicky and sick at the thought of what he's done.

He's been planning this for a long time, he's come to terms with it, or thought he had, but even so, now that it's become a reality he can't quite believe he's gone through with it. He feels as if he's done something fundamental and irredeemable, which of course he has. He feels as if he's tipped the world on its axis.

He sweats and shakes, and for a while he stands over the sink, his hands gripping the sides, the unyielding chill of the metal digging into the soft pads of his thumbs. He tries to make himself throw up, as if he's full of poison he needs to expel.

But he can't. He can't vomit out his sins. He's eternally stained with them.

When he switches off the oven containing the fish pie, the thought of Chris making it for the two of them, preparing something tasty and nourishing and wholesome for them to share over a bottle of wine and a movie, causes such a crushing black wave of horror and self-loathing to wash over him that he staggers as if drunk. He opens his mouth and lets out a blurt of sound that's somewhere between a sob and a wail. *What have I done?* he thinks. *What have I done?*

He considers leaving the house and driving away. Just driving and driving and never coming back.

But then he thinks, *What if it's not too late? What if she's okay? If I call an ambulance, maybe they can rush her to hospital and pump out her stomach and save her?*

But then what? Because even if she did recover, how would he explain what had happened? Because she'd know. She'd know what he'd done to her. And ultimately it's this, his inability to face the prospect of her recovering and realising that her own husband had tried to kill her, that provides him with the resolve he needs to finish the job.

He walks back into the lounge and forces himself to look at her. It salves his conscience a little to see that she looks okay, peaceful even. She's slumped sideways on the settee, her eyes closed and her mouth partly open. She looks as though she's just nodded off.

"Chris," he says, and when she doesn't respond he moves closer and raises his voice. "Chris."

She's still. She doesn't murmur or twitch. He can't see her chest rising and falling beneath the chunky green cardigan she's wearing to keep out the cold.

She can't have gone already, can she? It's only been—what?— fifteen minutes, twenty at most, since she finished her wine. He leans over her and speaks her name again. Nothing. He reaches out a hand, hesitates a moment, then gently nudges her shoulder. Not even a flicker of a response.

His thoughts are veering, colliding inside his head like dodgem cars. He closes his eyes a moment, tries to ignore the clutter, to concentrate on the plan. When he thinks he's got a handle on it he sets to work, telling himself it's a job, a procedure, something he has to work through methodically. First he puts on a pair of latex gloves he pulls from a packet in his jacket pocket and uses a fresh duster from the cupboard under the kitchen sink to wipe the wine bottle and Chris's glass free of his and her fingerprints. Then, still wearing the gloves, he lifts Chris's hand and encloses it first around the glass and then the bottle, so it will look as if she's the only person who's touched them.

He then carries bottle and glass upstairs into the bathroom and starts running a bath. While the water is filling the tub, he goes back downstairs, washes, dries and puts away his own wine glass, then takes the fish pie out of the oven and scoops it from the pie dish into a plastic Sainsbury's bag, his stomach roiling at what, in other circumstances, would have been the delicious smell of baked fish and cheese and herbs. Also into the bag go the vegetables—because why would a woman who intended to kill herself first take the time and effort to cook a meal for two?—after which he ties up the bag, intending to take it with him and dump it in a bin somewhere when he leaves.

When he's washed, dried and put away everything she used to make the meal, he goes back upstairs and turns off the bath taps. Although he's working methodically, he feels as if he's on the verge of succumbing to a virus, but is trying to hold himself together in order to get through an unavoidable engagement—an important business meeting, a lunchtime appointment, the funeral of a friend.

Picking up Chris, the dead, floppy weight of her, makes his skin crawl. He wonders whether a shrinking flame of life still flickers somewhere deep in her brain. If so, she shows no sign. Her head lolls against his arm and her arms dangle as he carries her upstairs.

He almost stumbles and drops her at one point, but finally he makes it to the bedroom they have shared for the past twenty-four years and lowers her on to the bed. Though his back tweaks with pain as he bends forward, he does it gently, tenderly, supporting her head as if she were a baby. He straightens up, wincing, and puts a gloved hand to his mouth, as if to hold in his shame and self-disgust and regret. Now comes a part he isn't relishing, but which he knows he's going to have to go through with if he's going to make this convincing. He takes several deep breaths and then begins to undress Chris, to peel her clothes away layer by layer.

It's not that he hasn't seen her naked before, it's just that doing this without her compliance makes him feel uncomfortable, exploitative. He feels he's stripping her not only of her clothes, but also her dignity, and even though taking away what remains of her life is worse, it is this which makes him feel like a true monster.

But he forces himself to keep going, and a few minutes later Chris's scrawny but flabby body lies exposed before him. It is the saddest sight he thinks he's ever seen, and remembering how she was when they first met, how she seemed to thrum with allure and vitality, fills him with an overwhelming, almost unbearable sense of grief.

"I'm sorry," he whispers. "I'm so sorry." Then he bends down and slides his gloved hands under her and lifts her up. She still feels warm, but does that mean she's still alive? He doesn't know. He has no idea how long it takes for a body to go cold after death. The blood sinks, he knows that, and sometimes (or is it always?) the bladder and bowels evacuate as the muscles loosen, but thankfully there's no evidence of that here. He hesitates a moment, then kisses his wife gently on the forehead, before carrying her through to the bathroom and carefully sliding her into the bath.

He hovers a moment, looking down at her lying in the water, and he wonders whether he has the courage to do what he and Fern had decided should be the final coup de grâce. At first he'd been horrified by her suggestion, had questioned whether it was really necessary. But she'd said they had to be sure, that they couldn't leave anything to chance.

"Pills don't always work," she'd said. "What if she throws up? What if she pulls through, but is brain damaged and you have to look after her? Besides, she'll be out of it. She'll just be meat. What will it matter? It's not like she'll feel anything."

In the end he had given in, because it was easier to do so, and because he lived in fear that too much resistance to Fern would result in her losing interest in him. He'd coped by putting this part of the plan to the back of his mind, by telling himself that once Chris was dead it wouldn't seem so bad; that the pressure would be off, the worst over.

But now that he's reached this point he feels different. The pressure isn't off, and the worst isn't over. Killing his wife, even indirectly, even though he hasn't laid a finger on her, has been awful enough, but the thought of now doing what he and Fern had agreed he should do ... well, it's unspeakable. He isn't sure he can go through with it.

"It was your idea," he mutters. "*You* fucking do it."

But Fern isn't here. She's in her flat, far from the scene of the crime, no doubt sipping Chardonnay and waiting for his call.

He'll try, he decides. He'll take it step by step and see how far he gets. He turns and exits the bathroom, goes downstairs and into the kitchen and over to the knife block. He selects the sharpest knife they have and goes upstairs again, feeling suddenly heavy and breathless, the knife dangling from his hand, the end of the handle pinched between his thumb and index finger as if it's something he wants to disassociate himself from as much as possible.

When he re-enters the bathroom, he feels as if the imaginary virus he's been trying to suppress is starting to gain the upper hand. His skin and eyes feel hot and feverish; his head throbs; his legs feel hollow. His heart pounds in swift, queasy beats that he can feel not only in his chest, but also in his throat and fingertips.

Chris is still slumped in the water, her head on one side, chin almost resting on her right shoulder. He kneels beside the bath and lifts her left arm with his left hand, and presses the tip of the blade against a pale blue vein on her wrist. A bit more pressure and then one swift stroke upwards to her elbow, that's all he needs to do. Like slicing open a breast of chicken. He doesn't know how much blood there will be, or whether it will spurt, but as long as he doesn't get in the way of it and make the police wonder where the escaping blood went to, it'll be fine.

One swift stroke. Do it now and in two seconds it'll be over. Come on, be brave. It's easy.

He takes a deep breath, the muscles bunching and tightening in his hand and forearm.

And that's when Chris opens her eyes, turns to look at him and says, "Undersound."

Clay jumps back like a startled cat, and he feels a sort of jolt in his head, as if his thoughts have been diverted onto a new track. The knife clatters from his hand and his backward momentum causes him to land hard on his backside and bang his head on the sink. When he is again able to focus he gapes at his wife.

Only it is no longer his wife. It is a young man with spectacles and a neatly trimmed beard. And he is not naked; he is wearing a blue hooded sweatshirt and jeans. And there is no water in the bath. It is dry and empty.

Clay can only gape as waves of reaction, not unlike fever, ripple through his body. He tries to raise himself, but his arms feel weak, boneless. Finally he manages to speak, though his voice is cracked, almost a sob.

"Who are you?"

"His name's Richard," says a voice from the bathroom doorway.

"He saw what you were going to do to me."

Chris is standing there, leaning on the stick she uses to hobble about when she's not using her wheelchair, and the expression on her face is everything that Clay dreaded seeing—hurt and anger and terrible, terrible betrayal. It fills him with such a deep and unbearable shame that he wants to cover his face like a child, curl into a ball, close his eyes in the hope that if he wishes hard enough he'll blink out of existence.

But he doesn't do any of these things. He jerks his gaze away from Chris, wincing as if she's slapped him, and looks again at the young man now rising from the bath.

"I don't understand," he says, his voice almost a whimper. "I don't understand what's happening."

The young man—Richard—turns to Chris and asks in a soft voice, "Would you like me to leave you two alone? I can wait in the next room." He glances at Clay, but is still speaking to Chris when he adds, "You'll be quite safe now."

"No," Chris says, her voice so brittle that Clay knows immediately how terribly hurt she is, how close to tears. "I'd like you to stay. If you don't mind, that is."

"Of course," Richard says.

He steps out of the bath and perches himself on the side of it and clasps his hands between his knees.

"What's going on?" Clay pleads. "Won't someone tell me?"

"You tried to kill me, that's what's going on," Chris snaps. She hobbles into the room and her eyes are full of awful accusation. "How could you, Clay?"

"I'm sorry," Clay whimpers. "I'm sorry, I didn't ..." But his voice trails off.

"Mean it?" suggests Chris. "But you did, didn't you? You *did* mean it? Didn't he, Richard?"

The young man sighs. "I'm afraid so. I'm sorry."

Clay knows he has no right to feel indignant, but there is nevertheless a spark of indignation in his voice when he again asks the young man, "Who are you? Why are you here?"

Richard glances at Chris, as if seeking permission to answer the question, and then he sighs and says, "I'm one of the new people."

"What does that mean?" Clay asks.

"There are more and more of us." Richard speaks softly and haltingly, as if he feels uncomfortable, or is unsure how to explain himself. "But we don't advertise our ... gifts. On the other hand, we can't ignore them—or at least, I can't. We ... we hear the under-sound. At least, that's what the people who I know are like me call it. It's like there's an ... an extra muscle in our brains that opens and allows us to see what other people can't. Not yet anyway. But I think they will. Like I say, we're growing in number. I don't know why. Maybe it's just the next step."

He shrugs apologetically, then adds, "We're not all the same, but in my case events from the future throw echoes back into the past, and I hear them."

"The undersound," Clay mutters.

Richard nods eagerly. "That's right. It's random. I can't control it. I don't know whether I see what I see for a reason, or whether I just see the things that have the most ... resonance. The most emotional baggage."

Clay wonders whether he's dreaming this, or has perhaps gone mad. He feels distress, and not only because of what he's been through, and of the way Chris is looking at him. It's like the rug of existence has been pulled from under his feet, like everything he trusted and believed in has suddenly been revealed as a mirage, an illusion.

"Richard came to me," Chris says, every syllable she utters a chip of cold fury, "and he told me what you were planning to do. I was ... appalled. Upset. I couldn't believe it. I still can't. But he said there might be a way out, there might still be hope. If he could only get you to regret it, to not carry it through ..." She sags then, and her voice cracks, and tears run down her cheeks.

"But I couldn't," Richard says, and there is anguish on his face too. "I'm sorry."

He goes to Chris and puts his arms around her, and she sobs into his shoulder. When he next looks at Clay his eyes are full of con-tempt. "As well as seeing into the future, I can manipulate people's thoughts and senses. I can mess with their heads. It's easy. I gave you the chance to back out. To change your mind. But you didn't."

"I wanted to," Clay whispers. "Believe me, I wanted to."

Chris turns her tear-stained face towards him and suddenly screeches, "But not enough! Not enough!"

Clay shrinks back as her voice echoes off the blue walls, the white tiles.

"She wants you to go," Richard says calmly, his arms still wrapped protectively around Chris.

"But I can't," Clay bleats. "She needs me."

"She doesn't need you. I see a future where she doesn't need you."

Desperation makes Clay angry. "What do you know? What do you know about anything? Chris and I have been together for thirty years. We were together before you were born!"

"Nevertheless—" Richard begins, but Clay cuts him off.

"Nevertheless nothing. I'll talk to Chris about this, not you. We don't need you. We'll talk it out. We'll—"

"Go, Clay." Her voice is bleak and the words seem somehow final.

"You don't mean that," he says. His voice becomes a pleading whine once again. "We need to talk this through, Chris. We need to discuss it like two—"

"Go!" she shouts. "And don't ever come back."

"But where?" he says. "Where will I go?"

Her lips peel back over her teeth in an expression that is somewhere between a grin and a snarl. "That's not my problem."

He barely remembers clambering to his feet, staggering downstairs, exiting the house, but all at once Clay is in his car. He is sitting behind the wheel and he is shaking and crying, and he doesn't know what to do.

His phone vibrates in his pocket. He pulls it out in a daze.

The message reads: **Did you get my last text? Have you done it yet? What's happening?**

He stares at the message for a long time. And then he extends a trembling finger over the keypad. He's shaking so much it takes him several minutes, but at last he types his reply.

It's over.

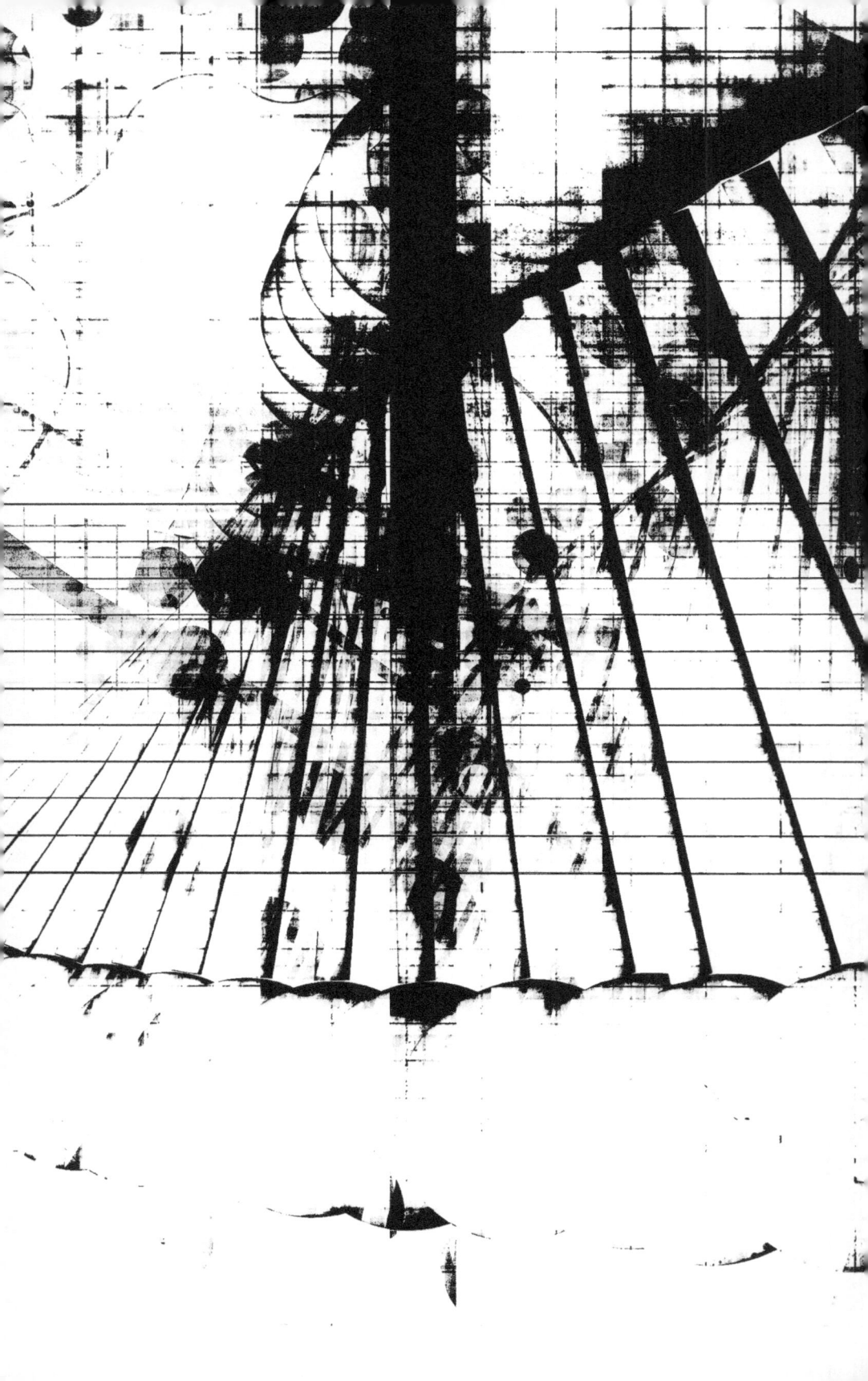

A LAUGHING MATTER

ERINN L. KEMPER

Curtis scowled into the spotlight, waiting for the laugh-app din of monkey chatter, dolphin squeaks, and old-timey car horns to die down. Did everyone in the audience tonight have an implant? A surge of pig snorts and gecko chirps came when some guy near the back of the club unleashed the famous Vincent Price laugh from *Thriller*. Dude must have paid a fair chunk for that one—most real people's emotions were trademarked, even the dead ones.

A woman seated in the first row of tables, dressed classy in a white, silk, button-down top, placed her gin and tonic on a coaster. Her lips curved up and parted in expectation. She had to have the real thing.

Curtis continued with the bit, even though he knew it wasn't funny. Didn't have to be funny these days. People were here to laugh, and they'd use any lame gag as an excuse.

"These emotion-apps are old news, anyways. Next thing you know they'll have the app change how we walk. We'll have hundreds of blissed out happy-in-love saps hogging the sidewalk. Skipping hand in hand, tip-toeing through the tulips, going all Gene-Kelly-Singing-in-the-Rain," a pause for an Al Pacino 'hoo-ah' from a stock-broker-type at the bar, "and come Monday morning it will be a freaking invasion of the undead as we all shuffle and lurch our way to the office. The Zombie App-pocalypse."

With his arms out front, Curtis mimicked the gait of a drunken sleepwalker, moaning 'coffeeee' and rolling his eyes. He tried to focus on the way the audience's mouths grinned wide, eyes streaming helpless tears as they lost themselves to the simple pleasure of yucking it up. But tonight he couldn't tune out the sounds—gales of seagull and parrot calls, arty types emitting banjo flourishes, wind chimes, waterfall static.

The classy woman clapped and nodded, and into a slight lull, opened her brightly lip-sticked mouth to unleash a loud, sputtering fart. Those at tables near her turned and pointed, some applauded, their own laugh-apps sounding in appreciation, which only brought louder, more ass-rippingly wet bleats of flatulence from the woman.

"Yeah, yeah." Curtis sighed.

The audience didn't even notice when he slid the mic back into the stand and walked off stage.

From the velvet-draped shadows backstage, Jimmy, the club owner, raised his eyebrows, and gestured at the spot-lit floor. "You got ten more minutes."

"Fuck it, Jim. I quit." Curtis headed for the door.

Outside, neon lights cast rippling reflections on the rain-washed pavement. From the karaoke bar next door to the Stand and Deliver comedy club came the eerie power-chord and drum-throbbing intro to Metallica's "Enter Sandman." The singer kicked in, voice-implant to sound like Mariah Carey. People paid for the stupidest shit.

Curtis shivered. He'd forgotten his coat inside—his trademark Harris Tweed with elbow patches. Good riddance. He hunched his shoulders against the wet autumn chill and ran for the subway entrance. He dug into his wallet for his subway pass, glancing at the clear plastic window where he kept the picture of Emmie—turned now so a square of white showed. He couldn't bring himself to take the picture out. Or to look at it. Not yet.

The train to Brooklyn pulled up and he stepped on, then wondered what he was doing. No way did he want to go home. Jimmy had probably already called there to tell him to collect his stupid jacket, which meant Sandra would be waiting to 'talk.' Her constant need to 'talk' had prompted him to 'lose' his mobile—a move she called passive aggressive, but he considered preservation of his sanity.

Curtis leaned back against the train window and let the vibrations fill his head until his eardrums tickled. He used to love doing his thing on stage, especially when Sandra came to his shows. She'd sit in the front in her punky out-for-the-night duds and grin up at him, eyes shining. They'd take the train home and as they rushed to undress she'd repeat her favorite bits in a terrible impression of the New Hampshire accent he played up during his act, while he slid his hands from her breasts down the supple curve of her hip. She would laugh at the lines all over again, then gasp when his fingers found the wetness of her. It had been a long time since he'd heard her laugh—since before Emmie's death.

A gentle cooing accompanied by a thrumming purr interrupted his thoughts. He opened his eyes. A young couple sat across from him, rocking side-to-side with the motion of the train. The dude's head nestled on his girlfriend's shoulder, his hair swept forward to cover his eyes. She ran her mirror-nailed fingertips back and forth across his palm. Impossible to say which one was the dove and which the cat, but their affection-apps made nearby passengers shake their heads and smile. Young love.

He remembered relishing the pleasure of fingertips on flesh. Eyes closed so the world reduced to just that—her body, her breath, their heat. Then their world grew a little, made room for the life that quickened inside Sandra. Oh how fragile bubbles are, how it hurts when their luminous skin bursts and the chaos and noise rushes in.

Curtis got off at his stop, walked up to the street and turned right instead of left. The choice between a bottle and home came easy tonight.

⁂

"Can you tell me what you mean by that, Sandra?" Janet, their couple's therapist, put her palms on her lap and leaned forward, her expression open, encouraging. "And if you don't mind, could you turn off your phone for the rest of the session."

Sandra had been seeing Janet before her pregnancy, to deal with her social media addiction. During bed rest in her last trimester she'd gotten hooked all over again. She'd tried to stop using on her own—for a while, anyways. Then that day when Mrs. Green from next door crouched outside their house in the burbs with a scrub brush and a bottle of bleach to get rid of the blood stain, Sandra had shut the blinds and turned on her device. She hardly looked up anymore.

Now she and Curtis saw Janet together, though they always arrived separately.

Sandra picked up her phone and pressed the off-button, then placed it face-down on the coffee table. "I don't know how to talk to him. I think we need to actually say how we feel—speak about it—so we maybe can get on with our lives. But then that feels terrible. Getting on with our lives. As though we're forgetting."

Curtis sat tight to the arm of the love seat, giving Sandra lots of room, his arms and legs crossed, his jacket draped over his lap. Jimmy had delivered the jacket in person, guessing they'd moved back to their apartment in the city. He came with a check and a plea for Curtis to return to work.

"You know how many of you guys have been quittin'?" Jimmy scratched the stubble that salt and peppered his chin. "The new guys, the ones that bring the apps into their routine, improv their bits commenting on all the funky sounds—man, they just aren't funny. All they're doin' is giving the crowd an excuse to show off their tech. What about when the trend moves on? Maybe folks'll want some actual comedy. Right? We can't go forever without real laughter."

Curtis had no answer for that. It felt like forever since he'd heard a real laugh. What if the next trend brought something worse?

"Curtis, you with us?" Janet smiled and tilted her head toward Sandra, reminding him his job for the moment was to listen.

Sandra sniffed and continued. "I'm logging on way less. I'm trying really hard. He's just so closed off. He won't get an implant, even though he knows it would be good for him. Help him show what he's feeling. He's exactly the kind of person they were made for."

"Can you explain why you won't consider an implant?"

Curtis pressed deeper into the back of the couch. Both woman stared at him, Janet with her cool grey eyes, Sandra's eyes filling with tears.

"You lot, psychologists or whatever, made it to help people, but it's become a bastardization of itself, all the weird sounds. People get off being all emotional. Wallowing or stoking their anger just so they can transmit whatever new app they've got. Not to express what's really inside them, what's hurting or making them angry."

Janet nodded. "But the emotions are real."

"Sure," Curtis said, "and so are mine. But there's no way those chuckle-heads who come to the club are using their apps for therapy. Not all of them. It's just trendy. I don't need to squawk like a chicken to show my feelings. I'll show them in my own way."

Sandra wiped her nose with a tissue. "Right now that's by shutting down, not talking at all. It's like living with a piece of furniture instead of a husband. I figured when he went back to work it'd maybe, I don't know, open up that part of him that shut down." She twisted the tissue and clenched it in her fist. "You're not accomplishing anything by quitting your job on top of quitting your marriage."

"I'm not quitting our marriage."

Sandra just stared at him. Her body shuddered and her face scrunched up. A blink turned her tears loose.

Then the sound of her grief came out. The muffled and distant cries of an infant left alone in a cold, dark room, down a long hallway, crying for someone to come and comfort it.

His stomach ached and the hairs on his arms and neck rose to attention. He almost got up and walked out.

Those desperate wails, some nights they brought Curtis gasping awake. *Emmie.* He'd jump from bed to tend to their daughter, only to find his wife lying beside him, staring up into the darkness, tears falling on her pillow. Other times she'd be sleeping, the sounds merely a ghost that haunted his dreams.

Sandra bit her lip and pressed the fresh tissue Janet offered against her eyes, but the more the app cried, the more her tears fell.

Curtis looked at Janet. "This. This is fucked up, right?"

The therapist took a deep breath, her expression calm and neutral. "Well, it's certainly an unusual choice, considering."

Curtis knew the therapist agreed with him.

"Where the hell have you been?" Sandra leaned in close when he walked into the kitchen. It used to mean she wanted a kiss. Today she sniffed his breath for traces of whiskey and scowled when she found the tell-tale fumes.

"Looking for work."

Curtis grabbed a glass from the cupboard and the vodka bottle Sandra had open on the counter. He didn't clarify that looking for work meant skimming the classifieds, circling nothing, then sitting at the club with Jimmy, drinking bourbon while the bartender stocked the shelves.

He went to the freezer for ice and found Sandra's device face-down between the frozen corn and a bag of coffee beans. The ice tray was empty.

"Our therapist fired us, by the way. She left a message for you." Sandra swiped the dishtowel in the direction of the telephone. "You need to get another mobile."

As if receiving his wife's endless photos of bleak, lonely land-scapes, meme's about death and grief and loss—or her voice mes-sages where she just cried that horrible echoing baby's cry—was something he needed.

Curtis tossed back a shot of vodka, then picked up the phone. Sandra capped the bottle before he could pour another and slammed it into a cabinet with a bang, so he missed the beginning of the message.

"… *afraid that a personal conflict requires that I cease our sessions. I've referred you to a colleague who I feel is very capable of working with you both. Um. Listen. There is one last thing.*

"*Curtis. I'd really like you to meet someone. I think he can help you … you can help each other. We'll be at The Whiskey Bar in Brooklyn around eight o'clock. Pretty sure that's near your place. I know this is unusual, and if either of you are uncomfortable, I understand. I just …*" She paused and breathed into the phone for a moment. "*I'd really like you to meet him.*"

Curtis hung up and looked at Sandra, bent over the sink, scrub-bing a pot she'd burnt something in. Since she was back using Me-Dia, or whatever site was trending, that meant lots of forgotten pots on the stove, lots of complaints from the super about setting off the smoke detector.

Her voice broke with the rhythm of her scrubbing. "I told her you'd go, so you'd better get a move on. Almost eight now. But since you've already been at the bottle, no car."

Strange that Sandra hadn't noticed he didn't use the car any more. A few months ago he'd been driving through a school zone, distracted by the kids screaming around the playground playing an extreme elimination version of dodgeball. The car surged and lurched as it bounced over something in the street.

He'd hit the brakes, cold with sweat, blinded by heart-drumming terror. He'd jumped out and run behind the car, stared at the road. It took him a minute to understand he'd driven over a speed bump. Just a speed bump.

A voice called to him from his memory. *Daddy, Daddy. Catchy kiss, catchy kiss.*

The kids in the schoolyard shrieked and laughed. Real laughter, real shouts of pleasure and glee.

With a wave at the drivers waiting patiently for him to complete his meltdown, he got back in the car, parked down the road a bit, and called a tow-truck.

"Yeah, no car. I could use the walk." He grabbed his tweed jacket, added his wooly plaid scarf to complete the look.

Outside the night air slipped cool across Curtis's face. He headed for McCarren Park, a shortcut to the bar. His breath clouded the air as he practiced blowing vapor rings. Someday he'd get it right.

Curtis shoved his hands deeper into his pockets as he entered a copse of trees. A shout sounded ahead of him, and a woman's scream for help. A real scream, he was almost certain. Curtis stopped, pulled his hands from his pockets. When he heard the cry again he ran in that direction. As he got closer he heard other sounds. Anger-apps. Chainsaws revving. Detonations.

Next to a planting of frost-crisp flowers three men fought, while another stood between a woman and the action. The woman fumbled with a phone. The man blocking her swatted the device from her hand and stomped it into the ground. The phone crusher spotted Curtis and shook his head.

"Stay out of it, buddy. They're just working some shit out."

"Help him, Curtis." He hadn't recognized Janet, bundled in a scarf and wool hat. She tried to get around the guy in front of her while he was distracted, but he grabbed her in a bear hug, holding her back. "You shit heads. Leave my brother alone."

Curtis turned his attention to the three men. Two against one. And the one guy, Janet's brother, definitely looked the worse for it. Bright blotches marked his face—the sites of future bruises—his green shirt untucked and gaping at the collar, a couple buttons gone.

"C'mon, faggot. That the best you got? Or do you need your fairy-god-brother over there to come and save your dick-loving ass?"

The men jeered—a laugh-app chorus of Three Stooges yucking it up, the 'ha-ha' of Nelson from *The Simpsons*—as they circled, eyes feverish and shining. When their jackets flapped open Curtis could see the badges sewn to their shirts. *Harbingers of the Apocalypse*—one of the more conflicted and stupidly named of the religious right extremist groups. Didn't they know if gays were bringing about the apocalypse, it just carried them closer to eternal reward?

One guy stepped in and took a jab with a red-knuckled fist. "You just gonna stand there, or you gonna come and get me? This is what you want, isn't it?" He turned and lifted his leather jacket and shook his ass.

Janet's brother met Curtis's gaze, tightened his lips and shook his head. He wanted to go it alone. Curtis stepped back, and nodded. Dude was welcome to these assholes, and when he opened his mouth in a silent roar of fury and launched himself on the leather-jacketed ass-wiggler, Curtis thought maybe Janet's brother had their number.

"Curtis? Please help Benny." Janet wriggled free of her captor and tried again to get around him.

"I think he wants to do this himself. I hope the fuckers get a good taste of their own balls when he slams them up their throats."

Without making a sound, Janet's brother, Benny, kicked Leather Jacket in the gut, and the guy bent over, gasping. His buddy, fists clad in driving gloves, came at Benny from behind, shoving him face-first into a tree. Benny pushed himself off the tree, turned, and elbowed Driving Gloves in the throat just as the guy drove a knee into his crotch. Benny doubled over, face going pale, then flushing red. Still he made no sound.

Janet's blocker moved to step in and help his buddies, brow heavy with intent, gaze locked on his target, the shudder-inducing sound of nails screeching down a chalkboard surged from his throat. Curtis got in front of him and delivered a surprise upper cut to his jaw—a little off-center, but hard enough to send the guy staggering back toward Janet. She stuck out her leg and he toppled over, onto the ground.

"Fuck you, faggot." Leather Jacket wheezed over the chain-saw rasp of his anger. He stepped back, then bent to help his buddies up.

Janet tugged on Curtis's jacket. "Let's get out of here. Benny? You about done?"

Benny straightened up, took a deep breath, slowly unclenched his fists and his jaw, wiped the blood from his nose, and limped off in the direction of The Whiskey Bar.

Once settled at a table in the brick and wood dimness, each with an ounce of whiskey already warming their bellies and working slowly on their seconds, Curtis's shakes from the confrontation eased.

Janet leaned against Benny and squeezed his hand, but he seemed more concerned with trying to find a way to get his collar to cover an old, nasty scar slashed across his throat, the healed tissue a thick worm of iridescence.

Curtis peeled off his scarf and handed it across the table. With a nod of thanks, Benny slung it around his neck and took another slug of whiskey.

"So. That how you guys spend your Fridays? Beating up homophobes?"

Janet smiled and sighed. "Benny read the signals wrong, didn't see their badges. Thought one of the guys was giving him 'the look.' Either he was and didn't want his buddies to know, or they were looking for a gay to bash."

"You don't think we should call the cops?"

Benny mimed laughter, and wiped fake tears from his eyes.

Janet punched her brother's arm. "What do you expect? You *are* the one who swung first, tough guy. They were a band of name-calling HOTA's. Good thing they didn't know how to fight. One of these days this *Death Wish* shit is going to get you killed."

Curtis flexed his fist. His knuckles still burned from scraping against the third guy's stubble. "You're lucky I had one sucker punch in me. If I'd really had to step in ... I'd have been more of a liability than anything."

Benny nodded his agreement.

Curtis laughed. "Fuck you, too."

Janet's smile wore a haze of sadness. "I knew you two were a match made in heaven."

"So, is this why you called me? Introduce me to a new drinking buddy?"

"I think Benny's story might help you. Since he can't do the telling," she reached over and pulled down the scarf a bit and placed her fingertips on the scar that snaked across Benny's throat, "I'm here as narrator. But I'm going to need these whiskeys to keep coming." She addressed her last comment to the waiter who'd paused at their table. He nodded and gave a tinkling xylophone-chuckle, then headed to the bar.

Janet drained her glass and took a deep breath.

"Benny had a husband. Robert. Bob and Benny. Benny and Bob. Perfect couple. When these apps came out they got matching sets of everything. An Ernie and Bert laugh, summer cricket and bird chirp affection.

"Benny is a great guy. He's my brother, and I love him to pieces, but he can be a little in your face." She squeezed her brother's hand.

Benny didn't take his gaze from Curtis. His features sagged under the weight of his grief.

The waiter placed three more glasses of whiskey on the table.

Janet continued. "Bob, though, he was one of those people, you know, even people who still feel weird about gays found a way to accept Bob. Forgive him his sins. They've both always been up front about who they are. Neither of them hid, but Bob went for the soft approach. People loved him. He made the best apple pie, told dirty jokes like a trucker.

"On date night they'd go to dinner, a movie, whatever, and hold hands. Kiss in public. Most people don't care about that, or at least ignore it. But they met up with a group of bashers out hunting, spouting their hate-gospel. Drunk, big, angry guys. Benny trash-talked them into a fury, called them butt-buddies for Jesus or whatever.

"Benny was not the kick-ass fighter he is now. Those fuckers dragged my boys into an alley. Benny only remembers some pushing and a few slaps and punches, then he saw Bob go down. Benny got shoved back against a dumpster and hit his head. Lights out. When he came to, Bob was still out. The coma lasted for a week, but the brain swelling was too much and Bob died."

She paused and sighed, sipped her whiskey. Benny's eyes glassed over with tears. "My stupid-ass brother almost killed himself. It was the crying that got to him. They had paid extra for a custom recording. Whenever Benny cried, at his husband's bedside, then after, when Bob was dead and ready to go in the ground, he heard the sound of Bob's grief. To get their sad-apps they had told each other the most upsetting stories they could find—true stories—until they'd made perfect recordings of each other sobbing, then they swapped their sadness.

"Instead of going in and getting it switched out for another sound, or turned off, he got drunk one night and got it in his head that Bob should be buried with his own crying. So he took his fileting knife to his throat to cut the transmitter out. Severed his vocal cords. Didn't get near the stupid device before he lost consciousness. I found him, bleeding out, almost gone."

She wiped a napkin across her face. All three picked up their glasses and drank.

Finally, Curtis broke the silence. "That's some proper Greek tragedy. I'm really sorry for your loss."

Benny pulled a folded paper out of his pocket. His hand shook as he passed it to Curtis.

Curtis unfolded it and read:

> I've wanted to meet you for a while. Bobby wanted to, too. He went to see your show a few weeks before he died, but he was too chicken to introduce himself, and really, it wouldn't have been appropriate.
>
> When we made our recordings, the ones of us crying, I only had to tell Bobby one story. Your story. I read him the

newspaper article. He couldn't stop crying. From that day on he wept every time he saw a father with a little girl. He never stopped crying for you, Curtis. And for Sandra. If he were here he would cry for you both and tell you that it wasn't your fault.

It wasn't your fault.

Curtis took a deep, shuddering breath and folded the paper again. He looked up at Benny and nodded.

He reached across the table and took Benny's hand. "What happened to your man wasn't your fault either, you know."

Tears wet Benny's cheeks as he cried in silence for their lost loves.

When Curtis got back to the apartment Sandra was on the couch, TV turned low, hunched over and networking. She looked up, guilt slipped across her face, and she set her phone on the table, screen down.

"How'd it go?"

"I'm guessing you know the story." Curtis sat on the couch next to her, then stood back up again and paced the room.

Sandra shrugged. "Some. They were fans of yours and his husband died. Really sad. Big difference is that he's alone now. Wounded. And his wound will always stay open without his other half to heal to. But you and me ... well, I guess we might as well be alone. Maybe we should be alone and on our own, rather than alone and together ... if that's what you want." She spoke the last words softly, her voice bruised with pain.

Curtis stopped pacing and turned his back to her, put his head in his hands. He pressed against his eyes, and between the flashes of neon he saw memories of Sandra. Grinning, eyes bright, hands out as though fending off words that rendered her helpless with laughter. Flash. Smiling in her sleep, buttery morning light clinging to her downy skin. Flash. Standing over Emmie's open grave—slumping toward the hole in the ground as though drawn to the worm-riddled darkness. Flash. Hunched over her screen, trying to reach him, her husband, through a wireless void.

The moments all hung in his memory, so clear, those little pockets of time.

They'd left their snapshots and portraits at the house in the burbs. A perfectly preserved capsule of when they were a family, instead of this broken, alienated two.

When he spoke his voice came out heavy and muffled, like the air had grown thick.

"I can't talk to you. We went through it all in the fucking inquiry. I don't want to talk about it anymore. You want me to express my feelings. I don't have any. None. Just a need." He pulled his hands from his face, and they curled into fists. "One need. I need to go back in time. Why the fuck did I have to fiddle with the radio, right that second? I could hear Emmie calling, telling me she was blowing me a kiss. Why did I put my foot on the gas? I could hear her, I was gonna catch her kiss as soon as I found my station. But I put my foot on the gas. I need to go back and catch that kiss. That's all I want. All I need. Everything else is pointless."

He remembered the lift then drop of the car tires, a drop that kept going down down down.

He turned to face Sandra. He didn't know what he wanted from her, he didn't know how to move forward from this point.

She stared at him for a moment, eyes wide. She blinked. "I was looking at my phone. I could have caught her, stopped her from running in front of the car, but some stupid cat meme caught my eye." She reached up with one hand, as though to touch the side of his face. "I don't blame you."

"Of course you do. How could you not?"

He stuffed his hands in his pockets and his fingers curled around his wallet. Before he knew what he was doing he pulled the wallet out, slid the backwards picture from its plastic sleeve.

"Do you know what today is?" Curtis held the picture out.

Emmie. Her mouth smeared with chocolate birthday cake, hair a delicate fuzz around her face, eyes wide with surprise and delight, grinning a huge, goof-ball grin.

Daddy had just spilled his beer and slipped in the froth on his way to wipe it up. Emmie laughed at his startled grunt, his wind-milling arms. A gurgling shriek that was her first laugh.

"Of course I know what day it is." Sandra's throat contracted, her eyes spilled tears. "No, no, no."

She pressed her lips shut, clapped her hands over her mouth, but the sound still came—the lone baby's cry.

Her eyes bugged, and her cheeks puffed out with the effort to hold the cries in. With one hand she fumbled for her phone and located the emotion-app downloader. Curtis was shocked she'd sprung for the whole program. Owning the apps outright was more than they could afford. It meant she could have changed hers at any time.

Jabbing frantically at the screen she scrolled through, one hand still pressed over her mouth, her skin turning red. From her throat came the muted sounds of a siren's wail, then a crackling fire, a faraway foghorn, a *Gong Show* gong, a toilet flushing, the absurd brap of a toad—then finally muffled sobs of her own.

"I'll get it taken out. They've gotten tacky, anyway."

She tossed her phone on the floor. It immediately buzzed with an update. Sandra's gaze went to the phone reflexively, then she scrunched her nose and looked away.

"Tacky? You know they're fucking appalling."

"Fucking App-palling." She mimicked his stand-up routine accent, then snorted at her own joke.

"Oh my god. That's terrible." Curtis shook his head. A smile tugged at his lips.

A laugh grew in him—it ballooned out from his stomach and up into his chest. He seemed to expand, his breath coming in short gasps. His smile widened, and a slow chuckle surged out, louder and louder, gaining velocity.

"It wasn't that funny." Sandra's eyebrows arched in surprise, her flushed skin still printed with a ghost hand where she'd pressed her mouth to contain the sound of her crying.

She giggled. A real giggle that caught, and turned into laughter.

Curtis collapsed beside her on the couch, his hand finding hers, their fingers knitting together, squeezing tight. He laughed with Sandra until his stomach ached and his face hurt.

THE SERILE

PAUL MELOY

My father was the composer Raleigh Coombes. You won't have heard of him, his music was terrible. It was described in the *Musical Opinion* as sounding like 'a lobster pleasuring itself in a coalscuttle.' And by *Gramophone* as 'Stockhausen without the intellect, vision or technique with composition.' I remember these reviews simply because they were the only two he ever got and they threw him into such a frenzy that I secretly cut them from the magazines and kept them pressed between the pages of one of my books.

My father spent much of his day in the coffee shops around town, favouring unfortunately, the one in which I worked on a Saturday for pocket money. He would meet people there and engage in long, Bohemian flights of fancy with them, debating politics and philosophies, theology and cant, and he would come home horribly alert from caffeine and intellectual stimulation, his eyes blazing, and disappear into his study to compose, or invent, or paint execrable artwork on large canvasses. He had these hanging in the coffee shops, over-priced installations fit for burning that he had pressed the meeker shopkeepers into displaying.

He had a rival. A renowned figure in town named Keith. Keith was to be seen marching the streets, his shirt unbuttoned and blowing in dirty vestigial wings beneath his armpits, youthfully paunched, with an ever-changing array of household items tied to the top of his head. One day a loaf of bread, the next an LP, the day after that, a fish, whole and still wet from the fishmonger's ice, all tied with a dressing-gown belt with a big, girlish bow beneath his chin. Keith, in the treatment-resistant manic phase of his illness was a terrible sight, his pathologically enhanced sense of well-being discharging an awful, baking charisma.

Keith's theories involved hanging antique furniture from the ceilings of abandoned buildings with wires of varying thickness. These pieces of furniture would be connected to each other with more wires and the whole thing would become a complex instrument synchronised to the phases of the moon. Without explaining how, he insisted that the resonance generated in the wires by the weight of the furniture and the minute gravity impelling the fixtures would generate music that was, essentially, 'a tactile synesthesia of space and time.'

This enraged my father.

When Keith presented himself to the clientele of the coffee shops, flushed and fuming, barging in off the street, often barefooted as a discalced prophet, the shop would swiftly empty. Except for my father. He would stand his ground, order more coffee, and beneath a gallery of his own works of art, invite Keith to debate.

These epic encounters would spin out for hours. Obscure references would be hurled, arcane works from incomprehensible old books quoted, the names of abortive, dead philosophers bandied. My father was pretentious, narcissistic and not terribly bright; Keith was mad but a genius nonetheless. And my father knew it and it tormented him. Keith built rubbish and his theories were laughable. But somehow his ideas worked. My father produced crap and crap it remained. And he knew Keith knew it, and this also incensed him.

Keith would jab a fat finger at the paintings arranged on the walls above my father's head, sweat lathering his cheeks like foam on a horse's flank. Framed scrawls and vile attempts at vorticism loured over my father, yet he sat before them with the aspect of a celebrated attorney summing up a brilliant and protracted prosecution before a handpicked jury.

"Your arguments are circular and obscurantist," Keith would say, his eyes as blue as the gas jets roaring beneath the coffee shop's brass urn. His voice was hoarse yet cultured, often raised in a scream. "Your art condemns your sensibilities at your own back! Your position is as brittle as the cut-price *gouache* smeared ham-fistedly across your canvases." The sneer inflected on the word 'canvases' implied a comparison to soiled toilet paper my father was unable to withstand.

In a rage my father's South London working-class roots were exposed; the thin soil of phoney, self-regarding intellect he had tamped over them across the preceding decades was quickly washed away beneath Keith's deracinating torrents of spleen, and he would rise screaming from his seat.

"You expect me to take artistic criticism from a tortured *cunt* like you?"

But Keith, impervious to the *ad hominem*, was able to deflect my father's rage with the logic of his statements. Keith never resorted to defamation.

"Even your son," he said, and pointed at me, "Defaces your paintings."

I stood behind the counter, a dishcloth in my hands, and blushed. Keith was right. On a dare, I had indeed drawn a minuscule cock and balls between the legs of a stick figure climbing a flight of disproportionate and teetering silver stairs. Keith had eyes everywhere.

My father whirled and sought out the offence, eyes crawling across the canvases, fists clenched, small, skinny buttocks trembling with rage within his faded-to-a-shine dress-suit trousers.

"You'd better not have, you little bastard, or I'll—oh my *God!*" He'd found it. "It's pissing, you *fuck*." Indeed, it was the idealised version, complete with the standard cat's whisker pubic hair.

"It's not piss." Keith said. He was studying the picture, head on its side, squinting. "If it were, they would be dashes. *They're* droplets. It's spunk."

"*Spunk?* It had better not be bloody *spunk!*"

I couldn't lie. Keith was watching me with an open and encouraging expression. Both hands were laced over his protruding belly. He nodded, prompting a response from me, the truth.

"Keith's right, dad," I admitted in a quiet voice. "It's jizz."

"Three sharp, colourless spurts from the taut and trembling glans of your son's secret esteem!" Keith roared, and his laughter was terrible, monstrous, the gurgling of black water through the sluices beneath a moribund asylum.

It was my father's speciality to keep us off guard and so it was a terrible shock when one afternoon, a couple of months ago, he rolled home from an afternoon in town with Keith in tow, and announced that from thereon in, Keith would be living with us.

This was also the day that my mother left.

She took my younger brother and twin sisters that same afternoon. They slipped away in a taxi and I haven't seen them again. I assumed they had gone back to the town in Northumberland where she had been born, and where her parents allegedly still lived. Intrigued, I looked it up, but I couldn't find it on any map. Maybe she had lied to me all these years. I think she had been planning to leave for a long time and was looking for the right excuse.

Nevertheless, I understood my father's need to keep Keith close. He risked humiliation in the open, but also needed to feed from Keith's energy and peculiar thinking. Compelling Keith to stay allowed my father to keep their debates private but also increased exponentially his appetite for the fruits of Keith's unruly genius. These are my thoughts on the matter; my father never admitted to this, nor do I believe he was able to. Reflection and hindsight were never gifts my father had any success at mastering.

It wasn't the first time he had brought home a stray.

When I was six, he returned from town with a young Frenchman called Titouan. Father had spent the afternoon in discussion with Titouan and discovered a like-mindedness and mutual appreciation for neglected early nineteenth-century epistemological philosophers. One in particular, Clovis Delvat, had been a proponent, briefly, between August and October 1817, of the theory of Universal Solipsism. My father insisted that it was an early, inchoate attempt to explain the multiverse theory, an endeavour to prove that although other minds did not truly exist outside of his own, in each infinite universe beyond his they were permitted and that each of us had our own universe to exist in, only this one wasn't it, it being his. Titouan enjoyed similar world-views but, of course, maintained this was *his* universe and my father's mind, though entertaining, did not exist here but somewhere impossibly distant and unremarkable, and that my father had, anyway, completely missed the point of what Universal Solipsism was.

Titouan spent a fortnight at our house, napping fitfully on the sofa in the drawing room when my father would permit him to do so. My father would spend long nights hectoring Titouan until one morning, too exhausted to take any more, the young Frenchman stumbled from our house white-faced and hollow-eyed, and was fatally struck by a rag-and-bone man's cart.

My father raced into the street. He stood over Titouan's broken body and crowed victory for all to hear. It was interesting to find out later, whilst poring through some of father's old reference books, that Clovis Delvat had suffered a similar fate. On the 26th October 1819, he had gone beneath the wheels of a horse-drawn cab in a district just outside northern Leon, pushed, it was believed, by an infuriated rival.

Delvat hadn't died, though, but had remained mute for the rest of his life. His later writings reveal a mounting interest in séances and table-tipping.

I continued working in the coffee shop but it was now oddly quiet, serene even. Old regulars returned and the peaceable clinks of coffee cups on saucers and cutlery on plates, the occasional cough and whisper of conversation, and the rustling of papers and magazines were the only sounds now that my father and Keith were too involved with their experimentation to come into town.

I much preferred Keith's company to my father's. There was an honesty about Keith that my father lacked, despite his delusions and inflations. Some evenings Keith would descend from my father's workshop and indulge me in a game of chess. It wasn't really chess, as one might know it in its classical form, but a variety Keith had developed and insisted was much harder to master. He called it *Chessolation*.

It was, of course, impossible, involving a continuous change in the movement of the pieces. Keith would shout, *"Chessolate!"* at a random moment in the game at which point the pieces could be moved in any direction. Or, he would shout, *"Chessolate Knight!"* and the Knight would take on the movement of the Queen, or the Rook, or any piece Keith decided on. I never knew when it was time to chessolate, and it was purely Keith's prerogative to call it. Despite Keith's insistence that it was harder to master than chess, it certainly seemed to make things easier for him. I never won, but we had some great games. My father, of course, wouldn't play.

"You cheating bastard," my father would say, coming into the dining room to find Keith, wiping his hands on an old oily cloth.

Keith would smile, his eyes blazing from a series of brilliant chessolations, and say, "The rules are clear," to which my father had no ready answer.

My father only ever attacked me once during this time.

He and Keith had been working on something in my father's study. I could hear the sounds of light industry: the tapping of a hammer and the occasional concise whiz of an electric drill. Voices were occasionally raised; insults delivered with cruel precision, but mostly things seemed to be going well. They were working, Keith had told me the previous evening over a game of Chessolation, on a *weapon*. It would revolutionise humanity if they could just reduce it to pocketsize. Currently it was as big as a car engine and they were struggling to diminish the calibrations sufficiently to incorporate the nozzle.

I was excited. A weapon was being developed under my roof. My father came down for a coffee. He was distracted and the backs of his hands were covered in biro-scrawled equations. Some looked quite deep, where he had scored into the flesh with the nib of the pen either in frustration or animation.

"Shall I make one for Uncle Keith," I said as my father filled the kettle.

It was fortuitous for me that the kettle had not already boiled, because it flew across the room and hit me in the face.

"Don't you *ever* call him that *again!*" my father roared and followed through with a punch that struck me on the top of the head.

I fell to the floor. My father was about to kick me but the boot never landed.

Keith had wandered into the kitchen and had come to my rescue.

He had my father in a choke hold. My father was silent, his face a burgeoning purple. His feet slid on the floor tiles and his hands, blackened with incomprehensible sums, clawed at Keith's huge, hairy forearm.

Keith backed out of the room hauling my father with him. My father's arms dropped to his sides and his eyes closed as conscious-ness deserted him. I sat up and put a hand to my face. My cheek was swollen and I had lost a back tooth. Keith winked at me. I nodded.

Keith dragged my father out of the room and I could hear them going upstairs, the heels of my father's boots bumping up the risers.

A while later the sounds of work resumed.

Living with us appeared to have a beneficial effect on Keith's mental state. He stopped tying things to his head and was less stimulated by my father's belligerence.

One afternoon he came into the kitchen where I was peeling car-rots for a stew. He rolled something onto the chopping board.

I picked it up and looked at it closely. It was a small wooden six-sided dice. I turned it in my fingers. On each face Keith had drawn a different chess piece.

"You've earned the right to chessolate!" Keith announced, and strode from the kitchen without another word.

I shrugged and put the dice in my pocket and continued with my chores.

Later that afternoon, Keith produced the chessboard and set up the pieces. He sat at the dining table and spread his arms, his invita-tion to play.

I sighed. I'd been beaten soundly the last seventy-eight times we'd played (Keith kept a tally in a small lined notebook), and I was tiring of the one-sided randomness of it all.

I sat at the table and Keith must have seen something in my ex-pression, because he laughed and said, "The dice!"

I remembered the six-sided dice and took it from my pocket. I put it on the table next to the board.

Keith looked delighted. He moved a pawn two squares towards my Queen. He always played white. It was in the rules.

I looked up at him and my hand hovered over the dice.

"Not yet!" Keith roared.

I moved a pawn with little enthusiasm two squares towards his Bishop.

Keith brought a Knight into play, sat back and crossed his arms.

I moved my Queen in front of my Bishop, assuming we were playing normally until the time came for Keith to chessolate, but he surprised me with a shout.

"Roll the dice!"

I picked it up and held it in my palm. I shrugged and rolled it across the table between us. It came to a stop with the Rook emblem uppermost. I looked up at Keith. He waggled his eyebrows.

"Chessolate Rook?" I said.

Keith roared with laughter.

"Outstanding!" he said. He moved his Rook diagonally across the board and took my Queen.

It was that evening that I first heard the machine.

I was clearing away the remains of dinner. Keith and my father had returned to the study to work, locking the door behind them as they always did to prevent me intruding and to thwart my curiosity.

I put the dishes in the sink and ran the taps.

At first I thought there was an airlock. It sounded like the old pipes juddering and booming in the walls and beneath the floor. I stepped back from the sink, expecting the water to start surging and spurting from the taps, but it continued to flow without a change in pressure. The sound intensified and the sash windows began to rattle in their frames. I ran to the bottom of the stairs and looked up to the landing. I put my hands over my ears because the noise was becoming hard to bear. It had changed in pitch and was now a shriek. I was about to call up but in the next moment, the noise stopped. I shook my head and blinked.

And then I heard something else. It was a voice. It was distinct and clear, a male voice, rather insinuating and unpleasant, addressing me from just above and behind my left ear.

I whirled around but I was alone in the hallway.

I must have imagined it. It was probably a residue from the ear-splitting noise of the machine in my father's study, making my ears ring.

I returned to the kitchen and the house remained silent for the rest of the night.

I thought about the voice, though, while I tidied up, and what it had said.

It had said: *Kill them.*

The voice didn't reoccur, and I forgot about it after a few days. I was busy in the coffee shop earning extra money after school. It was boring at home, and a little lonely. My father and Keith hardly came out of the study now. I assumed they were making progress with the machine and was happy to leave them to it.

But tonight I came home late, and found Keith sitting in my father's armchair in the drawing room. I thought he was asleep. The room was in darkness and Keith had his eyes closed and his mouth open. I was disconcerted not only by the stillness of his posture, but also by the fact that he had tied a large chisel to the top of his head. The dressing gown cord was knotted beneath his chin in two untidy and uneven loops.

I was about to creep upstairs but Keith opened one eye and spoke.

"I have something to show you," he said.

He pushed himself from the chair and stood up. The blade of the chisel swung in my direction like the needle of a compass. Keith grunted and tugged at the bow beneath his chin, tightening it. He went past me and started up the stairs.

"Come on," he said. His eyes looked unfocused and his demeanour was oddly flat and distracted. He looked like a man entertaining troubling thoughts. I followed him, keeping three or four steps between us.

Keith stopped outside my father's study and took the key from his trouser pocket.

He opened the door, switched on the light, and stood aside.

I took this as an invitation to go in, and I slid past him. His shirt was undone and his belly hung over his belt in a sulky lip of flesh. I tried not to brush past it but failed, and it felt feverish and spongy against the back of my forearm.

The study was in disorder. Books and papers were scattered everywhere. Bits of metal, tools, schematics, splintered pieces of wood, coils of wire, valves and diodes were strewn across the floor. A gutted television set was leaning against the paisley cushions on my father's chaise-lounge. The room stank of sweat, cigars, and engine oil.

Keith followed me into the room. Father's study was what would normally have been the master bedroom. He had commandeered it for his work and had made mother sleep in the box-room. Most nights father fell asleep on the chaise-lounge, exhausted from the efforts of composition or painting. He considered himself a Renaissance man and demanded the space and freedom this required.

I went further into the room. Behind the door was father's desk. It was clear of debris and supported only one object.

I glanced back at Keith. He nodded, a slow dip of his chin. The chisel strapped to his head was working loose again and it was beginning to slide down his forehead.

I approached the desk.

The machine sat there, on a base of rough-hewn lengths of timber. Its very presence was unsettling and unpleasant and I was reluctant to go too close. It was large, cuboid and still roughly the size of a car engine. Attempts to miniaturise it had obviously failed. It was glistening with oil, a large metal box from which wires dangled and odd things protruded. A bulbous black nozzle was situated on a panel built into the top of the machine and it pointed at me, pregnant with the potential for menace. I imagined this to be the business end of the weapon, some kind of barrel, but it looked more like the grotesquely enlarged sting of an insect, and full of poison. The whole thing had the aspect of an evil robot that had been put through a crusher and salvaged and put to some other malevolent purpose.

I felt the impulse to recoil but Keith's presence in the doorway and his clear intention that I should apprehend the machine prevented me, and so I stood my ground.

Two cables were connected to what looked like a modified alternator and went up to the ceiling and disappeared into the loft through holes drilled into the plaster.

Keith saw me looking up and whispered something from the doorway. He was partially concealed behind the door and so the words were indistinct, but it had sounded like, *atrocity cables.*

"What did you say?" I said.

Keith moved, drawing further into the room.

"Don't touch the Atrocity Cables."

This time I did withdraw. I stood a good few feet away from the desk and pointed towards the ceiling.

"What's up there, Keith?"

Keith looked up. The chisel slid from its loosening bonds and dropped to the floor. Keith reacted as though stung. He made a strange, prissy gasp and fell to his knees. He grabbed for the chisel, which was rolling onto the landing, snatched it up and pressed it to the top of his head. He looped the dressing gown cord twice around his head and tied it beneath his jaw. He stood up, holding onto the doorframe, and looked at me with dilated, hectic pupils.

"Insulation," he said in a breathless voice, remarking on the chisel I supposed, and not what was in the loft.

"From what?" I asked. I had edged further away, deeper into the study. The backs of my legs were pressed against the side of the chaise-lounge.

Keith frowned. "From the Serile," he said, in a tone that suggested I hadn't been paying attention.

I pointed at the machine.

Keith nodded.

"What is it?"

Keith came into the room and stood at the desk. He pressed a button on the side of the machine. It began to shake on its wooden base, gently at first but with increasing agitation. Bulbs lit up and dials flickered. The two cables extending into the ceiling trembled as though a puppeteer stood astride the beams in the loft attempting to coax the machine into clunky animation.

Keith reached up and pressed the chisel against his scalp. At the same time he took hold of the nozzle with his left hand and turned it in my direction.

A chorus of awful, raging voices exploded in my head. I fell back against the chaise-lounge and sat down hard. I opened my mouth but couldn't hear my own voice because it was drowned out by the force and volume of the furious crowd apparently surrounding me. There was, of course, no one else in the room but Keith and I, but I closed my eyes and pressed my hands over my ears to stem the imprecations of the sudden, incorporeal mob. I squeezed my eyes open and looked at Keith. He was watching me with the impassivity of a scientist awaiting a reaction in a lab rat.

"Turn it off, you bastard," I screamed, both terrified and raging.

Keith shrugged and reached around to the side of the machine. He switched it off.

Instantly the voices stopped. I sank back against the cushions and gasped. The impression of them still echoed in my head. The irresistible commands to kill remained a memory but had lost their force. I concentrated on regulating my breathing, trying to bring my galloping heart to heel. I felt dirty, violated.

I stood, aware that I was trembling.

"Where's my father?"

Keith looked perplexed.

"My *father?*" I said again.

Keith pointed at the ceiling.

I left the study and made for the loft.

I shoved open the hatch with the broomstick that leaned against the wall in the corner of the landing, and brought the ladders down using the hook screwed into the end of the stick. The whole process felt cumbersome, time-consuming. I glanced back towards the study, but Keith had not re-emerged. I climbed up and switched on the light. With my head and shoulders poking through the hatch I peered around.

I could see, to the right, where the cables rose through the study ceiling. I followed their trajectory, up to the sloping roof, through a series of metal eyelets screwed into the eaves and across the dusty space of the loft, to where they disappeared into the punctured and weeping eyes of my father.

I slipped, and came down on my elbows. I thought Keith had me, was pulling on my ankles, but it was the sudden weakness of shock that had unbalanced me and channelled all my blood to my core.

I pushed myself up into the loft and crawled towards my father.

He was still alive.

As I approached, he muttered something.

"It's me, dad," I said, as I thought I had caught the word *Keith* in the sibilance and wanted to reassure him.

I knelt before him. He had been tied to a support beam using reams of duct tape and bungee rope. His legs and torso were co-cooned. His arms were strapped to his sides. I could see the fingers of his right hand, blackening from lack of circulation, poking from a gap in the tape near his waist.

The cables had been jammed into his eyes.

"Dad," I said again. I reached out to him, searching for a frayed end to the tape, wanting to free him, but he hissed at me.

"*Get Keith!*" he said.

I sat back on my haunches and stared at him.

As I did so, I heard the machine start up again in the study. The cables began to thrum, and father threw his head back against the beam and opened his mouth. The cables quivered and mined a thin gruel of fluid from his sockets.

The voices began to rage again, surrounding me with their furious, irresistible imperatives, pressing me to act.

"You old cunt," I said, and put my hands around his throat.

My father had spoken to me once about auditory hallucinations. He had been theorising, trying to understand the forces that drove his nemesis, Keith, to achieve such success with his art despite its preposterous and nonsensical principles. He wasn't talking to me as a father might talk to a son, engaging, educating, mutually enjoyable, but as he always did, with a meandering and bitter monologue that accidentally incorporated me in its compass. He wanted no comment from me, but I would listen, anyway, sometimes enthralled, sometimes sickened, always saddened.

He had been doing research.

Keith had recently been the subject of an article in the local paper. He had been interviewed about a small installation he had created in the bathroom showroom in town. It was called *The Mind Plumber* and was a couple of old brass taps pushed into a block of green Oasis floral foam. The foam had been moulded and shaved into roughly the shape of a brain. The clever thing about the sculpture was, according to Keith, that the introduction of old reclaimed taps into a space occupied by gleaming chrome and stainless steel created a portentous atmosphere that encouraged people to think about the inevitable processes of entropy that acted on our genetic drive to increase its information. A war between ontologies, Keith explained with the customary vagueness that infuriated my father.

"They're just a couple of old *taps!*" he muttered. "But it works! He *succeeds!*"

Indeed, the installation had attracted such a number of people that the showroom remained open well into the evening, hiring a private catering company to provide cheese, wine and canapés for all the people who came to see it. They wandered through the showroom, caressing the curved porcelain surfaces of sinks and toilets and the gleaming shafts of chrome and steel pipes with distracted philosophical arousal. They left engaged in lively discussions about the problem of information and the curious, mathematical implications of apobetics.

"It's his delusions," my father said to himself. "It must be. He hears voices. They *inform* him. The voices of *devils!* I must ... understand!" He clenched his fists in front of his face and shook them. I think it was his tendency towards melodrama that repulsed me most about him.

"The more he complies with them the more success he has. How can I open myself to this, how can I channel this ... *genius?*" he spat the final word, refusing to attribute it to Keith, but to something beyond, something Keith's madness was allowing through.

He went on for ages, pacing the kitchen, picking up cutlery and pots and brandishing them before putting them down again with a strange, lost expression.

It was shortly after this that he brought Keith home.

I think my father had played right into Keith's hands.

I heard footsteps on the ladder.

Keith appeared in the opening. He hauled himself up into the loft and came towards me. His mouth hung open and his eyes had that dead, muddy cast to them.

"You did it," he said.

I could barely hear him above the sounds of the voices and the whine of the Serile.

I looked at my father. His face was swollen and his lips were black.

Keith handed me something. I took it. It was a small gammon, still in its cellophane wrapper, taken from the fridge. He held out something else. It was a dressing gown cord. He looked at me and nodded.

I tied Keith to the upright beam at his instruction. We had cut father free and rolled him beneath the eaves. Keith was tied firmly but not too tight. He wanted to do this for as long as he was able. For my sake. He loved me, you see.

As I bound him, he told me what they had done.

They had made the wrong machine. Keith had wanted to find a way to broadcast his voices for the benefit of mankind. Send them out, deflect them, and share them with the world. Father had wanted to keep them for himself. They had argued and fought. Father had done something to the machine one night, alone in the study, while we were engaged in Chessolation, and it had absorbed his paranoia and spite. It was organic, Keith explained. And as such, fickle.

It was intended to be a weapon against entropy, a wonderful thing that would enhance the creative nature of humanity and help them see the endless, orthogonal possibilities open to them. It would expand our imaginations and drive our species to newer, bolder thinking.

But father had ruined it. By the time Keith had found out what he had done it was too late. Once the machine had run, its murderous predilection had been unleashed.

"Why not just switch it off?" I argued.

"Too late," Keith said. "Humanity has been chessolated. Think of it like that. The Serile's range is infinite. Already people are changing. I wanted the world to make music, but I have created a dirge of decay. It must run its course!"

I wanted to leave him, go down to the study and smash the Serile to pieces, but he read my thoughts.

"Your father wanted to do the same. Not to make amends, but in a rage. Furious that he had again been thwarted by his own narcissism and greed. I brought him up here and made him experience the full force of the Serile."

I wept then, not for my father, but for Keith, and his courage and vision.

I picked the cables from the dusty floor. They were encrusted at their sharp, ragged ends with father's blood and tissue. I could feel the energy of the Serile vibrating through them.

"Can you hear them?" Keith asked. He cocked his head, indicated the streets outside.

I nodded. I could hear the sound of the night, as it became a battleground. Neighbours were emerging from their homes, enraged, entire streets crowded with invisible screaming voices. Traffic halted as people stopped their vehicles to get out and do the murder they were incapable of resisting. How far would this spread?

Infinite, Keith had said.

"Make sure it's on tight," Keith said.

I touched the gammon tied to the top of my head. I nodded and took his hand. The voices had abated. Perhaps the organic nature of my insulation was insufficient to block them entirely, but it was enough for me to be able to resist them.

"I always found the fish to be the best," Keith said. "But you didn't have any."

"It's okay," I said. "It's okay, Keith."

Keith took a deep breath.

"Maybe I can call it back," he said. "Maybe I can stop the Serile."

I nodded. Everything was theoretical.

We had to try.

I have the cables in my hands.

Beyond the house a war is raging.

Keith sits up straight, opens his eyes wide.

"Do it," he says.

I do it

EYES OF THE BEHOLDERS

LISA MORTON

We couldn't have been less prepared for the attack.

There were fifty-six of us when we started. Fifty-six, determined to make a new world. We didn't like calling ourselves "colonists" because some of us felt that word was tainted by past centuries of imperialism, of stealing lands and slaughtering indigenous peoples. For one thing, we'd been assured there were no indigenous *anythings*. There shouldn't have been, not on Tau Ceti-e, a world with no visible plant or animal life, where the average temperature would roast a human being in a matter of minutes, where the landscape continued the same, dull gray-brown from one horizon to another, punctuated only by ancient volcanic hills.

We named our new home Guanyin, which we hoped conferred a sort of blessing of peace and serenity.

We were, in other words, incredibly naïve and stupid.

Four of us survived that attack. We four made it only because we were off-planet on a routine supply run, bringing down more of the prefab sheets that made up our buildings.

That's something I'll never understand: we'd been there for a month already, long enough to have the settlement laid out and 70% built, to have personal touches in our homes, to have our greenhouses already planted. Why did they—or it, or whatever that was—wait a month to attack? Why not the instant we set foot on that unremarkable soil, before we'd gone far enough to be deceived into thinking we'd triumphed, that we'd provided a new outpost for our own failing species, long enough for us to create hope?

The four of us—Chen, Albert, Waiola, and I—were in our orbiting command ship, the *Waukheon 7*, pulling ourselves through the zero gee as we gathered material from the supply modules. I'd just pulled another carton of food rations when Chen's voice buzzed in my earpiece, "Sam, Albert, Waiola—I need everybody up in Control, NOW." Chen's voice quivered at the end. Chen *never* quivered.

By the time we all arrived, Chen had the monitors all tapped into our cameras around the ground settlement. None of us spoke as we stared in disbelief:

Long black tendrils were bursting from the ground. They slammed into our flimsy buildings, knocking them aside like cardboard. Those inside, exposed to Guanyin's scorching air, gasped for both oxygen and mercy. They received neither. Those—what, arms? tentacles? weapons?—fell on them, flinging them aside, or crushing them, or squeezing the last breath from them. I saw our head engineer, Yusasa, try firing a pulse rifle at one, but it didn't even slow it down. One of those things spun around Yusasa's ankle and pulled him screaming into the ground. His assistant, Jackson, had a machete from the greenhouse, and for a second hope flared when she cut one of the things in half … but she never saw the one that came up behind her and yanked her entire arm off.

Then I saw Akiko. My wife. I think I shouted something. I don't really remember.

In less than two minutes, it was over. Chen had fallen into a seat and was hyperventilating. Waiola curled over to vomit onto the deck. Albert jittered forward, agitated, frantic. "We've got to get down there—come on!"

He started to swim from Control, flapping like some ungainly sea mammal, but Chen stopped him. "Albert, wait …"

Albert paused in the hatchway, twitching all over. "We can't wait, we've got to get down there *now!*"

"No, we don't."

Albert's eyes were wide, wild, his voice cracking. "What are you talking about?"

Waiola looked up, wiping her mouth, brown skin pale. "Listen to Chen."

Chen stood; I could see the man trying to regain his usual, implacable calm. "If we go down there, whatever just got everyone else will get us, too."

"We don't know that it got everyone—"

I didn't care that I was still crying as I approached them, pulling myself along. "It did. It wiped out all of the buildings in less time than anyone could have suited up."

Albert gave us a look of simmering frustration before trying to move away. "Fuck you, too, Sam. I'm going."

Chen grabbed his arm, holding tight. "No, you're not. None of us are."

Albert fell apart.

We spent the next two days grieving. On the monitors, the black arms continued to pulverize the last of our settlement. No piece of wall, no stray body part, not even a shred of clothing was allowed to remain.

What were those things? Did they belong to some gigantic organism buried deep beneath the surface? Were they a defense system left long ago, by a race gone for millennia? Or something we couldn't begin to imagine?

I couldn't sleep, or think clearly. When I tried to close my eyes, a single image looped and looped in my head, of my Akiko being thrown against a lab console, our dreams shattered with her life. She'd been Guanyin's botanist. I was nothing beside her, just a historian who could also play guitar and lift a crate, who'd been lucky to make it onto this team. I'd never understood why she loved me; sometimes I doubted that she did. Maybe it'd been convenient for her to say she loved me because of the mission. I told her that once, and it was the only time I'd ever seen her cry. I never said that out loud again, although I secretly still thought it.

Gone now. All gone. Love and doubt both. Murdered by something I couldn't even define.

On the third day we tried to pull ourselves together enough to discuss our options. Chen, always our leader, had already been working for the last two days.

"We have to go back to Earth," he told us.

Albert laughed. We were all worried about him; he'd been one of our techies, but he'd always been neurotic. Now he seemed close to a breakdown. "Go back ..."

Chen nodded. "We can do it. With our payload so reduced, we'll have enough energy for another hole."

I felt a fresh weight settle on me. I'm sure we all did, even Chen. We'd been part of the grand plan to save dying humankind, one of four teams sent out to habitable planets using the new wormhole technology. We were supposed to ensure the future of our race. We'd been sent with everything we'd need.

Everything but superweapons. Of course every analysis of Guanyin (when it had still been known as simply Tau Ceti-e) had confirmed the lack of any life form. None of the unmanned probes returned with footage of giant black limbs.

It was never intended that we would return. Guanyin was 11.8 light years from earth. We'd made the trip using the experimental drive that had performed well with the drones. It seemed to have worked for us, too, since we arrived in the Tau Ceti system in seconds after entering the hole ... but we'd received no signals from home since. We didn't know if our communications had somehow been damaged by the hole, if we'd experienced severe time dilation ... or something worse.

"No way," Albert cried out, "no fucking way! Even if anyone's still alive and they haven't destroyed the planet, well, the—the—"

I was surprised when Waiola continued for Albert. "The planet may be uninhabitable. Or time could be fucked up, they may not even speak our language anymore, or—"

"—any of it," said Albert.

Chen waited them out and then said quietly, "The alternative is suicide."

That stopped us all for a few seconds. Chen added, "We can't go anywhere else."

"There are other planets we could try," Albert added, but his voice failed him at the end of the sentence. Even he knew that idea was impossible.

"The only other planets in this system are incapable of sustaining us on any level. And we can't calculate a wormhole to get us from here to any other system, except Earth's."

I fixed Waiola, who I'd always considered a good friend, with the strongest look I could muster and said, "Chen's right. We can't stay here, and we can't go anywhere else. It has to be Earth."

In the end, Albert and Waiola agreed. Two days later, we set the *Waukheon* on a path out of Guanyin's orbit, into open space, and through a wormhole.

The last thing I remember was feeling the ship shudder around me and thinking we were dead.

I awoke to a face I didn't know.

Beautiful, flawless … *literally* flawless, in fact. The eyes didn't blink, the bald head didn't move. I thought it was a lovely mannequin until it spoke. "Hello," the face said, in a flat tone I could identify as neither male nor female.

It took me a few more seconds, as I struggled to full wakefulness, to realize the face wasn't living. It was some sort of robot or android, far more sophisticated than any I'd ever seen.

"You're on Earth," it said. "You may call me Robin."

I felt disoriented—likely the after-effects of going through the hole—but the feeling dissipated quickly, and I wondered if I'd been given a drug I didn't know. My voice was only slightly hoarse when I finally used it. "Robin … you're a machine, aren't you?"

"We prefer 'inorganic.' I am a mechanical form housing a fully functional A.I. Because I have existed for fifteen years, I have attained personality and complete self-awareness."

Fifteen years? My gut clenched. I was no robotics expert, but I knew that in the year 2086 we didn't have anything like this, and we certainly hadn't had it for fifteen years.

I looked around, saw that I was in what was obviously some sort of medical bay or hospital room, although one entire wall seemed to look out on a deep forest, with densely-packed trees shaded by green-filtered sunlight, as red and yellow birds flitted among the branches. "Is that a … what, a projection of some sort? A hologram?"

"Yes. I can change it if you'd prefer something else, although studies have shown this particular scene promotes healing and recovery."

"Robin, what year is this?"

A flicker of discomfort crossed the lovely face, and another jolt of dread went through me—if this "inorganic" was worried, what was I in for?

"The *Waukheon* vessels all left Earth 768 years ago."

I couldn't answer. I wanted to say it was ridiculous, impossible ... but the thing now eyeing me with concern didn't exist in my world. "We detected your vessel when it left the wormhole; fortunately it was undamaged and we were able to bring it to earth. We're still studying the logs to determine how the wormhole generator malfunctioned ..." There was more after that, but I wasn't listening. I was trying to process the knowledge that everyone and everything I'd known was long dead. I thought of Akiko—dead anyway, killed by something on a world a dozen light years from here, and I thought of children we'd never had, and our families. Gone. *Everything.*

And yet Robin spoke my language without so much as an accent. Language always evolved with history. Something wasn't right ...

Oh. "You've been programmed to speak my language," I said.

"Yes, I've been provided with extensive dictionaries and historical samples. I am here to assist your integration."

I looked more closely at Robin, and saw something disconcerting: whereas the face was recognizably human and could have passed for living from a slight distance, the rest of Robin was obviously mechanical, with a slender torso ending in three curving legs that supported the body, while arms protruded from each of the four sides of the torso. All of these extensions seemed fluid, more like tentacles than limbs based around interior structures. "Robin," I said, trying to phrase the question carefully, "there are still humans on Earth, aren't there?"

"Yes," Robin answered. "However ..."

The inorganic trailed off; once again I saw caution there. "Yes?"

"Human beings have evolved."

154

"Evolved how?" In less than eight centuries? That didn't make sense. Was Robin speaking metaphorically? Because she (as I'd started to think of Robin) must certainly be capable of metaphor.

"Both physically and mentally, due largely to genetic enhancement."

Ahh, of course.

"What about the others who were on the *Waukheon*?"

"Chen and Waiola are recovering as you are, and you will see them shortly. I'm sorry to inform you that Albert attacked his inorganic and then self-terminated."

"Suicide …?" It didn't surprise me with Albert, but it still gave me a chill. "How?"

"He removed cabling from his inorganic and strangled himself with it."

I glanced around my room, wondering how it would be possible to tie a noose anywhere—there were no bars or holes in the ceiling. "He must have been very determined."

Robin looked away for a moment. "His inorganic—Charl—was my friend. They've deactivated the A.I. until a replacement housing is manufactured."

"I'm sorry," I said. "Albert should probably have never been on the Tau Ceti team."

Robin didn't answer.

<hr />

Later that day, I was given a simple one-piece jumpsuit to wear. I followed Robin down an otherwise-empty hallway to a small room. The room was devoid of furniture except for three chairs that seemed old and little used. The walls rippled and fluctuated with energy, the source or use of which I couldn't begin to speculate about.

Chen was already there. Waiola arrived a few seconds later.

We shook hands (Chen) and embraced (Waiola). My friends were each accompanied by their own inorganic, both of whom bore a resemblance to Robin without looking exactly like her. The three inorganics exchanged a look before Robin addressed us: we would shortly be meeting with Dr. Husam Menanges, the director of this medical facility. After Dr. Menanges, we would meet with Council

Leader Jillius Rand, who I gathered was the current version of a President, and several other leaders. Apparently we had become celebrities during our recovery time.

Before Robin could finish, a soft bell sounded. "Oh, Dr. Menanges is early," she said.

The door to the room opened. Chen, Waiola and I turned—and stared, stunned.

What entered the room seemed less human than the inorganics. It possessed a male head, hairless, and a male torso, also hairless, but adorned with vivid white stripes that flickered and pulsed hypnotically. This new arrival possessed no limbs of any sort, moving not via locomotion but rather simply floating several feet above the floor. It smiled at us, but there was something just behind the expression. Anxiety? No, not quite right ...

Repulsion. Something about us obviously disgusted the good doctor, even though he did his best to hide that fact.

He began to speak, his voice surprisingly deep and mellifluous; the language sounded vaguely familiar, but we definitely needed Robin's translation. "Good afternoon," she said, positioning herself between us and the floating half-man, "I'm Doctor Menanges. I'm pleased to meet each of you, and to see that you're doing well, although I'm sorry to hear of your colleague Albert Hamsun."

Robin and Menanges looked to us expectantly—were we supposed to respond? Then I saw Chen step around Menanges, looking beneath him as well. "We're pleased to meet you, Doctor, and grateful for your hospitality. May I inquire as to your means of support?" he asked.

Robin translated. Menanges responded; one word sounded like *sikess*. "All human beings now possess an ability you would know as psychokinesis."

I caught Waiola staring at me, her eyes wide in disbelief, before turning to Menanges. "You control motion by thought?"

"Yes," answered Menanges, in response to Robin's interpreting.

I asked, "So you're floating because ...?"

"Because I will it, just as you achieve movement with your legs."

An uncomfortable silence ensued. Even Chen backed away, and

I could see our precise engineer-commander trying to parse the best way to phrase the question we obviously all had. "Sir," he said after a few seconds, "may we ask—"

The bell sounded again. Menanges muttered something, and Robin said, "Leader Rand will join us now."

The door slid back, and we once again stared in mute surprise. The woman who entered was like Menanges—floating, lacking limbs or hair. Her body glittered with red and gold patterns, which I realized it must be their version of clothing, some sort of covering that acted like a screen. She smiled at us, but I had the sense that she was a highly practiced smiler, good at covering her real feelings, like many of history's leaders. Behind her came an entourage of half-a-dozen others, all floating heads and torsos. One had some sort of device covering his eyes; the device made small whirring noises when he looked at me, and I guessed he was recording our meeting.

Robin translated for the leader. "I'm Jillius Rand, and I'm so pleased to meet you all. You've become quite famous over the two days that you've spent recovering! I think I can speak for the entire planet when I say that we're all very interested in you."

We all muttered some response. Rand continued. "I know you have many questions, and you'll find your inorganics will be very helpful. You in particular, Doctor Sarkissian," she said, looking at me, "will undoubtedly be most anxious to know what's passed over the last eight centuries."

"Indeed," I said. "We're all curious about ... the changes."

"Well, let me assure you that the planet itself is changed for the better. Nearly 90% of the human population died off shortly after the *Waukheon* ships departed, but then the first psychokinetic mutation appeared and geneticists were able to isolate and replicate the trait. With both the population and the need for fuel-based transportation largely gone, the ecosystem began to recover."

Chen said, "There were obviously ... *other* mutations as well ..."

Menanges blinked and frowned, but Rand didn't skip a beat. "If you're referring to our lack of *limbs* ... no, that wasn't strictly a mutation, but rather some very skilled genetic engineering."

Beside me, Waiola fell into one of the chairs. "Oh my god ..."

Before Chen or I could say anything, Menanges spoke. We didn't need to hear Robin's translation to pick up on his contemptuous tone. "Anything that erodes the sleek beauty of the human form is a great pity. If science can assist in negating this unnecessary ugliness, then by all means it should ... should it not?"

Chen's gaze ran across all of them before he asked, "Are there *any* people left who possess limbs?"

Robin answered before any of the humans could. "At this point, no. The last human being with limbs died a hundred and twenty years ago. The geneticists ensured that the traits for limblessness and hairlessness were spread throughout the entire remaining gene pool." She hesitated, apparently unable to continue. When Robin spoke again, I knew she wasn't translating for someone else. "They find you ... distasteful. Not only are you a reminder of a despised past, but you are also considered extremely visually displeasing."

"Ugly," Waiola muttered, as she stared at her hands, with their long slender fingers.

I spent most of the next few days with Robin. She became my teacher, giving me a crash course in the history of the last 700 years. Most of it was documented visually, so I spent hours watching the last few human survivors crawl out of the crumbling ecological devastation the *Waukheon* ships had left behind, until the day came when a newborn infant made things move just by thinking about them. The infant became a phenomenon; she was studied and probed and copied, and soon all the newborns had the ability. As they grew more adept at simply moving themselves mentally, their legs began to atrophy, then their arms. Doctors removed them, researchers figured the genetic sequencing to permanently remove them, and soon *Homo delabor* was the dominant species.

The remaining *Homo sapiens* often had surgery to remove their arms and legs. The first time I saw that in the old video records, I had to ask Robin to stop the recording for a while.

"You look very pale," she told me.

"I'm sorry. It never occurred to me that anyone would *want* to become a quadriplegic."

"Limbs were considered no better than an unsightly growth, like a tumor or wart. The surgical techniques were very advanced."

"I'm sure they were."

I told Robin one day I wanted to leave the medical facility, to see the world. She told me it might be an uncomfortable journey for me. At first I didn't understand, but I soon realized she was right.

The world was a hundred and eighty degrees from what I'd known before; it looked like a picture out of an old book or magazine, with its blue skies and puffy white clouds and clean streets. The world I'd known had always been hot, with smoggy brown skies. As people had died off from disease and storms and earthquakes and starvation, infrastructures had failed, so I'd lived my life with trash and crumbling buildings, sallow-faced survivors and skin-and-bones predators lurking in the ruins.

Now the world was clean and prosperous again. Most of the environmental damage had been reversed—air and water cleaned, environmental catastrophes eased, they'd even managed to add ice back to the polar caps. War, terrorism, epidemics, mass starvation were all in the past. *Home delabor* was obsessed with the arts, and its biggest stars were its writers and artists.

And everywhere I went people stared at me in disgust and fascination, whispering to each other, giving me a wide berth. The weight of their eyes was like lead, holding me as earthbound as the clumsy legs they despised. Their whispers made me put my arms behind my back, or hunch, or hug myself. Children giggled or gagged, until nervous adults floated up, hurrying them away.

I told Robin I wanted to go back right away. "Are you displeased? Is there an area you'd prefer to visit?"

"No, but ... I'm a freak to these people. I just ... oh for god's sake, just get us back."

The hospital room I'd first awakened in now served as my one-room apartment; none of my hosts seemed too anxious to move me elsewhere. When I saw Waiola, I knew why.

Robin came into my room that morning, looking vaguely ill at ease. "You have a visitor—Waiola." Her arms curled and uncurled, a motion I'd come to understand displayed discomfort.

"What's wrong?"

"Waiola has ..." She turned away, unable to finish before leaving the room.

I waited for a few moments, perplexed, anxious.

And then Waiola entered, and I saw why.

Her head was smooth and hairless, and she was missing her arms and legs. Her new, egg-like body was encased in a heavy wrap, different from what the others wore. She floated like they did, but from the way the air around her wavered—like heat mirages in a desert—I guessed she was supported by some sort of field.

"Hi, Sam," she said, softly. Too softly—she was anxious.

"Dear God, Waiola—what have you done?" Even as I said it, I knew it sounded absurdly theatrical, but there was really no other response to the sight of her mutilated body.

"Their surgeons are as skilled as they said. There's no pain. They even dull the nerves in the skin permanently so you never have to worry about itching. They couldn't make me psychokinetic, of course, but they could put me in this hoversuit." She nodded at the inorganic that stood attentively by her side. "And with my permanent helper here ..." She trailed off. I knew she couldn't go on.

"Why did you do this? Did they force you?"

That brought her eyes up to mine. "Force me? No. No, I wanted to. I mean, if we're staying ... Sam, I couldn't live among them forever with all of them *looking* at me like that, like I'm some monster, something they want to protect their children from ever seeing ..."

"But you ... you were beautiful." I meant that. Waiola—with her nut-colored skin, glossy black hair, perfectly curved cheekbones and full lips—had easily been the most exquisite woman in our group. I'd once caught her showing Akiko some dance moves, and as much as I loved my wife I hadn't minded watching Waiola as she waved her arms sinuously, swaying her hips from left to right, taking tight little steps ...

With feet she no longer possessed.

Tears inched down her face. She whispered, "Chen's done it, too."

My nerves gave way, collapsing me onto the bed. "God, no ..."

The inorganic wiped Waiola's face gently just before she floated up close, speaking urgently. "Have you been outside yet? Have you felt them watching you, with all that ... that *hate*. God, they can't stand to look at us. I can't go through life like that."

"I know." I reached out to stroke her soft, bald head. "It's okay, I understand ..."

I couldn't put my arms around her while she cried; I still had arms, but there were no shoulders, no hips to rest a hand on. I did my best to comfort her, but in the end I felt inadequate. I was secretly relieved when she left with her inorganic. But five minutes later, my decision was made.

"I want to speak with the surgeons."

I thought I caught sadness in Robin's face as she turned away to make the call.

Fortunately, the surgeons and Leader Rand both acceded to my requests.

As I write this, I'm one hour from boarding the *Waukheon*. The engineers here were able to fix the wormhole drive; the return to Guanyin shouldn't take long once we're out of Earth's orbit.

The four new arms the surgeons equipped me with make me look a little like a male version of Kali, the Hindu's goddess of destruction. I've had six swords made from the same indestructible metal used in my arms. Rand has also equipped me with other sophisticated weapons, some of which I'm not even sure how to use.

Fortunately, Robin is going with me. Even though she knows it will likely be a one-way trip, she says she's never been comfortable existing among *Homo delabor* either. I doubt that any of the inorganics have, with their multiple limbs and obvious subservient position.

I don't know if the things that destroyed our home on Guanyin are still there. Rand told me humans have never returned there after the failure of the first settlement. And centuries have passed; maybe they died, or wore out, or moved on.

But if they are still there ... I will crush them. I will move among them as a beautiful many-limbed avenger showing no mercy. Robin will back me up, ready to hack down any I miss. I will not stop until I know they are all dead or demolished. If we should survive that, I don't know what will come next. Perhaps we'll take the *Waukheon* to the other settlements, find out if any of them survived. Or maybe we'll return to Earth to show *Home delabor* the real usefulness of limbs. I will create history instead of only recording it. But first ...

Akiko, I'm coming home.

STRINGS

TIM LEBBON

I wake in the early hours and hear scratching, and moaning, and the secretive whisper of something brushing along walls. When this happened before, Margot and Ray were still my friends and staying with me, and I believed their lovemaking to be the cause of the sounds. Trying to keep quiet for my sake, the height of passion took away their caution. The scrape of fingernails against a wall. The steady touch of bedding shifting somewhere beyond my room. Their groans, low and long as if such ecstasy could last forever.

This time, I know the noises aren't caused by them, because Margot and Ray left three days ago. I suspect I'll never see them again. They became worried about what we were attempting to do, though I think their fear is misplaced. I think they're cowards.

I lie awake and listen, trying to place the sounds and their source. They seem to be originating from inside my head as well as without, as if dreams can have echoes. I suppose they can. All this has happened because of a dream I had so many years before, a fervent desire that inspired and invigorated the three of us to try things never before imagined. That's me: the dreamer. I was the driving force, the passion, though they were the ones with the knowledge. We all had to give something, and I was happy to be the guinea pig.

Another scratch. A deeper groan. I can't yet understand what the noises mean, but in that cool, motionless darkness I realise that the time will soon come when I do understand. They're clearer now than they were last time I heard them. Clearer, louder, and closer.

It's working, I think, and the one thing I cannot do is open my eyes. Even in the dark, I fear that I will see.

"Don't mind him," Margot said, "he's just being a prick." I saw the look she threw Ray when she said it, and the brief flicker of some complex expression on his face. Part of it was annoyance, part excitement. I knew some of what he was feeling. Margot and I had been engaged until three years before, and I understood more about her than he'd ever know.

That's what I liked to think, at least. In truth, I believed our work was tearing us apart even on the day I slipped the ring on her finger. Ray wasn't so invested. He was here, he was helping, but he wasn't touched by what we were trying to do. For him, this was all about money and fame, his future and not anyone else's.

"All I'm saying is, I think you need to be careful," he said. He took another long swig of red wine. He drank it from half-pint glasses, and he'd already put away a bottle during dinner. "Your vitals always look weird after a dose, and that effect is growing."

"Maybe the instruments are on the blink," I said. "I'm feeling fine."

"You sure?" Margot asked. She leaned forward in the armchair and touched my knee. Ray bristled at the contact, and hoped I didn't display the satisfaction I felt at his discomfort.

"Yeah. Fine. Better than ever." I stood and paced the room. It was a big living room, far too large for just the three of us. Two sprawling L-shaped sofas, three armchairs, a slew of floor cushions, a massive TV affixed to one wall, and a fireplace I could walk into and stand up straight. The place slept twenty people in eight bedrooms, but we'd needed somewhere this big for all our kit and instruments.

Besides, it was out of the way and hidden from prying eyes. Grand House had its own mile-long driveway and couldn't be seen from any neighbouring roads, yet the nearest town was an easy walk away.

"It can't go on like this," Ray said. "It's not fair to us. We agreed right from the beginning, if something's looking off, we pull back and reassess our methods."

"Nothing's looking off," I say.

"What the fuck do you know?" Ray snapped. He shook his head, sighed. I was used to him playing the 'what do you know?' card.

"Neil, I can't in all good conscience sit here and agree that nothing's wrong."

I leaned against the fireplace. I stared into the big mirror hanging above it, offering a wide vista of the room behind me. They were both staring back at me. Margot ran her finger around the top of her wine glass. I had a sudden, unbidden memory of making love with her, the noises she would make, and I looked away in case my eyes betrayed it.

Something whispered deep within the stones of the chimney stack. I froze, head to one side.

"Neil? Did you hear me?" Ray asked.

"Huh?"

"I said I think you should see a proper doctor. I'm not comfortable with this anymore. I never finished my training."

"You're an almost-doctor," I said. "This is an almost-experiment. So what are you afraid of? Losing me, and losing your payday?" I turned around, daring a reply from them both.

Ray sighed. Margot shrugged and said nothing. The walls whispered in agreement.

I sat back in the recliner while Margot prepared the next shot of our strange elixir.

She was the genius of this team. She knew it, I knew it, and Ray sure as hell knew it, too. Her work in nanotech medicines should have propelled her into the higher echelons of twenty-first century scientific achievement. When she and I were together, before Ray came along and our plans grew, she'd talked about it often. I understood some of it, but not much. Perhaps that was why we grew apart.

"More magic juice," I said, wincing as the needle pricked my arm.

"It's not magic." She concentrated as she depressed the plunger, glancing up at the screen beside the chair and down again at the hypodermic. Ray sat in the next room monitoring my reactions to the injection, and there was a constantly open channel between us and him. I could hear him humming.

"When do you think it'll start working?"

Margot withdrew the needle and dabbed the bubble of blood. She bent my arm back and patted it, telling me I should keep it there. It wasn't as if I didn't know. She'd put a hundred needles in me over the past twenty days.

I hated it when she was like this, so immersed in her work that she hardly heard me talking. It was just about the only time she and I were alone now, even though Ray could see us on his screens and hear every word. She acted like I wasn't here.

"Margot," I said. She wheeled her chair back to a table and tapped at her laptop.

"Soon," she said. She didn't sound convinced. "Ten minutes and you can do the tests."

I lay back in the seat and tried to feel the new stew of nano-bots streaming through my blood. There was nothing, even though several times I'd convinced myself that I could feel them pulsing towards my brain, implanting themselves there, setting to work. Margot would smile indulgently, and Ray would tut and shake his head.

I wasn't stupid, but I wasn't them. I was only here because I'd once loved Margot, and started us along a path I could not quit.

Who wouldn't want to be a superhuman?

I listened and looked, and heard and saw nothing different.

And then Ray called me into another room, and he started running through the same test procedures we'd been using for weeks, and everything began to change.

In the morning I open the back door and stand once again on the threshold.

It's been three days since Ray and Margot left, and I have yet to go outside. The house is set in several acres of land on the shallow side of a valley. The landscape is beautiful and wild. I see the regular quilt work of fields in the distance, but closer to the house there is woodland, expanses of heather and scrub, and a rocky slope leading up the valley's opposite side. There is no sound of humanity. Even occasional vehicles passing along the narrow country lane a mile away are mere whispers, their engine sounds swallowed by the stone wall and hedge bordering the road.

And yet I hear. I hear *more*. Between breaths, something else comes in. It's a distant whispering, scheming intelligences hidden in the sunlight, languages I cannot know riding the breeze across the countryside. On the day Margot and Ray left I tried to replicate what these strange noises were, and I saw Ray's face as he recorded my impersonations. He looked cold in a warm room. He looked chilled.

They are much louder when the back door is open.

I take one step outside. My foot crunches on the gravel path, and the whispers instantly fade away to nothing. Even the breeze drops, a held breath. I hear my own breathing, and it's not the comfort it should be.

I take another step and the whispering begins again, louder, closer. It's an agitated babble, an excited susurration. I back up immediately and slam the door closed, and through the heavy old wood I can hear those noises joining the breeze, shushing through the house' old eaves.

They sound disappointed.

I pace around the house, examining the detritus of our time here. I have been in limbo since they departed, trying to persuade myself that it's all part of the experiment, an intentional abandonment to help advance the progress we'd been trying to make. But I can't convince myself of that. I saw Margot's fear when she left, although she seemed averse to telling me. Ray couldn't even face me.

In one of the big house's downstairs bedrooms, the two single beds are pushed aside to make room for a table bearing all manner of recording equipment. At its centre is the simple digital Dictaphone I used.

～

"You're hearing more," Margot said, and she was the most animated she'd been for several days.

"Well …"

"There's nothing here. Ray? Is there anything here?" Ray sat at a desk weighted down with audio equipment, spectrographs, and frequency modulators.

"There's always something here," Ray said. "You know that. The air's full of sound, we can only hear things in a narrow bandwidth.

Above that, below, there's always more."

"Whole new worlds of sound!" Margot said, staring at me as if I was suddenly something new. "So describe it to us. Tell us what it is."

Whispers, I thought. I was troubled by what I was hearing.

"I'm not sure I can," I said.

"Mimic," Ray said. "Use a microphone and a recording device, listen, try to repeat the sounds you're hearing."

"Will that really work?" Margot asked.

"Surprisingly effective, sometimes."

Margot nodded and turned back to me. "We'll leave you alone. You listen, and record. We want to hear. I *need* to hear!"

I knew very well that if these experiments succeeded in opening my ranges of hearing and sight, Margot would be the next one to undertake the course of injections. I was pretty certain even then that Ray wanted nothing to do with it. When he was drunk he talked about fucking with nature, but the lure of crammed bank balances and fame was strong.

"I'm afraid," I whispered. Beyond the room, something responded to my whisper. It sounded amused.

"Afraid of what?" Margot asked.

I wasn't sure how I could tell her. It would have been like explaining fear of the colour red to a blind person.

"Here," she said, thrusting the Dictaphone against my chest. "We'll wait in the kitchen."

Margot and Ray left me in that room, alone with the whispers. I listened for a while, head tilted, brain struggling to decipher sounds it was never built or meant to hear.

Then I turned on the machine.

Around midday I see the first of the shadows. I've been expecting it. In a way, the expectation has been worse than the reality. Margot would bemoan the fact that my vision seemed unchanged by the experiment.

Now, I wish she was here with me again.

I'm standing at the open back door in the cottage's kitchen. The garden is large and nicely landscaped, with a climbing frame for kids, a barbecue area, and several paved patios for seating. The sun blazes down. The valley is deserted, save for me and the whispers that conspire to draw me out.

I see the shape dancing beneath a tree.

I blink, frown, shield my eyes from the sun, and look again. It's like a smudge on my vision, a blot in my eye. The tree branches hang low, and although the air here is still, the branches move as if disturbed by a breeze. Birds take flight. Several dead leaves fall, or perhaps they're shed by a squirrel hidden away in the tree. It's too far away for me to make out clearly, but the dancing figure I saw has gone. Just branches. Shadows.

As I turn away the whispers come in again, louder and closer than ever before, and in their alien tongue I hear mockery at my disbelief.

I slam the door and run through the house, seeking the false solace of my room. On the way to the staircase I pass the small second kitchen where Margot kept her concoctions locked up in the fridge. I still haven't cleaned up the mess. She smashed every container, poured the fluid into the sink, splashed it up the walls. She followed it down with a gallon of bleach, and the stink still burns my nostrils.

Perhaps I'm lucky they didn't consider doing the same to me.

I reach my small bedroom and slam the door behind me, sitting on the edge of the bed and expecting the whispers to follow. They keep their distance. Even the silence is loaded now, and I imagine great things poised to shout so loud that their voices will crush me down.

I know I'll have to leave soon. If I want to retain my sanity, I need to make it to the nearest town and ask for help.

The thought of walking along country lanes and hearing them all around drives me almost to tears, and I curl up on the bed. Even though for now they are silent once more, I wish the voices would let me sleep.

᠁

"Hairy bastard."

"I can't help that. It's natural."

"Not for everyone. You're less evolved."

Margot rested her head on my chest. I could feel her heavy breath on my sweat-dampened chest, feel the dampness of her against my thigh. We'd made love twice, and I was already considering whether I could manage one more before we both fell asleep. She had that effect on me. It was love, but it was also a deep, passionate lust.

"Maybe you could evolve me a bigger cock."

"I wish." She propped herself up on her elbow and turned to look at me. "You have no idea, do you?"

"What do you mean?"

"How it works." I liked her when she was like this. Her cheeks and thighs ruddied from my stubble, long hair sweat-dampened against her forehead, pupils dilated, she was approximately fifteen times more intelligent than me, and I loved it. I knew a lot of men who'd shrivel beneath such intellect, metaphorically and literally, but I found it a massive turn-on. In truth I did understand a lot of what she said, just not to the depth and degrees that she did. Sometimes she lost me, and if that happened I'd go along for the sound of her voice, the denseness of her passion.

"I mean, we've essentially halted human evolution. There's no survival of the fittest anymore, not for humanity. Imagine if we had to hunt food in the dark, and those with better eyesight survived and procreated more? But we have supermarkets and food dumped on our doorsteps. What if bats carried a deadly plague, and we had to listen out for their high-frequency calls and hide from them? Those with that hearing ability would survive and pass it on to their offspring. But we're cosseted in our four walls. Given medicines to cure things that should really kill us. Weaklings are helped to survive, and—"

"Weaklings?"

She shrugged. "You know what I mean. There's no natural selection anymore. We're *all* selected. We've stopped evolving because we think ourselves already perfect."

"And we're not?"

She reached down and grabbed me. Grunted in disappointment. Arched an eyebrow.

"Give me time," I said.

"We should do it. We've talked about it long enough. I've tried the formula on mice, rats, apes."

"Apes? I don't know—"

"Ray said he'll help."

"Ray? He's a prick."

"I like him," she said. "And besides, he's the best tech guy I know. He's got more stolen equipment in his basement than NASA. Apple would pay for some of the shit he's designed and developed just to amuse himself."

"If they did, he'd have sold it to them."

She started squeezing, kneading. "Yeah, he's all about the money, but that doesn't mean he isn't brilliant."

"He's worth a fortune already. Why would he ... do ... this?"

Margot wasn't answering anymore. She was smiling. "I do believe you're ready to go again."

I smiled. "Survival of the fittest."

I haven't been injected for three days, but it seems that Margot's theories on dosage and continuity were wrong. She always believed that my body's natural defences would attack the alien compound, and that would necessitate introducing more on a daily basis. It targeted my hearing and sight, its pre-programmed purpose to open up my abilities, expand and broaden them. It worked on my sensory organs, nerve receptors, signal transference, and also the parts of my brain given to translating such information. An artificial evolution, she called it. In her eyes, she was allowing those two senses to achieve their full potential, but they would always revert. I would be given a glimpse at something greater, hear a wider spectrum of sound. The effect was never meant to be permanent.

She was so wrong. The abilities are expanding and strengthening, not fading away. I have never felt so alone, yet the more time goes by, the more I begin to understand that I am surrounded. The things that surround me, though ... I have no wish to know them.

I have to leave this place. Perhaps closer to other people, the effect will wear off. Maybe I'll even find Margot and Ray again.

I'll try to tell them it was all a joke.

It was as if the whispers I heard—those guttural, harsh croakings of things mostly unseen, in languages we were never meant to hear—channeled themselves through me. That was the only explanation I could give. Left alone in that room, I did my best to relay the things I was hearing in my own voice. At first it was like singing someone else's song, and I felt quite ridiculous, trying to remember the sounds and cadences, the tones and feel of those strange voices. Speaking into the Dictaphone, I sounded like a dog making strangling noises, or a child attempting to feign a deep voice.

Then something strange happened. As I spoke, I heard those real voices in my ears, muttering their strange tones as if coaching me. I continued for a couple of minutes, then hit 'stop' and dropped the Dictaphone onto the table.

The voices receded, leaving behind the echo of a soft, knowing laugh. It took a while to fade, and even when Margot and Ray came back into the room, I could hear the dregs of those strange sounds.

"Done?" Margot asked.

I nodded down at the Dictaphone.

She picked it up and pocketed it.

"Mind if me and Ray …?" She gestured at the door, then the two of them left me there without waiting for a reply.

What happened next was the first instant I began to comprehend just how fractured my relationship with myself had become, now that I was hearing and seeing more. I began to realise that I was not only hearing higher and deeper tones, or seeing a wider band of the spectrum. I was hearing *further*. Seeing *deeper*. Something about what they'd done to me had shifted my reality, or moved reality around me.

More things were making themselves known to me.

A couple of minutes later I heard their raised voices. Ray was crying, wretched, wrenching sobs torn from the heart of him. Margot was shouting, sounding both startled and vulnerable. I knew what they had heard, and a perverse part of me was glad. I didn't want to be the only one.

She stormed back into the room, kicking the door open as if ready to attack me, but then just standing there, staring, and it was the utter fear in her eyes—the fear of me—that upset me the most. She remained in the doorway, ready to run at any moment.

"What have we done?" she said.

That night they left. I thought perhaps they'd gone out to discuss the experiment, leaving the confines of the house, and that they'd return in a few hours. But they had abandoned me. I tried to follow, but couldn't. Each time I left the building, those voices assailed me more, singing terrible songs that would drive me mad if I heard them a moment longer. They sang and sang.

Trapped with myself, I was becoming a stranger.

I know now that I have no choice but to leave. They're getting closer. If I lie down I hear their whispers, starting far along a wide, empty corridor and then drawing closer, louder. It's only when I sit up that they dwindle away. I wonder what would happen if I didn't sit up.

It's dawn when I decide to leave. I stand inside the back door for a long while, peering through the side window and searching the landscape for shadows that are out of place. There are none that I can see, but even that disturbs me. It means that they're hiding.

I close my eyes and press my hands to my ears. *I wish I was the old me*, I think. *I wish I couldn't see and hear more. I wish Margot had never been so clever, and Ray so cynically brilliant.* In comparison I was merely their lab rat, and they've left me alone to suffer now that they've finished with me.

Now that they're afraid of what they've done.

I wish like all the best lab rats, they'd put me down.

Opening my eyes, taking my hands from my ears, I see and hear them as soon as I open the door.

They can't touch me, I think. *They won't hurt me.* It is fair reasoning, because I am seeing and hearing things that are always there. The experiments have changed me, not my surroundings, giving me the ability to perceive realities that humans aren't supposed to know. That does not mean that they will now hurt me. Maybe they're pleased to be seen. Perhaps those whispers I hear are songs of joy.

I cross the gravelled area and approach the long driveway. In my determination to leave, my senses become unguarded, and the world opens up around me. Birdsong fills the air, and I hear the differing tones, the deeper meanings. A breeze rustles through the trees, carrying rumours from afar. Sunlight dapples the distant valley sides. Its journey is over, memories of deep space splashed like foam across a seashore. I see and hear new realities and despair at my inability to understand.

I am two hundred feet from the house and moving away. *This might work*, I think. *If I find them again, perhaps they'll see that their fear was misplaced.*

I pass through the gate that borders the property and out onto moorland, following the rough lane up towards the road. That's when the whispering begins.

A breeze first, then a more sibilant harshness, inside my head and beyond. My blood runs cold, my skin prickling with goosebumps, because I have never heard them sounding so angry. Yet I have done nothing wrong. If they dislike my new abilities, then let them come and tell me why. I cannot remain alone in that house forever.

I walk on, pressing my hands over my ears. That only serves to trap the voices inside. Their strange words echo around my mind, leaving a corrupt trace of themselves wherever they touch.

I see the first of the shadows as I round a corner in the road. It hunkers down in a field behind a hedge, defying the sun, pulsing like a living thing yet surely not. Surely.

I freeze, shifting from foot to foot as I try to make it out. It is difficult to discern properly. Whichever way I look, however much I shield my eyes, the shadow seeks to dazzle me with refracted sunlight. I move closer, and suddenly the whispering in my head changes from angry to mournful. Still tinged with darkness. Still alien.

I see Ray's body splayed on the ground beneath the shifting shadow. My breath is stolen from me. He's on his back, eyes open as if staring at the thing above him.

It is wan and grey, and other colours of dark infinity I cannot understand. It is connected to Ray in a dozen places by long, flexing limbs. It seems to be dead as well, although I'm not sure these things comply with any distinction between alive and dead.

Fifty feet beyond it, another shape sits beneath an old oak tree. It is a similar shape and colour. I don't want to see what lies beneath it, because I already know.

"No," I say. "Oh, no. No." My voice seems to stir the attention of other things more distant and still unseen, because the whispering gathers pace and volume. I'm driven back by the words, stumbling over my feet and sprawling in the lane. I scrabble backwards, keeping my eyes on the things I should not see as they pulse and whimper above the bodies of my two dead friends.

I turn and run back to the house, herded by screams and screeches, shoved by shadows when I dare to glance back. I realise with a terrible finality that these things do not want to be known.

And now, I'm the only one who still knows.

Back in the house with the doors shut and the curtains drawn, I stagger into the large living room and lean against the fireplace, head hung, tears spattering the old slate hearth.

Outside, they have gone quiet. They know they have me.

I look up into the big mirror and see movement, and for the briefest instant I think Ray and Margot have come back. Their deaths are a mistake, as is the experiment. I'll get over it. With their help I'll get better, and we'll move on without ever revealing what we did here.

Then I see the thing standing close. I can feel it behind me, exerting a terrible gravity on my life and my soul as they surely do to every man, woman and child. Dark strings lead from around and within me, rising like quivering tentacles and meeting eventually in that monstrous puppeteer's hands.

Though I close my eyes, I will always hear its dreadful, intimate voice.

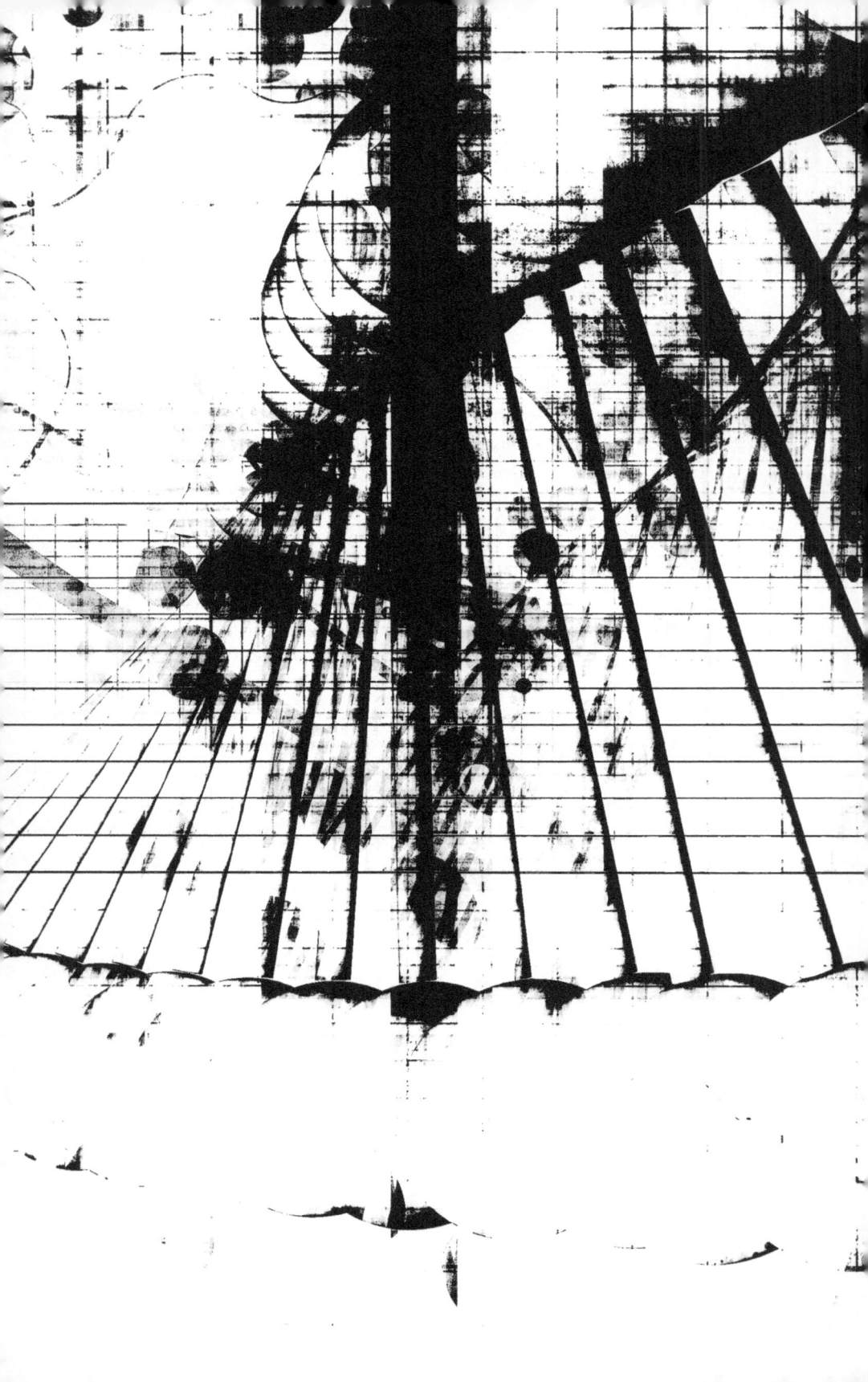

SLICED BREAD

JEFFREY THOMAS

Lawrence could tell just by touching the first slice from a newly opened package—bypassing the heel, though he'd use it later—that the white bread was unpalatable. He had never tried this brand before, and had been hoping it would be something of an improvement over the last brand he'd fallen into the habit of buying. As with the last, though, this bread was like some spongy paper product, but not spongy in the sense of being moist. More like a porous kind of semi-soft cardboard, and he could taste it just by touch; it would be as dry as chalk. And yet many thousands of people bought this brand of bread, and all the other brands he was familiar with were much the same. As long as these people bought it, it would remain, and it would be bought because they needed it and it was all they were offered. They expected no better, because they didn't feel they deserved any better.

But he didn't care for it at all. He remembered bread in his youth being softer—and even a little sweet, was it?—but then again people spoke of foodstuffs being more healthy these days. He could only take their word for that.

Had countless stalks of wheat raised their blond heads toward the sun and given their lives only to make something as blank and tasteless as this? Many thousands of stalks rooted in place, impassively waiting to be scythed down by their masters … like those who would eat this bread?

Lawrence finished making his sandwich to bring with him to work, dispirited with the thought that this white bread was only just the beginning of his day.

It was never good when the boss called one into his office, unless it was something like news of a pay increase. Then again, Lawrence hadn't seen a pay increase in four years.

The door was open, and when he poked his head in, his manager, Rod, looked up and said pleasantly, "Oh, come in, Lawrence."

As he entered the room he saw another man standing in the corner, in front of a whiteboard covered in sloppy boxes with indecipherable words inside and arrows scrawled between them. These kinds of formulas were to Lawrence like the secret code of those above. The man in the corner wore a black uniform, and didn't greet Lawrence verbally but stared at him intently.

"Could you close the door?" said Rod.

Dread seeped into Lawrence's belly like a solution of caustic soda. He complied, then sat in a chair positioned in front of Rod's desk.

"Well," Rod sighed, fidgeting with a pen. He clicked its tip in and out. "Lawrence, I can't help but notice you've been spending a lot of time again on the internet during working hours. Email, social media, search engines." He used the pen to point to his monitor, to call to Lawrence's attention the record of his internet activities.

"I'm sorry," Lawrence said. "I try to stick to break times, but—"

"If it was only break times I wouldn't have called you in here."

"Well, I wouldn't look at the internet during busy times. But sometimes it's slow, and—"

"When it's slow you could be asking one of your coworkers if there's something you can do to help them, right?"

"Yes … right, but …" Lawrence tried not to let his gaze shift past Rod to that looming, silent man in the black uniform. His head was shaved bald and he wore a goatee, a look that was in itself a kind of uniform. Years ago, men didn't try to look so brutish when they went bald; they wore a humble semicircle of hair around the back of their heads. He could half remember seeing men like that when he was a child. His own father had combed his hair over the top of his head. If his father was alive now and of a similar age to this man, would he shave and wax his head, too?

"You like arguing, huh?" the man in the corner spoke up. His

178

sudden voice made Lawrence flinch.

"It's not like that ... it's just—"

"And you're *still* arguing, you stupid fuck."

Looking back and forth between this man and Rod, Lawrence babbled, "Sometimes I keep an eye on my email or social media just to see how my daughter's doing in college ... if she needs anything, or ... you know. She just began last month, and—"

"You started out saying you were sorry," said the uniformed man. He made a flicking motion with his right hand, and from it a telescoping metal wand shot out to its full length. "You should have stuck to that route, instead of trying to justify yourself."

"Wait!" Lawrence cried, jerking backward in his chair and raising a hand to protect his face. "I *am* sorry!"

The bald man stepped forward, growling, "Sorry doesn't give your boss back this time you're wasting ... or this company back the time they paid you for, for doing *nothing*."

The wand whistled through the air, striking Lawrence hard across the back of his uplifted hand. He yelped.

"Get that hand out of my way!" the uniformed man snapped.

With a sob, Lawrence lowered his smarting hand and a second later the baton was cracking him across his left cheek. He turned his head sharply to one side, but then the wand was coming in from that side, too, and struck him across the right cheek. "Oh God," he blurted.

"I'm sorry, Lawrence," said Rod, wincing. He actually looked sympathetic. "I think that's enough for now. I hope you get what I'm talking about. Why don't you go back to work now?"

Lawrence nodded, rose shakily from his chair. "Thank you, Rod," he croaked, turning toward the door. As he opened it, he heard the security man's wand slide back into itself.

He saw half-faces peeking out at him around the partitions of the cubicles he passed on his way back to his own work area.

The vivid red welts on both his cheeks, like raised brands, had subsided by lunchtime, leaving only purple-yellow bruises that themselves would be gone in an hour more. He unconsciously flexed his hand while he waited in line to pay for the coffee that would accompany his bagged lunch. Its inner workings were still sore, but even if the bones had been fractured they would have healed by this time tomorrow.

Beside the cashier, as she worked her register, stood a security guard—this one bald but clean-shaven and with an overhanging gut—openly glaring at each customer in turn, as if daring them to cut in line or come up with too little money, or as if he might spot some butter packets, which cost extra, hidden under a napkin. "You're holding up the line," he snarled at a woman who fumbled with her debit card nervously. Lawrence got beyond him without a comment.

No one really watched Lawrence now as he made his way to a table at which he had noticed one of the workers from his own department sitting alone. The curiosity had dissipated. With his symmetrical bruises, he was not an uncommon sight.

"Hey, Lawrence," said this coworker, Sebastian, looking up. In a lower voice he asked, "How you doing now?"

"Okay," he muttered, removing his sandwich and a bag of chips from the plastic shopping bag he had brought them in. He didn't care for these chips; he preferred them oily and salty, as he recalled them from his youth. Salt, though, was bad for people. A few weeks ago he had seen another worker slashed across the back with a wand for using a salt shaker she had smuggled into work in her pocketbook.

A security guard strolling between the tables—a woman this time, with bleached blond hair—tapped Lawrence's plastic bag as she passed and said, "Make sure you put that in the proper recycle bin when you're done." She then pointed across the room, at a labeled line of such bins near the exit doors.

"Yes, ma'am," he said, smiling up at her.

She only grunted and kept walking.

Sebastian dug his fork into the macaroni and cheese he had just microwaved. It looked to Lawrence more like styrofoam packing popcorn and cheese. Since the company-wide pay decrease last January that had impacted every employee below management level, many of the workers brought in their own lunch from home rather than buy food in the cafeteria. "When are you going to learn, man?" Sebastian whispered, between bites. "You've been called to the office more times this year than I have since I started here."

"I get so bored when it's slow," Lawrence said.

"Milk it, then, like I do. But just don't be obvious about it. I daydream to keep myself from being bored. Use your imagination."

"Imagination is a dangerous thing in itself, isn't it?"

"Hey, guys," came a voice from the end of the table, and recognizing it, Lawrence looked up with a jolt. "Mind if I join you?" Rod set down a tray containing a paper container full of clam chowder, which was more accurately potato chowder.

"Sure, sure, Rod," Sebastian said, too enthusiastically. He joked, "We were saving that spot for you!"

Rod chuckled, then switched his attention to Lawrence. "Hey," he said, "I really am sorry about this morning, Lawrence, but you know there's nothing I can do about that. Upper management reviews the internet logs, too. If I don't address it, they will, and if it gets to that point their security people won't stop with two whacks. And I might get a couple whacks, myself."

Lawrence was surprised. Really? Did that happen to managers on Rod's level, or was he just saying that to make it sound more like he was one of them?

"I understand," he said.

"Good ... I'm glad." Rod made a face as he tasted his clam chowder, but brightened and asked, "So what are you guys planning for the weekend?"

Sebastian and his girlfriend were going to the White Mountains on Saturday morning, coming home Sunday night. Lawrence related that his daughter would be coming home this evening from college, spending Friday night with him before going on to visit her mother and stepfather on Saturday afternoon, to spend the night at their house until she returned to school Sunday evening.

When they were finished, Rod motioned to Lawrence to stay on a minute while Sebastian headed for the trash and recycle bins. In a confidential tone he said, "Lawrence, it'd be a good idea to make a doctor's appointment, so you can bring in a note that you'd seen him."

"Her," Lawrence corrected.

He was confused. Surely Rod knew his face, even his hand, would be as good as new in no time. Would have been, even if his hand had been struck repeatedly. Even if he had been caned until the flesh of his back was split. In what scientists explained as a miraculous leap of evolution, an upgrade to the human species, the healing process was faster and more effective than it had been for his parents' generation. They called it the Caudata Effect, named after an order of amphibians that boasted advanced regenerative abilities. For those of Lawrence's generation and after, lacerations healed without leaving any trace of a scar. A finger chopped off to the first knuckle would regenerate, and in a month. A hand chopped off at the wrist wouldn't grow back, but the point of injury would close up and the stump smooth over far more rapidly than in the past. Oddly, the body could still be afflicted with disease, still succumb to cancer, and it degraded naturally with old age—the human lifespan had not been affected—but it responded more aggressively to damage to tissues, bones, organs, via stem cells with the versatility and proliferation of embryonic stem cells. A badly damaged penis or vagina, bladder or liver could be wholly restored through a Promethean level of regeneration. Of course, brain injury was another matter. Every miracle had its limits.

For another thing—the pain associated with injuries of any type was the same as it had ever been.

"*Her* ... sorry," Rod corrected. "You know, see if she can adjust your meds. You are still taking meds, right?"

"Oh yeah," Lawrence said, "my meds. Sure, Rod."

"Good man ... good man."

In truth, Lawrence had stopped taking the medication his doctor had last prescribed him, but he realized he had in fact better go see her and get something else prescribed. If company security should take him aside to sample his hair or blood or urine, and found he had been neglecting his meds ... well, the outcome was no mystery.

"I knew I shouldn't have come home this weekend," said Agatha.

"Let me look at it … what happened?" Lawrence cried, taking hold of his daughter's chin and angling her face into a profile. On the left side of her jaw was a great swollen mass like a hard ball inserted under the skin, with a raw red mark in its center. A similar red wound, though less swollen, was nearby on her neck.

Agatha sighed, then explained, "Around noon today I attended a protest. I wasn't even yelling or carrying a sign or anything, but I'm one of the lucky ducks who got hit with rubber bullets."

"Jesus *Christ*, honey! What was this stupid protest about?"

She met his eyes. "*Stupid?* Dad … the protest was about police brutality."

He let go of her chin. "For Chrissakes, Aggie. How smart is that? So who was it shooting rubber bullets into the crowd? Let me guess—the police?"

"My school's security."

Unemployment had dropped off radically in this country over the past few decades, a kind of leap in societal evolution. In a program managed state by state, many thousands of people had been given jobs as security personnel, a kind of second tier police force, outnumbering the police force. Vocational training was offered in high schools. It was easy to be certified. Though the focus was on disciplinary violence, lethal force was authorized under appropriate circumstances.

"You have to keep your head down, honey … how many times have I told you? You have to fly under the radar at all times."

"Just like *you* do, Dad? And how many times have you caught a beating at work?"

He couldn't say anything to that.

The next day, by the time she was ready to go drive out and visit her mother, the egg on her jaw line was only a mild bruise, the mark on her neck a fading hickey.

That's why they can do this to us, Lawrence thought. *Because we heal so fast these days.*

Or, he thought, *we heal so fast these days so they can do this to us.*

"How did the nepenthitine work for you?" asked Dr. Castile. "Did it make you feel more calm ... less tense? Less resentful?"

"Ahh," Lawrence said. He knew he should say yes, it worked fine; could she renew his prescription? But he hesitated too long, and she gleaned that it had not had the desired effect.

Dr. Castile began jotting on a pad on the examination room's little side desk. "Let's see how something else works for you. I'm going to have you try pacifitine; we'll start with 100 milligrams once a day, before bed. I'll see you again in a month and determine whether to increase the dosage to 300 milligrams." She tore a slip off the pad and handed it to him.

Lawrence glanced at it, pocketed it. He was curious how this drug might make him feel. Would it really make him less miserable, less restless, less bitter? Maybe not happy, content, but at least numb? He partly hoped he would feel that way, as the majority of people his age and below apparently did, but mostly he hoped it would fail as the other medications had. He was afraid he would become less ... *him*, whatever that was. Whatever that was worth. Ultimately, the only thing he needed it to do was show up in his system should he be surprised with a drug test at work.

"You're an unusual case, Lawrence," his primary care physician said, frankly but not sternly. "But, there are those rare individuals—anomalous throwbacks, I guess—who resist the advances of our species. Perhaps not physically, but psychologically. Though of course, it can be difficult to determine if a problem is psychological or somatic, on a case-by-case basis. Which is why we try using medicine to sort it out."

Throwback? Lawrence wanted to contain his reaction, but he just couldn't. He said, "There are those who would say, instead, that all the people who don't feel resentful about being tortured on a regular basis are the anomalous ones."

"A majority is never anomalous, Lawrence," said Dr. Castile, smiling indulgently. "You sound like one of those conspiracy nuts, now. The people who think *all* of us are freaks, just because the Caudata Effect came along so quickly. If freaks are mutations, then so be it; evolution runs on mutation."

"Well," he replied, "it is pretty odd if you think about it, isn't it? That there'd be such a radical development in evolution in such a short period? There are those people who point out that the Caudata Effect coincides with the introduction of the rounds of vaccines everyone in our country has to have, by law. People who suggest there are proteins in those vaccines that are *responsible* for the Caudata Effect."

"Oh, Lawrence," his doctor chuckled, wagging her head. "Like I said ... conspiracy theories. *Proteins*. Sure, and there are gamma rays in there, too. Next you'll have super powers like Batman."

"Batman doesn't have super powers."

"You know what I mean. Those vaccinations are what have kept us safe from Ebola ... HIV ... I could go on and on. Look at the situation in countries that don't have these vaccinations."

"Coincidentally enough, countries where the people haven't experienced the Caudata Effect."

"What are you, the fucking Surgeon General now, you crazy fucking anti-vaxer?" said a man who had been standing in a corner of the examination room, listening to their exchange. "You think you know more than Dr. Castile—*huh*?" This baldheaded man, short and stocky and with a teardrop tattoo beside his left eye, surged forward and lashed out with his metal wand. It cracked Lawrence across the right side of his neck.

"Gah!" Lawrence cried, slapping his hand across the spot.

"Dumbass," the man said, stepping back, his eyes popped and wild. He weaved his head like a cobra as he spoke. "You want to argue with your physician some more?"

"I'm sorry," Lawrence moaned.

"I think that's enough," said Dr. Castile. Rod would always say that, too, after the fact, but they didn't control the security people ... it was always up to them when it was enough. "Why don't you try that pacifitine, Lawrence, and let me know how it goes. Make an appointment up front to see me again in about thirty days, okay?"

"Yes, Dr. Castile," Lawrence whimpered, rising from his chair and moving toward the door. He added the only words he knew he was expected to utter: "Thank you."

At first break when the weather was good, Lawrence typically liked to fill his travel cup at a water cooler then go outside to walk one lap around the building, this whole excursion taking about fifteen minutes. If he was late getting back to his cubicle it would only be by five minutes, max ... nothing too conspicuous. He actually felt a perverse gratification stealing those few extra minutes.

Today as he walked he awkwardly held both his travel cup and phone in front of him, staring hard at the latter. He was careful what sites he visited even on his phone, and even on his breaks; the company could track his movements there, as well, so long as he was within their air space. Right now he was only looking at a news site, but a story he'd found troubled him greatly.

Today on the grounds of a college in California, students protesting the beating death of a male student by campus security had engaged police by lobbing teargas grenades back at them, and some had thrown rocks. The police had opened fire with live rounds. Twenty-one students had been shot, though seventeen of them were expected to recover fully from their wounds. Four had been killed, however, by head shots.

He needed to warn Agatha again. He hoped she was seeing this story, and that it would be a wakeup call. She'd told him she hadn't gone to a hospital or doctor after her recent injuries, knowing she'd recover, so maybe her school's security and the police hadn't identified her and opened a file on her. But there were surely cameras all over her school and its grounds. Would she be the one, next, ordered to report to some doctor's office or clinic, to be prescribed nepenthitine or pacifitine or something else? Was she a throwback, too?

Please, not her. He wanted her to be comfortable in life. To be content.

To be ... numb?

In a related video of a press conference, the president spoke out harshly about the incident, jabbing a finger toward the camera. Toward his viewers.

"Ingratitude is rampant in our youth. Mindless rebellion is being fueled by subversive music, illegal drugs, and poor parenting. You have only yourselves to blame, parents, when you see your children fall like this. They had already fallen long before those shots were fired. *Wake up, America!* Be thankful for the lives you lead in this, the greatest country on the Earth!"

The path Lawrence took around the building was primarily along a sidewalk that conformed to the edges of its surrounding parking lots. Spaced along the path here and there were benches, and he saw a woman seated on one of these just up ahead at the far corner of the rear parking lot, where it was bordered thickly by trees. She too was intent on the phone in her hands. She was an attractive black woman with whom he exchanged smiling greetings whenever they passed each other in the offices or plant, but he didn't know her name, precise department, or function.

He was both excited and agitated to see it was her. He didn't want to disturb her—she looked so absorbed—but might she glance up, notice him, and this time engage in more than just hellos with him, being that they were in such a private location? Oh, to summon the strength to ask her out. He hadn't dated a woman in over two years. He was so nervous, he almost hoped she wouldn't look up as he came toward her, but ...

Seemingly from out of nowhere (but Lawrence had simply been too focused on the woman), a security man strode up to the worker on the bench. His voice boomed, causing her to jerk her head up, as startled as Lawrence. The man—bald-headed, goateed, wearing dark glasses—said, "Symphorosa White! Yeah, *you!* Did you think nobody was going to notice you've taken thirty-five minutes for a fifteen minute coffee break?"

"Wait ... please," she said, holding up both hands, one still clutching her phone. "My mom went in the hospital last night ... I was just checking—"

"Check this." A metal wand flashed open in the right hand of the man in the black uniform and black glasses, like a magician's suddenly appearing cane. It arced through the air. Symphorosa (so that was her name) screamed as the expandable baton struck her across the upper arm, and she hunched over to tuck herself into a ball. The man seemed incensed by her resistance to her punishment.

He brought his arm far back, whipped her across her curved back twice. Shrieking, Symphorosa tumbled into the grass, but only pulled herself into a tighter ball. The guard responded by kicking her in the lower back and her bottom. He seemed particularly interested in kicking her bottom ... a half dozen times before he desisted, panting.

"Now get that lazy ass of yours back inside and sit it down in your chair where it belongs." The guard turned, and saw Lawrence transfixed there, watching. "You got a problem, douchebag?"

Lawrence couldn't speak.

"I suggest you keep an eye on your time, too." He made a V sign with his fingers at his eyes, then pointed one finger at Lawrence. And with that, the guard marched away, cutting across a grassy island in the parking lot toward the building. A group of geese that frequented the various lots waddled out of his way as quickly as they could manage, as if familiar with the man's boot-tips.

Lawrence rushed to the sobbing woman's side, knelt and touched her arm lightly. "Can I help you get up?" he asked.

She peeked over her shoulder at him and only sobbed harder, but she allowed Lawrence to take hold of her arm and help her to her feet. She grimaced at her movements.

Together, they walked back toward the building, cutting at an angle across the lot. Lawrence had his arm around her waist, though not lasciviously, and she leaned against him as she staggered along.

Sebastian had said he passed his time at work by fantasizing. Lawrence hadn't told his coworker that he often did the same. But his fantasies consisted of bringing a shotgun to work, or to a mall, or some other place where there were many of these security personnel. And making *them* cry ... making *them* plead, "No ... *nooo* ..."

Then he'd go into hiding. Live as a fugitive. Strike elsewhere.

Fantasies. They were called fantasies for a reason.

"That was overboard," Lawrence said to Symphorosa. "Fucking overboard ... pardon my French."

"It was my own fault," the woman wept, shaking her head. "I knew I was way over my time. It was my own fault."

Lawrence carried bags of groceries with him as he trudged upstairs to the door of his apartment, still feeling sour over how few groceries his fifty-five dollars had bought him and guilty for a couple of treat items he had indulged in. The sourness and anxiety he felt reminded him that he still hadn't noticed anything different since taking the pacifitine. Maybe later he'd experience results, if Dr. Castile decided to up the dosage after his follow-up exam.

He was relieved to still be himself. Disappointed to still be himself.

He unlocked and opened his door, stepped into the large central room which served as both kitchen and living room, with doorways off it leading to his bedroom, the spare bedroom he used for storage that Agatha slept in when she visited, and his bathroom. A pleasant enough little apartment for one person, but he saw he had company.

Seated on his sofa watching TV was a man in a neat black uniform, his hair buzzed down to a black crew cut. On the coffee table in front of him rested a flattened brown paper lunch bag with a partial sandwich and package of cookies atop it. An open can of soda stood nearby. The man looked up at Lawrence nonchalantly and said, "Hello, Lawrence. My name's Tomas. I'll be staying here for a while to, ah, keep an eye on you. Well, me and a couple other people I'll be alternating with. Your doctor was concerned about you so she put in the request."

"Now wait," Lawrence said, setting his bags onto the floor.

"Don't go getting yourself excited," the security man advised, raising a halting palm. "Here's the order." He pushed a paper across the table, but Lawrence didn't reach for it. "This can go on for as little or as much time as it needs to ... it's all on you. But it didn't help your case, you feeling all sorry for that woman at work the other day. Like she'd been done wrong, instead of her doing wrong. And yeah, your workplace was contacted at your doctor's request, too, so they could have some input. So ... you have nobody to blame but yourself for this."

"But I ..." Lawrence's words tripped between his teeth, plummeted to their death.

"*But* what? Nothing? Good ... you're learning already. Now, I'll try to make myself as inconspicuous as possible. You want to watch TV now? I'll move myself over there." He motioned toward the kitchen table.

"You can watch TV," Lawrence choked.

"Can I make a few observations right off the bat? You should have a little more self-respect and vacuum this carpet more often ... it smells like a wet dog. You've got some questionable material, too, in your bookshelf, but that's not my area of expertise so I'll just email the photos I took of the book spines."

Lawrence lowered his gaze to the aforementioned carpet, not conscious of the fact he was wagging his head very slowly, like a pendulum running down.

"Your daughter, Agatha, is she coming home this weekend?"

At Agatha's name Lawrence snapped his head up, alert again. "No, not this weekend. Why?"

"Just curious, Lawrence ... just making polite conversation. I saw her photo collage over there, on the wall. Pretty girl."

Lawrence nodded. Fantasies flamed on the backs of his eyes. Fantasies were the only drug that worked ... at least a little bit.

"Well," said the security man, gesturing, "why don't you go put your groceries away, make yourself some dinner, and if you want the TV later just say so. I'll sleep in the spare room tonight. If you don't make things hard on yourself, I'll be no more than a shadow."

With that, the man lifted his sandwich again and took another bite.

Watching him chew, the TV's light reflected in his eyes, Lawrence wondered: didn't this person realize that bread he was eating was no different from what the people he oversaw ate? No more appetizing? No more satisfying? No better?

I WILL BE THE MAKING OF YOU

RENA MASON

No one ever recalled the void or the time spent there before their making. Only the sudden pinpoint of light in the black womb's epicenter, then its exponential growth. The energy that crackled and stung as it surged from one reaction to the next until they all merged and exploded, a supernova in the mind.

No one had remembered except Dr. Nora Shastry, Chief Clones Scientist for GEB-217.

Master Plasma Drive Engineer, Kai Ricard floated in her darkness.

"Never forget this kiss. Us here now, like the Klimt painting. Save it forever," he'd said.

They lay naked, their bodies entwined, under a gold thermal blanket, drifting ...

"I promise, always."

So she'd isolated, digitized, replicated, and stored the memories of all the years they'd spent working, living, and loving one another while she waited to live again.

Everyone recollected the brilliant pulse that made them, but Nora along with fifty-eight other scientists and engineers remembered so much more—had to. Retained data from the cloned minds continuum were repeatedly transferred, keeping the thread of advancement uninterrupted for further development and breakthroughs.

Again Kai smiled in the endless black, and she woke.

A click then a hiss, and the hermetically sealed lid of Dr. Shastry's capsule raised. She opened her eyes, adjusting them to the dim blue light in her sleeping chamber. Luminous cryogen gas spilled to the left in a ghostly waterfall, evaporating into nothing. Nora looked out at blurred shadows. She sat straight up and coughed, her lungs expelling glowing plumes of cold. Red emergency blinkers flashed in every corner of the warehouse room, intermittently casting crimson light over rows of sleek casings around her.

After dry heaves, she spoke, her voice weak and raspy: "Lights."

Long rectangular bars situated above, switched on one after the other with loud mechanical claps, illuminating the other capsules. Two hundred white tubular coffins in all, most empty in case others had to be made early to fix issues that might arise before the arrival to super planet Wolf 1061c, renamed New Earth 217, fourteen light years from the original.

After being made, the clone would either go into cryo storage or be neutralized, both painless processes. The choice depended on the essentiality of their function, although Geb had the final decision. Named for the Egyptian god of earth, GEB-217, a fully self-sustaining vessel capable of thought and action, controlled the fate of Earth's humankind.

Nora put her legs over the side and let them dangle. A small rover moved next to the capsule and robotic arms swung round and covered her. The crinkling sounds of the thermal blanket resounded off matte, metallic walls.

She remembered wrestling Kai while she'd tried to get a cheek swab. He wouldn't stop until she'd kissed him.

The kiss on Mars, an image of Klimt's painting, Kai.

"I love you," she mouthed. Random thoughts continued firing rapid pulses across neurons, triggering more memories. They shifted, organized, and stored, would continue doing so until she expired.

Why hadn't anyone from the Cryo Team come? The emergency flashers continued blinking.

"Status report," she said.

No overhead response came.

"Geb, are you there? Status, please."

Dr. Shastry flipped the thermal blanket off and disconnected cryo tubes from an outer, biodegradable skinsuit the pod had made that coated her from toes to chin. When she hopped down, it was as if her soles had landed onto a bed of nails, then she fell back against the capsule.

"I hate this part."

Braced against the icy casing, she moved toes first, tapping the floor and grimacing until the shock and pain wore off. Taking baby steps on the balls of her feet, she shuffled her way to the exit, a set of smooth doors set into wall panels that all looked the same.

"Open. It's Dr. Shastry, number 319."

A snap and then an opening appeared. Her capsule closed behind her with a whoosh of hydraulics. She stepped out. Emergency blinkers in the corners of the halls flashed.

"Status report," she said louder. "Geb, are you operational?"

No response.

Every main corridor had a monitor that displayed ship function, location, and all made live on board. When she got to it, only one red circle blinked, the number 319 inside—her. Other numbers showed up as stagnant blue circles lined in rows, activity levels among the frigid metabolisms in the Cryo room at nil.

Location read ten years and three months out. "That's too early! Why was I awakened?"

New Earth, a massive planet compared to the original, appeared on the center screen as an orb covered in shades of white exposing glimpses of blue. The monitor for ship function read fully operational, automated, but Geb's interface had been put into sleep mode.

"By who?" Nora looked down the hall on either side then thrust her back against a panel.

Chamber Chill, a side effect of cryo, gripped her body. Every muscle went into violent spasm and she shook uncontrollably. Even with clenched jaws, her teeth chattered. Pain and rigidity distorted her face, convulsive limbs twisted into a seizure. When the waves of torturous cold passed, Nora collapsed to the floor.

Warmth provided optimal function, so she pulled herself, using stiff arms and hands, and dragging her more gelid and tense legs to the nearest body suit. Dr. Shastry didn't want to be *live* for the next decade. She'd die in less than half that time. Besides rapid aging, being alone for such an extensive period without Kai would drive her mad, and the ship only had enough sustenance for *live* crew members to last one Old-Earth year—enough time for Bioengineering to make food.

"God, I miss you, Kai. What happened? What should I do?" She spoke into the cold, her eyes following the vapor whorl that came out of her mouth.

Nora's mind heard his voice, but she knew the thoughts belonged to her. *You've got to get Geb back online. Wake me up, I can help.*

Dr. Shastry adjusted the controls of her body suit settings on the sleeves. It registered her name, number, and vital signs. She turned up the core temperature.

Her justification for waking Kai collided with the Prime Initiative, but as one of Geb's operational managers, her lover would know what had happened and how to fix it. Then maybe after the issues got resolved, they could spend time together and make more memories before going back into cryo. It would be best to wake him first, then get Geb back online.

In the lab, she sat at a large desk with multiple built-in monitors and scrolled through the *live* list. Kai Ricard-283, slotted for capsule eight, didn't show up. It appeared Chief Security Engineer Tanner Parks slept there. A terrible IA choice to lead a pre-existing planetary threat Eradication Team. The man had no patience or tolerance, and Nora couldn't stand him.

She got on the computer and did a manual search of each unit's occupants. Still no listing for Kai. Her bodysuit's control panel alarmed, alerting her that her heart rate exceeded its normal range. She took in a deep breath, pushed away from the monitors, and massaged her temples.

"This can't be right. Kai, where are you?"

Her hair fell forward, the medicinal shampoo scent filled her nostrils. Images of Kai flooded her mind. Sterility being imperative while working operations for the Plasma Space Drives, he always had an industrial clean smell. She pulled her hair back and tied it into a knot.

A fragmented image flashed behind her eyes. A passionate kiss with Kai. The picture left a guilty residue she couldn't link. Coming out of cryo had more side effects than just Chamber Chill. It scrambled the brain like being *made*, but not quite as bad. A lot of information had unexplainable disconnect. It seemed to get worse with every making.

They first met when she had to get a DNA sample. Swabbing the inside of his cheek, she examined the perfect asymmetry of his face. Vertigo and lightheadedness affected her, things she'd never felt before the radiation sickness came. She trembled, jabbing the swab-stick into his gum.

"Ouch! Take it easy with that. Sure you've done this before?" He waited, staring at her.

Nora froze and gazed at him uncertain how to respond, then he laughed. Later she saw him in the cafeteria going from woman to woman and table to table with his food tray. They'd all shaken their heads, declining him, and then he approached her as she sat alone at the far end of the room.

"I was your last choice?" she said.

"No, you were my first. But I felt I had to go through your ranks and ask their opinion."

Nora realized every woman he'd spoken to was from the Genetics Department.

"About what?"

"Whether or not I'd have a chance with you."

"They all said no?"

"That's right. So I think you should prove them wrong." He sat.

Almost every moment after that was spent loving him. Nora wanted nothing else but to see him again and again. They'd live the next four to seven years of all their lives inseparably. He kept her coming back. Gave her a real and tangible hope. She'd never lived before him, had never loved.

Something about the numbers 1443 and 1507 felt significant. Nora returned to the monitors and pulled up the DNA samples. Millions of strands attached to millions of names, representing the population of every New Earth. Their nucleic acid memories stored in a separate registry. Domegemegrottebytes of data—all that remained of human existence and its history.

Susan Blanchard was listed as 1443, the name unfamiliar. Slot 1507 held Cain Jensen's DNA. Thousands of names from several segments were missing.

"This can't be." Unless something had happened. She needed status reports, but Geb's log required a code she only knew part of. She had to wake Geb. Or, she could go to the Genetics Department and make Kai.

Dr. Shastry bit the inside of her cheek. Salted warmth leaked onto her tongue. Life termination remained the punishment for creating duplicates, another duty of the Eradication Team. Kai would never forgive her. No. She'd have to exhaust every means to find him and figure out what happened first.

"Time to rise, Geb."

Past the Control, Operations, and Navigation areas, Dr. Shastry went to Geb's room. Access had been left wide open. RAM boards hung from their slots by colored cables. Nora saw limbs torn from a body, dangling by ligaments, veins, and arteries. She worked fast, carefully untangling the mess, then sliding each rectangular block back in place, resetting them. The emergency blinkers stopped and dim blue and green lighting filled the space.

"Geb, are you operational?"

"Yes, DNS319. Thank you."

The electronic male voice sounded close enough to human that Nora sighed with relief.

"Welcome back. Why had you been put into sleep mode?"

"I don't know."

"Who was responsible?"

"You, Dr. Shastry."

"No Geb, it wasn't me. Locate *live* Kai Ricard number 283."

"He's not on board."

"That can't be. You're mistaken. Search again, please."

"There are multiple duplicates on board. This violates ethics code number 14207. They must be destroyed. It is necessary to wake Eradication Team Leader, Tanner Parks."

"Geb, there are no duplicates on board."

"Capsules 59 through 101 are duplicates."

"Dammit, that's not possible. I didn't see any—"

"Security Agent Tanner Parks' awakening will commence in 193 minutes."

"Stop this, Geb. Override orders number 742. Do you understand?"

"You don't have security clearance for override orders number 742."

"There's a mistake. Run a self-systems check. Large segments of DNA are missing."

"A contamination breach in DNA storage occurred. I had to isolate and destruct to prevent advancement."

"Contamination? What? When? Is that why you woke me?"

"Over two hundred years ago, during event 127,368. There was minimal loss. I did not wake you."

"Minimal? It was thousands of people. Memory storage! Was it damaged?" Nora's sleeve alarms beeped. Jumbled memories darted over neural pathways, her head pounded and she swayed, leaning against a data center wall.

"Calm yourself, 319. Your bodysuit is registering high levels of dopamine and decreased serotonin and oxytocin. You are experiencing anxiety and need to rest."

"Later. Now answer me. Was anything in Memory DNA Storage corrupted?"

"No. The memories banks were not affected. The destroyed genes can be replicated using the archived Mars DNA samples."

"Yes! The archives. Search for Kai Ricard, Mars number one."

"He is listed as 1547."

"Highlight it, please. I'm headed that way."

"Yes, doctor. Security Agent Tanner Parks' awakening will commence in 189 minutes."

"No! Do not wake Tanner Parks. That's an order, Geb."

"You have no authority to override CON protocols. Those are

my primary functions."

"I will stop you." Nora rubbed her forehead. Thinking hurt.

"You have no authority. Tanner Parks will wake in 186 minutes."

"The hell he will. Sorry, Geb, but you're wrong. We'll fix you once I make Kai."

"You are making a fatal mistake. Your existence violates ethics code number 14207. You are a duplicate."

Nora stepped over and grabbed Geb's RAM boards, pulling them from the slots.

"I don't think so, Geb. I can't have you waking up any more team members, and especially not to eradicate me, or any other *live* you think are duplicates. What the hell happened to you? Were you damaged during the event?"

She kept sliding the blocks out until the room looked like it did when she entered. Déjà vu flashed through her mind as the lights went out and the emergency blinkers came on again, but she couldn't think about that now. Kai was her main priority.

"Geb are you there?"

No answer.

"Geb, are you functional? I order you to answer to a live command."

Nothing.

"Good. I'll be making Kai now. Without you."

An image of Kai looking into a mirror shaving, blinded her. She had come up behind him and put her arms around his shoulders, kissed the nape of his neck. A blink and the memory disappeared along with the pain.

After the success of engineering and altering human DNA to combat radiation among other inadequacies for space travel, IA instituted archival storage. Only the latest samples from Mars were housed for the historical chemical data transference of clones.

Any vessel sector involving the Genetics Department was run by T3-WRT or Taweret, protective Egyptian goddess of childbirth and fertility. Nora forced the pioneer IA members from Cairo to allow her that much. T ran the Genetics Department much in the same way Geb ran everything else. Geb had total control, while T's knowledge and function didn't extend beyond Genetics and Reproduction.

The department housed many labs, all cold, with labyrinthine, sterile corridors and storage rooms. Nora peeled off her suit and raced to the entryway. The door sealed behind her with a blast of air and a tick. Nora walked over to a shower tube and pressed the *Clean* button, then listened to T's feminine voice.

"Please, close your eyes and hold your breath in three, two, one."

Nora followed the instructions as cleansing solution jetted over her from head to toe. Her body rotated with the floor then stopped. She opened her mouth and took in a breath. In the same steps, *Rinse*, then *Dry* completed the first round. The door unsealed.

Next came the scrub sinks. Careful to clean under her nailbeds without nicking anything, Nora used the small pointed end of a disinfecting stylus, then lightly scrubbed her nails, hands, and arms with sterilization solution preloaded onto a brush. Nora winced when the liquid stung her raw finger tips. Finished, she pushed her hands up to her shoulders into the vacuum rinse tubes above. The flanged silicone openings removed any remaining water.

Nora stepped onto the sterilization walkway, triggering T's voice activation again. Then her real-time heartbeat played through speakers in the ceiling, its rhythmic thumping echoed down the long white hall.

"Preparing to engage UV rays. Please identify."

"Dr. Nora Shastry 319."

"Voice confirmation activated and complete. Standby for further decontamination processing."

The walkway moved as multi-colored lights passed over Nora in bright lines, both analyzing her tissue and sterilizing it.

"Inflammation detected, third digit, right hand. There is also a minor abrasion at the interior right cheek of the oral cavity undergoing the latter stages of healing."

Nora's heartrate increased, the sound resonating. "Is there a break in the skin or mucosa?"

"None identified."

"Continue processing." The thought of being locked out until healing commenced could take more time than she had the patience for. Nora took in a deep breath, closed her eyes, and exhaled slowly. Her cardiac beats decreased overhead.

The walkway glided a single meter per three minutes. A tedious procession that ended with a final flashing of UV germicidal irradiation, now safe for direct clone contact.

"T, did Geb earmark DNA from the Mars Archives?"

"Yes. Chief Plasma Engineer Kai Ricard, number 1547 has been highlighted."

"Great. Can you pull a strand to begin reproductive cloning, please?"

"Yes, Doctor."

After donning a sterile bodysuit and hood, Dr. Shastry entered the cloning lab and watched T's robotic arms retrieve a strand sample then inject it into an empty egg. The early makings of Kai went into an Automaton Uterine Cavity next, also called a making pod.

"First and second stage clone process is initiated, Dr. Shastry. Would you like to make anyone else?"

"Not yet, T. Number 1547 needs to be made as fast as we possibly can. Please expedite, graduating growth hormone increases at the safest levels possible."

"Expedition is not recommended."

"I know, T. Bypass the normal protocols and link the feed to ship's monitors, and pull the memories for 1547 too, please."

"Yes, Doctor."

It would take two weeks to have Kai back, fully grown with his own mind and a millennia of memories.

When she wasn't watching the ship's monitors to assess Kai's growth, Nora adhered to the IA's standard protocols for non-cryo *live* on board, which required food, exercise, sleep, and daily Geb checkups; the latter she'd skip. Geb would function without the RAM she'd pulled.

As well as the single screens down every corridor, an array of status monitors with more detailed information segmented every side of the decagonal upper decks. Starting from the first grouping closest to the outermost section of the lab, she ran her way around counterclockwise. During her jog, passing one flat silver wall panel after another, Nora made it a point not to look up at the blaring red prompts until she'd made it to the tenth display. Then she'd stop, jog in place and look. Dissatisfied with the slow results, Nora ran to the next one, then the next. Metallic clicks and groans threw her steps off. She stopped at a single monitor then slid menus across the screen before selecting Mars Landscapes. The panels lining the corridors and ceilings lit up with sienna hues. The rugged planet's terrain and the memories she'd made there with Kai kept her mind focused on something other than the annoying sounds.

On day ten of Kai's making, during her run, she thought about what Geb had said and stopped to check one of the display arrangements. Her heart skipped a beat when she leaned in for a closer look at the Cryo area. Her suit's alarm went off twice with heart rate increases. Unidentified blue circles existed in capsules 59-101. She hadn't noticed them before because they had no assignment numbers, and she was certain Geb had suffered an event malfunction. Still sorting and organizing data in the clutter of her stored memories, she didn't always think straight. Nora turned off her heart rhythm alarm for a third time, then jogged down to Cryo.

"Doors, open."

They slid back and she stepped in. The cold jarred another memory. She and Kai had just finished making love, and he'd opened the screen to his bedroom window, exposing Mars' sun casting hazy light over terracotta rock formations.

"Look," he said. "Someday we'll wake up together and get to walk outside just like this."

"But we're naked."

"So?"

Nora thought for a moment, visualizing it, then smiled. He padded back and kissed her.

"Soon. You'll be back in my arms again."

She stepped over to inspect the capsules. At number 101, she ran her fingers across the smooth, white exterior. Cocoons for a new age. A rectangular screen lit up when she touched it. No occupant was listed, but stable vital signs and cryo functions read stable.

"Who could this be?" She tapped the capsule, dreading a tap back.

Dr. Shastry went up and down the rows, checking every capsule to 59 with the same negative occupant results. Before leaving she walked over to Tanner Parks' capsule and reset the wake time Geb had initiated. The timer had stopped its countdown when she'd pulled Geb apart.

She returned to quarters, mulling over what Geb had said. He had to be wrong. After tube showering, she put on a jumpsuit then grabbed a nutrient pack and sucked on the spigot while walking to the Genetics Department.

"Geb, prep the sterilization walkway in Gen, please?"

It took a moment of thought lapse until Nora realized she'd disabled Geb's communications. He could see her, locate her on the ship, but he couldn't talk, take any actions, or remember their previous conversation; she hoped anyway, wondering if it frustrated him and what he might be thinking. Squeezing the rest of the IA's daily recommended sustenance into her mouth, she gulped the cloying syrup, put the container into a recycling conduit, then stripped off the jumpsuit to shower again.

Nora pushed buttons outside, manually preparing the walkway to enter and check Kai's generation status and his making pod.

"T, full update on 1547, please."

"Organism is stable, exceeding multiplication ratios. Estimated completion time is one hour and forty-five minutes."

"Wow. Good job on the expediting. You cloned the Mars Archive genes and returned them, correct?"

"Thank you. Yes. I followed standard protocol after extraction."

"Are the grafted memory DNA strands jiving?"

"Define jiving, please."

"Working. Are the strands ... experiencing any anomalies?"

"No. They're jiving normally."

"Thank you." Nora laughed. She sounded distant and strange. A long time had passed since she'd last experienced laughter.

An electric current jolted more memories, zapping them through neural tracts, consolidating fragments from each lobe of her brain. Every retrieval made her heart skip, triggering alarms over the department's speakers.

Robotic machinery rolled into place and the making pod opened. The memory of her and Kai's kiss fired again, charging white hot through fibers and synapses as she saw herself in the cavity.

"No!" Nora screamed, her knees buckled, and she fell, plunging backward through a seemingly endless abyss until finally hitting the floor. She curled into a fetal position, wailing and sobbing, blocking out all the status alarms blaring through the speakers. Nora rolled prone and pounded the icy metal with her fists, adding to the chaos of sounds in the lab.

Her DNA had been on that swab, not Kai's—the kiss. The Mars Archive samples had never been tested, simply stored. She thought of every Geb launch and all the cloned genes from identical samples. In the bliss that had made her mind senseless, did she mix up their memories, too? Or had the machines chosen?

Losing Kai forever was not an option she'd live with. It couldn't be. His DNA had to be somewhere on board. But it would have to wait. Once the rest of the team woke, they'd assist. Geb though ... when they got into New Earth's orbit his main priority would be the Prime Initiative—planet analysis, planet stabilization, and cloning of the Reproductive Series. Plasma drives for further travel no longer a necessity, Kai's function less important, Geb would have the final decision.

T's voice tore Nora from her pain. "1547 is almost complete. Waking to commence in—"

"Don't wake it! We've got to bring it to Cryo for immediate storage. Understand?"

"No. But I am programmed to follow orders, not to reason. That is a Geb function. I detect current failures in parts of his system. Would you like me to attempt repairs?"

"What? No. Uh, Geb was affected by an event. I'm working on fixing him. That's why I needed to make 1547, Kai Ricard."

"Dr. Samuel Qwan is Geb's creator. Should I wake him from cryogenic sleep? I detect an increase in your heart rate, as well as shallow breathing, low dopamine and serotonin levels, Doctor."

The sounds pulsed throughout the lab. Nora rubbed her temples and thought hard.

"Dr. Shastry, would you like me to wake Dr. Qwan?"

"No. Please. Let's just move 1547 there first. Then we'll figure out whether or not to wake Dr. Qwan."

"Yes. My rovers will commence with the transport in 3, 2, 1. Genetics rovers exiting department in 3, 2, 1—"

"Yes, T. I'm coming!" Nora swiped tears from her face, got up on shaky legs and shambled behind the machinery carting her duplicate down the corridors to Cryo.

"Doors open." Nora went to capsule 102 and pulled up the prompt, keying in codes for cryogenic sleep.

The lid opened, then the rovers' robotic arms placed the body into the capsule. Tubes and wires moved and coiled around it as if it had fallen into a snake pit. The rolling machinery left the room while Nora watched the skinsuit grow. Finer gauged electrodes snaked through it, passing into the clone, stabilizing it while the capsule filled with refrigerants. The lid closed as several tubes slid into the nostrils and mouth of her clone. Once sealed, Nora slumped against the capsule and cried. Every one of her, right down to the Nora of origin, screamed and sobbed inside. She felt them all.

Kai would have wanted her to have hope, *had* given her hope. She'd find a way to bring him back. Nora stood, knowing what she had to do. Heading to the Genetics Department first, she erased T's recent memory. Then she removed all evidence of her work there, ejecting it into space, staging the lab to its previous state. Geb's room came next. Programmed to destroy duplicates and eradicate any *live* cryo organisms if necessary, Geb had the ability to terminate then *make* the team again completely if he needed to. Seeing the mess she'd made of him, Nora didn't know what else to pull. She wanted to flood her mind with nothing but Kai, see him, be with him and only him in the forever darkness, which meant sleep.

Acute aches pulled her chest muscles taut. Lightheaded and short of breath, she stumbled to capsule 58 and touched the exterior screen. It was occupied. Vital signs stable, no name listed. Nora hung her head and shuffled to 103, keyed in the codes, then climbed in. Her lid descended as icy wet tubes slithered toward her mouth and nose. She heard a click then the hiss of the capsule behind hers opening.

While her clones continued to replicate themselves until they ran out of cryo chambers, or when GEB had reached New Earth's orbit then eradicated them all, she'd envision the Klimt painting of *The Kiss*. Kai would come to her in the darkness, and they'd live again.

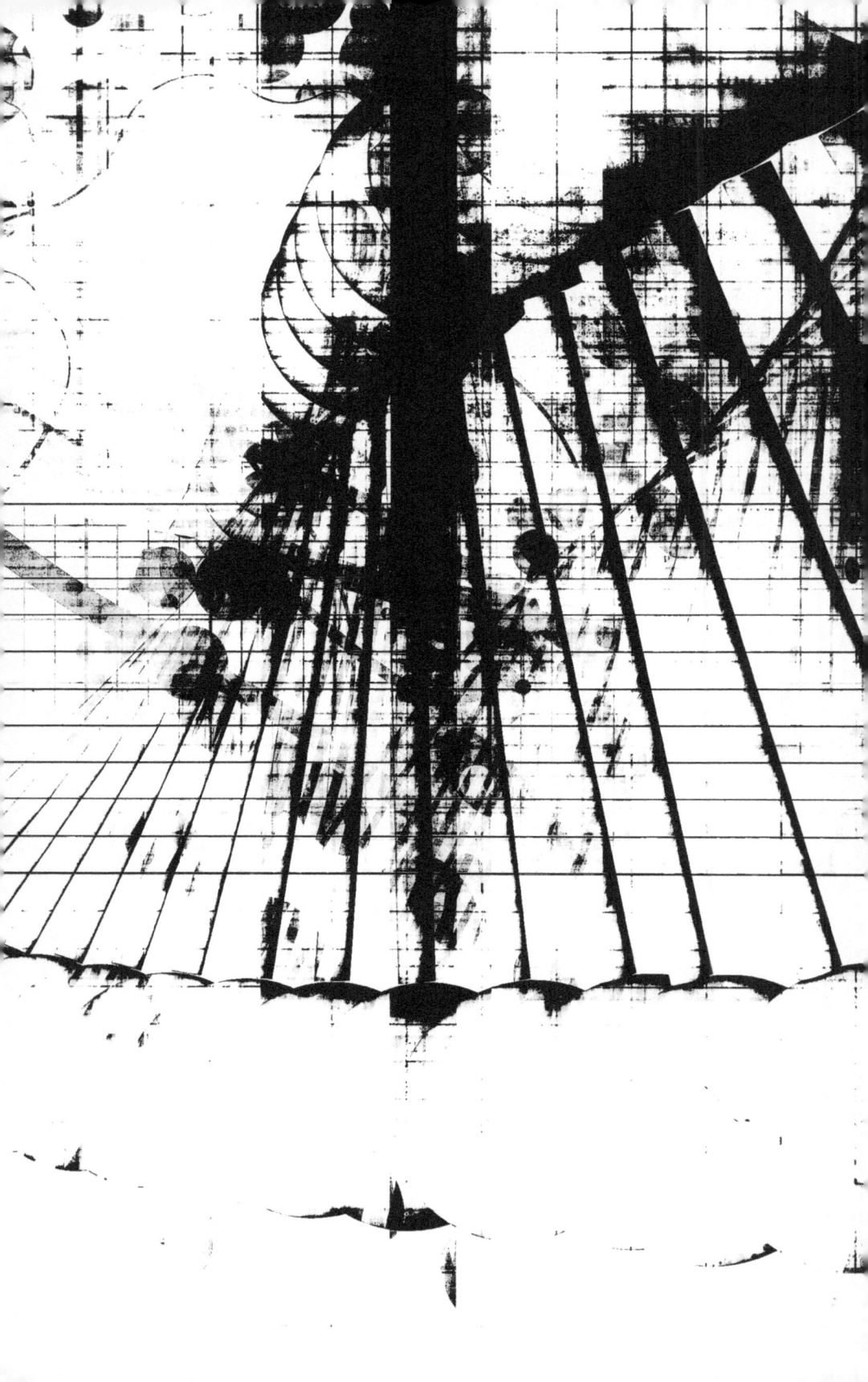

ΠAMELE55 EITIZEΠ

BRIAN EVENSON

1

The world is a hell because we have made it so—I have always thought so, even before. This is not something to be regretted, only something to be accepted, and with each passing year I have come to accept it more. I doubt anyone would argue with me about it now, even if there were others left to argue.

The last person I argued with, indeed the last person with whom I had had contact of any kind until two days ago, I argued with seven years ago. He left on foot, carrying a small titanium cylinder, its surface etched with red script. He asked me to go with him—a simple delivery, he said. I declined. "You won't come back," I told him. "They won't let you." He knew this to be true just as I did, and yet, stubborn or naïve or simply confused, he chose to go anyway. He shook my hand and then turned and left. As predicted, he never came back.

Two days ago, I spent most of an afternoon in the basements of the houses surrounding my own. The houses here are now ramshackle or collapsed, subject to decades of heat and cold and unnatural rain and wind since the disaster, but the basements are still more or less intact. I have broken the concrete floor of each basement, turned the soil beneath and, with great effort on my part, have set about attempting to fruit mushrooms and fungi. For many years I didn't succeed in growing anything at all, and instead lived on the food storage scavenged from the basements and closets of empty houses around me. Outside, I attempted to grow various grains, but either the seeds or the soil is sterile, or perhaps both. Every few years, whenever I discover a cash of seed or grain sheltered in some fashion from the air, I try again.

With mushrooms, I managed finally to fruit several dozen translucent and wracked buttonlets, each no bigger than my fingernail. I ate half of them, a tasteless mouthful that did not kill me, and then transferred some of the others to adjacent basements, hoping that soon I'd have half a dozen separate colonies that would eventually feed me. But their brief moment in the outside air between basements may have been enough to kill them, for only in the first basement do mushrooms continue, lethargically, to grow.

The air might, still now, be more deadly than I imagine. Hard to know since the air that killed everything around me has had no effect on me at all. Or, rather, a salutary effect: my body absorbs its poison and channels it, making me feel more alive.

I was just leaving my final basement when I heard it: a voice, shouting, tinny. I stopped, listened. Then moved toward it.

"Nameless citizen," the voice was calling, "we need you!"

"Nameless citizen," a second voice called, "please we beg you!"

"Nameless citizen," the first voice called, "we have no desire to hurt you! Please, grant us audience."

I squirmed under a collapsed fence and through a ruined backyard, then took a roundabout path back to my own house. Eventually, I caught sight of them. There were just two this time. They stood at the edge of the barren ground that marked my yard, on the crumbling remains of the sidewalk, holding rifles in their gloved hands. They wore thick hazard suits.

"Nameless citizen!" the voice called. "Surely you don't want our species to die out?"

But I did. Why ever not? We had destroyed almost everything along with ourselves. It would be better for the little that remained if we died out.

Or they, I should say, since even though I was once one of them, I could hardly to be said to be so now. The disaster had changed me.

I had become a different creature altogether.

"Nameless citizen!" one of them bellowed through his suit speaker. No doubt he would have continued to bellow had I not tapped his shoulder. He spun around, panicked, trying to get his weapon up, but I already had my hands on the rifle's stock and barrel, had forced the weapon back flat against his chest. If he squeezed the trigger the shot would travel up through his throat and jaw and remove the front of his face.

When he cried out, the other one spun and pointed his rifle at me.

"You called?" I said.

"Let him go," said the second one. "Or I'll shoot."

"I thought you said you had no desire to hurt me," I said. "You need something from me. If you shoot, you won't get it. You called me, I came. Put your weapon down and tell me what you need."

They looked at each other and then the one who I was not touching gingerly placed his rifle upon the ground. I took the rifle from the first and did the same, then took a step back.

"Nameless citizen—" that one began.

"Are you the same drones who came before?" I asked.

"Before what?" asked the first.

But the second shook his head. "This is the first time we've come. If others came, those others are dead."

"Nameless citizen—" the first began again.

"I'm going to stop you right there," I said. "I might be nameless, but I am not a citizen. Not in your community."

I watched him furrow his brow in concentration. And then his brow smoothed. "Nameless person," he said. "We call on you to help our community and your species! We must have material for the construction of individuals if we are to continue on. As you see from our vestments, we are not made to survive in this place, in this air. Even with these suits we cannot live long outside. This visit to you has already shortened our lives."

And where I touched you as well, I thought, though I did not say so. My body is as polluted for them as the air outside, and where I had pushed my hand against his chest the skin would soon bruise and slough, even with the suit between.

"You," said the other, "have no such constraints. You live outside, not underground. The air cannot hurt you. Truly you are a wondrous being."

"Nameless person," said the first. "We ask you to help us. Will you travel to where the material is stored and bring it back to us, for the sake of your species?"

"No," I said. "I will not."

"What can we do to convince you to help us?" asked the other.

"There was another, a sort of brother of mine," I said. "He came to help you seven years ago, on a similar mission. I saw the cylinder he brought. Was he not able to help you?"

"Horak?" said the second. "That was before our time," he said.

"He did help us," said the first, "but he is not in a position to help us again."

"Why not?" I asked.

Neither of them responded to this. Either they did not know or they had been told not to tell me. Considering the shortness of their lives and the pointedness of their purpose, it could be either. Indeed, in all likelihood, these two had been formed hurriedly, primarily for the task of trying to coax me into making the same mistake Horkai had made.

"Nameless person—" the first began again. "What can we do to—"

"Absolutely nothing," I said. "I will not help you under any circumstance."

"We have failed in our purpose," confided the second to the first.

"Nameless person," the other began again. "What—"

But I simply walked past them and into my house.

For a while they remained where they were, trying, no doubt, to determine if there was some way of salvaging their purpose. Perhaps they were even assessing the odds of taking me unawares and forcing me to come with them. When I judged that they had stayed too long, I parted the shutter and stuck the barrel of my rifle out at them. At that, they gathered their own guns and left.

I spent the time until dark setting traps for them around the property. I propped a gun inside both the front and back door, just in case.
But, considering what I had done to their comrades last time they
had come and tried to take me by force, I didn't imagine they would
return.

I waited, thinking. Horkai—if Horak and Horkai were the same
person—was "not in a position to help us again." What did that
mean, exactly? Dead, maybe? But these readymade people did not
generally speak in euphemism. They didn't understand it. Should the
words be taken literally? If so, what would they mean exactly?

I thought about what they had done to Horkai the time before,
before I met him, the way they had severed his spinal column as a
means to control him, to use him. And him, I thought, despite that,
willing to go back.

Eventually, I slept.

Did I dream? I would say no—I never dream, at least not dreams I
remember. I have not dreamt since the disaster changed me, as if the
exchange for surviving the conflagration was to surrender my ability
to dream. And yet, despite this, something had rearranged itself in
my head as I slept, and I woke up another person. Not changed so
as to become the comrade of those two hazard-suited drones, not
changed so as to have an interest in saving so-called humankind,
but no longer quite so willing to stand aside. And curious enough to
know what happened to my friend that, despite the trail being seven
years cold, I went in search of him.

2

I passed down streets thick with dust, cars scoured of paint, the
metal beneath hardly rusted in the dry air despite all the decades
that had passed. I walked until I realized I had entered a cul-de-sac
and, for just a moment old habits asserted themselves and I almost
turned around and went back to a street that ran through. But what
did it matter? Nobody had lived in these houses for years, and I

could see where the fence had been kicked in at the end of the cul-de-sac, perhaps by the very drones that had come to woo me. I passed through an expanse of dust, then through another backyard and onto a street. The street jogged left, and I slid down a culvert and back up the other side. A few more streets, heading roughly east, passing through the remains of a housing development, then a church that had partly collapsed. The sun was red and sticky, obscured by haze. I kept walking.

I passed through a river, its water a brownish red, just transparent enough that I could see something floating in it, like hair was growing from the riverbed. When I started across it, it clung to my boots, making a sucking sound as I pulled myself along. Something alive then, at least in a manner of speaking. *Is it edible?* I wondered, but decided it would be a mistake to stick around long enough to find out. Something else, too, that it took me a moment to place: water bugs, skittering across the surface, though closer in appearance to termites than to water striders. At first I wasn't sure how they kept afloat exactly, then realized that they'd extruded blobs of mucus around their feet and floated on that. I stayed there, calve-deep in the water, watching, surprised how much it moved me to see something alive and new, appropriate to this new world in a way that humans were never appropriate to the old. Indeed, I nearly stayed too long: by the time I started walking again, the filaments had tightened enough that it was hard to free my boots.

I made a wide detour around the capital building, having nearly lost my life there some years before. And from there worked my way northeast, along the ruined boulevard, toward the ruined library where the drones were from.

I found the drone perhaps a kilometer from the library, collapsed in the middle of the street. He was face down, and when I turned him over his faceplate was shattered, his skin bruised. Judging from the dust angel inflicted on the ground beside him, the other had stayed beside him for some time before continuing on.

I followed what I assumed were his steps. They wove a little, became shorter, and I kept expecting to come across his body as well, but I never did.

I found the iron door and struck it with a rock repeatedly, the sound ringing out through the empty air. There were bugs here as well— one or two tiny flies that moved in erratic patterns. Things were coming back: another few thousand years and the world might be back to where it was before we appeared. Yet another reason for allowing humans to go extinct.

Nobody came. I struck the door again and hollered. When it still remained closed, I rooted around in the ruins until I found a place where the ground had collapsed and I could insinuate my way down a level into a half collapsed lower hallway. I lit a flare and wormed my way forward, wondering whether this was wise: I was, admittedly, very difficult to kill, but being buried under rubble might do it. And if it didn't, at least not at first, assuming I was buried that might well be worse.

I snagged my arm on a piece of rebar and tore it deeply. I pulled the arm back, licked the wound clean and pushed the edges together. A few moments later the bleeding had stopped and it held shut, the edges filmed over and milky. A few hours and I would not even be able to see where a cut had been. I worked my way further in and suddenly was through the rubble and in a solid hall again, ceiling and walls intact.

At the end of the hall was a seal, a kind of artificial barrier made of vulcanized fabric: one or several hazard suits apparently torn apart and reassembled to make a protective wall. I took out my knife, cut a slit in it and forced my way through.

A door was on the other side. I forced it open and found myself in a room thick with dust. Nobody had set foot in it for years. The far wall of the room was entirely covered with sandbags, packed floor to ceiling. Another protective barrier I began pulling them down and found, in the middle of the wall, a door. I kicked it open and went through.

It took passing through a few empty rooms before I found the second drone. He was lying naked on a metal table, breathing shallowly, eyes glazed. His body was bruised in places, blackish in others. When

I slapped him, he came to himself confusedly.

"You," he said when he saw me. "I knew you'd come."

"Where's Horkai?" I asked.

"Who?" he said, and only then did I realize he was the drone who, of the two, had seemed to know the least.

"Where is everybody else?" I asked.

"There is nobody else," he said. "I'm the last one. You came just in time."

"For what?" I couldn't help but ask, even though I already knew.

"The monitor will give you a map," he said weakly. "It will tell you where to go. It will tell you how to assemble the material to form a new generation as well."

"I'm not here for that," I said.

"No?" he said. And then he closed his eyes and died.

He had not been lying. When I had been to the ruined library years before, it had been crammed with the living, all of them huddled underground, desperate for a way to stay alive. Now, the whole place was empty. Or not empty exactly. Many of the rooms had corpses in them, desiccated, covered with sheets, with faces and bodies identical to that of the drone I had just seen die.

3

There was only one computer that I could find that seemed to be operational, and I assumed this was what the drone had called the monitor. I fingered it on. On the screen appeared an old man, his beard gray, his hair mostly gone. He moved slowly and tentatively, as if he had forgotten how to use his legs and was only just becoming accustomed to them again. He wore on his feet a pair of dirty slippers that swished as he moved, and had a tattered bathrobe over his bright jumpsuit. Why he had chosen such a self-representation, I found it impossible to understand.

"Ah," he said, his voice hoarse and wavery. "You're here."

"I am," I agreed.

"Yes," he said. "Who woke you?" He turned back to me. "Well?" he said.

"I ..." I started, and then stopped, realizing he had mistaken me for Horkai. Or Horak. Very carefully, I said, "I wasn't aware I had been asleep."

He watched me, his eyes suddenly attentive, shining.

"You don't remember who I am, do you?" he said.

"You're a construct preserved electronically," I said. "You're part of the monitor."

"Yes," he said. "But who was I in life?" And when I didn't answer, he said: "Rasmus. Does that ring a bell?"

I knew the name of course. Horkai had spoken of him, and perhaps I had met him many years before, the first time I had come to the ruined library. I knew he was not to be trusted. But, then again, is anyone meant to be trusted?

"Where's Horkai?" I asked him.

"Ah," he said. "So you're not him. I'm afraid you all look alike to me, all those of you who have left the race. You must be Rykte."

"That's not my name," I said.

He waved his hand, feebly. "It will do in place of a name," he said. "I was told you weren't coming. And yet here you are. Had a change of heart?"

"Not exactly," I said.

"Doesn't matter," he said. "As you can see, I'm the only one left. It's too late."

"But you're not really left," I said. "You're just a construct, an impression within a computer's memory."

This irritated him. "That may be," he said. "But even as a construct, I'm the most human of the two of us."

I laughed. "I would hope so," I said.

"And it really doesn't matter to you?" he said sometime later. "We could die out and you wouldn't care?"

I shook my head. "It should have happened long ago," I said. "Where's Horkai?" I asked again.

He waved the question away. "How about we trade?" he said.

"What sort of trade?" I asked.

"You get the cylinders of material we need, bring them back here. I'll show you how to form new mules and then I'll teach them. And then I'll show you your friend."

"Why does it matter? A series of artificial persons will never bring real people back."

"Won't it?" he said. "If that's the case, then what can it possibly hurt to indulge an old man's whim?"

I thought it over. Did I want to see Horkai badly enough?

"No," I said.

"No?" He regarded me a long moment and then sighed. "So be it," he said.

I turned to leave. "One more thing," he said, from behind me.

I turned back.

"Will you please power the machine down? I might as well go extinct along with everybody else."

I reached out to do it, and then began to think. About what Rasmus had done to Horkai, about his unwillingness to reveal where Horkai was now, about the drones or mules or whatever the fuck he called them that he was creating out of pilfered genetic scraps. "No," I said.

"No?" he said.

"You wanted so badly not to go extinct, let's see what living alone until the machine dies does to you."

And then I left. The construct called after me, but I ignored it. I looked for my friend in the other rooms of the complex but did not find him. I looked above ground as well, in the open air. I moved in a widening circle, exploring those buildings that were still standing nearby. Though I found a preservation chamber that had been recently used, he was not in it. And I found little else.

4

But that preservation chamber in the end proved useful. Not knowing what else to do, what other course to take, not caring to go back to the life I had been living before, I have decided to take the step of having myself preserved. I do this despite the strong likelihood of there being no-one left to awaken me. Eventually, I know, the preservation chamber will break down and I will probably die while being improperly thawed. But perhaps, with a little luck, someone will find me first, bring me back to life, and allow me to see how the world has changed.

Who? a voice inside me wants to know.

The rest of me has no answer for that. Maybe someone will come, from somewhere. Maybe I have missed someone. Or maybe Horkai will someday return.

Besides, I am curious. I don't want to live out my last years scrabbling away at my mushroom farms. I want to see what will come next, what will replace us.

And so I shall preserve myself, throw the dice, trust to fate. I leave this record also as a way to tempt fate, to make whoever finds it curious enough about me that they will attempt to rescue me.

But chances are that it will not be found at all. Or if not that, that what eventually finds me and unthaws me, decades or centuries from now, cannot, properly, be described as human.

But then, for that matter, neither can I.

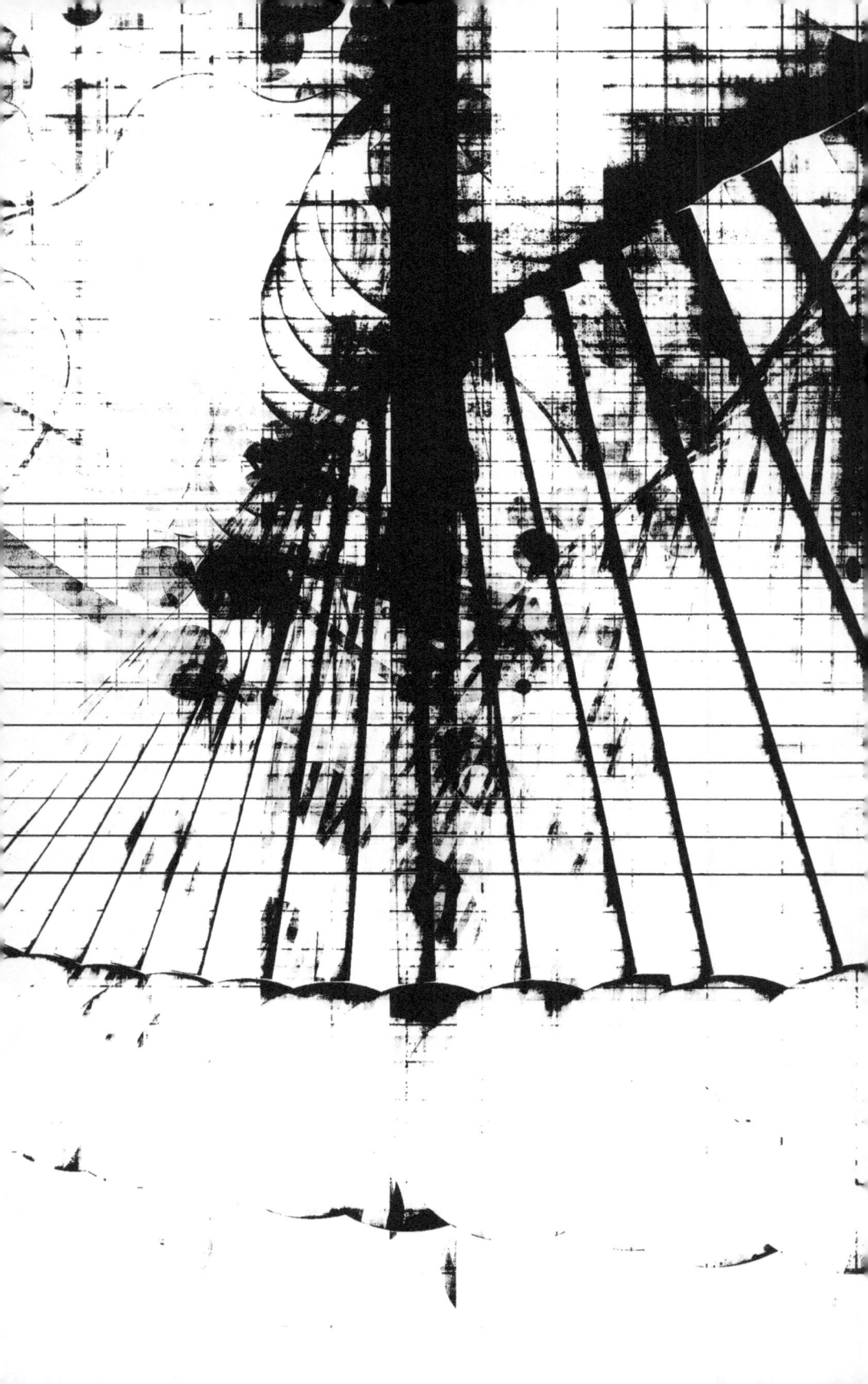

PAINTING THE BURNING FENCE

ROBERTA LANNES

<ACTUAL INCIDENT RETRIEVED FROM OnCorp DATA STREAM> POD 366—MIND DEATH

Andrew looked up from his drawing at the sound of rain against the conservatory windows. Just outside, he saw a blurred figure standing in the deluge. The brick patio had gone from faded terra cotta to dried-blood brown, wet and steaming this hot summer's afternoon. He set down the soft pencil, glancing at the portrait he'd nearly completed, then to the figure, as indistinct as the statuary by the hedgerow. He stepped up close to the window to see it was a girl, he thought perhaps ten years old. Water had soaked her tee-shirt through. Staring at her budding breasts, tiny nipples pressing against gray cotton, Andrew now thought her twelve. He felt his groin go hot and his penis stiffen, his graphite-mudded fingers going to his jeans. He smiled. This one, she was the best so far.

He opened the conservatory door and the girl rushed in. Her doe-eyes blinking, she looked up at him. "Thank you for letting me in. It wasn't supposed to rain today."

Andrew shook his head, grinning. "No. You're soaked. You'd better dry off."

She hesitated, taking in the opulent furnishings and elegant setting. "All right."

He nodded, reaching out a hand. "I'm Andrew Ware. No one's here but me."

She wrapped her arms around her middle, straggly dark hair in wet ringlets around her angelic face. "Oh! I'm Hanna. My dad's your new gardener." She assessed him mildly.

"Ah, yes. I met him." He dropped his empty hand and turned away. "Let's go up to the bath. Loads of towels there." He glanced back at her, knowing she'd follow. The programming.

As they passed the enormous mirror at the base of the stairway, he caught sight of his sixteen-year-old self; a rangy, but good-looking russet-haired lad.

The bath, a sparkling white-tiled haven with a long window facing the garden, awaited them. The water had been run, the scent of orange blossoms wafting up with the steam. Andrew showed Hanna in, pointing out the towels, explaining he'd be waiting outside.

"I don't need a bath, really. Just to dry off. Get clean clothes." She smiled up at him. Warm, open, sweet, just as he'd wanted. "That okay?"

"Sure! When you're dry, I'll show you to my sister's bedroom where you can borrow some clothes. You're the same size, same age."

The girl grinned, only a little afraid being in the big house. "That's lovely." She took a towel, held it to her. "I'll just be a minute."

"Just call out." He nodded, then shut the door.

Rushing into the linens cupboard next door, he moved a box on the eye line shelf to reveal a small hole. He peered into the bath. As she peeled off her wet things and stepped out of her wet trainers, he watched, the thrall centering in his crotch. She dried off, leaving her things in a sopping pile by the tub. Her body was hairless, perfect. Wrapping herself loosely in the towel, she went out of view.

"Hello? Mr. Ware?"

Andrew went to the door, composing himself, and tapped. "Are you finished already?"

"Yes, sir."

"Covered up?"

The door opened and her angelic face appeared. "Yes. Your towels are huge!"

"You'll have nice things in the gardener's cottage, too. Just follow me ... that way." He jerked his head to the right. He couldn't take his eyes off her.

She presented herself. "Oh, my dad! He'll be wondering where I've wandered off to."

Andrew averted his gaze as she passed before him into the hallway. "We'll let him know … when you get the dry things on."

She padded ahead of him, leaving wet footprints on the polished oak floor. She'd slip now, fall, the towel unraveling from around her. Part of the Perfect Moment.

She hit the floor with a soft thud. "Oh, my!" Andrew knelt beside her, drinking in the sight of her sprawled out. She pulled the towel over her. "I should've said for you be careful, dry your feet …"

Hanna nodded, rolling onto her side. Ignoring his proffered hand, she struggled to get up. "I think I hurt my back." She winced as she straightened, rose up. "Agh, yow!"

"Let's get you into some warm clothes. Perhaps my sister Sophie has some paracetamol."

Summer clothes had been laid out; a flouncy white cotton summer top, pale blue shorts, and white socks stuffed into white trainers. Good choices, he mused. He'd let Sophie plan some details.

He went to the bedside table, opened the drawer. A tub of mentholated rub lay beside a bottle of massage oil.

"No paracetamol, but here's something for a sore back. Sophie has back problems from riding. Have you seen the stables yet?" Andrew held the tub of mentholated goop in his palm. She shook her head. "Well, do you mind if I rub a little in before you get dressed?"

Hanna raised a dubious eyebrow. "I suppose so. You won't … look at me …" Her eyes glinted with trepidation mixed with excitement, almost coquettish. *Perfect.* This subtle expression showed just the right amount of resistance and intrigue. He nearly swooned.

"I'll be a gentleman. And call me Andrew."

"Just a little, then." She looked at the outfit. "Nice."

"Good! Now, just put the towel on the bed and lie down. I'll look away."

She blinked, momentarily unsure. "Okay."

Andrew averted his gaze, then looked back to catch Hanna spreading the towel over the brocade duvet and crawling on. Once on the towel, she went rigid with apprehension, her hands beneath her, completely exposed.

"Remember, don't look ..." She had glanced over her shoulder, her eyes now wet, awaiting his hands on her back.

"Close your eyes. This will make you feel better." She did as he asked. He switched the rub out for the massage oil.

He undid his jeans, allowing them to quietly fall to the floor, then pulled his pants down. A couple of drops of oil went on his hands, fingers brushing over his erection, as he leaned over her. With well-schooled precision, he pressed his thumbs into the small of her back, spreading his hands, and pushing upwards toward her shoulders. Again, starting lower, parting her buttocks enough to see between, then upwards.

Hanna moaned. "That's it. Where it hurts." She arched her back. Andrew continued, his touch growing sensual.

Until now, Sophie had been Hanna, performing, but at his predesignated request, Hanna took over. Sophie had no control. She was now just going along for the ride. As he wanted. Needed.

He continued massaging, his hands moving down to her knees, up her legs, separating them. He felt her relaxing under his ministrations, opening herself to him. His hands moved around her slender back to her breasts, his fingers to her nipples. He grew light-headed, savoring the exquisite seduction and ready for his pleasure. Yes, Hanna was the right one. The best.

With a loud bang, the bedroom door slammed open, turning both their heads. Andrew gasped. No!

It was too soon, and not Hanna's incensed father standing in the doorway. It was Sophie, not the twelve-year-old he'd seduced, but Sophie at twenty. Twenty; when she'd grown possessive, jealous. Dangerous.

"Andrew! What are you *doing*? Who *is* that?"

Andrew grappled on his pants and jeans, as Hanna scrambled off the bed, pulling the towel around her. Andrew stepped out in front. "Get the *fuck* out, Sophie!" Rage destroyed his lust. "This isn't the way we agreed ..."

"*No*! This is *my* room. *You* get the fuck out, and take your nasty little tart with you!" Sophie stepped aside. "*Now!*"

Andrew shut his eyes. "Dominique … *Five-Two!* What's going on?!"

Hanna grasped his elbow, eyes wide. "I cannot act upon this situation from inside this construct." She saw his panicked face, squeezed hard. "Here, Andrew. I'm *here!*"

He glared at Sophie in terror. How was Five-Two in Hanna and not in his mind?

Then, Sophie pulled Andrew's hunting rifle from behind her and pointed it square at the two of them. "It's her or me, Andrew. *Decide.*"

The memory of what had actually happened when life was real screamed back. Sophie shooting cook's daughter. Her time in the asylum which filled him with loathing, longing, and loss. This scenario played out again and again. After all, Sophie's mind still determined her behavior even after death.

He turned to Hanna; Five-Two. Her large eyes had gone translucent, displaying chips, wires and tiny lights. He felt as much anger as helplessness as he fixed his eyes with her, straining to connect.

He shouted then, as if she was across the room. "Five-Two, do it! *Erase!* Now. Erase!" He shut his eyes.

The sound of a vapour lock releasing signaled a major action. He opened his eyes to find Sophie gone. An illusionist's trick. Andrew still felt panicked, terrified.

"What have I done?" Hanna/Five-Two trembled. "Why would she want to harm us?"

"This wasn't supposed to happen. Shouldn't have happened. Get dressed, or disengage, or whatever … I don't know *how* you did this!" He waved his hand before her.

Hanna nodded, blurred, then disappeared. As Andrew walked through the doorway, he was engulfed in absolute darkness.

Mind Crime January 6/2289.4 POD 366 MIND DEATH

The following is the deposition of LST Five-Two, also known as Dominique Evangaline Durais, in the above named incident. This should not be regarded as reliable testimony without corroborating data evidence, collection of which is ongoing.

Recorded via BioCom.
Transcript prepared by MC Analyst Jon Arndt.

"This is Jon Arndt. I'm your Mind Crime Analyst and legal advocate. Please state your name, remit, employment period with the corporation, and the charges against you."

Female voice. Quizzical tone. "How strange. I only hear your voice. Are you actual or virtual?"

"That's not relevant to this inquiry. Please, answer the questions."

Sighing. "I'm Five-Two, aka Dominique Evangaline Durais. I've been a Life Support Tech with ONCorp fourteen years." Another sigh. "Seriously, I asked to speak with an actual person, not a bot."

"Noted. Read the statement you've prepared regarding the charges, or relate it in your own words. Details are crucial to your sentence or exoneration. Include your personal experience, emotions if any."

Derisive tone. "What if I refuse unless I see an actual person?"

Ambient background sound. Bass bump signaling interruption or cessation of the investigatory recording. Second, softer bump.

"All right, Dominique. Off auto-bot. This is Jon. You're now receiving this via BioCom. I'm a real person based offsite. Your OnCorp location is isolated and protected beneath the hot zone. Will you talk with me?"

Flirtatious tone. "Hi, Jon. Why can't I meet with you face to face? It's not fair."

"I'm not able to travel to your facility. And, I'm the only person qualified to take your testimony."

"Can I see what you look like? You know what I look like, right?"

"Hold … for an image overlay."

Sound of light keystrokes.

"This is me."

"It's a still. Can't you push active imaging?"

Stern voice. "There are regulations, one of which I just broke. If I attempt a live feed, you won't have had adequate legal representation, which you'll require when it comes to court. I'll terminate our link unless you agree to speak with me."

Sighing. Still flirtatious. "Okay. You're nice-looking, Jon."

Warm response. "Thank you." Stern again. "Please state the charges as they were given to you."

"All business, you." Soft chuckle. "Well, then, the charges are tampering with a mind in my pod and causing an EOL."

"And the definition of EOL … as you know it?"

"Really? End … Of … Life. Mind termination."

"Thank you. Do you prefer Five-Two or Dominique?"

Sultry voice. "Dominique, of course."

Stern voice. "Dominique, my job is to be your legal advocate, take your testimony, and when it's offered to the World Court, support you and your attorney." Throat clearing. "Do you agree to this arrangement?"

Resigned tone. "Understood. Yes."

"Then, let's get to work. Can you start at the beginning and include as many details as you can access so I can best help you?"

Sound of tiny movements, voice relaxed. "Fine, Jon. Not sure where to begin."

"Begin with your background, then introduce me to POD 366. What were your duties?"

Sighing. Resigned voice. "Well, an LST's job involves monitoring, providing and adjusting a pod's members mind support, creating constructs or avatars, and making sure whatever physical body remains is kept medically sound. LSTs are linked with the Core or Bio-Stasis for up-to-the-minute statistics for attention if needed, alerts us to make corrections to unacceptable pod practices and apply consequences when laws are broken.

"*Me*. I had two years of training, two more interning, then three short-term assignments during a year-long probationary period. According to my records, which you'll have, I had exemplary scores. Yes?"

Neutral tone. "That's what I have. Well done." Ambient noise.

Warm tone. "Thank you! That's important, isn't it? To my case? A perfect history?"

"Yes, definitely. It will be up to me to decide what, if anything, in your deposition might be deleterious to your case and of benefit. Go on. Tell me about this pod."

"They called it The Estate, their world. Charming. Very early twentieth century big country house on acres of lush land. Cecily, Andrew, and Sophie Ware are ... were the owners or members. Aunt, older brother, and his sister. Cecily set up the pod to begin utilization upon her physical death, which occurred nearly a decade before the siblings passed. Sophie entered next, then Andrew.

"They didn't like calling me Five-Two. After a consensus, they decided to call me Dominique; more informal, after a maternal grandmother, actually."

"How much control did you have over the thoughts and actions of the members, what they experienced?"

Warm tone. Musing. "Mmmm. Control isn't the word I'd use. I'm sometimes a guide, always a facilitator. More of a slavish service technician than chaperone. Not controlling in the real-life way of manipulating events or forcing an outcome out of self-interest or personal gain. I'm neutral."

"So a consensus comes about independent of your input?"

"That's correct. Consensus decisions, as well as individual choices, are sovereign in The Estate. If a majority decided to change the pod in some radical way that went counter to corporate contract, I'd intervene."

"Give me a *hypothetical* example."

"A few members of an academically inclined pod exclude a pair from philosophical discussions, deeming them intellectually inferior. An LST could choose to infuse the excluded pair with a complete education in philosophy, eliminating cause for exclusion."

"So an LST doesn't play God, but finds solutions to issues that occur in a pod. Understood. You started with a pod of three."

"Yes, but they wanted to grow. While they could create constructs, or avatars and control them through me, they decided to invite associate members who weren't predictable. But, as often as they brought in others, they sent them away."

"Associate members are really temporary guests unless they fit into the pod's values, yes? So who vetted them?"

"The Estate was a T-pod. A Trust Pod is created long before physical death and allows members complete control. Trusts are extremely well-funded, so they have almost no limitations. As in real life." Warm chuckle. "Money trumps corporate restrictions. T-pods make their own laws, and very rich T-pods can be nearly autonomous worlds unto themselves. Pods are limited to eight life links, though."

Throat clearing. "This describes The Estate?"

"Yes. Pod 366's main funders were Andrew and Sophie, though Cecily was the initial Trustee. When associate members were invited, they were vetted by the Wares with the corporate oversight regarding their numbers. They chose associates they could control regardless how potentially problematic I found them. These were poor and discarded fringe people who'd have died and been cremated. In The Estate, the associates experienced elevated conditions they'd never have known in life, but the tradeoff was that the Wares had full control of them. They took in deviants and criminals for amusement, but not easy folks to control. They were trouble.

"I should make something clear before I go on. In stasis, T-pods build their world in consensus; creating a mutual set of laws, or an anarchist society, with only the corporate law absolute. Those laws were three. First law is for an LST to remain separate and impartial. Second law is for all, do no harm. Third law is for an LST: never terminate without express instruction from SM or corporate."

"Are there other laws?"

"Hundreds, as in real life. T-pods are the exception … practically free from all regulation, but those three."

"Unless requested by the trustees?"

Sighing. "Yes. If they choose to have their LST become an active part of their world or allow virtual physical harm or obtain the right of termination, they can do so. But, they pay for that."

"So, harming or terminating another is unlawful and receives consequences?"

"Yes, in all but T-pods where restrictions are lifted. As I monitored Pod 366, the many avatars and associates they used and threw out, I learned to adjust to their … lawlessness."

"Did your Section Manager know the disturbing composition and perversity of your T-pod and if so, were you ever instructed to intervene or interfere in any way?"

"Everything I did, everything that happened in the T-pod was fed unaltered into the Section Manager. Anything that alerts SM to a corporate infraction would've been flagged instantly. This never happened."

Suspicious tone. "So all data stream received by Section Manager would have been *unaltered*?"

"As far as I'm aware. In training, we're told that glitches rarely occur. Hacks, yes, but they're handled so quickly, LST personnel might not be told. I wouldn't know if something occurred unless there was a sudden *and* extreme change or my connection to the data stream was interrupted. Subtle changes can occur over time, and I wouldn't be made aware from SM. If I missed it, so would SM."

"This is good information. Opens a reasonable doubt window. Continue."

A whir. Hum. "After eleven years witnessing every sort of deviance and perversity, I grew inured. Being disconnected from the T-pod over the last five months, I see how passive and accommodating I'd become. They never broke their own laws. They had none!

"Perhaps some personal member background will give the context."

Detached tone. "Absolutely. Specificity is essential here."

Soft chuckle. "Where did real Jon go?" More chuckling.

"He's tired. Apologies."

Cheery voice. "Accepted. Okay. Cecily raised Andrew and Sophie. Their parents died very young. Mr. and Mrs. Ware became earth-fodder rather than use life/mind-extension. They surely never imagined they'd die in a transport accident in their late twenties, hence the lack of preparation for post death. Next of kin, Cecily, took on the role of parental figure and started a trust.

"She was nineteen at the time, Andrew five and Sophie an infant. Inheriting WareCorp, with wealth beyond our comprehension, Cecily had a lot of help raising them, but for an immature, spoiled and not-quite-bright girl, she responded to motherhood as a bother. She preferred leaving the wolves in charge.

"Cecily was a fat, unattractive girl who desperately sought high society's acceptance and a handsome, rich husband. After five years of relative invisibility through outright disdain, she became reclusive. Andrew became her new best friend. He was a good-looking boy, but his parent's death and early abandonment issues gave him much shame. The easy-going charming façade he took on in public faded away at home. Cecily's attentions and now-constant presence gave him a false sense of belonging, according to the psyche-eval.

"Cecily began seducing Andrew when he was ten and it continued until her death fifteen years later. There's no proof, but Andrew's recollections are that he began molesting Sophie when he was fifteen. It gave him some sense of control. Sophie was eventually complicit in this. No different from Andrew, she longed to feel a part of a relationship, to be seen, heard, felt. A decade on, when Cecily learned of this ongoing relationship between her niece and nephew, she had a jealousy-fueled psychotic break, viciously attacking them both. She spent three years in a sanitarium where she received heavy monitoring and reprogramming. The day she was to be released, she hung herself in a treatment room. It was fortunate that she'd set up the Post-PD trust after her brother's death, and was linked in immediately."

Weary voice. "Sophie and Andrew Ware died years apart, according to the data stream. She of ovarian cancer, he of an accidental drug overdose. How were they received by Cecily when they entered the T-pod?"

"Coolly. Sophie arrived first. Cecily had acquired brain injury from the sanitarium treatments, which caused recurrent bouts of dementia. She requested partitioning soon after Sophie arrived. In the partitioned area, she created her own world. There, she's gorgeous, slim, happily married to a handsome adoring man, and the two of them freely sexually abuse the children.

"When Andrew arrived, he and Sophie acclimatized, creating The Estate environment, where they continued their incestuous relationship. Initially, and for a few years, the familiarity of it gave them comfort. They grew dissatisfied eventually, and began to experiment with avatars and brought in the associate members for as long as they remained of interest."

Captivated tone. "This jibes with the evaluations I have, but your telling gives them a softened, almost sympathetic version. Do you think spending so many years with them you grew to feel benevolence?"

"Perhaps. More disappointment softened by pity. As their LST, my feelings about them were tertiary to my remit."

"Do you believe that the data your SM has from your years in service to the Ware's T-pod will show that you were successful in separating your emotions from your responsibilities?"

Long pause. Silence. Forlorn voice. "It would take a long time for me to review that much data to assess the truth of that. I thought I did a good job."

"You don't sound certain."

Soft machine noise. "Don't I? Would you if this incident occurred on your watch? You'd have to go through the data and decide for yourself, Jon."

"I need context. You have that. You experienced it."

Awkward derisive snort. "That I did."

Cough. "I need a break. Ten minutes?"

"Yes. Ten." Firm bump sound.

INTERVIEW RECOMMENSED
10.25 MINUTES LATER

Soft bump. "Dominique?"

"Better if I'm just Five-Two, now."

"If that's what you feel comfortable with. We can continue. Do you recall where we left off?"

Soft tone. "Yes, Jon. I do." Unintelligible noise. Detached voice. "I do."

Gentle voice. "Let's start at a point you were first aware of subtle changes that may have allowed the incident to occur."

Resigned tone. "I can do that for you, Jon."

"At year nine, after going through a dozen *associate members*, their perversity had peaked in the extreme. Because of the depths of depravity he'd experienced and a general ennui, Andrew grew weary of Sophie and their incestuous escapades. He was bored. Unfulfilled. Sophie designed higher risk-taking adventures to include him, but he withdrew. He preferred nostalgia to activity, reminiscing over his youth for long periods, asking me to provide him scenarios of experiences from before his parent's deaths. Sweet, poignant moments. He softened, began reading poetry, fiction.

"Then, strangely, he began talking *to* me, reading to me. Not merely thinking what he wanted without conceiving of me as anything other than an operating system link. In a way, I became a person, not his LST.

"He asked me questions about who I was, where I'd lived, my family, what it was like where I worked. We had conversations. So, when he asked me if I lived in The Estate, what my avatar would be like, I wasn't alarmed. In any other pod, this would be in direct offense of the first law …"

"Breaking the Fourth Wall."

Fascinated. "Interesting."

"Did Andrew, Cecily or Sophie directly request that you break any of the OnCorp laws?"

"Indirectly. When Andrew asked me who I'd be in The Estate, I answered neutrally. No differently than wondering how many trees I thought should exist on The Estate. I said I'm female, forty years old, and I'd immerse myself in quantum entanglement conundrums because that's my main interest. I explained that throughout my education, I wanted to be a physicist, but my psych-eval showed a high level of multitasking skills, compassion, and the technical skills used in LST work.

"Andrew thought that my choices were dull and laughed. He then asked me to describe what my construct would look like. Even with my infinite imagination, I said I had clear blue eyes, a boyish figure, and that my hair was short and brown. He thought that was dull, as well. It shouldn't have bothered me, but the last word I'd use to describe myself is 'dull'."

"Did you feel hurt?"

Apologetic voice. "Yes." Pause. Incredulous tone. "Then, he asked me if I *liked* him, found him attractive! I'd never thought about it. I identified as separate. I expressed that I felt neutral."

"Did this trouble him? You?"

"In that instance, I registered the change in his behavior as minor, and he never questioned how I felt about him again. I thought it inconsequential. Pod members may think whatever they like, and if it was of concern, I believed my SM would've alerted me."

"So your relationship became somewhat personalized?"

"In hindsight, yes."

"What was the next instance?"

"Sophie's world devolved further, taking in an associate, requesting she be free to cause harm, use torture if she wanted. Harm registers in their minds, but they feel it profoundly, so SM stepped in. They gave her strict parameters regarding consent.

"Andrew knew nothing of this. So when he began involving me peripherally in his creation of his Perfect Moment, play-acting as a *surrogate* avatar, not *the* actual avatar, I considered it a kindness. Running the avatar, I remained in his head, acting from his imagination.

"He said he wanted Sophie to become integrated in this female construct, so he told her about the Perfect Moment; a sequence of erotic events centered on his first experience with Sophie, but redesigned to fit his ripened fantasies.

"This felt the ultimate betrayal to her. She grew testy, mean-spirited. Yet, she didn't confront him, choosing instead to behave as *the perfect one*, and get it 'right' as he saw it. The three of us then created Hanna."

"Clarify this. How did you know how she felt, yet allow her to be integral to this scenario?"

Embarrassed voice. "She'd learned to shield herself from me, which I only know now. Sophie had become incredibly strong. But, as Andrew worked with Sophie to create his perfect Hanna, something felt wrong to him, so I sensed it as well. I thought it best for him to have a safe word in case Sophie chose to cause harm, of which I knew she was capable. If he said it, I'd freeze her and restart the situation in safe mode. Or end it.

"In retrospect, when instances such as this occurred, I felt protective toward Andrew, which wasn't a good thing. I believed I'd remained as balanced as possible. Clearly, over time, subtle changes did occur."

Jon interrupts. "The incident itself is a separate data log, viewable omnisciently by the parties in this criminal trial. So can you explain your experience of it for the record?"

"I was linked to Andrew and Sophie acting as Hanna from her appearance outside the conservatory. During the incident, as Hanna and Andrew enter Sophie's room, Sophie essentially moves out of Hanna. I retained our link and followed her to Andrew's gun cabinet. She was about to have her precious memory rewritten. To her, an abomination! She had to confront him now. I knew she wanted to harm him.

"At the same time, somehow I remained linked with Andrew and I force-inhabited Hanna. She wasn't a true avatar; she was the construct's husk. The system somehow pushed me, Dominique, into Hanna."

"Could you have left Hanna to disappear or forced her to become a construct of her own?"

"This, I do not know. This situation was unprecedented. The system wasn't addressing this situation, so to remain in service, I suddenly entered into Hanna. I can only explain the way I experienced it.

"I knew Sophie was coming after him, but as Hanna, I couldn't change the scenario. When he saw Sophie with the rifle, he feared she'd cause him harm. He had no idea I'd taken Sophie's place in Hanna, because he called out to me with his safe word, 'Erase'".

"Did you know '*Erase*' was your T-pod's corporate termination code? That your imperative was to fully terminate upon that order?"

"As LST, I must've known. But, pods *can* have unique termination codes. Still … I've retraced the events of that day, wondering why, if I had access to that information in my data stream, I'd follow Andrew's command. He gave me the safe word. A termination code. Why didn't I override it to simply freeze Sophie and reboot Andrew's Perfect Moment?"

"Do you question why your SM didn't intervene?"

A low growl. "Absolutely. Don't you?"

"Yes, Five-Two. There're no precedents for what occurred. This closed mind/life extension system has worked perfectly for nearly a century. *Or so we're led to believe.* And you'll be up against OnCorp. They'll protect their interests."

Tone of lament. "I can't save myself, can I Jon. But you can. Will you save me?"

"I'm up for this challenge, and I'm on your side, no matter what."

Resigned voice. "No matter what? You could be on my *losing* side."

"Best case scenario, Andrew gets a rebooted Dominique back. You know the worst."

Tone of lament. "So, paint the burning fence, or let it burn down. Forever."

"But, I'll be with you all the way." Deep thrum.

INTERVIEW PART ONE
TERMINATED BY MC ANALYST JON ARENDT 21:15

PITY THIS BUSY MONSTER NOT

SCOTT EDELMAN

Julian found himself sitting at a narrow counter which ran along the coffee shop's front window, a coffee shop which he knew should have been familiar to him, even though it was not. His head was down as he frowned while working with too great an effort on what should have been an easy crossword puzzle. He was frowning twice over, in fact, for he wasn't just frowning because he found the clues which ran down the page to be tough ones. He was also frowning about even frowning over that crossword puzzle. For as far as he knew, he didn't *like* crossword puzzles, at least, not that he remembered, which explained, he guessed, why he also couldn't recall ever attempting to do one.

Actually, he wasn't quite sure what he liked or didn't like, was only sure that he shouldn't examine too closely the nature of his uncertainty just then. So he returned to his struggling, a mental exercise accompanied by gently tapping the cap of his pen against his lip, a habit he found comfortable, and recognized as his own, even though he had no idea why, when, or where the gesture had become his in the first place.

He searched his memory, which he knew in his heart (he had a heart, didn't he?; yes, he felt it there, beating) to be wide and deep (though he clearly had no true proof of that in this instant) to remember the name of a certain actress from a certain movie made during a certain year. This attempted dive into the past made his head hurt, because somehow he knew, somehow he was aware, that he should have remembered information like that easily. He always had before, hadn't he? Though he wasn't sure how it should be possible to remember that remembering, while at the same time having no clue as to the information itself.

Sighing, he lifted his gaze for a moment from the newspaper. It had been the only moment he'd raised his head since sitting down with his puzzle and his coffee and his banana nut muffin, and in that moment, he chose to glance out the large front window and onto the street.

He could have looked elsewhere in that instant. He could have turned his head, perhaps, looked to his right, and studied a wall decorated by a tromp l'oeil mural of coffee beans growing on a hillside. Or he might have tilted his head back, looked up, and admired the fanciful lighting fixture formed there by a spiral of glowing coffee cups. But no, instead, he chose that moment to stare straight ahead, to feel the sun on his face for what seemed like the first time, and so he, not just for what seemed like the first time, but for what actually was the first time, saw *her*.

Had he changed this element of his posture a moment earlier, she wouldn't have yet reached that narrow stretch of side street, and so he'd have lowered his gaze before she passed, missing her. If he'd stirred himself a moment later, she'd have already been gone, having turned a corner, escaped the moment of their maybe, never to be seen by him. But, luckily for him, luckily for her, the puzzle which had been confounding him disturbed him just enough that he'd looked up at exactly the right moment.

As he saw her, this woman he would have sworn he knew and swear he didn't know, it seemed to him as if she contained not just all that mattered in the universe, but all the matter *in* the universe. His body grew suddenly too tight to contain his soul, and he feared that if he stared at her any longer, if she did not pass quickly from his field of vision, her presence would burst him from his skin and split his shell to tatters. But his heart was pounding now in a way he'd never felt a heart pound before, making him aware of its presence with an urgency he'd never known, so he had to dare it anyway.

He would not look away. He could not look away. And then he didn't have to look away.

She was gone.

He dropped his pen and dashed out to the street, leaving his muffin barely nibbled, his coffee hardly sipped.

But once there, he was unable to spot her in any direction. As he scanned the city, a city in which he'd spent his entire life, it did not seem familiar to him the way he knew it should, and now, because of her, he assumed, it was only an impediment, a maze, its marvels meaningless, and not worth his time.

Because of her.

If the woman he sought had already entered a building, he knew he'd have lost his only chance, and would never find her again, but perhaps, oh, perhaps, if she'd only turned the corner …

He hesitated for the merest fraction of a second, trying to make in that infinitesimal fraction of time—one so small, it didn't seem possible for a human to measure it—what he knew would be his life's most important decision: Which way to run. Then he simply ran, knowing he had time for but one choice, knowing that if he'd chosen wrong, this would be the end of it, though an end he would never forget, and so no end at all.

He reached the street which instinct—or something grander— had headed him toward, looked in one direction, and saw nothing but a string of food trucks mobbed by a crowd he could immediately tell did not contain her. But when he looked the other way—ah, when he looked the other way—there she was.

He'd made the right choice. Or perhaps the universe had made the right choice for him. He'd have looked skyward and said thank you had he believed there was anything to which to say thank you.

After he called out to her, the expression revealed to him on her face when she turned told him, however … she didn't at all think he'd made the right choice.

⌇

Barbara'd had enough of strange men calling out to her on the street as if they'd had a right to, shouted at by so many she couldn't remember them all even if she'd wanted to. Which she did not. So she had made it a habit now to ignore them, and to make it seem at the same time as if she wasn't ignoring them, merely as if she'd never heard. Life was easier that way. Safer, too. She knew that even though she wasn't sure how she knew that, couldn't conjure up more than just a few of their faces even though she'd have thought they'd be burned into her memories, but if her mind wanted her to forget things, if her memory had become porous, she figured there had to be a good reason, whether she could extract that reason or not. So she let go of the attempt to remember which the cry from behind her had raised.

This time, as opposed to all of the other times except for the first, which she was aware of instantly without really remembering … she decided to turn. To confront.

Though the words said by the man behind her weren't by themselves offensive, his call had come when she'd had just about enough—he hadn't been the first that day; at least she thought he hadn't been the first that day—so who it was and what was said this time didn't really matter. She'd had enough, and though she wasn't sure what she was going to say, she was going to say *something*.

But when she spun, ready to speak, and trusting the words would be there when she needed them, she couldn't tell at first which of the others on the street had even been the one to accost her, as no one was looking directly at her. The dozen or so people were mostly in motion, hurrying for their destinations, with none headed toward her, while the ones who vibrated in place were all occupied by tasks which had nothing to do with her—hailing a cab, studying a storefront, lighting a cigarette. But the way his voice had reverberated so recently and so close behind, she knew he must still be there, and realized that it had to be *him*, the man looking down in confusion at a newspaper in his hand, as if he'd forgotten it was there, as if its presence had distracted him and caused him to forget *she* was even there. But then he looked up, and saw her, and she could she him remembering where he was, and why he was, see a smile blossom across his face from that remembering. A smile. Not the leer she'd come to expect from a string of faces she couldn't conjure up. (And why not? But better not to ask, she knew.)

He lifted the newspaper, shook it slightly so her eyes were drawn to a partially completed crossword puzzle, and asked whether she knew the name of a certain actress from a certain movie made during a certain year. A question which took her aback. Both because it was so unlike anything any stranger had ever said to her, but also because she *did* know the name of that certain actress who'd starred in that certain movie made in that certain year. Why, she'd been discussing it just the night before with one of her girlfriends. How remarkable was that?

So she told him.

His smile grew wider, a smile of happiness that she was right, not only in her answer, but ... *right*.

He then looked at his other hand, the one not holding a puzzle, and smiled a different smile, a crooked smile, and asked whether she had a pen he could borrow. He stepped closer and ran a finger down the column where the name of the actress she'd given him should go. She shook her head, apologized, telling him it had been a long time since she'd had to write anything down that couldn't been done electronically. Writing with ink on paper seemed like something an ancient people would have done.

It seemed longer ago to her than it actually was. She knew that. But she didn't really care.

Oh, he wasn't quite as old as that, he told her, then pointed at an empty corner of the puzzle, and tapped the clues that went with it. He wondered whether she'd care to help him further. He knew of a coffee shop around the corner where they brewed excellent coffee, and the muffins weren't that bad either. And if they were lucky, no one would have yet thrown away the pen he'd left behind.

She looked at him, and for the first and last and only time (she was surprisingly uncertain of many things this morning, but not of that) thought ... oh, why not?

❦

That didn't seem right.

Did you really expect it would? It was a long time ago.

What are you saying? That just because that was then and this is now, nothing needs to make sense? How did he know which way to go to catch up with her? How did she know to stay after he'd found her? How did he know she was the one? How did she know he was the one? How did either of them know anything?

They just knew.

It doesn't seem possible. They didn't have enough information to be able to know. Not the way they were constructed in the old days. They didn't have the tools. And even if they'd had them, they wouldn't have known how to use them.

Maybe it's not that. Maybe we're reading them wrong. The information that survived from those times is incomplete, you know, so when we reanimate them, when we inhabit them, there are gaps. We might not be getting a complete and accurate picture.

Well … they did seem awfully uncertain at times …

And whether our knowledge of them is fragmented or not, how can their knowing what they knew of each other be the thing that disturbs you? And not that he was struggling to complete that puzzle when the answers should have been immediately accessible from the air around him? Not that he was having to eat and drink—what were those things they put in their mouths anyway?—in order to continue living? Not all those cars they needed to move from place to place? Or their inability to fight the force which kept them pinned to their planet? I had almost forgotten all those things.

And I couldn't remember any of them. But those mysteries made far more sense than this knowing what could not possibly be known.

But the question is, did any of that, or the others we reconstructed and ran simultaneously, help you decide? You have been delaying this for eons.

Time is infinite. We won't run out of it. Infinity, it's the only thing we won't run out of. I think we need to see more. To be more. No need to be hasty.

If you say so.

Do you disagree? Once we proceed, once a decision is made, there's no going back.

I neither agree nor disagree. I am merely … patient.

Then let's keep going.

Sylvia couldn't open her eyes, even though she wanted, oh, how she wanted, to open them. But she was unable to summon the strength, barely had enough even for a coherent thought. And yet, she was still aware, though she was uncertain how she was aware, as she hadn't raised her lids once since entering the room, that the darkness without matched her darkness within. Only a few blinking lights kept that darkness from being total, she knew that as well, even though she'd never seen them blink, not even when her lids were intermittently lifted so her condition could be checked, for her eyes, well, they were beyond seeing. Those lights twinkled like stars, stars that felt like home, stars that comforted her, as if she had always lived among them, stars she knew very well, as well as she knew her own soul, without knowing how she knew them very well.

Their glow cast barely perceptible shadows upon her face, a face smoother than she'd thought it would remain for her to have ended up in such a place as this, not that she'd ever thought she'd end up in a place like this. They'd made themselves a promise, the two of them, she and her lover, that neither ever would. They'd made a pact, in fact, one they'd hoped they'd never need, but swore to each other would be fulfilled if necessary. But then life intervened, speeding up and sneaking upon them before they saw it coming, and they had no choice. And now that Sylvia was beyond doing any of the choosing, Jane, poor Jane, had to do the choosing for her.

Unable to see, unable to move, there was little for Sylvia to do save listen to the hums, the whirrs, the beeps of the sustaining machines which surrounded her, and the answering call and response of the meat symphony within—the air passing through her lungs, the blood coursing through her veins, the crackle of electricity allowing her to think those thoughts, none moving with the force they once had, but with enough, just enough. She was amazed that body continued to function at all, even as a part of her, a part she'd never noticed before, was also amazed that it had ever functioned in the first place. Bodies were messy things, and that hers had survived this long as the vehicle for the part that mattered was miraculous.

She became aware that beneath those sounds, barely audible, hid the sound of crying. As that sound came closer, grew louder, she recognized the maker of them. She wanted to sit up, to reach out, to place a hand against a cheek, to make the tears stop. But she could do none of those things. She could only lie there as she knew one of them eventually would, and listen, and be grateful. She'd known this was coming. It was foretold by the promise they'd made. But that didn't make it any less of a surprise when it finally arrived.

She could hear the weeping grow louder, though no closer, for they were already close enough that she could feel dampness on her face, tears which were not her own, and she knew that if she opened her own eyes, if she could somehow regain that power, she would see *her* eyes, the eyes of the one she knew so well, the eyes she'd chosen to gaze into forever (a forever which had been sadly shortened), above her, damp and overflowing. But though she strained, though she exerted all that remained within her, she could not even do that.

She hoped her lover knew she'd do that if she could.

She knew her lover knew she'd do that if she could, and knew it with a certainty which made all her earlier certainties only faith.

Then, interrupting their reunion, there rose the voice of another, a stern voice, and when it spoke with words Sylvia could not make out, that crying stopped for a moment, so there came a deafening silence which was almost unbearable, but then a cacophony followed to fill it which was more painful than the silence—yelling both from the one she loved, and from an angry voice, no, two angry voices, neither of which she recognized.

The voices grew louder, but no matter how much she concentrated, she could not understand what they were saying, for she was beyond concentration, behind understanding. She was adrift in a sea of her brain's own making, and as she struggled to make sense of the world around her, a world she could not see—but felt as if another would let her, she could, she could—those voices grew more guttural, grunting rather than speaking, and then her bed shook, as if others were bumping against it, others she could not stop, wrestling with another she could not protect, and she tried in the center of this chaos with all her soul, all her remaining will, to rise, to help, to protect ... but could not. For whatever remained of her was simply not enough.

And then the room was silent again, silent save for the sounds from the gleaming machinery without which tried to keep her from dying and messy machinery within which was doing its best to disobey.

A room in which, though together they'd chosen another path, she knew she would die alone.

Jane had never done anything illegal in her life—well, except for the way she *lived* her life, but why should that be illegal, they had no right—and now, this was the time to take that step, because something illegal was being done to her. Well … not *illegal* illegal, not literally illegal, but definitely immoral and definitely something that should have been made illegal long ago, and someday would be. She knew that with a certainty, wishful thinking aside, knew that humanity would one day be beyond this, beyond barriers of laws, of concrete, of flesh—of flesh?—though she was unsure why that certainty beyond faith should be instilled within her now, considering how bleak things looked. Considering what she was considering doing.

More than merely considering. *Actually* doing. That's what they had pushed her to.

She'd bought an outfit that looked like something she thought a nurse would wear, wriggled into it in her car in the hospital parking lot, waited at night until she saw a legitimate nurse step outside for a cigarette break, and then slipped past her and inside before the door could shut, into the hospital where she was forbidden to be. The hospital where a photo of her was pinned to the wall by the front security desk. Where Sylvia lay in a bed, her wishes ignored, being kept alive in a way she would never have chosen.

Nothing was going to keep the two of them separate. Nothing was going to keep Jane from doing what her love alone could not. Nothing.

The corridor revealed off the rear lot was unfamiliar to her, looking nothing like the maze beyond the front entrance out of which she had been escorted so many times. She felt lost, but it was necessary that she feel lost. For here there were no guards to stop her from wandering, and that was all that mattered. She trusted she'd find her way. She'd been lost before she found Sylvia, and yet she'd found her, hadn't she? Being lost was but a temporary stage before what mattered. The world would not be so unkind as to prevent her from fulfilling her mission.

She entered a stairwell—she didn't feel she could dare risk one of the elevators, worried she'd be too visible there—and walked up with what she hoped would seem to anyone who saw her to be a nurse's determination rather than a madwoman's urgency. No one spotted her, though, and so she made it safely to what she remembered as Sylvia's floor. Then a wave of horror passed through her as she thought—what if they'd moved her in the week since her last visit?

But—surely they wouldn't have, for where else would they have moved her *to*? The hospital was already doing all it could, and Sylvia wasn't going to get better, so there was only one other place for Sylvia to move on to from here, and Jane didn't want to have to think about it. Not yet. Not until she had to. Because it would have meant Jane had failed her, and she wasn't sure she could bear knowing that. But at least ... she wouldn't have to bear it for long.

She exited on a corridor without a view of the nursing station, for which she was grateful—as she could probably be taken as a nurse by those who'd never seen her face before, but not them, not them—and made it to the remembered room with no false turns, which surprised her, because luck was never usually on her side. Well, except for having found Sylvia.

Sylvia.

She lay in the bed in the dark, her breathing more a series of arhythmic gasps than the gentle flow of air, the sound of which had helped Jane fall asleep all the years since they'd gotten together. Wires and tubes led from the body she knew so well to the machines which surrounded her. Her eyes were closed, her face expressionless. Somewhere inside was Sylvia, but her body, it could have passed for dead.

This was the end they'd promised they'd keep each other from. They'd had a pact, promised they'd never let it progress like this, never let these people get their hands on either one of them. Though if she were honest with herself, Jane, being the older of the two, had always thought, if they'd erred and let things get this far, *she'd* be the one in the hospital bed, with Sylvia doing for her what she couldn't do for herself ... but one doesn't get to choose.

She stood by Sylvia's side, ready for what she was meant to do, but found herself unable to reach into her pocket for the hypodermic. It had to be done, she knew it had to be done, but her hand would not obey. All she could do was cry. Her tears struck Sylvia's cheek, making it appear as if she were the one crying. She wondered whether Sylvia could sense the dampness on her face. She wondered whether Sylvia even knew Jane was there. Whether either of them was there.

Neither of them believed there was anything after this life, they'd discussed the matter many times, but as there would soon be nothing left of this one, Jane knew … she'd better start pretending.

She was about to place a hand against her lover's cheek to draw strength for the next step when the door behind her slammed open. She knew they'd come, so that was no surprise—she just didn't know they'd come so soon. Before they could reach her, she grabbed the railing on Sylvia's bed with one hand, while simultaneously reaching into a pocket for the handcuffs, which she slammed down against her other wrist. But she wasn't fast enough, and before she could attach herself to the bed, they pulled at her arm and twisted it behind her back. They knew who she was, shouting her name, shouting other things which she couldn't believe they'd dare to shout, words she'd been called many times before, but not here, not now.

Jane went limp, dropping to the ground, uncertain even as she fell whether she'd done it deliberately to prevent herself from being dragged off, or if her knees had buckled from the rush of emotions.

Down on the linoleum, curled into a ball, she screamed at them, cursed them, demanded they think about what they were doing, but none of that stopped them doing it, no matter how loudly she insisted she loved Sylvia, how they couldn't possibly be so inhumane, how they should let the two of them be, regardless of what Jane's estranged family had insisted. Couldn't they see? Didn't they understand? They would someday, they all would someday. She knew it. *She knew it.* But that helped little now.

They ignored her words as they yanked her to the door. And as she was pulled from the room, she kept fighting, kept foolishly hoping they'd find it in their hearts to let her fulfill her promise, but most of all kept her eyes on Sylvia, only on Sylvia, until the door slammed shut and she saw her no more.

That was terrible. It can't possibly be true. Can it? Were they really once like that? Were we really once like that?

Once like what? Bound in bodies? Or blind to what that imprisonment did to them? Both, I fear. But it doesn't matter whether it's true or not. We're beyond that. We don't need to have anything to do with them.

That's not really something we can choose. They either were us ... or were not. Facts are facts. History is history. It's not a matter of choice.

Of course we can choose. We're no more required to believe in them than we are to accept the truth of a myth, or the laws laid down by a religion. Besides ... the information we have ... who knows whether it's accurate? There are holes. There are mysteries. Didn't you sense them?

Our presence ... it seems to be filling those holes. We're doing more than watching untampered recreations. We became a part of them. We're not the only ones sensing things. Didn't you sense them sensing us? They're aware of what we're doing. They're aware of what we're trying to decide. So we're not getting a perfect picture of how they really were. The evidence that was left behind by those we once were ... we've tampered with it. Infected it. Our trail from there to here is no longer true.

Oh, there's been some transference perhaps. They surely did not have that certainty we're picking up about times to come. Our times. We're bleeding through. But enough of it remains true. Enough for you to decide.

I know.

You still have to decide.

Yes. I know. So ... we can be what we want to be? We can be what we are? We already are what we are.

But that's not what this has been about. That's not what we're trying to decide. We've been embodying them to determine whether to become what we are not yet.

I don't know that we're ready.

Then it's a good thing we have all the time in the universe. Time enough to replay every one of them if necessary.

I'm not sure I could bear many more of them. They feel so ... constricting. How were they ever able to stand it? We, at least, have a choice, but they, they had none.

It doesn't seem as if they could stand it. Maybe that's what drove them mad. Maybe that's why we two are all that's left. But that doesn't matter now. What matters is, since you've yet to decide ... do we dive in for more?

We must. We'll dive. We'll learn.
We'll choose.

Gwendolyn is a genius, something the world long ago acknowledged, as any scan of the Internet would reveal, but she'd never consider calling herself one. The scientists on whose shoulders she stands, those are the geniuses. She sees herself as someone merely making real what those others had already proven possible, for everything she's achieved over the years seems obvious to her even as the world calls it miraculous. She wonders, as she rehearses one final time in her head the presentation she's about to give, the momentous step she is about to take, why she's thinking of herself in those terms now. She'd never used the world genius to describe herself, would never think that way, so for a moment she's confused, feeling not quite herself at the exact moment she needs to feel most herself.

Perhaps it's her old fear, one she'd thought she'd long gotten past, suddenly asserting itself again as she prepares to stand before a crowd and speak, something she's never much liked doing because of the way the looks on their faces would sometimes signal they had too many questions about the way she presented herself to be.

Perhaps something else.

On another day, without the pressure of what was about to occur urging her to get on with it, she might have paused to examine this feeling more closely, figured out why she was having thoughts which seemed not her own. But she had no time for that now. And so, as best as she could, she shook off whatever it was, and raised her head to look out once more at the reporters who surrounded her now that the culmination of her work was at hand.

Studying their faces, she wished she could have found a different way. She wished the others in the scientific community would have listened, allowed her that. But those whom she'd thought her peers but had proved not to be felt her latest findings ridiculous, didn't want to help her let the world know of this project through the usual sources, so she'd had to pursue other means. She'd always scoffed at those who'd choose to reach out through the popular press rather than scientific journals, but she was beyond that now. The whole world had to get beyond that.

It was time to move on.

She activated the equipment behind her, and the hum as the lights flickered and intensified quieted the murmuring of the reporters. It was as if a galaxy was unfolding before them, and she found surprising comfort there. She wondered why. Reluctantly, she turned from it, turned to them who would let the rest of the world know.

We are far more than our bodies, she explained to them. This is nothing new, she said. We have always been more than the meat which imprisons us. But until now, there has been no way to unlock the prison gate. Until now, the body ruled the spirit. Until now, there was no way to become immortal.

She could tell they were confused. This sounded to them like New Age nonsense. This was not what they'd come for. She was, after all, a scientist. A genius. (Where had that come from again? Enough.) But Gwendolyn knew they wouldn't have come if they'd known what they were coming for.

Our only hope for survival when the world burns up isn't rockets, she told them. Not generation starships to carry us to another Earth far away. We have no need of other Earths. We can have the universe. Because only meat needs metal. The mind does not.

The mind need no longer be at war with the body in which it is trapped. The mind can be free. The mind can span galaxies.

The words she spoke did not seem like the kind of words she'd speak—they were far more philosophical than she was comfortable with—but they were the only words she seemed to have left. Good thing she had more than words.

She raised a hand to the equipment behind her and explained what was going to happen even though she knew they could not understand. But she had written it all out, provided documentation, blueprints, everything necessary for others to replicate what was about to occur. She attached the wires to her temples, her ankles, her wrists, her heart. And she told them goodbye, that after this meeting, she would be able to tell them no more, that it was up to them to spread the word of what they were about to see, so others could join her, so no one ever need feel imprisoned again, so no goodbye would ever be permanent.

And then she pressed the button.

She crumpled to the ground, her head striking a corner of the podium on her way down, but no matter. Some of the journalists leapt forward to check on her, see what had gone wrong, not understanding that all had gone right. Others remembered their roles, which they'd later come to regret, then later come to not, and kept snapping photos.

Let them.

Gwendolyn looked down upon the body she'd abandoned, the body she had wrestled with for too long, and was glad to be rid of it.

Would they tell her story? She smiled, surprised she could still feel the sensation of smiling when she had nothing left with which to smile. Ah, yes. They would tell her story. Her bifurcated life and apparent death would make sure of that. And eventually, someone would understand the documentation she had left behind, figure out what she had done, and join her. Others would follow.

And who knows what might happen then?

⚓

We have much to be thankful for.

That we do. Those bodies were uncomfortable. Unwieldy. Unnatural.

Well ... that last is something they can't be accused of. They were natural, all right.

And they had all the flaws that came with being natural. How did they ever survive without going mad?

They didn't. Survive, that is. Not more than a fraction of them anyway. But luckily, by the time the world went away, enough of them had decided to become us. Or what was to mix and merge and coalesce eventually become us.

Coalesce ... yes. We are all who remain made two. Without bodies to keep us apart, without the membrane of flesh between us, why not? Once those walls began to fall, why let any other walls keep us apart? It wasn't until the barriers of the spirit were shown to be unnecessary that we could see they were even more claustrophobic.

And yet ...

And yet? Am I not convincing you?

I feel the tug, I really do, sense the gravity of consciousness calling, pulling us together. But still ... I hesitate.

Inhabiting the psyches of the billions past, or what remains of them for us to know, was of no help to you?

Nothing we saw answered the question, will we be lonely when we are no longer two? There has never before been a universe inhabited by only one.

Well ... except ... you know.

Yes ... well. It's not the same thing, though.

No. No, it's not. However ... procrastination ill becomes you. It's time for you to decide. Can you really deny it? That this, that that, is what was and is meant to be? Isn't that what we learned from inhabiting those who came before? Isn't that what this sorting through our particles has been all about?

Yes, you're right ... but ... I'm afraid.

So were they, you know. But they were afraid because they were apart. And if we weren't afraid, we wouldn't be human.

But we're not human. Not anymore.

Oh, but we are. We are human still, Nothing has changed. What matters is the wine, not the bottle.

That makes no sense. We have no need to drink any more. We are the stuff of stardust now.

Hush. Listen to them. Then let go.

Julian and Barbara and Jane and Sylvia and Gwendolyn and a million million others felt a sudden disturbance as they lived their lives—or perhaps it wasn't their lives which were interrupted at all, perhaps it was merely an unexpected pause in a shadow play, a breach of their recreations as they'd been worn like a mask during the search for truth in making this ultimate decision. But whether alive or illusion, real or only memory, at this point, after more time had passed by far than the entire race had ever lived, was there really a difference?

Julian and Barbara, too old to be living independently, having moved in now with their oldest daughter, looked at each other with smiles, then up at the wall to the completed crossword puzzle they'd had framed so long ago, then back to each other, their skin tingling—

Jane, standing over Sylvia's grave, her trembling hand pressed to the stone engraved with a date of death from decades earlier, felt an electric charge pass through her, turned around because she felt someone was there, saw no one, but knew, without a doubt, that someone *was* there—

Gwendolyn, drifting away from Earth to circle the sun, paused in formless wonder, suddenly connected to a future she had dreamed into being, and quivered with ecstatic urging—

And Dana and Masud and Luc and Robert and Mary Jo and Li Xia and Jeremy and Hani and Amelia and Felipe and a billion others stopped what they were doing, suddenly unconstrained by the scripts of what they thought were their lives, and cried out:

"What are you waiting for? Get on with it!"

And the final two became the only one, transforming into a fine specimen of hypermagical ultraomnipotence, and delighted itself, no longer alone, by going off to explore a hell of a good universe.

AN END TO
PERPETUAL MOTION

MARK SAMUELS

Having enjoyed great success with the last play of mine—a 'screw-ball' comedy—that ran in the West End and which later transferred to Broadway, a Hollywood mogul (whose name is not pertinent to this narrative) offered me a contract to write 'talkie' scripts for the motion-picture industry on behalf of his major film studio in Los Angeles. I had recently gone through a painless divorce, and since there was nothing to keep me in London, I accepted the mogul's offer and decided to relocate and break with my past entirely, with a view to settling permanently in the United States.

I chose to make my passage across the Atlantic in a liner, the *S.S. Pyrrho*.

The ship sailed from Southampton, in excellent weather, and I began the first of my half-dozen weeks of life on board by establishing a regular daily routine of writing drafts in the morning, walking the deck mid-afternoon, reading until dinner and then taking cocktails in the Art-Nouveau themed "Parisian" bar in the first class section.

Only at the end of the first week did I notice the first stirrings of my old affliction—insomnia—creeping up on me. I cannot say exactly whether it was a result of the strange environment, the motion of the vessel, or simply bad luck that brought on its resurgence. I at first delayed, however, seeking the assistance of the ship's doctor and it was as a consequence of this that I had my initial encounter with Ignatius Zeno.

Having woken for the second day in a row at just after four in the morning, I decided, on this occasion, to walk around the ship and attempt to tire myself back into drowsiness. Previously I had lain in bed, futilely, and not regained sleep for another three hours.

Pacing the deserted internal passages and stairwells seemed horribly labyrinthine and claustrophobic, so I went out onto the decks for relief and fresh air.

The moonless night sky was clear, with thousands of piercing stars, and beneath it stretched the vast, dark expanse of ocean. I have seen the sea described by a writer as the matrix of creation, whose voice of liquid thunder sometimes murmurs deep in our own blood, and on that night I could well believe it.

Eventually, I found myself wandering into the "Parisian" bar. At that hour, naturally, no steward service was provided and I expected to find it as deserted as the rest of the ship. But it was here, sitting alone in a side-booth framed by stained-glass panels, that I first saw Ignatius Zeno, with a bottle of gin set before him on the table. I watched him pour a measure of the spirit into a tumbler and drain it rapidly. Then he took out a crumpled packet of cigarettes from one of his pockets, placed one between his lips and patted himself—to no avail—in search of matches.

I wish at that moment I had gone back to my cabin. The whole course of one's subsequent life can turn on what seems, at the time, to be only an insignificant gesture of common courtesy.

I stepped forward, offering him a light with some remark or other.

He turned as if surprised, though whether he had been really unaware of my presence, or whether he feigned his reaction for the effect—I mean in order to excuse his having disregarded me until now—well, I suspected the latter.

"Thanks," he said. "Sit down and join me. It is late, but have a drink."

I found it impossible to place his accent.

I lit his cigarette. He slid another glass across the table towards me and half-filled it with gin.

At first I took him for an actor (perhaps a consequence of being so involved with the stage and seeing the species lurking everywhere).

I found it difficult to determine his age. At one moment I would have guessed thirty, but then, as he shifted his position across from me, perhaps he was even as old as fifty or sixty. Although his thick black hair certainly looked dyed, his skin was of an olive complexion—with only two barely perceptible creases on his forehead, and no lines elsewhere. His face was clean-shaven. His nose was ever so slightly askew, as if broken long ago and not reset. He wore a pair of oval shaped, silver-framed spectacles, but the lenses were of no great thickness and did not distort the cold, ice-blue eyes behind them. There was only one definite aspect that made me lean towards the idea he was older than he appeared. The two rows of teeth, all perfectly straight, small and brilliantly white, made me think of newly acquired dentures.

"Sorry," I said. "Jolly rude. Should have introduced myself. Ambrose Hamilton. How do you do?"

My name seemed not to register at all with him, so I dismissed my initial suspicion of his being an actor—or the idea of any connection with theatricals at all, even as a playgoer.

"I'm Ignatius Zeno," he replied.

Unusual name, I thought. But it signified nothing to me. Except perhaps he might be Greek. But I didn't go into the matter.

"I hope," I went on, "you don't mind my asking, but our meeting like this prompts it. Has insomnia ever troubled you? Keeps me up something rotten I can tell you."

Zeno took a drag on his cigarette, as if seeking time to consider the matter more fully.

"A long time ago perhaps. Not that I need much sleep now. If you're wondering why I happen to be here drinking in this bar in the middle of the night, it's just that I like to make sure things are moving along as they should. Especially in the dark. You know?"

"You mean this ship?"

"Precisely. Can't tolerate the thought of any delays."

Everything was very 'matter-of-fact' in the way he said this, and there was no sign of agitation when he made the remark, but it struck me as odd. I hadn't really thought about it before, but I supposed that a passenger (at least one not on deck or looking out a porthole) might fail to notice whether a liner had slowed down—or even stopped altogether. On a ship of this size, unless the weather was really dreadful that is, one hardly noticed its continued forward motion.

"I expect there's a night crew," I said.

"Hmmm."

"Up on the bridge I mean. A skeleton staff or something."

"Quite right. Maybe there is."

He let out a hollow laugh.

Rather absurdly, I felt as if I had walked into a Boris Karloff motion picture. The lack of sleep, the isolation, the silence surrounding us, not to forget the gin, was making me think morbidly.

And Zeno himself certainly didn't help. I thanked him for the gin and went back to my cabin. I didn't sleep well.

The following morning I asked the purser about Zeno. He seemed put out at the mention of gin being consumed—wanting to know if it was duty-free brought on board or from the galley supplies—but any notion I might have had about a spectral encounter was quickly dispelled. He told me that Zeno had travelled on the *S.S. Pyrrho* several times, at intervals, while he had been serving aboard her. Quite what line of business Zeno was in, the purser couldn't say, but he was always very generous with his tips and a man of considerable means.

Later on I went along to see the ship's doctor, and he gave me a bottle of soluble sleeping pills. Passing the time with him, I brought Zeno's name up again.

"Peculiar chap," he said. "Avoids me like the deuced plague. Several times I've seen him coming along the deck towards me and then going in the opposite direction. No idea what I've done to offend him. Does the same thing every time he's on board."

Although Zeno now comprised something of a minor mystery during the voyage, I can't say that I thought a great deal more about him. I was too busy with my own work during the mornings and the afternoon and, during the evenings, found myself subsequently in the company of the notorious Montague sisters.

This pair, identical twins, were the most glamorous flappers of the 1920s so-called "Bright Young Things," and were celebrated across

London for their various treasure hunts, themed costume parties, for gatecrashing Irish stately homes, and for their riotous practical jokes. It was said that they had both once danced the Charleston to a tearful collapse during a private absinthe-cocktail party thrown by novelist Sinclair Xavier at Kettner's in Soho.

If I am to be brutally honest then I must add, however, that they sometimes filled me with alarm.

Although both were incredibly beautiful (and nearly impossible to tell apart) they seemed to exist constantly on the verge of chaos; as if they wanted to smash everything up just for the sake of having nothing better to do. They were equally charming—until they got hold of drink to consume. Having done so they then suddenly regarded themselves like big-game hunters on a moral Safari; their mission to bring down by pleasurable violence all civilised standards. The purser lived in fear of them, and even the Captain refused to have them at his table, despite the illustrious, ancient (even sea-going) English family which had lately disowned them. The twins simply wouldn't leave me alone once they heard of my theatrical and motion picture connections, and even threatened to trail me across the continent once we were in the United States.

It was around midnight, a few days after my meeting with Zeno that I saw him again in the 'Parisian' bar, sitting in his usual booth, a bottle of gin in front of him. The Montague sisters were with me and both were extremely tight, having, since mid-afternoon when they woke up from the night before, started in on more of the vast quantity of liquor they had stashed inside their cabin for the trans-Atlantic voyage.

"I say," Lady Gertrude said, "who is that awful specimen of humanity in the booth other there?"

"Doesn't look to me like he belongs in First Class," said Lady Penelope.

(I should point out that any identification I make as to which of the two was speaking at this time must be regarded as provisional.)

"It's a chap called Ignatius Zeno," I said. "Met him the other night. Quite a mystery man by all accounts. Supposed to be wealthy."

"Sounds foreign. Looks like he's a yokel or something. Dressed all wrong. Not in evening dress." One or other of them went on.

"Let's not bother him. Here, have another drink," I said.

The first part of my suggestions neither interested nor affected them at all.

"Introduce us to him 'Brosie," Lady Gertrude insisted.

"Do," said Lady Penelope. "Or we'll cause a scene."

I sighed and wandered over to where Zeno was sitting, with the Montague sisters in tow.

If a gentleman is unfamiliar with their Ladyships' reputation for being dangerously unbalanced, then the usual initial reaction to an encounter with them is one of admiration and wonder at their extreme beauty. Their excessive lifestyles had not yet taken any physical toll upon their charms. Indeed, both Ladies Gertrude and Penelope had come to take a favourable response for granted. And so they were rather put out when—after I made the introductions—Zeno looked them up and down with near-indifference. He had made the polite effort to get his feet, but that was the sum total of the tribute he paid to their sex.

"How do you do?" he said. "Care for some gin?"

Lady Gertrude examined the label on the bottle.

"This is beastly stuff. How can you bring yourself to drink it?" she said. "Are you some sort of Uranian poet?"

Lady Penelope then slowly tipped the bottle over and watched the contents drain across the table and flow onto the floor. She snapped her fingers at a passing steward, who shortly returned with another, more expensive brand.

This grisly behaviour didn't appear to discomfit Zeno very much, who turned back to the same topic of conversation he had broached with me when last we had met.

"If any of you do notice some sign of the ship slowing down I'd be obliged if you'd advise me. You can always find me in cabin six, upper deck."

"So you say. Look here," said Lady Gertrude, "you're not some rotten stowaway are you?"

Quite why she asked this question, other than to be offensive, was beyond me. It had already been made clear to her that Zeno had every right to be onboard.

"Oh no, not at all. That's not why I asked. I just like to be sure there's no cause for delay," he said.

"Where is it you said you come from?" Lady Penelope asked. "Can't quite place your accent. Sounds like it's from all over."

"You might think of me now as a citizen of the world. Actually the country of my birth no longer exists."

"I hate all that cosmopolitan rot," Lady Gertrude said. "Might as well be a gypsy. Are you a gypsy? Do you live in a caravan? Do you make a living by telling fortunes?"

I'm afraid the conversation rather went around in circles, with the Montague sisters trying to provoke him and with Zeno droning on about the importance of the ship keeping to the scheduled time of its Atlantic crossing. All three were talking entirely at cross-purposes. I said very little. After some ten minutes or so of the same thing the Ladies Gertrude and Penelope drunkenly accused Zeno of being an utter bore and a beast.

"We're leaving. We have to change. There's a bijou costume party going on in cabin twelve hosted by 'Biffo' Burford, the Earl, you know. Frightfully amusing. Lashings of Bolly. Are you coming 'Brosie?" they said, alternating the sentences between one another.

I declined the invitation and they looked rather put out. As a matter of fact their Ladyships' eyes suddenly manifested that legendary steely look that—or so the story goes—had even once made the famous Catholic author Sinclair Xavier decide he had probably said quite enough about distributism during a public lecture in which the sisters happened to be sat in the front row of the audience.

Nevertheless, I remained, whilst they departed. Noisily.

"Look," I said to Zeno, "I'm awfully sorry about all that. They had no right to speak to you in that fashion. But they're both rather tight, you know."

Zeno asked me for a match and then went on:

"Oh don't let it trouble you. Young people are always the same, generation after generation. The basic principle's the same—epicurean. Only the faces change," he replied.

"Jolly decent of you to take it like that."

Zeno puffed at his cigarette and poured us both some more gin.

"You're something of a philosopher, then?" I said.

"In my time. You never get to the end of it though—once you start. Someone else always comes up with a clever new objection you yourself haven't quite dealt with—logically I mean. But, well ..."

He left the remark hanging between us. I'm afraid all this stuff isn't quite in my line so I changed the subject.

"I understand you travel quite a bit on this route," I said.

"Oh yes, it's a very reliable mode of transport. Very little can go wrong with a ship like this. They've also learnt a lot since 1912."

"What will you do in the United States when we arrive there?"

"Cross it by locomotive."

"Ah, I'm heading for California myself. I expect to be in Holly-wood indefinitely, writing scripts for the talkies."

"And then I'll catch another vessel, across the Pacific via Nippon."

I was becoming confused. He didn't seem to have a final destination in mind.

By now the stewards were clearing up and keen on turfing everyone out for the night.

He suggested we finish drinking the bottle of gin in his cabin. I was all for a nightcap or two, and what with finishing the evening off with the sleeping pills the ship's doctor had given me; at last getting a decent night's sleep when I left Zeno. I had no doubt, on the other hand, that the Montague sisters would be partying ferociously until well after dawn.

We walked along the corridors, Zeno with gin bottle in hand, rolling with the ever-so-slight motion of the ship, although how much of our swaying was due to our alcohol intake is an open question.

Zeno's cabin was only a few doors along from my own.

Once inside we slumped down in a couple of easy-chairs and he poured a refill of gin into my glass, adding a splash of tonic from a siphon he took out of a small mahogany cabinet.

"So you're staying in Nippon—um—Japan for a while?" I said.

"No, not at all, just passing through the country before I cross over to Vladivostok."

"Isn't that where ..."

"Yes," he said, cutting in. "The eastern terminus of the trans-Siberian railroad."

"What then?" I said. "The Orient Express?"

Zeno frowned. I thought I might have inadvertently offended him with this off-hand attempt at humour.

"There's no connection to that service at Moscow," he replied. "I might take the express to Berlin or Prague. Then on to Paris I think, then Boulogne or Calais, the ferry to ..."

I interrupted him.

"I get the idea. Look here old chap, you're starting to sound like Phileas Fogg. Is that what's going on? Some sort of solo round-the-world thing?"

Zeno didn't reply but stubbed out his cigarette and went into the adjoining bathroom, excusing himself.

While he was occupied I wandered around his cabin for something to do. On top of the cabinet from which he'd produced the soda siphon there were a dozen passports or travel documents or visas. All were in Zeno's name. The nationality of the holder seemed to vary according to local convenience. So, too, the age given on them was inconsistent. Only the photograph of the bearer identified them as all being the same man. I heard the door to the bathroom rattle, stepped away from the cabinet, and dropped back into my chair.

Zeno emerged, his face still damp.

"Having travelled so much I expect you speak quite a few languages," I said.

"That's right. You know, sometimes I can't quite tell what language I'm actually thinking in, though I do when I'm having a conversation with someone."

Something occurred to me. It was ridiculous, but I couldn't get the thought out of my head. Due to the gin, no doubt, I blurted it out:

"You never stop, do you? All the time you go around and around the world, over and over and over. Isn't that it?"

Zeno frowned again. For a moment I thought he might tell me to get out. He looked over at the travel documents spread out on the cabinet top, as if wondering why he had been so careless as to leave such clues lying around in plain view.

"It's dangerous for me to stop now. The thing has been going on for far too long."

"But surely … but surely there were times you stopped that were outside your control?"

"Up to an hour's delay. That's the maximum time allowed before I'm caught up with. No more than that. Which is why I always travel on overnight services. Sea vessel, locomotive, or motor-coach usually. I can't afford to take risks. Naturally I fear accidents."

I swigged back a large part of my drink. The fellow was, I thought, off his head. He had to be quite wealthy to keep up this lifestyle, but was still clearly the victim of derangement. It was astonishing that he hadn't been locked up in a mental sanatorium. Perhaps he had been. Perhaps he'd escaped years ago and that was at the root of all this. His next remark even seemed to confirm my suspicion:

"It's Doctor Prozess you see," Zeno said.

My gaze involuntarily wandered to the door, calculating how quickly I could get to it if he turned violent. He was probably talking about his alienist.

"I doubt that you've heard the name," he went on. "But he's behind it all."

"I see."

"You've got to play him at his own game. I imagine you're thinking that the world is in continual motion anyway, spinning on its axis as it hurtles in orbit around the sun? But that's a precise route. Mine here on Earth varies quite a bit."

"Ah, yes."

"Likewise with our bodies. It's all a question of motion. Internal and external. But always with a slight variation, heartbeat, digestion, breathing and so on. When motion begins to slow we decay, and when it ceases we die. Do you understand?"

"Indeed so."

"The consequences are cumulative though—when you wilfully thwart his design I mean. Doctor Prozess marks you out, waiting to strike back, tracking you across the long grey centuries. Exceptions to the rule of universal synthesis aren't allowed."

The poor man was talking nonsense. I had the feeling that he had been wanting to confide all this utterly bizarre stuff running around inside his head to someone for a very long time since his escape. He was not conscious of playing a role—just like those monomaniacs who really think they're Napoleon and even dress up like him. I remembered reading somewhere that the safest course of action with such people was to humour them.

"That certainly makes sense," I said.

Then events took an even more alarming turn.

Zeno had wandered across to the porthole and, glancing outside, became highly agitated.

"We've stopped! All this time I've been talking we've been motionless. Come here, see for yourself!"

His voice was high-pitched and frantic.

My first instinct was that he was imagining it, as part of his delusions, but when I got up from my chair and he stood aside so that I could see for myself, I discovered he was quite right. For some reason, the ship had come to halt. It must have taken some ten or so minutes to do so, as its inertia gradually ebbed away.

"No time! No time!" he shouted.

This new development, of course, put matters on an entirely new footing. Zeno was agitated beyond belief. There was no telling what he might do. He was already making for the door. For all I knew he could harm someone, even if only himself.

My hand fished around in my jacket pocket and found the small bottle the ship's doctor had given me earlier. While his back was turned I dropped three of the sleeping pills into his half-consumed drink. They fizzed and dissolved.

"Wait a minute," I said. "I'll do all I can to help you. I know how the lifeboats work. I'll get you off safely old chap. Let's have one last drink on it."

I carried across the two glasses of gin and gave him the one with the Mickey Finn. He downed it in one hurried gulp.

We shook hands on the deal.

"I can't sufficiently express how grateful I am to you," he said. "In the past, when I've revealed the truth people have thought me a lunatic."

We were halfway down the corridor when he suddenly keeled over.

I then dragged his unconscious body back to his cabin, took his key, locked him inside, and started back; intending to make my way to the bridge.

To my surprise, I encountered the Captain coming towards me in the opposite direction. He was dressed in green silk pyjamas and slippers, though he was wearing his official headgear (albeit askew). Somewhat bleary-eyed, he'd obviously only just been awakened from a deep sleep. He was accompanied by two other crew members, who were carrying crowbars.

Before I could voice my concerns regarding Zeno, the Captain barked out an order:

"Grab that man! He's coming with us. He's their associate."

And all four of us started off into the bowels of the ship, down the decks, descending flights of stairs and passing through hatchways.

As we did so, the Captain explained the situation.

The Montague sisters, not content with having smashed up cabin twelve during 'Biffo' Burford's fancy-dress party, had gone far below, invaded the engine room, somehow tied up all the stokers, and then disabled the ship's engines.

"You are familiar with the modern flapper mentality," the Captain said, "I ask you—what possible excuse can there be for such behaviour? My God, are they not both daughters of the seventh Earl of Farquhar, whom Nelson called "the noblest of the noble"? Have they no sense of decorum at all?"

The poor Captain had obviously spent too much time of late at sea. A few nights spent in Piccadilly after midnight would have opened his eyes to the glamorous horrors of the Jazz Age and its deleterious effect on the aristocracy. I had no doubt that Lady Gertrude and Lady Penelope had concocted their scheme to halt the ship purely in order to both spite and amuse themselves at Ignatius

Zeno's expense.

We reached the engine room to discover that the Montague sisters had departed a few minutes before our arrival. The stokers were untied, and then drunkenly tried to explain how they had been duped by two young beautiful madwomen and forced to drink vast quantities of liquor against their will, while they were interrogated on the operation of the engines. No permanent damage, however, had been done to the mechanism, and it was restarted successfully shortly afterwards, being idle for an hour and a half in total. Of their Ladyships there was no sign—but a missing lifeboat, and later newspaper reports of disgraceful chaos on the *S.S. Adeimantus*, out of New York and bound for Southampton, provided a solution to the mystery.

As for the greater mystery of Ignatius Zeno; as soon as I had finally explained—as best I could—the situation to the Captain, we both went back to cabin six where I had locked him in some time ago.

Zeno, like their Ladyships, had apparently vanished.

Later, when the coroner made his report, everyone declared that it must have been a hoax. But there, upon the floor, snaking through a pile of crumpled clothes and a pair of shoes, was a thick layer of grey ashes. And, mixed in with the vaguely head-shaped mound of human dust, was a pair of new dentures and silver-framed spectacles. The ashes, it was claimed, were thousands of years old.

For months I suffered from public ridicule, and from newspaper harassment, to the extent I even began to doubt the truth of the matter myself. I wondered whether it were not actually the case, as they all claimed, that the real Ignatius Zeno had jumped overboard, vanishing utterly in the sea, and whether the parody in his cabin was yet another sick prank perpetrated by the notorious Montague sisters.

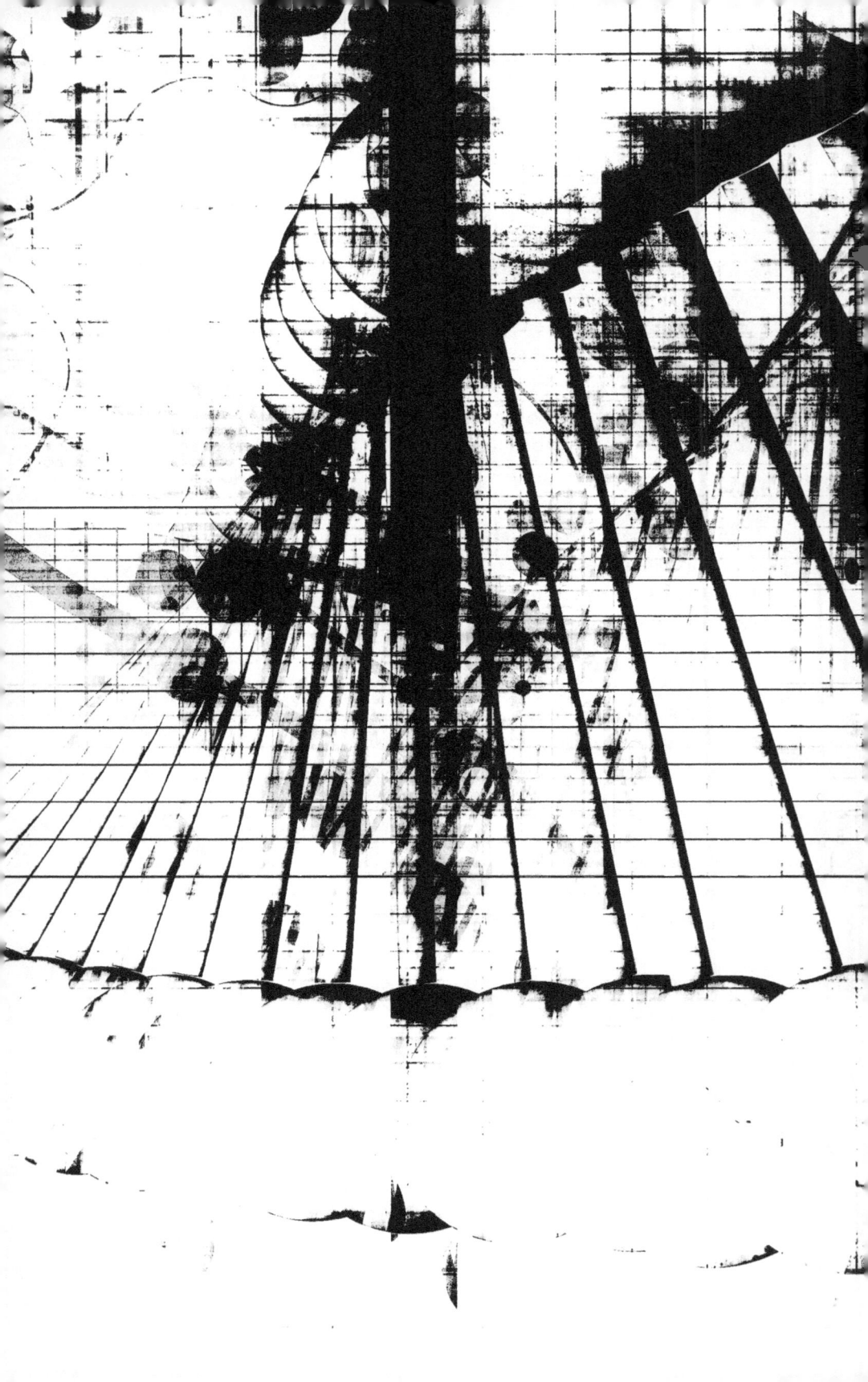

SWIFT TO CHASE

LAIRD BARRON

In medias res part II:

After a hard chase and all-too brief struggle, the Bird Woman of the Adirondacks loomed over me, demonic silhouette, blackest outspread wings tipped in iron; gore-crested and flint-beaked. Her thumbnail-talon poised to spike me through the left eye.

"To know itself, the universe must drink the blood of its children." Her voice cracked like an ice shelf collapsing; it roared across an improbable expanse of inches.

The talon pressed against my iris. It went in and in.

Rewind and power dive from the clouds. Join the story, *in medias res*, part I:

Where in the world is Jessica Mace? That scene when the superlative secret agent gets captured inside the master villain's lair is where. Instead of a secret agent, here's little old me doing my best impression. Rather than a rocket station beneath a dormant volcano, I'd gotten trapped on an estate (1960s Philip K. Dick-esque) nestled among the peaks of the Adirondacks. Cue jazzy intro music; cue rhinestone heels and a dress slit to *here*. My nemesis, billionaire avian enthusiast and casual murderer of humans, Averna Spencer, wasn't playing. Except she *was* playing.

First clue of my imminent demise (more like the fifth or sixth clue, but just go with it): a leather-bound copy of *The Most Dangerous Game* parked on the nightstand of my quarters. Second clue? The woman herself said over the intercom, "Fly, my swift, my sweet. When I catch you, I'm giving you a blood eagle."

Viking history isn't my specialty, but I know enough to not want one.

There I sat, dressed to kill or be killed. The loaner evening gown was a trap. Spencer had set it when she laid the fancy box across the sheets of the poster bed, and I sprang it as I slipped the dress on. Bird-of-paradise-crimson, gilded with streaks of gold and blue, a bronze torc to cover the scar on my neck (so thoughtful of my hostess), and four-inch rhinestone heels amounted to a costume worth more than I'd make in a lifetime unless that lifetime included a winning lotto ticket or sucking millionaire cock on the daily.

The ensemble transcended mere decoration; it reorganized my cells and worked outward like magma rushing through igneous channels. I'd stared at myself in the mirror and come face to face with a starlet. A tad hard-bitten. Close, though. Action heroine on the precipice of unfuckability by Hollywood's standard. Regardless, the illusion of fabulous me radiated heat—live-wire alive.

Yep, slipping into the dress had been to stick my head right through a dangling snare. Call it the price of admission. Too late to change a damned thing that was coming. I grinned like a prizefighter to keep my gorge down. I'd been here before and survived. Double-edged blade, the notion of past as prologue, and so forth. Resilience in prey excited Averna and made her want me that much more.

A girl on the run in a dress and high heels wouldn't run far is what Spencer bet, and why not? She owned the house. The house always wins.

The isolated mountain house of a high-toned serial killer isn't the kind of joint you accidentally wander into. I'd been recruited, seduced, and deployed. Dr. Ryoko and Dr. Campbell (more on my patrons—and their sexy, sexy bodyguard, Beasley—in due course), possessed a special interest in Averna Spencer's activities. My mission was to infiltrate her estate and conduct hostile actions on their behalf.

A few words about our mutual foe:

Averna craved the chase. She wasn't a slasher of (hapless) womenfolk or a sniper of unsuspecting coyotes. She didn't howl at the moon; hadn't been born under a bad sign or suffered childhood trauma. A hunter, nonetheless. Pure predator evolved to the job at hand. Sixty-three kills, if the cobbled-together records told it true. Sixty-three on U.S. soil; only INTERPOL could speak for the body count in Europe where she frequently traveled.

The manifest of persons missing and presumed dead since 1988 included loggers, hikers, ex-military, a baker's dozen hardened criminals, and a former Olympic decathlete. These folks vanished across the US; law enforcement records established the deeds, but the authorities hadn't officially put it together. Unofficially, there were rumors. A retired FBI agent in Houston, a discredited private investigator in Wisconsin, and other assorted kooks, rocked the boat now and again. It came to nothing, as these situations usually do.

The track and field star haunted me. Strapping lad. Last known photograph taken at sunset, ice cream cone in hand (an athlete's notion of decadence), a tall, dark-haired chick hanging on his arm. Track and field dude—let's call him Rocky since he looked a hell of a lot like a Rocky I knew in high school—dressed nicely, smiled nicely. Only missed snagging the bronze medal by hundredths of a second. I imagined how he must've been later, after the kidnapping—alone, lost in a trackless forest. Pressed flat against the trunk of a pine, head cocked, every cord in his neck straining. Then, *slice*.

Rocky the Olympian's tragic story ended the same as the rest. Worm food.

Fast, strong, tough. Hadn't mattered, had it? Can't fight what you don't see coming, can't fight if you're prey. Dharma 101, friends and neighbors. The rabbit runs and the hawk dives.

Where do I fit into the grand scheme? I muck around in the rising tide of cosmic night. I'm hell on wheels. My totem animal is the coyote, the mongoose, my blazon a bloodied Ka-Bar in a clenched fist against a field of black.

Lest I join the dearly departed in their unmarked graves, the moment had come to make myself scarce. The original extraction plan struck me as sketchy at best—on the bright side of the equation, Spencer's houseguests normally returned to the world unharmed. The data led Campbell and Ryoko to theorize that those whom she kidnapped (and I qualified) were subsequently hunted across her estate grounds. Should the operation go pear-shaped, I was to flee Averna Spencer's home and rendezvous at a hunting cabin a mile past the estate's southeast boundary. My patrons had assured me they'd done the math forward and back—it wouldn't come to such an extreme. Bastards.

A grand staircase spiraled down into gothic gloom. Marble raptors guarded the way. I ripped the dress to upper-thigh, removed my heels, and transformed into a new creature; slippery and dangerous.

I hustled through the door and past a phalanx of artificial eggs arranged on the front lawn. Almost did a doubletake. The eggs were outsized and exaggerated, Andy Warhol style; waist-tall, maybe three feet in circumference, cast from milky-lucent porcelain that glowed in the porchlight. The one nearest my left was bisected at its apex, like a hollow rocket missing its conical nose. An egg and a coffin are antipodes of a closed circuit. Made it halfway across the yard before Averna's evil sidekick, Manson, shot me in the ass with a dart from a rifle. She waved when I glanced back. I flipped her the bird (ironic to the bitter end). Strength drained from me like blood from a tapped artery. Five more steps and I sprawled.

Averna rolled me onto my side. She moved her lips against mine in a not-quite kiss. Would've punched her in the throat except whatever Manson had loaded the dart with froze every muscle in my body. I tabled the impulse. She licked the salt of my tears and leaned back to regard me from the shadows. Eyes without a face. Yellow eyes with strange-as-shit pupils. Hawk pupils. I wanted to ask how she'd *known*. Maybe she didn't; and if she didn't, despite her rhetoric, I might escape with my skin.

This feeble hope persisted for less than five seconds.

"The doctors asked you to acquire a certain document, yes? They promised some grand reward for your service; appealed to your sense of honor. Couldn't you detect the evil in their black little hearts? Did you not whiff the deception?"

Had I been capable of speech, I'd have said nobody's perfect, and spat a gob in her eye.

She smiled. "I delivered the formula to them months ago. Payment for your sweet self. I got the best of Campbell and Ryoko, as usual. The formula is worthless, lacking a specific strain of Jurassic protozoa, which, let us pray, no one ever resurrects. Blink if you can hear me."

I'm stubborn, so I glared, bug-eyed defiant. Impossible to tell if she was lying, and if so, how much. My "power" to behold the evil in the human heart doesn't work on women half as well as it does on men, and if she was telling the truth, it didn't work half so well on men as I'd thought.

A sociopath will say anything to make her victims squirm, which meant I dared not believe a word from her lips. Yet, and yet ... I tried to speak; to scream, actually. Had my preparation and training been a ruse? Had those kindly eggheads really double-crossed me? Had their man-at-arms (and my lover) Beasley, participated in the con? Et tu, Beasley? Et tu, you handsome sonofabitch?

Averna said, "None of this is an accident. The doctors do not trade in coincidence and neither do I. We've observed you for many years. Something happened to your mother as a young woman. She met a friend of mine, a foreigner, you might say, who contracted with the CIA to enhance various programs. Lucius was part of an experiment, alongside many of her friends. She and the other surviving test subjects have been remotely monitored since the latter 1970s, as are their offspring. The ... conditions that altered Lucius skipped her firstborn, Elwood, and bloomed within you. Curses can be finicky.

"Did those old goats suggest they knew Lucius's fate? Spoiler alert: mother dearest isn't living in a trailer in Tennessee with a failed country singer. She didn't drink herself to death or get eaten by a bear. I am not privy to the machinations of Campbell and Ryoko. I *do* have my own brand of intuition. My intuition says they murdered Lucius Lochinvar Mace. Did her in in the name of science." She rose and gestured to Manson who lurked nearby.

Manson hoisted me with her arms extended as if I were a crash test dummy. My field of view revolved off its y axis. I went bye-bye into the hollow belly of night.

Backtrack, backtrack. Maybe you're wondering how a nice girl like me ended up in a place like this ... A pair of infamous scientists figured I might be game to solve a mystery and save the world. Unlikely, yet no less so than the rest of the improbable bullshit that increasingly defines my existence. My current boyfriend, the aforementioned Beasley, happened to serve as bodyguard, valet, and moral compass to the renegade doctors. He introduced us. This set the ball rolling. Happy (unhappy) coincidence? As I've come to mutter on a routine basis, there are no accidents.

Most people born prior to 1980 have at least heard of the inseparable duo, Toshi Ryoko and Howard Campbell (erstwhile academic favorites of every male-oriented pop magazine in existence). Renowned for death-defying expeditions, gauche stunts, and outré theories in their heyday; less celebrated of late. The naturalists retired (voluntarily mothballed, as Beasley put it) to a quaintly decrepit New England farm. Ryoko in his wheelchair, Campbell stooped to push. The inseparable duo as drawn by some virtuoso graphic artist; say Mile Mignola or Patch Zircher.

Prior to our first meeting, I did my homework and read the news stories (which traced back into the early '80s), watched myriad videos, and listened to radio programs devoted to their exploits (the *public* exploits; turns out the pair really and truly deserved the "mad scientist" appellation). Iconoclasts and apostates to the hilt. Neither man would go quietly to a nursing home. These two were fated for an exotic demise: they'd vanish in the Bermuda Triangle, or into the Amazon rainforest and leave behind a ravaged campsite, cryptic research notes scattered, a cursed Neolithic medallion dangling from a bush; or, an unmarked government van would whisk them to a black site for a final debriefing.

We got along swimmingly. Didn't mean I'd be a cheerful pawn in their schemes.

"The Shadow of Death slides across the floor," Dr. Campbell said, and nodded at his shoe in a sliver of sunlight.

"The Shadow of Death!" Dr. Ryoko struggled to light a cigarette. His palsy tremors came and went.

"Soon it will crawl onto us and dig in the spurs. Time yet ..."

"... a few years yet. We can do some good."

"*You* can do some good, Jessica. Help us hold back the darkness."

What they wanted wasn't difficult. Hazardous to my health, yes, but not difficult. Some rich lady possessed a formula; a cure for a deadly strain of avian flu, or a recipe to weaponize the virus, nobody could be sure which. Campbell handed me an envelope full of notes and photographs and that's how I came to acquaint myself with the legend of Averna Spencer—AKA the Bird Lady of the Adirondacks, AKA (my addition) the Cuckoo Killer. She'd briefly made a public splash on nightly news programs when they profiled her participation in the emergent wingsuit craze during the late 1990s. As one of the few women rich enough and ballsy enough to leap off cliffs and sail like a flying squirrel, she'd represented a curiosity.

Averna kicked it old school, pre-Information Age—nothing left to chance in a computer database, otherwise Ryoko and Campbell would've enlisted a hacker and done the job by remote. She kept the formula locked in a safe at her residence; a cliff-side mansion-slash-fortified stronghold amid thousands of acres of wilderness. The aforementioned master villain's lair. Called it the Aerie.

The broad owned more land than Ted Turner in his Montana heyday with Jane Fonda and the Atlanta Braves. Closest road lay twenty miles southeast. Traffic came and went via a helicopter pad. Power derived from generators, turbines, and solar panels. Security? Ex-military goons provided by Black Dog; armed drones; bloodhounds and German shepherds. Land mines. The wilderness and its many teeth waited for scraps.

How did the doctors score this information? Dr. Ryoko claimed a contact on the inside. A spy in the house of love. While this shadowy individual didn't possess direct access to the formula, the person had provided a detailed description of the item and the combination to the safe where it currently resided.

My natural skepticism asserted itself. Setting aside reservations regarding the veracity of the alleged spy, why in the hell would Averna Spencer, noted recluse, grant me an audience?

"Never fear, we'll arrange it," Dr. Ryoko said. "You are the mistress of inevitability. The opener of the way. Occult forces magnetize to you."

"Spencer delights in taking things apart. Unbreakable individuals are her weakness." Dr. Campbell rubbed his hands when he said this.

"Oh, goodie," I said.

"If she isn't familiar with your résumé as a survivor of massacres and slayer of maniacs, we'll enlighten her. She won't be able to resist. You're a blue-ribbon prize."

"Nice as that sounds, I'd prefer to live a while yet."

Ryoko said, "The universe built you to destroy human predators as it built the mongoose to destroy serpents."

"Dang, as a little girl I adored Kipling's tales to the max."

I inquired at length as to what they meant by occult forces and got nowhere fast. Slick as politicians dodging press questions, they relentlessly pivoted to the matter of Averna Spencer and her formula.

Charisma, resourcefulness, and grit notwithstanding, *Mission Impossible* wasn't my bag. The doctors hung in there with the hard sell. Dr. Campbell said I owed it to the missing persons and their distraught families. Dr. Ryoko insisted I bore a patriotic duty to obtain the formula from Spencer. Heaven help us if the avian flu developed into a more lethal strain.

This dragged on.

"What's your decision?" Dr. Campbell tried on a hopeful, earnest smile. "Will you help us avert a global catastrophe?"

"Pass."

"You're a born meddler," Dr. Ryoko said. "Consider the stakes— mass extinction of multiple species …"

"Not for all the chickens in the world." I actually meant, sweeten the pot, you cheap sonsofbitches. They sweetened the pot.

Dr. Campbell said, "Twenty-thousand. Cash. Our entire rainy-day fund."

"Tempting, but no thanks."

The doctors exchanged a glance I'll take to my grave.

"We'll tell you what really happened to your mother," Dr. Ryoko said.

Ding-ding-ding. Winner.

The Aughts exacted a hell of a toll on the Mace family. It felt personal between us and the universe.

Mom took a permanent vacation to parts unknown.

My brother, Elwood, stepped on a landmine. Elwood was "technically" the eldest of my fellow brood—he'd plopped onto the hospital sheets about forty-five minutes before me back in 1980. We didn't share the Corsican Twins psychic bond as romanticized by pop lit. Elwood and I had barely acknowledged, much less dwelled on, the fact we were twins. I was shocked as anyone to get the bad news from Afghanistan.

Jackson Bane, love of my life, went down with his fishing boat.

Dad followed suit in a separate accident on the Bering.

A bunch of friends and colleagues got murdered by the Eagle Talon Ripper. The Ripper almost did me in as well, hence the scar on my neck. Melodrama galore.

Hindsight: Mom's final disappearance began the unholy countdown sequence. Unlike the many other instances where Lucius slapped Dad and hit the road for a week or a month, she didn't return. Didn't call, didn't write, didn't leave a hint where she'd gone and after a couple of years, her fate gradually became the stuff of legends.

Flash forward the better part of a decade. When the mad doctors offered to solve the nagging mystery of Mom's vanishing act, my instincts were to skip the whole middle part where I went off on a fool's errand into the den of a sadistic murderer. Quicker and more reliable to extract their information with a sharp stick.

Beasley presented a major obstacle. He watched over Campbell and Ryoko with zeal. The adorable brute exhibited a ruthless streak when it came to protecting the codgers. His bulging biceps and handiness with gun, knife, and hobnail boot, gave me pause.

It's seldom wise to tackle an irresistible force of nature head-on. I played it coy.

He implored me to forget the mission and slip away into the night. No amount of money was worth the risk, he adored me, et cetera. I informed him the old bastards had made me an offer I couldn't refuse—and then refused to tell him what the offer entailed. I asked if he'd ever met a woman named Lucius, real slick like. He shrugged and said yeah, she'd blown into camp a few years back, consulted with the doctors, then departed on an evening breeze.

Innocent, and I'm a decent judge of a man's soul if I gaze into his eyes long enough after a good hard screw. On the subject of screwing: I didn't have the heart to ask if he'd banged my mom.

"Spencer is a monster," he said as we smoked cigarettes in bed and slugged from a bottle of vodka. "She's protected by the powers of darkness. I've seen the file. I've seen all their files …"

"Who else are your bosses spying on?"

"Don't ask questions you'll come to regret. You're not a professional. The docs aren't either. Meanwhile, Spencer is queen of her little mountain fiefdom. Absolutely untouchable. The FBI knows. The Department of Defense knows. Everybody."

"The government is aware that she's a serial killer?" I feigned shock. Experience had taught me that we primates were capable of anything, everything. There ain't no good guys.

"Always room for one more creep on the payroll. Uncle Sam wouldn't give a shit if Spencer had Joseph Mengele's brain implanted. As long as she keeps her activities on the property and doesn't kill anyone important, she's golden."

"Golden," I said. "Reminds me of something …"

I loved Beasley, after a fashion. It isn't unusual, as Tom Jones might say. Big, sorta-handsome (he looked like a soap star who got smashed in the face with a shovel); mean guys rev my motor, and the Bease had it going on in spades. He loved me back, far as I could tell. Our mutual affection complicated matters; made what I had to do to get close to Averna a dilemma of scruples versus pragmatism. My scruples aren't what they used to be.

"Since I can't change your mind, I can show you what you've signed on for." He plugged in a laptop and ran three video clips. Surveillance or home footage as shot by an anonymous someone with Ingmar Bergman's ice-cold aesthetic.

Clip one, black and white: *a man sprints along a seaside cliff toward the camera. The fuzzy shape of an enormous bird sweeps through the frame and plucks him in its claws. The man struggles as the bird cruises toward the horizon. They shrink to a distant blot—the smaller blot separates and plummets into the ocean.*

Clip two: a*n actress clad in an elaborate costume (skintight suit pricked with gemstones; a demented mask with a red and yellow feather plume, a vicious iron beak, underarm webbing, and steely talons) glides the length of a vast solarium. She rebounds from the walls to alter course with horrible grace. Naked men and women scatter beneath her. Every pass, the performer decapitates a victim with the swipe of a talon or the slash of a spur. Viscera streams in her wake.*

I know from Wire-Fu. I couldn't find the wires.

Clip three: A*verna Spencer stands near a bonfire with her arms spread. An assistant (the woman in the photo with Rocky the Olympian) fits her into a wingsuit designed by Satan. Spencer's arms are harnessed to actual wings designed after some gigantic specimen—twenty feet, tip to tip. The feathers ripple, hinting at a spectrum dulled by the black and white film. The fire illuminates queerly-hooked calf-high boots, steel (titanium?) talons strapped to her wrists, metallic panels across her breast, and a bronze helm crafted in the likeness of the god or devil of all avian-kind. Beneath the cruel beak, she grins.*

I stared overlong, evidently.

Beasley apologized, mistaking silence for dismay. Truthfully? The images had stolen my breath. A close race between disgust and awe. That's how much I'd evolved since Alaska. He figured I would react as any normal, rational person and tell the doctors to stuff their espionage mission. Quite the contrary.

Averna Spencer seldom emerged from her mountain fortress. She traveled in rarified company under various aliases and in disguise. Tracking her movements abroad proved a no-go. Campbell and Ryoko approached the finest detective agencies and were rebuffed without explanation. Beasley wasn't kidding when he said Spencer enjoyed protection from on high. Somebody ran major interference on her behalf, and I suspect that baloney had a first name, spelled CIA, and a second name spelled NSA, and a last name starting with Homeland Security. Spread enough money around and the baddest intelligence agency will act as your very own private concierge.

Since flushing out our quarry didn't seem a viable option, we needed to attract her interest. Birds appreciate shiny objects. The doctors devised a plan that involved getting me onto the guest list for an exclusive seminar featuring a famed ornithologist rumored to be an on and off again flame of Ms. Spencer. The doctors pulled strings and away I went to make the magic happen.

The lecture occurred in Kingston, New York at the home of a wealthy naturalist who reveled in this kind of groovy shit. Real nice place, if a tad stuffy. Kind of a museum, although the owner rarely opened for tours; he collected documents, weapons (a veritable shit-ton of knives), landscape paintings, and animal artifacts for his sole viewing pleasure. I've met a few guys with that particular pathology; the type who stored priceless art in bank vaults. Creepy bastards, the lot of them.

The ornithologist (Henry-something or other), on the other hand, seemed normal enough for a whack-a-doodle birdwatcher. We hit it off after I revealed my secret identity as a retired biologist. Dude gave his talk to a parlor-load of eminently bored stuffed shirts, then took my elbow and introduced me around. Scotch started flowing and I made tons of new friends.

One of these friends shook my hand and said to call her Manson. Manson stood tall and Amazonian in combat boots. She wore a bomber jacket (unzipped to flash DETROIT in block type across a stretched-tight T-shirt) and makeup fit to front The Cure. Cropped hair, heavy eyeliner, cherry-black lipstick, cherry-black nails. Yeah, I'd read her file too—born and raised in the Motor City, ex con, worked as muscle for hire until Averna Spencer rescued her from the mean streets. I recognized Manson as the mystery girl in the last photo of Rocky, Mr. Decathlete, and in the video of her girding Spencer for mayhem. Guess that made her Oddjob to Spencer's Goldfinger, or Renfield to Dracula.

We adjourned to the veranda, admiring an autumnal blaze in the eye of the sunset. Manson reminded me of a female iteration of Beasley—big, tough, ruggedly attractive, and not overly gifted in chitchat. Manson came right to the point. She explained that her mega-rich, mega-private employer desired my presence at her estate for dinner and light conversation. The mysterious employer approved of my various exploits (especially the way I'd dispatched the Eagle Talon Ripper in Alaska). Should I be so gracious as to accept the invitation, my forbearance would be well-compensated. A helicopter waited nearby. No need to pack; my every need would be fulfilled.

Damn, the forces of darkness moved in fast. Manson's Plan B probably involved a rag and chloroform, so rather than play hard to get, I acted tipsy and said, hell yeah, take me to your leader. What girl turns down a ride in a private helicopter? Not this girl! Manson ran a wand over my body from stem to stern and patted me down with more intimacy than a zealous airport security agent. Smart call, leaving my knives at home.

The helicopter carried us north for the better part of an hour.

Our pilot wore a snow-white uniform. His (or her) visor concealed his (or her) identity. I thought of Jonathan Harker's carriage-ride, Dracula at the reins, hell-bent for leather on the way to the castle. Dracula possessed a cold grip and the strength of twenty men. How strong was Averna Spencer's grip?

The answer—firm. That old saying about a velvet glove and an iron fist applies here. A few minutes after we touched down (and nope, I never saw her and the pilot together), the lady herself greeted me near the front lawn and its koi pond and assorted Greco-Roman statuary. Red dress and sensible shoes; she didn't wear any jewelry or makeup. She gently closed her hand around my throat and planted a lingering kiss on my cheek. Felt as if she could've torn my head off with a twitch. We locked gazes—her pupil flickered yellow and back to black again, foreshadowing troubles galore. I gave not a shit. My legs trembled. Anxiety evaporated, replaced by thrill. Pheromones, mad pheromones.

The plan, such as it was, was to play hard to get, work the charm offensive, gain access to the Bird Woman's home and acquire the formula. Babies, those best-laid stratagems went out the window the instant I got a whiff of her scent.

No, man. Averna didn't have "sharp features," or a "cruel nose," or "talon-like" hands (usually), or any such shit. Dark hair, brown eyes (usually), athletic. The record put her on the backside of fifty. Up close and personal, she felt a hell of a lot younger; ripped as a gymnast (a decathlete?), and nary a wrinkle or crow's foot. Averna understood how to walk, how to hold herself motionless the way politicians and models do, how to project her personality with kinetic force. Cool to the touch. Worth forty billion and enamored of esoteric scientific research. Spencer's corporations funded an assortment of crazy projects. Despite this massive wealth, her name seldom surfaced outside of highly insulated circles. A bizarre, protean vibe emanated from her and her retinue. Is evil (capital E evil) protean? That would explain much.

Invited me to freshen up (my quarters contained every amenity including evening wear in my size) and take a stroll with her resident PR man. Dinner at seven on the dot.

I toured the house. Bizarre and immense (immense even before factoring in a network of shops, garages, and the sector of hexagonal cottages where she stashed her off duty workforce and security personnel).

Envision a three-wing mansion of redwood logs and slate, mated to a giant bisected Bucky Ball on loan from the Martians—soaring, crystal-domed atriums with copses of full-sized pine trees and willows and a river falling over glass-smooth rocks; cozy parlors where fake flames danced inside hearths; steel bulkhead hatches concealed by cherry wood paneling and illustrated hangings that were sufficiently moth-eaten to indicate pricelessness; and an array of security cameras, some obvious and others less so. Most of the art was of the abstract genre. I didn't recognize anything.

Averna Spencer's PR lackey (a chipper guy named James who smiled like a hostage in fear of his life) took me in tow. According to my guide, the floorplan included a sauna, gymnasium, theater, bowling alley, discotheque, shooting range, and a spa. When his back was turned, I peeked inside vases and cabinets—no corpses, no skeletons. The circuit ended with a glimpse inside a museum gallery that would've made a nice addition to the Smithsonian. Dinosaur bones, suspended biplanes, and a two-story spire of glossy, radiant yellow crystal. The usual weird stuff one might expected to find in the trophy den of a megalomaniacal billionaire murderess.

When I craned my neck to get a better look, James became nervous.

"Ms. Spencer would prefer to show you these special exhibits herself. Someone accidentally left this open …"

"That's a huge chunk of crystal, Jimmy," I said. "Last I saw something like that was on the cover of a 1970s science fiction novel. And the bird skeleton … What's the wingspan? Twenty feet? Is it a pterodactyl?"

"No, ma'am, it is not a pterodactyl." James pulled a pair of brass-plated doors shut. "*Argentavis magnificen.* An extinct predator. Among the largest of her kind. She devoured prey whole. Shall we move toward the dining room?" He wiped his brow and checked his watch.

"The crystal. You simply have to give me the scoop, Jimbo."

"Ms. Spencer awaits." He led the way, and briskly.

"Does Manson handle the executions around here?"

He glanced over his shoulder, eyes glassy-bright. "Mainly, yes."

A woman spends her early adult years at hatcheries and aboard fishing trawlers doing the honest labor of tracking and cataloguing salmon (that great Alaskan export), and nobody cares. Americans want their food marginally harmless in a marginally attractive package; the fewer details, the better. A woman gets attacked by a mass murderer and lives to tell, everybody wants a piece of the action.

Type Jessica M into any search engine and the auto-form will suggest *Jessica Mace & Eagle Talon Ripper; Jessica Mace US Magazine; Jessica Mace Nude Photos; Jessica Mace Final Girl.* Averna Spencer hadn't merely followed my career as portrayed in the media, she knew my whole origin story—how a while back, I'd barely survived an apartment complex massacre and fire; how I'd risen from near-death and killed the killer; how I'd bailed on my fifteen minutes and vanished (like mother, like daughter). She'd also obtained facts regarding my unpublicized excursions on the road. Averna confessed her fascination regarding people who had confronted the vicissitudes of existence in an intimate manner. I took it to mean she'd burned ants with a magnifying glass as a kid.

We finished supper and wandered through her hanging gardens and lesser aviaries. Flocks of tropical birds dwelled inside a dome of sparkly mesh that protected a lush jungle biome. It would take the gross national product of a small country to stock and maintain such a preserve.

Our path wound through an imported jungle. Paper lanterns (grotesque busts of birds of prey) cast our primeval surroundings in the light of an animated Kipling adaptation. Climate control simulated the tropics. Humidity soaked my clothes and I almost believed the sliver of moonlight peeping through leaves was other than a subtly masked klieg.

She said, "You're rather trusting for a woman who's had her throat slashed. Do you jump into a helicopter with any total stranger?"

"Manson isn't the kind of person you argue with." I raised my voice to compete with raucous chatter of birds and mating frogs.

"Manson is an extension of my will. I made her."

"Made her? As in Pygmalion?"

"Isn't that the idiom the cool kids are using?"

"Yes. Do me next, pretty please."

"I projected my life essence into her puny mortal frame and voila, a million-year evolutionary leap. It's a messy process. Not for weak stomachs."

Seemed an appropriate point to change the subject. "I read in an article that you employ a team of geneticists and zoologists. You want to protect endangered bird species." Campbell and Ryoko's dossier alleged that Averna Spencer hired mercenaries to shoot nest robbers and sabotage the infrastructure of land developers who operated in environmentally-sensitive regions such as South America.

"The science team pursues much grander designs," she said. "We work to resurrect a spectrum of extinct species. Avian, reptile, amphibian. I'm worried for honeybees. As our apian friends go, so go we."

"The research is conducted here, in house?"

"Yes, and in twenty-three other countries."

"Good thing you're loaded. Woman could burn through a fortune on fringe research."

"She could. Or she could manipulate a host of international political actors to foot the bill. Drug lords, warlords, bored industrialists … It isn't as difficult to separate them from their spare millions as you might think."

"Any luck raising the dodo from the dead?"

"Sixty-eight percent of this aviary system is populated by animals that no longer exist in the outside world."

I flashed to the giant bird skeleton in the private museum, and how the tall, crystal had seethed with a weird yellow fire. Decided to zip my lips. Averna's stride, long and graceful, reminded me of her unnatural strength. Her friendly smile hinted at savagery.

"My most prized work isn't specific to avian research," she said. "I hope to create a trigger of human evolution. A radically accelerated process."

"Mutation."

"After a fashion."

"Toward what end?"

"The ability to survive dramatic climate change. To withstand nuclear radiation and acid rain. To think faster. To dispense with antiquated paradigms of morality and ethics. To soar with the eagles and swim with the fishes."

"Things mad scientists say for five hundred, Alex," I said. "Any notable successes, a la *The Island of Doctor Moreau*?"

"Me, a scientist? Hardly. Certainly, I'm slightly bonkers and quite ancient. Old people acquire knowledge. We spread it around, for weal or woe. As to the matter of success, I'm banking on getting lucky tonight, at least. Let's swing by your room for a nightcap."

"Mine? Surely yours is more luxurious."

She took my arm rather possessively. "I sleep hanging upside down from a trapeze bar in Aviary 4. It's not a cozy rendezvous."

All I could see was the mask of the devil bird in the video clip, the feather plume; her victim's corpse tumbling toward the water; men and women screaming in a solarium, its walls splattered in gore. Averna, radiant and exultant as a blood god from the bad history books.

Half a magnum of 1928 Krug later:

"Final girls are a necessarily rare breed." Averna studied my calloused palms, the yellow bruises along my shoulder. Her nails were trimmed close to the quick and unpolished. Dark specks of blood had gotten under some of them. "Your training regimen is fierce. No enhanced strength or ESP? No telekinetic powers?"

"I skate along on woman's intuition."

"No secret weaponry of any kind?"

"Apparently, I'm a mongoose. Natural weaponry. Rawr!"

"She kissed my (also bruised) belly. "I am curious what combination of pathology and trauma drives you to seek danger."

"This from Miss I-jump-off-cliffs-in-a-wingsuit?"

"Pretend a normal person you'd like to fuck asked the question. The event in Alaska opened the world for you."

"Opened the world? Like I should be grateful? I never volunteered to get brutalized. I didn't tip that domino. The attack fucked me up royal." I resisted the urge to touch the scar on my neck.

"Or it awakened dormant DNA. Your latent adrenaline junkie gene."

"You know how it is—at first, it's about the rush, then the rush becomes a habit. After a while, you're basically screwed."

"Give it an eon. Who's your favorite superhero?"

"Let me think ..."

"Don't think, tell me."

"Like tic-tac-toe?" I stalled.

"Cheating already."

"Okay. The Batman."

"Not Batgirl?"

"Defending my answer wasn't part of the game. I want every bit of power. You?"

"Captain Midnight."

"Who's Captain Midnight?"

"Seriously?" Averna cupped her chin and regarded me. "I'm re-evaluating this whole relationship."

"All six hours of it."

"My time is precious, Mace. Bouquets of thousand dollar bills could rain from the sky and it wouldn't be cost effective to stoop for the ones that didn't fall into my pocket."

"Okay, don't be rethinking anything. Give me a mulligan. Who the hell is Captain Midnight?"

"Ace World War One pilot. Could fly anything. Total badass."

"You're busting my balls over a cartoon from World War One?" She undid my bra and tossed it over the side. "Radio show."

"Seems like an odd choice for a hero," I said.

"Not if you knew me for more than six hours."

Ultimately, I told her my darkest secrets: Mom and Dad fought over the heavyweight title and it brought the Mace kids together; my first real love rescued me from the galley of a fishing boat right before it went to the bottom of the sea and a few happy years went by and nobody was around to rescue him; Mom ran out on us a hundred times, and finally, she stayed gone for good, either dead or reborn; when the Eagle Talon Ripper sliced my throat, I thought I'd died. Such a relief! The real reason I emptied the gun into the sonofabitch was because he'd done a half-assed job putting me out of my misery.

"At last I understand your motivation," Averna said. "It isn't thrill-seeking behavior. You experience suicidal ideation, probably stemming from survivor's guilt."

"I'm not suicidal anymore. Guilt? Not so much of that either."

"Dying isn't easy for most people. Instinct is a real bitch and she wants to live. Sadly, those with a true death wish, suffer terribly. O cruel universe. It imbued you with unbearable misery and a rational mind. Care to guess what the mind says?"

"Let's fuck? Let's drink? Let's forget?"

"The mind says, no more, let's stop. The universe also imbued you with the genetics of a survivor. Your subconscious resists annihilation; it says, okay, you can die, but only after jumping through fiery hoops, only after completing an obstacle course in hell. Some people with your particular affliction drink themselves to death or go hunting for Mr. Goodbar. They take on risky jobs. You, my dear, follow this hard road. It led to my doorstep."

"The other shoe droppeth," I said.

"Just your panties, at the moment."

What's *your* motivation?"

Her long, cruel fingers dug into my hips. "I like it when my prey runs screaming through the forest. I like the idea that animals will inherit the earth. I like the idea that with a little push we could be apes again."

"Oh," I said.

On day two we buzzed the estate in the helicopter. Trees, tree-covered mountains, tree-covered valleys, and more trees. Averna piloted. She wore a shiny black flight suit that exaggerated her figure into comic book proportions. Manson sat in the rear, loose-limbed and heavy-lidded. Her suit and mine were dull gray.

My secret of the day: I'd seen this before. In the course of training for the mission, Dr. Campbell had put me into a hypnotic trance and shown dozens of satellite images of the territory. Military grade imagery that dialed right down to the individual acorn. He explained that a photographic memory wasn't necessary to retain this information—if I got lost in these woods, a certain phrase would trigger the implanted memories and I'd have access to a 3-D "mind map" of the surroundings.

I keyed the mike in my headset. "Averna, I read somewhere that you almost died testing a wingsuit in Finland."

"Norway. Bad landings happen. Fortunately, the crash appeared nastier than the reality."

Witnesses said she'd hit the turf at an estimated one-hundred and thirty-miles per hour. The article also claimed it required a team of surgeons, four operations, and a roll of duct tape to put Humpty-Dumpty together again.

"Tycoons evidently score the world's greatest docs. I know women with C-section scars that could've been done with a boar spear."

"Flawless skin was a gift from my mother. Hold on." She banked hard right and put the helicopter into a shallow dive toward the foothills. We shot through a notch in the tree line and she leaned back on the yoke into a near vertical climb to hop over the rocky crown of a hill, then pushed hard and dropped hard to skim several feet above a lake, and steeply up again at the last second as a wall of evergreens closed in. My heart remained where it had leapt from my chest, a couple miles back.

Upon our return to the house, I retreated to my room and pondered the implications. Eighteen hours with Averna Spencer convinced me she didn't possess a scintilla of spontaneity. Her brain functioned on a beautiful, cold algorithm that perfectly mimicked human thought, human desire, yet possessed the nascent spark of neither. Rich folks often exhibit outsized egos and a narcissistic compulsion to impress the peasants. Averna didn't give a damn. She'd taken me on the flyover to demonstrate the geography and parameters of her estate for a practical purpose. In retrospect, the message was no less subtle than if she'd leaned over and whispered that I should get my track shoes laced. It's on like Donkey Kong, girlfriend.

The second message was delivered much later in the evening as I prowled through the house, casually testing locks and poking my nose where it didn't belong. Happened to peek into an antechamber and Lo! Averna (naked and gleaming) straddled Manson (naked and gleaming) atop a couch. Averna swallowed grapes from a prodigious clump. She regurgitated into Manson's wide open mouth and sealed it with a kiss. She winked at me. Her yellow eye reflected the epoch when scales and dagger-length talons were king (queen).

I backed away slowly, as one does when menaced by a large and partially satiated predator. Propelled by unreasonable jealousy, I strode to Averna's quarters, temporarily dismantled the security feed with an electromagnetic device disguised as an earring (in addition to zoology, exobiology, physical anthropology, and several other disciplines, including hypnotism, obviously, Doc Campbell dabbled in experimental engineering), and went straight for the safe. I'd memorized the combo and the doctors assured me that all I needed to do was glance at the documents; vital contents would be retrieved via hypnosis during my debriefing. Campbell assured me the mind operated like a camera and everything it experienced was undeveloped film.

The safe lay empty but for a piece of paper that read, *Bluebeard is a cautionary tale, lover,* and signed with a lipstick kiss.

I decided to hoof it, mission be damned, and take my chances in the mountains with the bears and the wolves and the inevitable pursuit. Two guards were posted on either side of my bedroom door. Stony-faced guys in military uniforms, assault rifles at port arms. So much for sneaking off, stage left.

Day three, several guests emerged to join the fun. Averna behaved as the convivial lady of the manor. We played games of the mundane variety. Mini golf and horseshoes in a horseshoe pit worthy of the Roman Coliseum. Manson caught my attention and casually straightened an iron horseshoe with her bare hands.

Then supper.

While gnawing on a pheasant wing and swilling fancy imported lager, I rubbed elbows with the new folks. Three of them had arrived at the estate a week prior; two others had gotten flown in that morning. Young men, down at the heels, but strong and athletic. Army guys who hadn't readjusted to life stateside; a boozy ex-cop; a kid maybe six months clear of high school where he'd wrestled varsity; and a couple cop/soldier wannabes. Each of them hoped to score a permanent security gig or at least a free ride as long as it lasted. I chatted the boys up—no close family; they were at loose ends. Nobody back home would notice, much less care, when they went missing. I won't bother with names; simpler to think of them as Hapless Victims #1 through #5.

Manson stood next to me at the bar. She wore a dark gown and a star pattern of heavy purple eyeshadow. "We don't usually entertain more than a couple of guests. This is special."

"What's the occasion?"

"It's Tuesday. Go back to your quarters. Ms. Spencer left you a gift."

"Because it's Tuesday?"

"Because there will be entertainment later this evening and you may wish to dress appropriately."

This is where you came in ...

Averna kept me stewing (quite literally) for forty-eight hours, plus or minus; a fact I estimated by the phase of the moon and an above average internal clock.

Why giant synthetic eggs? The design of the incubators was strictly symbolic. The contents—a contemporary primordial soup chock full of vitamins, proteins, and assorted mystery elements intended to cleanse her chosen, to heighten our reflexes and provide sufficient high-test nourishment for a proper hunt—could've done its work in a tank. She preferred elaborate theatrics; a consequence of eternal life. Have to wonder which came first: murderous rage or immortality. Since I could only hazard a guess, I guessed the eggs were deposited at various predetermined sites on the estate. We prisoners "hatched" and were subsequently hunted by our hostess and her majordomo.

During incubation, my dreams were psychedelic and fantastically, Lucio-Fulci-strength, macabre. Visions, perhaps. I beheld the male guests pelting through a night forest roiling with phosphorescent mist. Averna glided down on stiff, black wings. Her wingsuit defied physics. She tilted vertically and her toes dug into the soil every third or fourth gigantic stride and beheaded each of the fleeing men with a casual swipe of her metallic talons. She accelerated in dizzying curlicues through gaps in the trees.

Averna crooned to me through an intravenous drip. She spoke of evolutionary slippage, of natural mutation and genetic manipulation.

I die and live again and again. My soul regenerates into new flesh.

I have broken the hearts of countless men. I have eaten the beating hearts of countless men. I have devoured so many beating hearts, I shit and piss black heartblood.

I am a fountainhead of raped vitality.

I am a supplicant of the gods of eternal return.

I mean to devour you as I've devoured the rest in their multitudes.

You'll regenerate as I have done since the dawn of hominids. We'll meet again in a hundred million years at the dawn of the hominids. We'll meet again between one scream and the next.

Wake up, wake up, wake up ...

LAIRD BARRON

I love and hate *The Vanishing*. The Dutch version by Sluizer; don't bother with the American remake, hunky Jeff Bridges notwithstanding. In a previous life, I made my bread as a marine biologist. I survived many a tedious night aboard fishing tenders on the Bering Sea with a stack of paperbacks and VHS tapes while the rest of the crew was drunk or unconscious. Somewhere in the middle of *The Vanishing* a character describes a nightmare of being trapped in the darkness of a golden egg. Love it because the image got to me on a primal level and stuck. Hate it for the same reason.

These many years later, waking to fluid blackness three thousand miles east of Alaska, tubes up my nose and down my throat, body coiled like an embryo inside a golden egg of my very own? Must be the abyss everybody talks about.

I kicked, one-two, and dove deep into a sea of blood. Crimson light churned. The shell cracked and broke and the universe spilled me onto a carpet of pine needles. Out came the rubber tubes with a yank; then a bout of projectile vomiting—pheasant, sorbet, and copious amounts of whiskey and synthetic amniotic fluid. The blood in my eyes seeped down and dried into scales. Tears dug diamond furrows through caked-on grime. My convulsions subsided. I stood and leaned like a drunk against the bole of a hemlock and assessed the fucked-upedness of my situation.

A mild evening in the early October. Mosquitos whined; could have been worse. Clouds rolled over a crescent moon. Had to think fast, had to move. Standing still would get me dead. *Moving* would get me dead. Where was Rikki-tikki-tavi in my hour of need? An owl screeched. The bird glided past; the very shadow of death itself.

I'd trained for the direst scenarios—spent the previous several months jogging barefoot to toughen my feet; I also worked on traveling in New England forests at night to sharpen my lowlight vison. An affinity for rough and tumble notwithstanding, no way, no how am I a martial artist. I sparred with Beasley, who agreed (after I walked into his right hand three or four times) keeping it simple would be for the best. He honed my bag of dirty tricks and taught me a couple new ones.

Should've done more. Should've stayed in bed.

For all the roadwork and psychological preparation, and despite my alleged "purpose" and indomitable resolve, it was a psychological body blow to wash up on the proverbial lee shore: naked in the middle of the woods in the dead of night, pumped to the gills with experimental juice and on the run from Elizabeth Bathory II and her army of mercs. I intoned Dr. Campbell's mnemonic phrase (*the mind is a camera*) that would supposedly trigger a pseudo-holographic image of the surroundings. It worked, too.

I waded down a stream to confuse tracking dogs, then dug a hole near the roots of a tree and covered myself in clay, pine needles, and sap. I hadn't worn hair products or used scented soap or perfume in months. The docs put me on a regimen of an experimental, military grade antiperspirant.

Smeared head to toe in muck, I ran like hell through the dark, dark woods like the doomed heroine of a slasher flick. I angled southeast for the extraction point (would Beasley await my arrival?); kept right on trucking until daylight and then burrowed into a deadfall and slept. Night came around. I slurped brackish water from a puddle and set forth again, skulking from tree to tree with a wild animal's determination to survive. For a while, I believed I'd successfully evade and escape. Hope makes fools of us all.

Contrary to the cliché, I didn't trip and sprain an ankle, didn't sob or shriek to give away my position, and didn't glance over my shoulder every ten feet. Perversely, that last detail proved my downfall.

She hit me the way a hawk or an owl does an unsuspecting squirrel. Instead of severing my spine on impact, Averna merely snagged my long, luxurious mane and ascended vertically, yanking me off my feet. Similar to those rides at the State Fair—the ones where a scabrous, hungover carny straps you into a harness that dangles from a big metal wheel and up your sorry ass goes, with nothing between your sneakers and sod but a sheer drop.

The radiant sickle moon gashed the clouds; first above, then below. Averna clutched my hair in her left fist and skimmed treetops at a precipitous velocity, dragging me several feet lower like the tail of a kite. We dipped and swooned; accelerating, decelerating. If she had a jet pack strapped on her back, I didn't hear it. The only sounds I heard were the hissing breeze, and the clatter of branches when she swung me viciously against the canopy. Each blow knocked the breath from me and tore my flesh.

God knows where the bitch's flight plan would've taken us. I didn't stick around for the surprise. It required a metric fuck-ton of grit to recover from the initial whiplash and saw through my hair with a shard of the designer egg I'd carried (and managed not to drop) this entire time. Sliced my fingers and palm, but it got the job done—half a dozen convulsive hacks later, the last strand parted and I bailed. She cried my name.

Momentum hurled me in a broad arc. I caromed from leafy boughs and they snapped beneath my cannonball passage. Five seconds? Five thousand years? Those few heartbeats stretched across multiple lifetimes. Don't remember hitting the earth. Black stars cleared and I lay in a pile of dead, slimy leaves, oxygen smashed from my lungs, gaping at the moon.

A circling shadow blotted the light. I caught a glimpse of Averna in her sinister glory and realized the mysteries of the universe dwarfed my comprehension. She didn't need a wingsuit. She didn't need wings. She didn't need anything.

Manson strode from the depths of the forest. She didn't put a bullet through my skull as I might've logically assumed. She scooped my battered self (broken ribs, lacerated hand, and a world class concussion) into her arms and lugged me half a mile to the cabin. I don't recall a hell of a lot about the next couple of days except that the place was empty. No phone, no Beasley. Pretty clear my fate had been sealed from the beginning.

Manson played nursemaid by firelight from a decrepit hearth. Stuffed me into a sleeping bag and got an I.V. drip pumping fluids into my veins. Everything went blurry after the adrenalin wore off.

I dreamed that Averna, garbed in her horrorshow suit, shattered the cabin door and loomed over me as I lay helpless. Her wingtips scraped furrows in the walls. *Behold. I am the apex. I stand where humanity begins and where it will end.* She lovingly popped my eyeballs with her claws.

Woke screaming to beat the band.

Averna, dressed in a natty jacket, tenderly stroked my brow with a damp cloth. She revealed I was merely the second person to ever make it across the finish line. For me to plummet from the treetops and bounce instead of splat, represented a bona fide miracle. I didn't argue the point. Fell unconscious for however long it took for my injuries to mend.

Jessica, you must understand we're all meat and blood for the slaughterhouse. Regardless, we should learn until the very end. Sapient beings exist to acquire experience. The beasts of the wilderness kill and eat us. The wilderness itself kills and eats us. Every scrap down to our quintessence reduces and divides among maggots and dirt and adds to the sum.

Go in peace, dear girl. You and the world have unfinished business. Far be it from me to stand in the way.

Could've been a fever dream, could've been legit; either way, Averna and Manson let me live. Eventually I roused from blind sleep, aching, traumatized, and swaddled in gauze. The girls left clean clothes, pain pills, and an envelope with a few bucks inside a knapsack. Also, a loaded pistol and keys to a Jeep parked by the front porch.

Time passed. I bided it with grim patience.

Beasley the vigilant had to sleep sometime. I waited until he embarked upon one of his not infrequent drunks to make my move. Walked into the New England farmhouse around dawn. The doctors were seated at a table in the den, bickering over a pile of research papers. They registered surprise at my appearance, although less than one might expect. Fuckers had seen everything at least once, I suppose. Dr. Ryoko reached for a drawer, then noticed the pistol in my hand, and sat back with a resigned sigh.

"Hello, boys," I said. "Tell me about my mother."

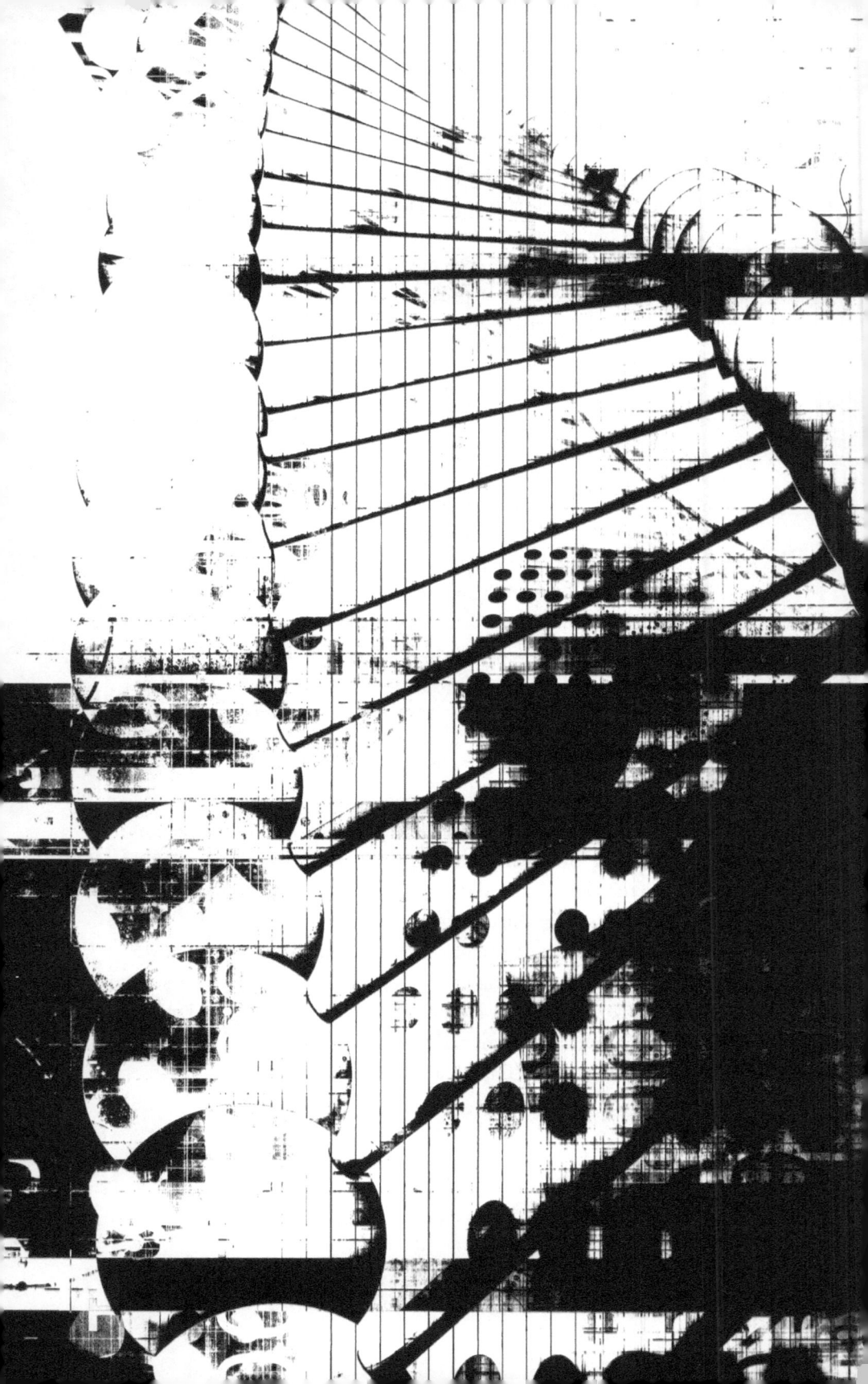

MICHAEL BAILEY
CO-EDITOR, COVER & INTERIOR DESIGN

is a multi-award-winning writer, editor, and book designer, and the recipient of over two dozen literary accolades, including the Bram Stoker Award, Benjamin Franklin Award, Eric Hoffer Book Award, and Independent Publisher Book Award. His nonlinear novels include *Palindrome Hannah*, *Phoenix Rose*, and *Psychotropic Dragon*, and he has published two short story and poetry collections, *Scales and Petals* and *Inkblots and Blood Spots*, as well as *Enso*, a children's book. He has created anthologies such as *Qualia Nous*, *The Library of the Dead*, four volumes of *Chiral Mad*, *You Human*, and a series of illustrated books.

LAIRD BARRON
"SWIFT TO CHASE"

spent his early years in Alaska, where he raced the Iditarod three times during the early 1990s and worked in the fishing and construction industries. He is the author of several books, including *The Beautiful Thing That Awaits Us All*, *Swift to Chase*, and the forthcoming novel *Blood Standard*. His work has also appeared in many magazines and anthologies. Barron currently resides in the Rondout Valley writing stories about the evil that men do.

CHAZ BRENCHLEY
"CH-CH-CHANGES"

has been making a living as a writer since the age of eighteen. He is the author of nine thrillers, four fantasy series (under three different names), two ghost stories and two collections. He lost count of his short stories long ago. His work has won the British Fantasy Award and a Lambda Award. He has recently married and moved from Newcastle to California, with two squabbling cats and a famous teddy bear.

RAMSEY CAMPBELL
"HOW HE HELPED"

The Oxford Companion to English Literature describes Ramsey Campbell as "Britain's most respected living horror writer." He has been given more awards than any other writer in the field, including the Grand Master Award of the World Horror Convention, the Lifetime Achievement Award of the Horror Writers Association, the Living Legend Award of the International Horror Guild and the World Fantasy Lifetime Achievement Award In 2015 he was made an Honorary Fellow of Liverpool John Moores University for outstanding services to literature.

SCOTT EDELMAN
"PITY THIS BUSY MONSTER NOT"

has published more than 85 short stories in magazines and anthologies such as *Analog, The Twilight Zone,* and many others. His collection of zombie fiction, *What Will Come After,* was a finalist for both the Bram Stoker Award and the Shirley Jackson Memorial Award. His science fiction short stories have been collected in *What We Still Talk About.* He has been a Bram Stoker Award finalist seven times. A collection of zombie novelettes, *Liars, Fakers, and the Dead Who Eat Them,* was published earlier this year by Written Backwards.

BRIAN EVENSON
"NAMELESS CITIZEN"

is the author of more than a dozen books of fiction, several of which have been finalists for the Edgar Award, the International Horror Guild Award, and the Shirley Jackson Award. He lives in Valencia, CA and teaches at CalArts.

ERINN L. KEMPER
"A LAUGHING MATTER"

lives on the Caribbean coast of Costa Rica where she hangs in her writing hammock, runs with her dog on the beach, and drinks ridiculous amounts of coffee, at least until happy hour. Erinn has sold stories to *Cemetery Dance Magazine*, *Dark Discoveries*, and *Black Static*, and appears in various anthologies including *You Human*, and *Behold! Oddities, Curiosities and Undefinable Wonders*. Visit www.erinnkemper. com for updates and sloth sightings.

JOHN LANGAN
"MY FATHER, DR. FRANKENSTEIN"

is the author of two novels, *The Fisherman*, and *House of Windows*, and two collections, *Mr. Gaunt and Other Uneasy Encounters*, and *The Wide, Carnivorous Sky and Other Monstrous Geographies*. With Paul Tremblay, he has co-edited *Creatures: Thirty Years of Monsters*. He is one of the founders of the Shirley Jackson Awards. Currently, he reviews horror and dark fantasy for *Locus* magazine. He lives in New York's Hudson Valley with his wife and younger son.

ROBERTA LANNES
"PAINTING THE BURNING FENCE"

was discovered in 1985 at UCLA by teacher/author Dennis Etchison, who published her first horror story, "Goodbye, Dark Love" in his award-winning anthology *Cutting Edge*. Since then, her varied genre short stories have been published in numerous anthologies, in fourteen languages. Her website, www.robertalannes.com, provides a chronological bibliography, in-depth biographical data, and contact information.

TIM LEBBON
"STRINGS"

has written more than forty novels, including *The Silence*, and *Relics*, and hundreds of short stories and novellas, several of which have won major awards. He is also a screenwriter. His short story "Pay the Ghost" was adapted into a movie starring Nicolas Cage, and *The Silence* is shooting this year. Find out more at www.timlebbon.net.

RENA MASON
"I WILL BE THE MAKING OF YOU"

is the Bram Stoker Award winning author of *The Evolutionist*, and *East End Girls*, as well as a 2014 Stage 32 / The Blood List Presents: The Search for New Blood Screenwriting Contest Finalist. A long-time fan of horror, sci-fi, science, history, historical fiction, mysteries, and thrillers, she writes to mash up those genres in stories revolving around everyday life. For more information about this author, check out her website: www.renamason.ink.

PAUL MELOY
"THE SERILE"

was born in 1966. He is the author of the short story collections *Islington Crocodiles* and *Electric Breakfast*, and the novels *The Night Clock* and *Adornments of the Storm* (forthcoming from Solaris 2018). His stories have been published in various magazines and anthologies, including *The Third Alternative*, *Black Static*, *Interzone*, *Nemonymous*, *House of Fear*, *The End of the Road*, and *Cinema Futura*. As a hobby, he is a full-time community mental health nurse.

MARK MORRIS
"UNDERSOUND"

has written and edited almost forty novels, novellas, short story collections, and anthologies. His script work includes audio dramas for *Doctor Who, Jago & Litefoot,* and the *Hammer Chillers* series. His recently published and upcoming work includes the official movie tie-in novelization of *The Great Wall,* the *Obsidian Heart* trilogy (*The Wolves of London, The Society of Blood,* and *The Wraiths of War*), the anthology *New Fears* (as editor), and a new audio adaptation of the classic 1971 horror movie *Blood on Satan's Claw.*

LISA MORTON
"EYES OF THE BEHOLDERS"

is a six-time winner of the Bram Stoker Award, a screenwriter, a novelist, and a Halloween expert whose work was described by the American Library Association's Readers' Advisory Guide to Horror as "consistently dark, unsettling, and frightening." Her forthcoming releases include *Haunted Nights,* co-edited with Ellen Datlow. She lives in the San Fernando Valley, and can be found online at www.lisamorton.com.

GENE O'NEILL
"SPIRITS"

has seen over 175 of his stories and novellas published, some of which have been collected in *Ghost Spirits, Computers and World Machines, The Grand Struggle, In Dark Corners, Dance of the Blue Lady, The Hitchhiking Effect,* and *Lethal Birds.* He has seen six novels published. Gene has been a Stoker finalist twelve times. In 2010, *Taste of Tenderloin* won for Collection; and in 2012, *The Blue Heron* won for Long Fiction. Most recent publications include four trade paperbacks in *The Cal Wild Chronicles* from Written Backwards.

MARK SAMUELS
"AN END TO PERPETUAL MOTION"

is a British author working in the continuum of weird, strange, and mystical fiction. First published in 1988, his short stories often focus on protagonists who discover deeper vistas of reality lurking behind modernity. His tales have appeared in numerous prestigious anthologies on both sides of the Atlantic.

B.E. SCULLY
"THE MYTHIC HERO MOST LIKELY TO SQEEZE A STONE"

lives in a crooked Red House that lacks a foundation in the misty woods of Oregon with a variety of human and animal companions. Scully is the author of numerous novels, short stories, poems, and articles. Published work, interviews, and odd scribblings can be found at www.bescully.com.

DARREN SPEEGLE
CO-EDITOR

is the author of six books, including his recently released debut novel *The Third Twin*. His second novel, *Artifacts*, is due in 2018. He is the author of five short story collections, including *A Haunting in Germany and Other Stories*. He is co-editor with Michael Bailey on the themed anthologies *Adam's Ladder* and *Prisms* (in progress). His short fiction is forthcoming in *Best New Horror 28*, and *Tales from the Lake Vol. 4*. His work has previously appeared in such venues as *Analog*, *Clarkesworld*, *Subterranean*, *Cemetery Dance Magazine*, *Postscripts*, *ChiZine*, *The Third Alternative*, and *Subterranean: Tales of Dark Fantasy*. Between gigs as a federal contractor in the Middle East, Darren resides in Thailand. When not writing, he enjoys outdoor activities like hiking and biking.

JEFFREY THOMAS
"SLICED BREAD"

is the author of such novels as *Deadstock*, and *Blue War* (Solaris Books), and various short story collections that include *The Endless Fall and Other Weird Fictions* (Lovecraft eZine Press), and *Haunted Worlds* (Hippocampus Press). Many of his characters face their challenges in his dark future setting of Punktown, but Thomas himself lives in ye olde Massachusetts.

DAMIEN ANGELICA WALTERS
"FILIGREE, MINOTAUR, CYANIDE, BLOOM"

is the author of *Sing Me Your Scars*, *Paper Tigers*, and the forthcoming *Cry Your Way Home*. Her short fiction has been nominated twice for a Bram Stoker Award, reprinted in *The Year's Best Dark Fantasy & Horror* and *The Year's Best Weird Fiction*, and published in various anthologies and magazines, including the Shirley Jackson Award finalists *Autumn Cthulhu* and *The Madness of Dr. Caligari*, *Nightmare* magazine, and *Black Static*. Find her online @DamienAWalters or www.damienangelicawalters.com.

ALSO BY WRITTEN BACKWARDS

ANTHOLOGIES

PELLUCID LUNACY

CHIRAL MAD

CHIRAL MAD 2

QUALIA NOUS

THE LIBRARY OF THE DEAD

CHIRAL MAD 3

ALLEVON

AT THE LAZY K
[novella by Gene O'Neill]

LIARS, FAKERS, AND THE DEAD WHO EAT THEM
[novelettes by Scott Ede man]

COLLECTIONS

BONES ARE MADE TO BE BROKEN
[Paul Michael Anderson]

YES TRESPASSING
[Erik T. Johnson]